The Treasure of Heaven

The Treasure of Heaven

A Romance of Riches

Marie Corelli

MINT EDITIONS

The Treasure of Heaven: A Romance of Riches was first published in 1857.

This edition published by Mint Editions 2021.

ISBN 9781513278230 | E-ISBN 9781513278698

Published by Mint Editions®

MINT
EDITIONS
minteditionbooks.com

Publishing Director: Jennifer Newens
Design & Production: Rachel Lopez Metzger
Project Manager: Micaela Clark
Typesetting: Westchester Publishing Services

The Treasure of Heaven

A Romance of Riches

Marie Corelli

MINT EDITIONS

The Treasure of Heaven: A Romance of Riches was first published in 1857.

This edition published by Mint Editions 2021.

ISBN 9781513278230 | E-ISBN 9781513278698

Published by Mint Editions®

MINT
EDITIONS

minteditionbooks.com

Publishing Director: Jennifer Newens
Design & Production: Rachel Lopez Metzger
Project Manager: Micaela Clark
Typesetting: Westchester Publishing Services

Contents

I

L ondon,—and a night in June. London, swart and grim, semi-shrouded in a warm close mist of mingled human breath and acrid vapour steaming up from the clammy crowded streets,—London, with a million twinkling lights gleaming sharp upon its native blackness, and looking, to a dreamer's eye, like some gigantic Fortress, built line upon line and tower upon tower,—with huge ramparts raised about it frowningly as though in self-defence against Heaven. Around and above it the deep sky swept in a ring of sable blue, wherein thousands of stars were visible, encamped after the fashion of a mighty army, with sentinel planets taking their turns of duty in the watching of a rebellious world. A sulphureous wave of heat half asphyxiated the swarms of people who were hurrying to and fro in that restless undetermined way which is such a predominating feature of what is called a London "season," and the general impression of the weather was, to one and all, conveyed in a sense of discomfort and oppression, with a vague struggling expectancy of approaching thunder. Few raised their eyes beyond the thick warm haze which hung low on the sooty chimney-pots, and trailed sleepily along in the arid, dusty parks. Those who by chance looked higher, saw that the skies above the city were divinely calm and clear, and that not a cloud betokened so much as the shadow of a storm.

The deep bell of Westminster chimed midnight, that hour of picturesque ghostly tradition, when simple village maids shudder at the thought of traversing a dark lane or passing a churchyard, and when country folks of old-fashioned habits and principles are respectably in bed and for the most part sleeping. But so far as the fashionable "West End" was concerned, it might have been midday. Everybody assuming to be Anybody, was in town. The rumble of carriages passing to and fro was incessant,—the swift whirr and warning hoot of coming and going motor vehicles, the hoarse cries of the newsboys, and the general insect-like drone and murmur of feverish human activity were as loud as at any busy time of the morning or the afternoon. There had been a Court at Buckingham Palace,—and a "special" performance at the Opera,—and on account of these two functions, entertainments were going on at almost every fashionable house in every fashionable quarter. The public restaurants were crammed with luxury-loving men and women,—men and women to whom the mere suggestion of a quiet dinner in their own homes would have acted as a menace of infinite boredom,—and these gilded and refined eating-houses were now beginning to shoot forth their bundles of well-dressed, well-fed folk into the many and various conveyances waiting to receive them. There was a good deal of needless shouting, and much banter between drivers and policemen. Now and again the melancholy whine of a beggar's plea struck a discordant note through the smooth-toned compliments and farewells of hosts and their departing guests. No hint of pause or repose was offered in the ever-changing scene of uneasy and impetuous excitation of movement, save where, far up in the clear depths of space, the glittering star-battalions of a wronged and forgotten God held their steadfast watch and kept their hourly chronicle. London with its brilliant "season" seemed the only living fact worth recognising; London, with its flaring noisy streets, and its hot summer haze interposed like a grey veil between itself and the higher vision. Enough for most people it was to see the veil,—beyond it the view is always too vast and illimitable for the little vanities of ordinary mortal minds.

Amid all the din and turmoil of fashion and folly seeking its own in the great English capital at the midnight hour, a certain corner of an exclusively fashionable quarter seemed strangely quiet and sequestered, and this was the back of one of the row of palace-like dwellings known as Carlton House Terrace. Occasionally a silent-wheeled hansom, brougham, or flashing motor-car sped swiftly along the Mall, towards which the wide stone balcony of the house projected,—or the heavy footsteps of a policeman walking on his beat crunched the gravel of the path beneath, but the general atmosphere of the place was expressive of solitude and even of gloom. The imposing evidences of great wealth, written in bold headlines on the massive square architecture of the whole block of huge mansions, only intensified the austere sombreness of their appearance, and the fringe of sad-looking trees edging the road below sent a faint waving shadow in the lamplight against the cold walls, as though some shuddering consciousness of happier woodland scenes had suddenly moved them to a vain regret. The haze of heat lay very thickly here, creeping along with slow stealth like a sluggish stream, and a suffocating odour suggestive of some subtle anæsthetic weighed the air with a sense of nausea and depression. It was difficult to realise that this condition of climate was actually summer in its prime—summer with all its glowing abundance of flower and foliage as seen in fresh green lanes and country dells,—rather did it seem a dull nightmare of what summer might be in a prison among criminals undergoing punishment. The house with the wide stone balcony looked particularly prison-like, even more so than some of its neighbours, perhaps because the greater number of its many windows were shuttered close, and showed no sign of life behind their impenetrable blackness. The only strong gleam of light radiating from the inner darkness to the outer, streamed across the balcony itself, which by means of two glass doors opened directly from the room behind it. Here two men sat, or rather half reclined in easy-cushioned lounge chairs, their faces turned towards the Mall, so that the illumination from the apartment in the background created a Rembrandt-like effect in partially concealing the expression of the one from the other's observation. Outwardly, and at a first causal glance, there was nothing very remarkable about either of them. One was old; the other more than middle-aged. Both were in evening-dress,—both smoked idly, and apparently not so much for the pleasure of smoking as for lack of something better to do, and both seemed self-centred and absorbed in thought. They had been conversing for some time, but now silence had fallen between them, and neither seemed disposed to break the heavy spell. The distant roar of constant traffic in the busy thoroughfares of the metropolis sounded in their ears like muffled thunder, while every now and again the soft sudden echo of dance music, played by a string band in evident attendance at some festive function in a house not far away, shivered delicately through the mist like a sigh of pleasure. The melancholy tree-tops trembled,—a single star struggled above the sultry vapours and shone out large and bright as though it were a great signal lamp suddenly lit in heaven. The elder of the two men seated on the balcony raised his eyes and saw it shining. He moved uneasily,—then lifting himself a little in his chair, he spoke as though taking up a dropped thread of conversation, with the intention of deliberately continuing it to the end. His voice was gentle and mellow, with a touch of that singular pathos in its tone which is customary to the Celtic rather than to the Saxon vocal cords.

"I have given you my full confidence," he said, "and I have put before you the exact sum total of the matter as I see it. You think me irrational,—absurd. Good. Then I am content to be irrational and absurd. In any case you can scarcely deny that what I have stated is a simple fact,—a truth which cannot be denied?"

"It is a truth, certainly," replied his companion, pulling himself upright in his chair with a certain vexed vehemence of action and flinging away his half-smoked cigar, "but it is one of those unpleasant truths which need not be looked at too closely or too often remembered. We must all get old—unfortunately,—and we must all die, which in my opinion is more unfortunate still. But we need not anticipate such a disagreeable business before its time."

"Yet you are always drawing up Last Wills and Testaments," observed the other, with a touch of humour in his tone.

"Oh well! That, of course, has to be done. The youngest persons should make their wills if they have anything to leave, or else run the risk of having all their household goods and other belongings fought for with tooth and claw by their 'dearest' relations. Dearest relations are, according to my experience, very much like wild cats: give them the faintest hope of a legacy, and they scratch and squawl as though it were raw meat for which they have been starving. In all my long career as a solicitor I never knew one 'dearest relation' who honestly regretted the dead."

"There you meet me on the very ground of our previous discussions," said the elder man. "It is not the consciousness of old age that troubles me, or the inevitable approach of that end which is common to all,—it is merely the outlook into the void,—the teasing wonder as to who may step into my place when I am gone, and what will be done with the results of my life's labour."

He rose as he spoke, and moved towards the balcony's edge, resting one hand upon its smooth stone. The change of attitude allowed the light from the interior room to play more fully on his features, and showed him to be well advanced in age, with a worn, yet strong face and deep-set eyes, over which the shelving brows stooped benevolently as though to guard the sinking vital fire in the wells of vision below. The mouth was concealed by an ashen-grey moustache, while on the forehead and at the sides of the temples the hair was perfectly white, though still abundant. A certain military precision of manner was attached to the whole bearing of the man,—his thin figure was well-built and upright, showing no tendency to feebleness,—his shoulders were set square, and his head was poised in a manner that might have been called uncompromising, if not obstinate. Even the hand that rested on the balcony, attenuated and deeply wrinkled as it was, suggested strength in its shape and character, and a passing thought of this flitted across the mind of his companion who, after a pause, said slowly:—

"I really see no reason why you should brood on such things. What's the use? Your health is excellent for your time of life. Your end is not imminent. You are voluntarily undergoing a system of self-torture which is quite unnecessary. We've known each other for years, yet I hardly recognise you in your present humour. I thought you were perfectly happy. Surely you ought to be,—you, David Helmsley,— 'King' David, as you are sometimes called—one of the richest men in the world!"

Helmsley smiled, but with a suspicion of sadness.

"Neither kings nor rich men hold special grants of happiness," he answered, quietly: "Your own experience of humanity must have taught you that. Personally speaking, I have never been happy since my boyhood. This surprises you? I daresay it does. But, my dear Vesey, old friend as you are, it sometimes happens that our closest intimates know us least! And even the famous firm of Vesey and Symonds, or Symonds and Vesey,—for your partner is one with you and you are one with your partner,—may, in spite of all their legal wisdom, fail to pierce the thick disguises worn by the souls of their clients. The Man in the Iron Mask is a familiar figure in the office of his confidential solicitor. I repeat, I have never been happy since my boyhood—"

"Your happiness then was a mere matter of youth and animal spirits," interposed Vesey.

"I thought you would say that!"—and again a faint smile illumined Helmsley's features. "It is just what every one would say. Yet the young are often much more miserable than the old; and while I grant that youth may have had something to do with my past joy in life, it was not all. No, it certainly was not all. It was simply that I had then what I have never had since."

He broke off abruptly. Then stepping back to his chair he resumed his former reclining position, leaning his head against the cushions and fixing his eyes on the solitary bright star that shone above the mist and the trembling trees.

"May I talk out to you?" he inquired suddenly, with a touch of whimsicality. "Or are you resolved to preach copybook moralities at me, such as 'Be good and you will be happy?'"

Vesey, more ceremoniously known as Sir Francis Vesey, one of the most renowned of London's great leading solicitors, looked at him and laughed.

"Talk out, my dear fellow, by all means!" he replied. "Especially if it will do you any good. But don't ask me to sympathise very deeply with the imaginary sorrows of so enormously wealthy a man as you are!"

"I don't expect any sympathy," said Helmsley. "Sympathy is the one thing I have never sought, because I know it is not to be obtained, even from one's nearest and dearest. Sympathy! Why, no man in the world ever really gets it, even from his wife. And no man possessing a spark of manliness ever wants it, except—sometimes—"

He hesitated, looking steadily at the star above him,—then went on.

"Except sometimes,—when the power of resistance is weakened—when the consciousness is strongly borne in upon us of the unanswerable wisdom of Solomon, who wrote—'I hated all my labour which I had taken under the sun, because I should leave it to the man that should be after me. And who knows whether he shall be a wise man or a fool?'"

Sir Francis Vesey, dimly regretting the half-smoked cigar he had thrown away in a moment of impatience, took out a fresh one from his pocket-case and lit it.

"Solomon has expressed every disagreeable situation in life with remarkable accuracy," he murmured placidly, as he began to puff rings of pale smoke into the surrounding yellow haze, "but he was a bit of a misanthrope."

"When I was a boy," pursued Helmsley, not heeding his legal friend's comment, "I was happy chiefly because I believed. I never doubted any stated truth that seemed beautiful enough to be true. I had perfect confidence in the goodness of God and the ultimate happiness designed by Him for every living creature. Away out in Virginia where I was born, before the Southern States were subjected to Yankeedom, it was a glorious thing merely to be alive. The clear, pure air, fresh with the strong odour of pine and cedar,—the big plantations of cotton and corn,—the colours of the autumn woods when the maple trees turned scarlet, and the tall sumachs blazed like great fires on the sides of the mountains,—the exhilarating climate—the sweetness of the south-west wind,—all these influences of nature appealed to my soul and kindled a strange restlessness in it which has never been appeased. Never!—though I have lived my life almost to its end, and have done all those things which most men do who seek to get the utmost satisfaction they can out of existence. But I am not satisfied; I have never been satisfied."

"And you never will be," declared Sir Francis firmly. "There are some people to whom Heaven itself would prove disappointing."

"Well, if Heaven is the kind of place depicted by the clergy, the poorest beggar might resent its offered attractions," said Helmsley, with a slight, contemptuous shrug of his shoulders. "After a life of continuous pain and struggle, the pleasures of singing for ever and ever to one's own harp accompaniment are scarcely sufficient compensation."

Vesey laughed cheerfully.

"It's all symbolical," he murmured, puffing away at his cigar, "and really very well meant! Positively now, the clergy are capital fellows! They do their best,—they keep it up. Give them credit for that at least, Helmsley,—they do keep it up!"

Helmsley was silent for a minute or two.

"We are rather wandering from the point," he said at last. "What I know of the clergy generally has not taught me to rely upon them for any advice in a difficulty, or any help out of trouble. Once—in a moment of weakness and irresolution—I asked a celebrated preacher what suggestion he could make to a rich man, who, having no heirs, sought a means of disposing of his wealth to the best advantage for others after his death. His reply—"

"Was the usual thing, of course," interposed Sir Francis blandly. "He said, 'Let the rich man leave it all to me, and God will bless him abundantly!'"

"Well, yes, it came to that,"—and Helmsley gave a short impatient sigh. "He evidently guessed that the rich man implied was myself, for ever since I asked him the question, he has kept me regularly supplied with books and pamphlets relating to his Church and various missions. I daresay he's a very good fellow. But I've no fancy to assist him. He works on sectarian lines, and I am of no sect. Though I confess I should like to believe in God—if I could."

Sir Francis, fanning a tiny wreath of cigar smoke away with one hand, looked at him curiously, but offered no remark.

"You said I might talk out to you," continued Helmsley—"and it is perhaps necessary that I should do so, since you have lately so persistently urged upon me the importance of making my will. You are perfectly right, of course, and I alone am to blame for the apparently stupid hesitation I show in following your advice. But, as I have already told you, I have no one in the world who has the least claim upon me,—no one to whom I can bequeath, to my own satisfaction, the wealth I have earned. I married,—as you know,—and my marriage was unhappy. It ended,—and you are aware of all the facts—in the proved infidelity of my wife, followed by our separation (effected quietly, thanks to you, without the vulgar publicity of the divorce court), and then—in her premature death. Notwithstanding all this, I did my best for my two sons,—you are a witness to this truth,—and you remember that during their lifetime I did make my will,—in their favour. They turned out badly; each one ran his own career of folly, vice, and riotous dissipation, and both are dead. Thus it happens that here I am,—alone at the age of seventy, without any soul to care for me, or any creature to whom I can trust my business, or leave my fortune. It is not my fault that it is so; it is sheer destiny. How, I ask you, can I make any 'Last Will and Testament' under such conditions?"

"If you make no will at all, your property goes to the Crown," said Vesey bluntly.

"Naturally. I know that. But one might have a worse heir than the Crown! The Crown may be trusted to take proper care of money, and this is more than can often be said of one's sons and daughters. I tell you it is all as Solomon said—'vanity and vexation of spirit.' The amassing of great wealth is not worth the time and trouble involved in the task. One could do so much better—"

Here he paused.

"How?" asked Vesey, with a half-smile. "What else is there to be done in this world except to get rich in order to live comfortably?"

"I know people who are not rich at all, and who never will be rich, yet who live more comfortably than I have ever done," replied Helmsley—"that is, if to 'live comfortably' implies to live peacefully, happily, and contentedly, taking each day as it comes with gladness as a real 'living' time. And by this, I mean 'living,' not with the rush and scramble, fret and jar inseparable from money-making, but living just for the joy of life. Especially when it is possible to believe that a God exists, who designed life, and even death, for the ultimate good of every creature. This is what I believed—once—'out in ole Virginny, a long time ago!'"

He hummed the last words softly under his breath,—then swept one hand across his eyes with a movement of impatience.

"Old men's brains grow addled," he continued. "They become clouded with a fog through which only the memories of the past and the days of their youth shine clear. Sometimes I talk of Virginia as if I were home-sick and wanted to go back to it,—yet I never do. I wouldn't go back to it for the world,—not now. I'm not an American, so I can say, without any loss of the patriotic sense, that I loathe America. It is a country to be used for the making of wealth, but it is not a country to be loved. It might have been the most lovable Father-and-Mother-Land on the globe if nobler men had lived long enough in it to rescue its people from the degrading Dollar-craze. But now, well!—those who make fortunes there leave it as soon as they can, shaking its dust off their feet and striving to forget that they ever experienced its incalculable greed, vice, cunning, and general rascality. There are plenty of decent folk in America, of course, just as there are decent folk everywhere, but they are in the minority. Even in the Southern States the 'old stock' of men is decaying and dying-out, and the taint of commercial vulgarity is creeping over the former simplicity of the Virginian homestead. No,—I would not go back to the scene of my boyhood, for though I had something there once which I have since lost, I am not such a fool as to think I should ever find it again."

Here he looked round at his listener with a smile so sudden and sweet as to render his sunken features almost youthful.

"I believe I am boring you, Vesey!" he said.

"Not the least in the world,—you never bore me," replied Sir Francis, with alacrity. "You are always interesting, even in your most illogical humour."

"You consider me illogical?"

"In a way, yes. For instance, you abuse America. Why? Your misguided wife was American, certainly, but setting that unfortunate fact aside, you made your money in the States. Commercial vulgarity helped you along. Therefore be just to commercial vulgarity."

"I hope I am just to it,—I think I am," answered Helmsley slowly; "but I never was one with it. I never expected to wring a dollar out of ten cents, and never tried. I can at least say that I have made my money honestly, and have trampled no man down on the road to fortune. But then—I am not a citizen of the 'Great Republic.'"

"You were born in America," said Vesey.

"By accident," replied Helmsley, with a laugh, "and kindly fate favoured me by allowing me to see my first daylight in the South rather than in the North. But I was never naturalised as an American. My father and mother were both English,—they both came from the same little sea-coast village in Cornwall. They married very young,—theirs was a romantic love-match, and they left England in the hope of bettering their fortunes. They settled in Virginia and grew to love it. My father became accountant to a large business firm out there, and did fairly well, though he never was a rich man in the present-day meaning of the term. He had only two children,—myself and my sister, who died at sixteen. I was barely twenty when I lost both father and mother and started alone to face the world."

"You have faced it very successfully," said Vesey; "and if you would only look at things in the right and reasonable way, you have really very little to complain of. Your marriage was certainly an unlucky one—"

"Do not speak of it!" interrupted Helmsley, hastily. "It is past and done with. Wife and children are swept out of my life as though they had never been! It is a curious thing, perhaps, but with me a betrayed affection does not remain in my memory as affection at all, but only as a spurious image of the real virtue, not worth considering or regretting. Standing as I do now, on the threshold of the grave, I look back,—and in looking back I see none of those who wronged and deceived me,— they have disappeared altogether, and their very faces and forms are blotted out of my remembrance. So much so, indeed, that I could, if I had the chance, begin a new life again and never give a thought to the old!"

His eyes flashed a sudden fire under their shelving brows, and his right hand clenched itself involuntarily.

"I suppose," he continued, "that a kind of harking back to the memories of one's youth is common to all aged persons. With me it has become almost morbid, for daily and hourly I see myself as a boy, dreaming away the time in the wild garden of our home in Virginia,—watching the fireflies light up the darkness of the summer evenings, and listening to my sister singing in her soft little voice her favourite melody—'Angels ever bright and fair.' As I said to you when we began this talk, I had something then which I have never had since. Do you know what it was?"

Sir Francis, here finishing his cigar, threw away its glowing end, and shook his head in the negative.

"You will think me as sentimental as I am garrulous," went on Helmsley, "when I tell you that it was merely—love!"

Vesey raised himself in his chair and sat upright, opening his eyes in astonishment.

"Love!" he echoed. "God bless my soul! I should have thought that you, of all men in the world, could have won that easily!"

Helmsley turned towards him with a questioning look.

"Why should I 'of all men in the world' have won it?" he asked. "Because I am rich? Rich men are seldom, if ever, loved for themselves— only for what they can give to their professing lovers."

His ordinarily soft tone had an accent of bitterness in it, and Sir Francis Vesey was silent.

"Had I remained poor,—poor as I was when I first started to make my fortune," he went on, "I might possibly have been loved by some woman, or some friend, for myself alone. For as a young fellow I was not bad-looking, nor had I, so I flatter myself, an unlikable disposition. But luck always turned the wheel in my favour, and at thirty-five I was a millionaire. Then I 'fell' in love,—and married on the faith of that emotion, which is always a mistake. 'Falling in love' is not loving. I was in the full flush of my strength and manhood, and was sufficiently proud of myself to believe that my wife really cared for me. There I was deceived. She cared for my millions. So it chances that the only real love I have ever known was the unselfish 'home' affection,—the love of my mother and father and sister 'out in ole Virginny,' 'a love so sweet it could not last,' as Shelley sings. Though I believe it can and does last,— for my soul (or whatever that strange part of me may be which thinks beyond the body) is always running back to that love with a full sense of certainty that it is still existent."

His voice sank and seemed to fail him for a moment. He looked up at the large, bright star shining steadily above him.

"You are silent, Vesey," he said, after a pause, speaking with an effort at lightness; "and wisely too, for I know you have nothing to say—that is, nothing that could affect the position. And you may well ask, if you choose, to what does all this reminiscent old man's prattle tend? Simply to this—that you have been urging me for the last six months to make my will in order to replace the one which was previously made in favour of my sons, and which is now destroyed, owing to their deaths before my own,—and I tell you plainly and frankly that I don't know how to make it, as there is no one in the world whom I care to name as my heir."

Sir Francis sat gravely ruminating for a moment;—then he said:—

"Why not do as I suggested to you once before—adopt a child? Find some promising boy, born of decent, healthy, self-respecting parents,—educate him according to your own ideas, and bring him up to understand his future responsibilities. How would that suit you?"

"Not at all," replied Helmsley drily. "I *have* heard of parents willing to sell their children, but I should scarcely call them decent or self-respecting. I know of one case where a couple of peasants sold their son for five pounds in order to get rid of the trouble of rearing him. He turned out a famous man,—but though he was, in due course, told his history, he never acknowledged the unnatural vendors of his flesh and blood as his parents, and quite right too. No,—I have had too much experience of life to try such a doubtful business as that of adopting a child. The very fact of adoption by so miserably rich a man as myself would buy a child's duty and obedience rather than win it. I will have no heir at all, unless I can discover one whose love for me is sincerely unselfish and far above all considerations of wealth or worldly advantage."

"It is rather late in the day, perhaps," said Vesey after a pause, speaking hesitatingly, "but—but—you might marry?"

Helmsley laughed loudly and harshly.

"Marry! I! At seventy! My dear Vesey, you are a very old friend, and privileged to say what others dare not, or you would offend me. If I had ever thought of marrying again I should have done so two or three years after my wife's death, when I was in the fifties, and not waited till now, when my end, if not actually near, is certainly well in sight. Though I daresay there are plenty of women who would marry me—even me—at my age,—knowing the extent of my income. But do you think I would take one of them, knowing in my heart that it would be a mere question of sale and barter? Not I!—I could never consent to sink so low in my own estimation of myself. I can honestly say I have never wronged any woman. I shall not begin now."

"I don't see why you should take that view of it," murmured Sir Francis placidly. "Life is not lived nowadays as it was when you first entered upon your career. For one thing, men last longer and don't give up so soon. Few consider themselves old at seventy. Why should they? There's a learned professor at the Pasteur Institute who declares we ought all to live to a hundred and forty. If he's right, you are still quite a young man."

Helmsley rose from his chair with a slightly impatient gesture.

"We won't discuss any so-called 'new theories,'" he said. "They are only echoes of old fallacies. The professor's statement is merely a modern repetition of the ancient belief in the elixir of life. Shall we go in?"

Vesey got up from his lounging position more slowly and stiffly than Helmsley had done. Some ten years younger as he was, he was evidently less active.

"Well," he said, as he squared his shoulders and drew himself erect, "we are no nearer a settlement of what I consider a most urgent and important affair than when we began our conversation."

Helmsley shrugged his shoulders.

"When I come back to town, we will go into the question again," he said.

"You are off at the end of the week?"

"Yes."

"Going abroad?"

"I—I think so."

The answer was given with a slight touch of hesitation.

"Your last 'function' of the season is the dance you are giving to-morrow night, I suppose," continued Sir Francis, studying with a vague curiosity the spare, slight figure of his companion, who had turned from him and, with one foot on the sill of the open French window, was just about to enter the room beyond.

"Yes. It is Lucy's birthday."

"Ah! Miss Lucy Sorrel! How old is she?"

"Just twenty-one."

And, as he spoke, Helmsley stepped into the apartment from which the window opened out upon the balcony, and waited a moment for Vesey to follow.

"She has always been a great favourite of yours," said Vesey, as he entered. "Now, why—"

"Why don't I leave her my fortune, you would ask?" interrupted Helmsley, with a touch of sarcasm. "Well, first, because she is a woman, and she might possibly marry a fool or a wastrel. Secondly, because though I have known her ever since she was a child of ten, I have no liking for her parents or for any of her family connections. When I first took a fancy to her she was playing about on the shore at a little seaside place on the Sussex coast,—I thought her a pretty little creature, and have made rather a pet of her ever since. But beyond giving her trinkets and bon-bons, and offering her such gaieties and amusements as are suitable to her age and sex, I have no other intentions concerning her."

Sir Francis took a comprehensive glance round the magnificent drawing-room in which he now stood,—a drawing-room more like a royal reception-room of the First Empire than a modern apartment in the modern house of a merely modern millionaire. Then he chuckled softly to himself, and a broad smile spread itself among the furrows of his somewhat severely featured countenance.

"Mrs. Sorrel would be sorry if she knew that," he said. "I think—I really think, Helmsley, that Mrs. Sorrel believes you are still in the matrimonial market!"

Helmsley's deeply sunken eyes flashed out a sudden searchlight of keen and quick inquiry, then his brows grew dark with a shadow of scorn.

"Poor Lucy!" he murmured. "She is very unfortunate in her mother, and equally so in her father. Matt Sorrel never did anything in his life but bet on the Turf and gamble at Monte Carlo, and it's too late for him to try his hand at any other sort of business. His daughter is a nice girl and a pretty one,—but now that she has grown from a child into a woman I shall not be able to do much more for her. She will have to do something for herself in finding a good husband."

Sir Francis listened with his head very much on one side. An owl-like inscrutability of legal wisdom seemed to have suddenly enveloped him in a cloud. Pulling himself out of this misty reverie he said abruptly:—

"Well—good-night! or rather good-morning! It's past one o'clock. Shall I see you again before you leave town?"

"Probably. If not, you will hear from me."

"You won't reconsider the advisability of—"

"No, I won't!" And Helmsley smiled. "I'm quite obstinate on that point. If I die suddenly, my property goes to the Crown,—if not, why then you will in due course receive your instructions."

Vesey studied him with thoughtful attention.

"You're a queer fellow, David!" he said, at last. "But I can't help liking you. I only wish you were not quite so—so romantic!"

"Romantic!" Helmsley looked amused. "Romance and I said good-bye to each other years ago. I admit that I used to be romantic—but I'm not now."

"You are!" And Sir Francis frowned a legal frown which soon brightened into a smile. "A man of your age doesn't want to be loved for himself alone unless he's very romantic indeed! And that's what you do want!—and that's what I'm afraid you won't get, in your position—not as this world goes! Good-night!"

"Good-night!"

They walked out of the drawing-room to the head of the grand staircase, and there shook hands and parted, a manservant being in waiting to show Sir Francis to the door. But late as the hour was, Helmsley did not immediately retire to rest. Long after all his household were in bed and sleeping, he sat in the hushed solitude of his library, writing many letters. The library was on a line with the drawing-room, and its one window, facing the Mall, was thrown open to admit such air as could ooze through the stifling heat of the sultry night. Pausing once in the busy work of his hand and pen, Helmsley looked up and saw the bright star he had watched from the upper balcony, peering in upon him steadily like an eye. A weary smile, sadder than scorn, wavered across his features.

"That's Venus," he murmured half aloud. "The Eden star of all very young people,—the star of Love!"

II

On the following evening the cold and frowning aspect of the mansion in Carlton House Terrace underwent a sudden transformation. Lights gleamed from every window; the strip of garden which extended from the rear of the building to the Mall, was covered in by red and white awning, and the balcony where the millionaire master of the dwelling had, some few hours previously, sat talking with his distinguished legal friend, Sir Francis Vesey, was turned into a kind of lady's bower, softly carpeted, adorned with palms and hothouse roses, and supplied with cushioned chairs for the voluptuous ease of such persons of opposite sexes as might find their way to this suggestive "flirtation" corner. The music of a renowned orchestra of Hungarian performers flowed out of the open doors of the sumptuous ballroom which was one of the many attractions of the house, and ran in rhythmic vibrations up the stairs, echoing through all the corridors like the sweet calling voices of fabled nymphs and sirens, till, floating still higher, it breathed itself out to the night,—a night curiously heavy and sombre, with a blackness of sky too dense for any glimmer of stars to shine through. The hum of talk, the constant ripple of laughter, the rustle of women's silken garments, the clatter of plates and glasses in the dining-room, where a costly ball-supper awaited its devouring destiny,—the silvery tripping and slipping of light dancing feet on a polished floor—all these sounds, intermingling with the gliding seductive measure of the various waltzes played in quick succession by the band, created a vague impression of confusion and restlessness in the brain, and David Helmsley himself, the host and entertainer of the assembled guests, watched the brilliant scene from the ballroom door with a weary sense of melancholy which he knew was unfounded and absurd, yet which he could not resist,—a touch of intense and utter loneliness, as though he were a stranger in his own home.

"I feel," he mused, "like some very poor old fellow asked in by chance for a few minutes, just to see the fun!"

He smiled,—yet was unable to banish his depression. The bare fact of the worthlessness of wealth was all at once borne in upon him with overpowering weight. This magnificent house which his hard earnings had purchased,—this ballroom with its painted panels and sculptured friezes, crowded just now with kaleidoscope pictures of men and women

whirling round and round in a maze of music and movement,—the thousand precious and costly things he had gathered about him in his journey through life,—must all pass out of his possession in a few brief years, and there was not a soul who loved him or whom he loved, to inherit them or value them for his sake. A few brief years! And then— darkness. The lights gone out,—the music silenced—the dancing done! And the love that he had dreamed of when he was a boy—love, strong and great and divine enough to outlive death—where was it? A sudden sigh escaped him—

"*Dear* Mr. Helmsley, you look so *very* tired!" said a woman's purring voice at his ear. "*Do* go and rest in your own room for a few minutes before supper! You have been so kind!—Lucy is quite touched and overwhelmed by *all* your goodness to her,—no *lover* could do more for a girl, I'm *sure*! But really you *must* spare yourself! What *should* we do without you!"

"What indeed!" he replied, somewhat drily, as he looked down at the speaker, a cumbrous matron attired in an over-frilled and over-flounced costume of pale grey, which delicate Quakerish colour rather painfully intensified the mottled purplish-red of her face. "But I am not at all tired, Mrs. Sorrel, I assure you! Don't trouble yourself about me—I'm very well."

"*Are* you?" And Mrs. Sorrel looked volumes of tenderest insincerity. "Ah! But you know we *old* people *must* be careful! Young folks can do anything and everything—but *we*, at *our* age, need to be *over*-particular!"

"*You* shouldn't call yourself old, Mrs. Sorrel," said Helmsley, seeing that she expected this from him, "you're quite a young woman."

Mrs. Sorrel gave a little deprecatory laugh.

"Oh dear no!" she said, in a tone which meant "Oh dear yes!" "I wasn't married at sixteen, you know!"

"No? You surprise me!"

Mrs. Sorrel peered at him from under her fat eyelids with a slightly dubious air. She was never quite sure in her own mind as to the way in which "old Gold-Dust," as she privately called him, regarded her. An aged man, burdened with an excess of wealth, was privileged to have what are called "humours," and certainly he sometimes had them. It was necessary—or so Mrs. Sorrel thought—to deal with him delicately and cautiously—neither with too much levity, nor with an overweighted seriousness. One's plan of conduct with a multi-millionaire required to be thought out with sedulous care, and entered upon with circumspection.

And Mrs. Sorrel did not attempt even as much as a youthful giggle at Helmsley's half-sarcastically implied compliment with its sarcastic implication as to the ease with which she supported her years and superabundance of flesh tissue. She merely heaved a short sigh.

"I was just one year younger than Lucy is to-day," she said, "and I really thought myself quite an *old* bride! I was a mother at twenty-one."

Helmsley found nothing to say in response to this interesting statement, particularly as he had often heard it before.

"Who is Lucy dancing with?" he asked irrelevantly, by way of diversion.

"Oh, my *dear* Mr. Helmsley, who is she *not* dancing with!" and Mrs. Sorrel visibly swelled with maternal pride. "Every young man in the room has rushed at her—positively rushed!—and her programme was full five minutes after she arrived! Isn't she looking lovely to-night?—a perfect sylph! *Do* tell me you think she is a sylph!"

David's old eyes twinkled.

"I have never seen a sylph, Mrs. Sorrel, so I cannot make the comparison," he said; "but Lucy is a very beautiful girl, and I think she is looking her best this evening. Her dress becomes her. She ought to find a good husband easily."

"She ought,—indeed she ought! But it is very difficult—very, very difficult! All the men marry for money nowadays, not for love—ah!—how different it was when you and I were young, Mr. Helmsley! Love was everything then,—and there was so much romance and poetical sentiment!"

"Romance is a snare, and poetical sentiment a delusion," said Helmsley, with sudden harshness. "I proved that in my marriage. I should think you had equally proved it in yours!"

Mrs. Sorrel recoiled a little timorously. "Old Gold-Dust" often said unpleasant things—truthful, but eminently tactless,—and she felt that he was likely to say some of those unpleasant things now. Therefore she gave a fluttering gesture of relief and satisfaction as the waltz-music just then ceased, and her daughter's figure, tall, slight, and marvellously graceful, detached itself from the swaying crowd in the ballroom and came towards her.

"Dearest child!" she exclaimed effusively, "are you not *quite* tired out?"

The "dearest child" shrugged her white shoulders and laughed.

"Nothing tires me, mother—you know that!" she answered—then with a sudden change from her air of careless indifference to one of coaxing softness, she turned to Helmsley.

"*You* must be tired!" she said. "Why have you been standing so long at the ballroom door?"

"I have been watching you, Lucy," he replied gently. "It has been a pleasure for me to see you dance. I am too old to dance with you myself, otherwise I should grudge all the young men the privilege."

"I will dance with you, if you like," she said, smiling. "There is one more set of Lancers before supper. Will you be my partner?"

He shook his head.

"Not even to please you, my child!" and taking her hand he patted it kindly. "There is no fool like an old, fool, I know, but I am not quite so foolish as that."

"I see nothing at all foolish in it," pouted Lucy. "You are my host, and it's my coming-of-age party."

Helmsley laughed.

"So it is! And the festival must not be spoilt by any incongruities. It will be quite sufficient honour for me to take you in to supper."

She looked down at the flowers she wore in her bodice, and played with their perfumed petals.

"I like you better than any man here," she said suddenly.

A swift shadow crossed his face. Glancing over his shoulder he saw that Mrs. Sorrel had moved away. Then the cloud passed from his brow, and the thought that for a moment had darkened his mind, yielded to a kinder impulse.

"You flatter me, my dear," he said quietly. "But I am such an old friend of yours that I can take your compliment in the right spirit without having my head turned by it. Indeed, I can hardly believe that it is eleven years ago since I saw you playing about on the seashore as a child. You seem to have grown up like a magic rose, all at once from a tiny bud into a full blossom. Do you remember how I first made your acquaintance?"

"As if I should ever forget!" and she raised her lovely, large dark eyes to his. "I had been paddling about in the sea, and I had lost my shoes and stockings. You found them for me, and you put them on!"

"True!" and he smiled. "You had very wet little feet, all rosy with the salt of the sea—and your long hair was blown about in thick curls round the brightest, sweetest little face in the world. I thought you were the prettiest little girl I had ever seen in my life, and I think just the same of you now."

A pale blush flitted over her cheeks, and she dropped him a demure curtsy.

"Thank you!" she said. "And if you won't dance the Lancers, which are just beginning, will you sit them out with me?"

"Gladly!" and he offered her his arm. "Shall we go up to the drawing-room? It is cooler there than here."

She assented, and they slowly mounted the staircase together. Some of the evening's guests lounging about in the hall and loitering near the ballroom door, watched them go, and exchanged significant glances. One tall woman with black eyes and a viperish mouth, who commanded a certain exclusive "set" by virtue of being the wife of a dissolute Earl whose house was used as a common gambling resort, found out Mrs. Sorrel sitting among a group of female gossips in a corner, and laid a patronising hand upon her shoulder.

"*Do* tell me!" she softly breathed. "*Is* it a case?"

Mrs. Sorrel began to flutter immediately.

"*Dearest* Lady Larford! What *do* you mean!"

"Surely you know!" And the wide mouth of her ladyship grew still wider, and the black eyes more steely. "Will Lucy get him, do you think?"

Mrs. Sorrel fidgeted uneasily in her chair. Other people were listening.

"Really," she mumbled nervously—"really, *dear* Lady Larford!—you put things so *very* plainly!—I—I cannot say!—you see—he is more like her father—"

Lady Larford showed all her white teeth in an expansive grin.

"Oh, that's very safe!" she said. "The 'father' business works very well when sufficient cash is put in with it. I know several examples of perfect matrimonial bliss between old men and young girls—absolutely *perfect*! One is bound to be happy with heaps of money!"

And keeping her teeth still well exposed, Lady Larford glided away, her skirts exhaling an odour of civet-cat as she moved. Mrs. Sorrel gazed after her helplessly, in a state of worry and confusion, for she instinctively felt that her ladyship's pleasure would now be to tell everybody whom she knew, that Lucy Sorrel, "the new girl who was presented at Court last night," was having a "try" for the Helmsley millions; and that if the "try" was not successful, no one living would launch more merciless and bitter jests at the failure and defeat of the Sorrels than this same titled "leader" of a section of the aristocratic gambling set. For there has never been anything born under the sun crueller than a twentieth-century woman of fashion to her own sex—except perhaps a starving hyæna tearing asunder its living prey.

Meanwhile, David Helmsley and his young companion had reached the drawing-room, which they found quite unoccupied. The window-balcony, festooned with rose-silk draperies and flowers, and sparkling with tiny electric lamps, offered itself as an inviting retreat for a quiet chat, and within it they seated themselves, Helmsley rather wearily, and Lucy Sorrel with the queenly air and dainty rustle of soft garments habitual to the movements of a well-dressed woman.

"I have not thanked you half enough," she began, "for all the delightful things you have done for my birthday—"

"Pray spare me!" he interrupted, with a deprecatory gesture—"I would rather you said nothing."

"Oh, but I must say something!" she went on. "You are so generous and good in yourself that of course you cannot bear to be thanked—I know that—but if you will persist in giving so much pleasure to a girl who, but for you, would have no pleasure at all in her life, you must expect that girl to express her feelings somehow. Now, mustn't you?"

She leaned forward, smiling at him with an arch expression of sweetness and confidence. He looked at her attentively, but said nothing.

"When I got your lovely present the first thing this morning," she continued, "I could hardly believe my eyes. Such an exquisite necklace!—such perfect pearls! Dear Mr. Helmsley, you quite spoil me! I'm not worth all the kind thought and trouble you take on my behalf."

Tears started to her eyes, and her lips quivered. Helmsley saw her emotion with only a very slight touch of concern. Her tears were merely sensitive, he thought, welling up from a young and grateful heart, and as the prime cause of that young heart's gratitude he delicately forbore to notice them. This chivalrous consideration on his part caused some little disappointment to the shedder of the tears, but he could not be expected to know that.

"I'm glad you are pleased with my little gift," he said simply, "though I'm afraid it is quite a conventional and ordinary one. Pearls and girls always go together, in fact as in rhyme. After all, they are the most suitable jewels for the young—for they are emblems of everything that youth should be—white and pure and innocent."

Her breath came and went quickly.

"Do you think youth is always like that?" she asked.

"Not always,—but surely most often," he answered. "At any rate, I wish to believe in the simplicity and goodness of all young things."

She was silent. Helmsley studied her thoughtfully,—even critically. And presently he came to the conclusion that as a child she had been much prettier than she now was as a woman. Yet her present phase of loveliness was of the loveliest type. No fault could be found with the perfect oval of her face, her delicate white-rose skin, her small seductive mouth, curved in the approved line of the "Cupid's bow," her deep, soft, bright eyes, fringed with long-lashes a shade darker than the curling waves of her abundant brown hair. But her features in childhood had expressed something more than the beauty which had developed with the passing of years. A sweet affection, a tender earnestness, and an almost heavenly candour had made the attractiveness of her earlier age quite irresistible, but now—or so Helmsley fancied—that fine and subtle charm had gone. He was half ashamed of himself for allowing this thought to enter his mind, and quickly dismissing it, he said—

"How did your presentation go off last night? Was it a full Court?"

"I believe so," she replied listlessly, unfurling a painted fan and waving it idly to and fro—"I cannot say that I found it very interesting. The whole thing bored me dreadfully."

He smiled.

"Bored you! Is it possible to be bored at twenty-one?"

"I think every one, young or old, is bored more or less nowadays," she said. "Boredom is a kind of microbe in the air. Most society functions are deadly dull. And where's the fun of being presented at Court? If a woman wears a pretty gown, all the other women try to tread on it and tear it off her back if they can. And the Royal people only speak to their own special 'set,' and not always the best-looking or best-mannered set either."

Helmsley looked amused.

"Well, it's what is called an *entrée* into the world,"—he replied. "For my own part, I have never been 'presented,' and never intend to be. I see too much of Royalty privately, in the dens of finance."

"Yes—all the kings and princes wanting to borrow money," she said quickly and flippantly. "And you must despise the lot. *You* are a real 'King,' bigger than any crowned head, because you can do just as you like, and you are not the servant of Governments or peoples. I am sure you must be the happiest man in the world!"

She plucked off a rose from a flowering rose-tree near her, and began to wrench out its petals with a quick, nervous movement. Helmsley watched her with a vague sense of annoyance.

"I am no more happy," he said suddenly, "than that rose you are picking to pieces, though it has never done you any harm."

She started, and flushed,—then laughed.

"Oh, the poor little rose!" she exclaimed—"I'm sorry! I've had so many roses to-day, that I don't think about them. I suppose it's wrong."

"It's not wrong," he answered quietly; "it's merely the fault of those who give you more roses than you know how to appreciate."

She looked at him inquiringly, but could not fathom his expression.

"Still," he went on, "I would not have your life deprived of so much as one rose. And there is a very special rose that does not grow in earthly gardens, which I should like you to find and wear on your heart, Lucy,—I hope I shall see you in the happy possession of it before I die,—I mean the rose of love."

She lifted her head, and her eyes shone coldly.

"Dear Mr. Helmsley," she said, "I don't believe in love!"

A flash of amazement, almost of anger, illumined his worn features.

"You don't believe in love!" he echoed. "O child, what *do* you believe in, then?"

The passion of his tone moved her to a surprised smile.

"Well, I believe in being happy while you can," she replied tranquilly. "And love isn't happiness. All my girl and men friends who are what they call 'in love' seem to be thoroughly miserable. Many of them get perfectly ill with jealousy, and they never seem to know whether what they call their 'love' will last from one day to another. I shouldn't care to live at such a high tension of nerves. My own mother and father married 'for love,' so I am always told,—and I'm sure a more quarrelsome couple never existed. I believe in friendship more than love."

As she spoke, Helmsley looked at her steadily, his face darkening with a shadow of weary scorn.

"I see!" he murmured coldly. "You do not care to over-fatigue the heart's action by unnecessary emotion. Quite right! If we were all as wise as you are at your age, we might live much longer than we do. You are very sensible, Lucy!—more sensible than I should have thought possible for so young a woman."

She gave him a swift, uneasy glance. She was not quite sure of his mood.

"Friendship," he continued, speaking in a slow, meditative tone, "is a good thing,—it may be, as you suggest, safer and sweeter than love.

But even friendship, to be worthy of its name, must be quite unselfish,—and unselfishness, in both love and friendship, is rare."

"Very, very rare!" she sighed.

"You will be thinking of marriage *some* day, if you are not thinking of it now," he went on. "Would a husband's friendship—friendship and no more—satisfy you?"

She gazed at him candidly.

"I am sure it would!" she said; "I'm not the least bit sentimental."

He regarded her with a grave and musing steadfastness. A very close observer might have seen a line of grim satire near the corners of his mouth, and a gleam of irritable impatience in his sunken eyes; but these signs of inward feeling were not apparent to the girl, who, more than usually satisfied with herself and over-conscious of her own beauty, considered that she was saying just the very thing that he would expect and like her to say.

"You do not crave for love, then?" he queried. "You do not wish to know anything of the 'divine rapture falling out of heaven,'—the rapture that has inspired all the artists and poets in the world, and that has probably had the largest share in making the world's history?"

She gave a little shrug of amused disdain.

"Raptures never last!" and she laughed. "And artists and poets are dreadful people! I've seen a few of them, and don't want to see them any more. They are always very untidy, and they have the most absurd ideas of their own abilities. You can't have them in society, you know!—you simply can't! If I had a house of my own I would never have a poet inside it."

The grim lines round Helmsley's mouth hardened, and made him look almost cruelly saturnine. Yet he murmured under his breath:—

> *"All thoughts, all passions, all delights,*
> *Whatever stirs this mortal frame;*
> *Are but the ministers of Love,*
> *And feed his sacred flame!"*

"What's that?" she asked quickly.

"Poetry!" he answered, "by a man named Coleridge. He is dead now. He used to take opium, and he did not understand business matters. He was never rich in anything but thoughts."

She smiled brilliantly.

"How silly!" she said.

"Yes, he was very silly," agreed Helmsley, watching her narrowly from under his half-closed eyelids. "But most thinkers are silly, even when they don't take opium. They believe in Love."

She coloured. She caught the sarcastic inflection in his tone. But she was silent.

"Most men who have lived and worked and suffered," he went on, "come to know before they die that without a great and true love in their lives, their work is wasted, and their sufferings are in vain. But there are exceptions, of course. Some get on very well without love at all, and perhaps these are the most fortunate."

"I am sure they are!" she said decisively.

He picked up two or three of the rose-petals her restless fingers had scattered, and laying them in his palm looked at the curved, pink, shell-like shapes abstractedly.

"Well, they are saved a good deal of trouble," he answered quietly. "They spare themselves many a healing heart-ache and many purifying tears. But when they grow old, and when they find that, after all, the happiest folks in the world are still those who love, or who have loved and have been loved, even though the loved ones are perhaps no longer here, they may—I do not say they will—possibly regret that they never experienced that marvellous sense of absorption into another's life of which Mrs. Browning writes in her letters to her husband. Do you know what she says?"

"I'm afraid I don't!" and she smothered a slight yawn as she spoke. He fixed his eyes intently upon her.

"She tells her lover her feeling in these words: '*There is nothing in you that does not draw all out of me.*' That is the true emotion of love,—the one soul must draw all out of the other, and the best of all in each."

"But the Brownings were a very funny couple," and the fair Lucy arched her graceful throat and settled more becomingly in its place a straying curl of her glossy brown hair. "I know an old gentleman who used to see them together when they lived in Florence, and *he* says they were so queer-looking that people used to laugh at them. It's all very well to love and to be in love, but if you look odd and people laugh at you, what's the good of it?"

Helmsley rose from his seat abruptly.

"True!" he exclaimed. "You're right, Lucy! Little girl, you're quite right! What's the good of it! Upon my word, you're a most practical woman!—you'll make a capital wife for a business man!" Then as the gay music of the band below-stairs suddenly ceased, to give place to the noise of chattering voices and murmurs of laughter, he glanced at his watch.

"Supper-time!" he said. "Let me take you down. And after supper, will you give me ten minutes' chat with you alone in the library!"

She looked up eagerly, with a flush of pink in her cheeks.

"Of course I will! With pleasure!"

"Thank you!" And he drew her white-gloved hand through his arm. "I am leaving town next week, and I have something important to say to you before I go. You will allow me to say it privately?"

She smiled assent, and leaned on his arm with a light, confiding pressure, to which he no more responded than if his muscles had been rigid iron. Her heart beat quickly with a sense of gratified vanity and exultant expectancy,—but his throbbed slowly and heavily, chilled by the double frost of age and solitude.

III

To see people eating is understood to be a very interesting and "brilliant" spectacle, and however insignificant you may be in the social world, you get a reflex of its "brilliancy" when you allow people in their turn to see you eating likewise. A well-cooked, well-served supper is a "function," in which every man and woman who can move a jaw takes part, and though in plain parlance there is nothing uglier than the act of putting food into one's mouth, we have persuaded ourselves that it is a pretty and pleasant performance enough for us to ask our friends to see us do it. Byron's idea that human beings should eat privately and apart, was not altogether without æsthetic justification, though according to medical authority such a procedure would be very injurious to health. The slow mastication of a meal in the presence of cheerful company is said to promote healthy digestion—moreover, custom and habit make even the most incongruous things acceptable, therefore the display of tables, crowded with food-stuffs and surrounded by eating, drinking, chattering and perspiring men and women, does not affect us to any sense of the ridiculous or the unseemly. On the contrary, when some of us see such tables, we exclaim "How lovely!" or "How delightful!" according to our own pet vocabulary, or to our knowledge of the humour of our host or hostess,—or perhaps, if we are young cynics, tired of life before we have confronted one of its problems, we murmur, "Not so bad!" or "Fairly decent!" when we are introduced to the costly and appetising delicacies heaped up round masses of flowers and silver for our consideration and entertainment. At the supper given by David Helmsley for Lucy Sorrel's twenty-first birthday, there was, however, no note of dissatisfaction—the *blasé* breath of the callow critic emitted no withering blight, and even latter-day satirists in their teens, frosted like tender pease-blossom before their prime, condescended to approve the lavish generosity, combined with the perfect taste, which made the festive scene a glowing picture of luxury and elegance. But Helmsley himself, as he led his beautiful partner, "the" guest of the evening, to the head of the principal table, and took his place beside her, was conscious of no personal pleasure, but only of a dreary feeling which seemed lonelier than loneliness and more sorrowful than sorrow. The wearied scorn that he had lately begun to entertain for himself, his wealth, his business, his influence, and all his surroundings, was embittered by a disappointment none the less keen because he had dimly foreseen it. The child he had petted, the girl he had indulged after the fashion of a father who seeks to make the world pleasant to a young life just entering it, she, even she, was, or seemed to be, practically as selfish as any experienced member of the particular set of schemers and intriguers who compose what is sometimes called "society" in the present day. He had no wish to judge her harshly, but he was too old and knew too much of life to be easily deceived in his estimation of character. A very slight hint was sufficient for him. He had seen a great deal of Lucy Sorrel as a child— she had always been known as his "little favourite"—but since she had attended a fashionable school at Brighton, his visits to her home had been less frequent, and he had had very few opportunities of becoming acquainted with the gradual development of her mental and moral self. During her holidays he had given her as many little social pleasures and gaieties as he had considered might be acceptable to her taste and age, but on these occasions other persons had always been present, and Lucy herself had worn what are called "company" manners, which in her case were singularly charming and attractive, so much so, indeed, that it would have seemed like heresy to question their sincerity. But now—whether it was the slight hint dropped by Sir Francis Vesey on the previous night as to Mrs. Sorrel's match-making proclivities, or whether it was a scarcely perceptible suggestion of something more flippant and assertive than usual in the air and bearing of Lucy herself that had awakened his suspicions,—he was certainly disposed to doubt, for the first time in all his knowledge of her, the candid nature of the girl for whom he had hitherto entertained, half-unconsciously, an almost parental affection. He sat by her side at supper, seldom speaking, but always closely observant. He saw everything; he watched the bright, exulting flash of her eyes as she glanced at her various friends, both near her and at a distance, and he fancied he detected in their responsive looks a subtle inquiry and meaning which he would not allow himself to investigate. And while the bubbling talk and laughter eddied round him, he made up his mind to combat the lurking distrust that teased his brain, and either to disperse it altogether or else confirm it beyond all mere shadowy misgiving. Some such thought as this had occurred to him, albeit vaguely, when he had, on a sudden unpremeditated impulse, asked Lucy to give him a few minutes' private conversation with her after supper, but now, what had previously been a mere idea formulated itself into a fixed resolve.

"For what, after all, does it matter to me?" he mused. "Why should I hesitate to destroy a dream? Why should I care if another rainbow bubble of life breaks and disappears? I am too old to have ideals—so most people would tell me. And yet—with the grave open and ready to receive me,—I still believe that love and truth and purity surely exist in women's hearts—if one could only know just where to find the women!"

"Dear King David!" murmured a cooing voice at his ear. "Won't you drink my health?"

He started as from a reverie. Lucy Sorrel was bending towards him, her face glowing with gratified vanity and self-elation.

"Of course!" he answered, and rising to his feet, he lifted his glass full of as yet untasted champagne, at which action on his part the murmur of voices suddenly ceased sand all eyes were turned upon him. "Ladies and gentlemen," he said, in his soft, tired voice,—"I beg to propose the health of Miss Lucy Sorrel! She has lived twenty-one years on this interesting old planet of ours, and has found it, so far, not altogether without charm. I have had seventy years of it, and strange as it may seem to you all, I am able to keep a few of the illusions and delusions I had when I was even younger than our charming guest of the evening. I still believe in good women! I think I have one sitting at my right hand to-night. I take for granted that her nature is as fair as her face; and I hope that every recurring anniversary of this day may bring her just as much happiness as she deserves. I ask you to drink to her health, wealth, and prosperity; and—may she soon find a good husband!"

Applause and laughter followed this conventional little speech, and the toast was honoured in the usual way, Lucy bowing and smiling her thanks to all present. And then there ensued one of those strange impressions—one might almost call them telepathic instead of atmospheric effects—which, subtly penetrating the air, exerted an inexplicable influence on the mind;—the expectancy of some word never to be uttered,—the waiting for some incident never to take place. People murmured and smiled, and looked and laughed, but there was an evident embarrassment among them,—an under-sense of something like disappointment. The fortunately commonplace and methodical habits of waiters, whose one idea is to keep their patrons busy eating and drinking, gradually overcame this insidious restraint, and the supper went on gaily till at one o'clock the Hungarian band again began to play, and all the young people, eager for their "extras" in the way of dances, quickly rose from the various tables and began to crowd out towards the ballroom. In the general dispersal, Lucy having left him for a partner to whom she had promised the first "extra," Helmsley stopped to speak to one or two men well known to him in the business world. He was still conversing with these when Mrs. Sorrel, not perceiving him in the corner where he stood apart with his friend, trotted past him with an agitated step and flushed countenance, and catching her daughter by the skirt of her dress as that young lady moved on with the pushing throng in front of her, held her back for a second.

"What have you done?" she demanded querulously, in not too soft a tone. "Were you careful? Did you manage him properly? What did he say to you?"

Lucy's beautiful face hardened, and her lips met in a thin, decidedly bad-tempered line.

"He said nothing to the purpose," she replied coldly. "There was no time. But"—and she lowered her voice—"he wants to speak to me alone presently. I'm going to him in the library after this dance."

She passed on, and Mrs. Sorrel, heaving a deep sigh, drew out a black pocket-fan and fanned herself vigorously. Wreathing her face with social smiles, she made her way slowly out of the supper-room, happily unaware that Helmsley had been near enough to hear every word that had passed. And hearing, he had understood; but he went on talking to his friends in the quiet, rather slow way which was habitual to him, and when he left them there was nothing about him to indicate that he was in a suppressed state of nervous excitement which made him for the moment quite forget that he was an old man. Impetuous youth itself never felt a keener blaze of vitality in the veins than he did at that moment, but it was the withering heat of indignation that warmed him—not the tender glow of love. The clarion sweetness of the dance-music, now pealing loudly on the air, irritated his nerves,—the lights, the flowers, the brilliancy of the whole scene jarred upon his soul,—what was it all but sham, he thought!—a show in the mere name of friendship!—an ephemeral rose of pleasure with a worm at its core! Impatiently he shook himself free of those who sought to detain him and went at once to his library,—a sombre, darkly-furnished apartment, large enough to seem gloomy by contrast with the gaiety and cheerfulness which were dominant throughout the rest of the house that evening. Only two or three shaded lamps were lit, and these cast a ghostly flicker on the row of books that lined the walls. A few names in raised letters of gold relief upon the backs of some of the volumes, asserted themselves, or so he fancied, with unaccustomed prominence. "Montaigne," "Seneca," "Rochefoucauld," "Goethe," "Byron," and "The Sonnets of William Shakespeare," stood forth from the surrounding darkness as though demanding special notice.

"Voices of the dead!" he murmured half aloud. "I should have learned wisdom from you all long ago! What have the great geniuses of the world lived for? For what purpose did they use their brains and pens? Simply to teach mankind the folly of too much faith! Yet we continue to delude ourselves—and the worst of it is that we do it wilfully and knowingly. We are perfectly aware that when we trust, we shall be deceived—yet we trust on! Even I—old and frail and about to die—cannot rid myself of a belief in God, and in the ultimate happiness of each man's destiny. And yet, so far as my own experience serves me, I have nothing to go upon—absolutely nothing!"

He gave an unconscious gesture—half of scorn, half of despair—and paced the room slowly up and down. A life of toil—a life rounding into worldly success, but blank of all love and heart's comfort—was this to be the only conclusion to his career? Of what use, then, was it to have lived at all?

"People talk foolishly of a 'declining birth-rate,'" he went on; "yet if, according to the modern scientist, all civilisations are only so much output of wasted human energy, doomed to pass into utter oblivion, and human beings only live but to die and there an end, of what avail is it to be born at all? Surely it is but wanton cruelty to take upon ourselves the responsibility of continuing a race whose only consummation is rottenness in unremembered graves!"

At that moment the door opened and Lucy Sorrel entered softly, with a pretty air of hesitating timidity which became her style of beauty excellently well. As he looked up and saw her standing half shyly on the threshold, a white, light, radiant figure expressing exquisitely fresh youth, grace and—innocence?—yes! surely that wondrous charm which hung about her like a delicate atmosphere redolent with the perfume of spring, could only be the mystic exhalation of a pure mind adding spiritual lustre to the material attraction of a perfect body,—his heart misgave him. Already he was full of remorse lest so much as a passing thought in his brain might have done her unmerited wrong. He advanced to meet her, and his voice was full of kindness as he said:—

"Is your dance quite over, Lucy? Are you sure I am not selfishly depriving you of pleasure by asking you to come away from all your young friends just to talk to me for a few minutes in this dull room?"

She raised her beautiful eyes confidingly.

"Dear Mr. Helmsley, there can be no greater pleasure for me than to talk to you!" she answered sweetly.

His expression changed and hardened. "That's not true," he thought; "and *she* knows it, and *I* know it." Aloud he said: "Very prettily spoken, Lucy! But I am aware of my own tediousness and I won't detain you long. Will you sit down?" and he offered her an easy-chair, into which she sank with the soft slow grace of a nestling bird. "I only want to say just a few words,—such as your father might say to you if he were so inclined—about your future."

She gave him a swift glance of keen inquiry.

"My future?" she echoed.

"Yes. Have you thought of it at all yourself?"

She heaved a little sigh, smiled, and shook her head in the negative.

"I'm afraid I'm very silly," she confessed plaintively. "I never think!"

He drew up another armchair and sat down opposite to her.

"Well, try to do so now for five minutes at least," he said, gently. "I am going away to-morrow or next day for a considerable time—"

A quick flush flew over her face.

"Going away!" she exclaimed. "But—not far?"

"That depends on my own whim," he replied, watching her attentively. "I shall certainly be absent from England for a year, perhaps longer. But, Lucy,—you were such a little pet of mine in your childhood that I cannot help taking an interest in you now you are grown up. That is, I think, quite natural. And I should like to feel that you have some good and safe idea of your own happiness in life before I leave you."

She stared,—her face fell.

"I have no ideas at all," she answered after a pause, the corners of her red mouth drooping in petulant, spoilt-child fashion, "and if you go away I shall have no pleasures either!"

He smiled.

"I'm sorry you take it that way," he said. "But I'm nearing the end of my tether, Lucy, and increasing age makes me restless. I want change of scene—and change of surroundings. I am thoroughly tired of my present condition."

"Tired?" and her eyes expressed whole volumes of amazement. "Not really? *You*—tired of your present condition? With all your money?"

"With all my money!" he answered drily, "Money is not the elixir of happiness, Lucy, though many people seem to think it is. But I prefer not to talk about myself. Let me speak of you. What do you propose to do with your life? You will marry, of course?"

"I—I suppose so," she faltered.

"Is there any one you specially favour?—any young fellow who loves you, or whom you are inclined to love—and who wants a start in the world? If there is, send him to me, and, if he has anything in him, I'll make myself answerable for his prosperity."

She looked up with a cold, bright steadfastness.

"There is no one," she said. "Dear Mr. Helmsley, you are very good, but I assure you I have never fallen in love in my life. As I told you before supper, I don't believe in that kind of nonsense. And I—I want nothing. Of course I know my father and mother are poor, and that they have kept up a sort of position which ranks them among the 'shabby genteel,'—and I suppose if I don't marry quickly I shall have to do something for a living—"

She broke off, embarrassed by the keenness of the gaze he fixed upon her.

"Many good, many beautiful, many delicate women 'do something,' as you put it, for a living," he said slowly. "But the fight is always fierce, and the end is sometimes bitter. It is better for a woman that she should be safeguarded by a husband's care and tenderness than that she should attempt to face the world alone."

A flashing smile dimpled the corners of her mouth.

"Why, yes, I quite agree with you," she retorted playfully. "But if no husband come forward, then it cannot be helped!"

He rose, and, pushing away his chair, walked up and down in silence.

She watched him with a sense of growing irritability, and her heart beat with uncomfortable quickness. Why did he seem to hesitate so long? Presently he stopped in his slow movement to and fro, and stood looking down upon her with a fixed intensity which vaguely troubled her.

"It is difficult to advise," he said, "and it is still more difficult to control. In your case I have no right to do either. I am an old man, and you are a very young woman. You are beginning your life,—I am ending mine. Yet, young as you are, you say with apparent sincerity that you do not believe in love. Now I, though I have loved and lost, though I have loved and have been cruelly deceived in love, still believe that if the true, heavenly passion be fully and faithfully experienced, it must prove the chief joy, if not the only one, of life. You think otherwise, and perhaps you correctly express the opinion of the younger generation of men and women. These appear to crowd more emotion and excitement into their lives than ever was attained or attainable in the lives of their forefathers, but they do not, or so it seems to me, secure for themselves as much peace of mind and satisfaction of soul as were the inheritance of bygone folk whom we now call 'old-fashioned.' Still, you may be right in depreciating the power of love—from your point of view. All the same, I should be sorry to see you entering into a loveless marriage."

For a moment she was silent, then she suddenly plunged into speech.

"Dear Mr. Helmsley, do you really think all the silly sentiment talked and written about love is any good in marriage? We know so much nowadays,—and the disillusion of matrimony is so *very* complete! One has only to read the divorce cases in the newspapers to see what mistakes people make—"

He winced as though he had been stung.

"Do you read the divorce cases, Lucy?" he asked. "You—a mere girl like you?"

She looked surprised at the regret and pain in his tone.

"Why, of course! One *must* read the papers to keep up with all the things that are going on. And the divorce cases have always such startling headings,—in such big print!—one is obliged to read them— positively obliged!"

She laughed carelessly, and settled herself more cosily in her chair.

"You nearly always find that it is the people who were desperately in love with each other before marriage who behave disgracefully and are perfectly sick of each other afterwards," she went on. "They wanted perpetual poetry and moonlight, and of course they find they can't have it. Now, I don't want poetry or moonlight,—I hate both! Poetry makes me sleepy, and moonlight gives me neuralgia. I should like a husband who would be a *friend* to me—a real kind friend!—some one who would be able to take care of me, and be nice to me always—some one much older than myself, who was wise and strong and clever—"

"And rich," said Helmsley quietly. "Don't forget that! Very rich!"

She glanced at him furtively, conscious of a slight nervous qualm. Then, rapidly reviewing the situation in her shallow brain, she accepted his remark smilingly.

"Oh, well, of course!" she said. "It's not pleasant to live without plenty of money."

He turned from her abruptly, and resumed his leisurely walk to and fro, much to her inward vexation. He was becoming fidgety, she decided,—old people were really very trying! Suddenly, with the air of a man arriving at an important decision, he sat down again in the armchair opposite her own, and leaning indolently back against the cushion, surveyed her with a calm, critical, entirely businesslike manner, much as he would have looked at a Jew company-promoter, who sought his aid to float a "bogus" scheme.

"It's not pleasant to live without plenty of money, you think," he said, repeating her last words slowly. "Well! The pleasantest time of my life was when I did not own a penny in the bank, and when I had to be very sharp in order to earn enough for my day's dinner. There was a zest, a delight, a fine glory in the mere effort to live that brought out the strength of every quality I possessed. I learned to know myself, which is a farther reaching wisdom than is found in knowing others. I had ideals then,—and—old as I am, I have them still."

He paused. She was silent. Her eyes were lowered, and she played idly with her painted fan.

"I wonder if it would surprise you," he went on, "to know that I have made an ideal of *you*?"

She looked up with a smile.

"Really? Have you? I'm afraid I shall prove a disappointment!"

He did not answer by the obvious compliment which she felt she had a right to expect. He kept his gaze fixed steadily on her face, and his shaggy eyebrows almost met in the deep hollow which painful thought had ploughed along his forehead.

"I have made," he said, "an ideal in my mind of the little child who sat on my knee, played with my watch-chain and laughed at me when I called her my little sweetheart. She was perfectly candid in her laughter,—she knew it was absurd for an old man to have a child as his sweetheart. I loved to hear her laugh so,—because she was true to herself, and to her right and natural instincts. She was the prettiest and sweetest child I ever saw,—full of innocent dreams and harmless gaiety. She began to grow up, and I saw less and less of her, till gradually I lost the child and found the woman. But I believe in the child's heart still—I think that the truth and simplicity of the child's soul are still in the womanly nature,—and in that way, Lucy, I yet hold you as an ideal."

Her breath quickened a little.

"You think too kindly of me," she murmured, furling and unfurling her fan slowly; "I'm not at all clever."

He gave a slight deprecatory gesture.

"Cleverness is not what I expect or have ever expected of you," he said. "You have not as yet had to endure the misrepresentation and wrong which frequently make women clever,—the life of solitude and despised dreams which moves a woman to put on man's armour and sally forth to fight the world and conquer it, or else die in the attempt. How few conquer, and how many die, are matters of history. Be glad you are not a clever woman, Lucy!—for genius in a woman is the mystic laurel of Apollo springing from the soft breast of Daphne. It hurts in the growing, and sometimes breaks the heart from which it grows."

She answered nothing. He was talking in a way she did not understand,—his allusion to Apollo and Daphne was completely beyond her. She smothered a tiny yawn and wondered why he was so tedious. Moreover, she was conscious of some slight chagrin, for though she said, out of mere social hypocrisy, that she was not clever, she thought herself exceptionally so. Why could he not admit her abilities as readily as she herself admitted them?

"No, you are not clever," he resumed quietly. "And I am glad you are not. You are good and pure and true,—these graces outweigh all cleverness."

Her cheeks flushed prettily,—she thought of a girl who had been her schoolmate at Brighton, one of the boldest little hussies that ever flashed eyes to the light of day, yet who could assume the dainty simpering air of maiden—modest perfection at the moment's notice. She wished she could do the same, but she had not studied the trick carefully enough, and she was afraid to try more of it than just a little tremulous smile and a quick downward glance at her fan. Helmsley watched her attentively—almost craftily. It did not strain his sense of perspicuity over much to see exactly what was going on in her mind. He settled himself a little more comfortably in his chair, and pressing the tips of his fingers together, looked at her over this pointed rampart of polished nails as though she were something altogether curious and remarkable.

"The virtues of a woman are her wealth and worth," he said sententiously, as though he were quoting a maxim out of a child's copybook. "A jewel's price is not so much for its size and weight as for its particular lustre. But common commercial people—like myself— even if they have the good fortune to find a diamond likely to surpass all others in the market, are never content till they have tested it. Every Jew bites his coin. And I am something of a Jew. I like to know the exact value of what I esteem as precious. And so I test it."

"Yes?" She threw in this interjected query simply because she did not know what to say. She thought he was talking very oddly, and wondered whether he was quite sane.

"Yes," he echoed; "I test it. And, Lucy, I think so highly of you, and esteem you as so very fair a pearl of womanhood, that I am inclined to test you just as I would a priceless gem. Do you object?"

She glanced up at him flutteringly, vaguely surprised. The corners of his mouth relaxed into the shadow of a smile, and she was reassured.

"Object? Of course not! As if I should object to anything you wish!" she said amiably. "But—I don't quite understand—"

"No, possibly not," he interrupted; "I know I have not the art of making myself very clear in matters which deeply and personally affect myself. I have nerves still, and some remnant of a heart,—these occasionally trouble me—"

She leaned forward and put her delicately gloved hand on his.

"Dear King David!" she murmured. "You are always so good!"

He took the little fingers in his own clasp and held them gently.

"I want to ask you a question, Lucy," he said; "and it is a very difficult question, because I feel that your answer to it may mean a great sorrow for me,—a great disappointment. The question is the 'test' I speak of. Shall I put it to you?"

"Please do!" she answered, her heart beginning to beat violently. He was coming to the point at last, she thought, and a few words more would surely make her the future mistress of the Helmsley millions! "If I can answer it I will!"

"Shall I ask you my question, or shall I not?" he went on, gripping her hand hard, and half raising himself in his chair as he looked intently at her telltale face. "For it means more than you can realise. It is an audacious, impudent question, Lucy,—one that no man of my age ought to ask any woman,—one that is likely to offend you very much!"

She withdrew her hand from his.

"Offend me?" and her eyes widened with a blank wonder. "What can it be?"

"Ah! What can it be! Think of all the most audacious and impudent things a man—an old man—could say to a young woman! Suppose,—it is only supposition, remember,—suppose, for instance, I were to ask you to marry me?"

A smile, brilliant and exultant, flashed over her features,—she almost laughed out her inward joy.

"I should accept you at once!" she said.

With sudden impetuosity he rose, and pushing away his chair, drew himself up to his full height, looking down upon her.

"You would!" and his voice was low and tense. "*You!*—you would actually marry me?"

She, rising likewise, confronted him in all her fresh and youthful beauty, fair and smiling, her bosom heaving and her eyes dilating with eagerness.

"I would,—indeed I would!" she averred delightedly. "I would rather marry you than any man in the world!"

There was a moment's silence. Then—

"Why?" he asked.

The simple monosyllabic query completely confused her. It was unexpected, and she was at her wit's end how to reply to it. Moreover, he kept his eyes so pertinaciously fixed upon her that she felt her blood rising to her cheeks and brow in a hot flush of—shame? Oh no!—not shame, but merely petulant vexation. The proper way for him to behave at this juncture, so she reflected, would be that he should take her tenderly in his arms and murmur, after the penny-dreadful style of elderly hero, "My darling, my darling! Can you, so young and beautiful, really care for an old fogey like me?'" to which she would, of course, have replied in the same fashion, and with the most charming insincerity—"Dearest! Do not talk of age! You will never be old to my fond heart!" But to stand, as he was standing, like a rigid figure of bronze, with a hard pale face in which only the eyes seemed living, and to merely ask "Why" she would rather marry him than any other man in the world, was absurd, to say the least of it, and indeed quite lacking in all delicacy of sentiment. She sought about in her mind for some way out of the difficulty and could find none. She grew more and more painfully crimson, and wished she could cry. A well worked-up passion of tears would have come in very usefully just then, but somehow she could not turn the passion on. And a horrid sense of incompetency and failure began to steal over her—an awful foreboding of defeat. What could she do to seize the slippery opportunity and grasp the doubtful prize? How could she land the big golden fish which she foolishly fancied she had at the end of her line? Never had she felt so helpless or so angry.

"Why?" he repeated—"Why would you marry me? Not for love certainly. Even if you believed in love—which you say you do not,—you could not at your age love a man at mine. That would be impossible and unnatural. I am old enough to be your grandfather. Think again, Lucy! Perhaps you spoke hastily—out of girlish thoughtlessness—or out of kindness and a wish to please me,—but do not, in so serious a matter, consider me at all. Consider yourself. Consider your own nature and temperament—your own life—your own future—your own happiness. Would you, young as you are, with all the world before you—would you, if I asked you, deliberately and of your own free will, marry me?"

She drew a sharp breath, and hurriedly wondered what was best to do. He spoke so strangely!—he looked so oddly! But that might be because he was in love with her! Her lips parted,—she faced him straightly, lifting her head with a little air of something like defiance.

"I would!—of course I would!" she replied. "Nothing could make me happier!"

He gave a kind of gesture with his hands as though he threw aside some cherished object.

"So vanishes my last illusion!" he said. "Well! Let it go!"

She gazed at him stupidly. What did he mean? Why did he not now emulate the penny-dreadful heroes and say "My darling!" Nothing seemed further from his thoughts. His eyes rested upon her with a coldness such as she had never seen in them before, and his features hardened.

"I should have known the modern world and modern education better," he went on, speaking more to himself than to her. "I have had experience enough. I should never have allowed myself to keep even the shred of a belief in woman's honesty!"

She started, and flamed into a heat of protest.

"Mr. Helmsley!"

He raised a deprecatory hand.

"Pardon me!" he said wearily—"I am an old man, accustomed to express myself bluntly. Even if I vex you, I fear I shall not know how to apologise. I had thought—"

He broke off, then with an effort resumed—

"I had thought, Lucy, that you were above all bribery and corruption."

"Bribery?—Corruption?" she stammered, and in a tremor of excitement and perturbation her fan dropped from her hands to the floor. He stooped for it with the ease and grace of a far younger man, and returned it to her.

"Yes, bribery and corruption," he continued quietly. "The bribery of wealth—the corruption of position. These are the sole objects for which (if I asked you, which I have not done) you would marry me. For there is nothing else I have to offer you. I could not give you the sentiment or passion of a husband (if husbands ever have sentiment or passion nowadays), because all such feeling is dead in me. I could not be your 'friend' in marriage—because I should always remember that our matrimonial 'friendship' was merely one of cash supply and demand. You see I speak very plainly. I am not a polite person—not even a Conventional one. I am too old to tell lies. Lying is never a profitable business in youth—but in age it is pure waste of time and energy. With one foot in the grave it is as well to keep the other from slipping."

He paused. She tried to say something, but could find no suitable words with which to answer him. He looked at her steadily, half expecting her to speak, and there was both pain and sorrow in the depths of his tired eyes.

"I need not prolong this conversation," he said, after a minute's silence. "For it must be as embarrassing to you as it is to me. It is quite my own fault that I built too many hopes upon you, Lucy! I set you up on a pedestal and you have yourself stepped down from it—I have put you to the test, and you have failed. I daresay the failure is as much the concern of your parents and the way in which they have brought you up, as it is of any latent weakness in your own mind and character. But,—if, when I suggested such an absurd and unnatural proposition as marriage between myself arid you, you had at once, like a true woman, gently and firmly repudiated the idea, then—"

"Then—what?" she faltered.

"Why, then I should have made you my sole heiress," he said quietly.

Her eyes opened in blank wonderment and despair. Was it possible! Had she been so near her golden El Dorado only to see the shining shores receding, and the glittering harbour closed! Oh, it was cruel!

Horrible! There was a convulsive catch in her throat which she managed to turn into the laugh hysterical.

"Really!" she exclaimed, with a poor attempt at flippancy; and, in her turn, she asked the question, "Why?"

"Because I should have known you were honest," answered Helmsley, with emphasis. "Honest to your womanly instincts, and to the simplest and purest part of your nature. I should have proved for myself the fact that you refused to sell your beautiful person for gold—that you were no slave in the world's auction-mart, but a free, proud, noble-hearted English girl who meant to be faithful to all that was highest and best in her soul. Ah, Lucy! You are not this little dream-girl of mine! You are a very realistic modern woman with whom a man's 'ideal' has nothing in common!"

She was silent, half-stifled with rage. He stepped up to her and took her hand.

"Good-night, Lucy! Good-bye!"

She wrenched her fingers from his clasp, and a sudden, uncontrollable fury possessed her.

"I hate you!" she said between her set teeth. "You are mean! Mean! I hate you!"

He stood quite still, gravely irresponsive.

"You have deceived me—cheated me!" she went on, angrily and recklessly. "You made me think you wanted to marry me."

The corners of his mouth went up under his ashen-grey moustache in a chill smile.

"Pardon me!" he interrupted. "But did I make you think? or did you think it of your own accord?"

She plucked at her fan nervously.

"Any girl—I don't care who she is—would accept you if you asked her to marry you!" she said hotly. "It would be perfectly idiotic to refuse such a rich man, even if he were Methusaleh himself. There's nothing wrong or dishonest in taking the chance of having plenty of money, if it is offered."

He looked at her, vaguely compassionating her loss of self-control.

"No, there is nothing wrong or dishonest in taking the chance of having plenty of money, if such a chance can be had without shame and dishonour," he said. "But I, personally, should consider a woman hopelessly lost to every sense of self-respect, if at the age of twenty-one she consented to marry a man of seventy for the sake of his wealth. And

I should equally consider the man of seventy a disgrace to the name of manhood if he condoned the voluntary sale of such a woman by becoming her purchaser."

She lifted her head with a haughty air.

"Then, if you thought these things, you had no right to propose to me!" she said passionately.

He was faintly amused.

"I did not propose to you, Lucy," he answered, "and I never intended to do so! I merely asked what your answer would be if I did."

"It comes to the same thing!" she muttered.

"Pardon me, not quite! I told you I was putting you to a test. That you failed to stand my test is the conclusion of the whole affair. We really need say no more about it. The matter is finished."

She bit her lips vexedly, then forced a hard smile.

"It's about time it was finished, I'm sure!" she said carelessly. "I'm perfectly tired out!"

"No doubt you are—you must be—I was forgetting how late it is," and with ceremonious politeness he opened the door for her to pass. "You have had an exhausting evening! Forgive me for any pain or vexation—or—or anger I may have caused you—and, good-night, Lucy! God bless you!"

He held out his hand. He looked worn and wan, and his face showed pitiful marks of fatigue, loneliness, and sorrow, but the girl was too much incensed by her own disappointment to forgive him for the unexpected trial to which he had submitted her disposition and character.

"Good-night!" she said curtly, avoiding his glance. "I suppose everybody's gone by this time; mother will be waiting for me."

"Won't you shake hands?" he pleaded gently. "I'm sorry that I expected more of you than you could give, Lucy! but I want you to be happy, and I think and hope you will be, if you let the best part of you have its way. Still, it may happen that I shall never see you again—so let us part friends!"

She raised her eyes, hardened now in their expression by intense malignity and spite, and fixed them fully upon him.

"I don't want to be friends with you any more!" she said. "You are cruel and selfish, and you have treated me abominably! I am sure you will die miserably, without a soul to care for you! And I hope—yes, I hope I shall never hear of you, never see you any more as long as you live! You could never have really had the least bit of affection for me when I was a child."

He interrupted her by a quick, stern gesture.

"That child is dead! Do not speak of her!"

Something in his aspect awed her—something of the mute despair and solitude of a man who has lost his last hope on earth, shadowed his pallid features as with a forecast of approaching dissolution. Involuntarily she trembled, and felt cold; her head drooped;—for a moment her conscience pricked her, reminding her how she had schemed and plotted and planned to become the wife of this sad, frail old man ever since she had reached the mature age of sixteen,—for a moment she was impelled to make a clean confession of her own egotism, and to ask his pardon for having, under the tuition of her mother, made him the unconscious pivot of all her worldly ambitions,—then, with a sudden impetuous movement, she swept past him without a word, and ran downstairs.

There she found half the evening's guests gone, and the other half well on the move. Some of these glanced at her inquiringly, with "nods and becks and wreathed smiles," but she paid no heed to any of them. Her mother came eagerly up to her, anxiety purpling every vein of her mottled countenance, but no word did she utter, till, having put on their cloaks, the two waited together on the steps of the mansion, with flunkeys on either side, for the hired brougham to bowl up in as *un*-hired a style as was possible at the price of one guinea for the night's outing.

"Where is Mr. Helmsley?" then asked Mrs. Sorrel.

"In his own room, I believe," replied Lucy, frigidly.

"Isn't he coming to see you into the carriage and say good-night?"

"Why should he?" demanded the girl, peremptorily.

Mrs. Sorrel became visibly agitated. She glanced at the impassive flunkeys nervously.

"O my dear!" she whimpered softly, "what's the matter? Has anything happened?"

At that moment the expected vehicle lumbered up with a very creditable clatter of well-assumed importance. The flunkeys relaxed their formal attitudes and hastened to assist both mother and daughter into its somewhat stuffy recess. Another moment and they were driven off, Lucy looking out of the window at the numerous lights which twinkled from every story of the stately building they had just left, till the last bright point of luminance had vanished. Then the strain on her mind gave way—and to Mrs. Sorrel's alarm and amazement, she suddenly burst into a stormy passion of tears.

"It's all over!" she sobbed angrily, "all over! I've lost him! I've lost everything!"

Mrs. Sorrel gave a kind of weasel cry and clasped her fat hands convulsively.

"Oh, you little fool!" she burst out, "what have you done?"

Thus violently adjured, Lucy, with angry gasps of spite and disappointment, related in full the maddening, the eccentric, the altogether incomprehensible and inexcusable conduct of the famous millionaire, "old Gold-dust," towards her beautiful, outraged, and injured self. Her mother sat listening in a kind of frozen horror which might possibly have become rigid, had it not been for the occasional bumping of the hired brougham over ruts and loose stones, which bumping shook her superfluous flesh into agitated bosom-waves.

"I ought to have guessed it! I ought to have followed my own instinct!" she said, in sepulchral tones. "It came to me like a flash, when I was talking to him this evening! I said to myself, 'he is in a moral mood.' And he was. Nothing is so hopeless, so dreadful! If I had only thought he would carry on that mood with you, I would have warned you! You could have held off a little—it would perhaps have been the wiser course."

"I should think it would indeed!" cried Lucy, dabbing her eyes with her scented handkerchief; "He would have left me every penny he has in the world if I had refused him! He told me so as coolly as possible!"

Mrs. Sorrel sank back with a groan.

"Oh dear, oh dear!" she wailed feebly. "Can nothing be done?"

"Nothing!" And Lucy, now worked up to hysterical pitch, felt as if she could break the windows, beat her mother, or do anything else equally reckless and irresponsible. "I shall be left to myself now,—he will never ask me to his house again, never give me any parties or drives or opera-boxes or jewels,—he will never come to see me, and I shall have no pleasure at all! I shall sink into a dowdy, frowsy, shabby-genteel old maid for the rest of my life! It is *detestable*!" and she uttered a suppressed small shriek on the word, "It has been a hateful, abominable birthday! Everybody will be laughing at me up their sleeves! Think of Lady Larford!"

This suggestion was too dreadful for comment, and Mrs. Sorrel closed her eyes, visibly shuddering.

"Who would have thought it possible!" she moaned drearily, "a millionaire, with such mad ideas! I *had* thought him always such a sensible man! And he seemed to admire you so much! What will he do with all his money?"

The fair Lucy sighed, sobbed, and swallowed her tears into silence. And again, like the doubtful refrain of a song in a bad dream, her mother moaned and murmured—

"What will he do with all his money!"

IV

Two or three days later, Sir Francis Vesey was sitting in his private office, a musty den encased within the heart of the city, listening, or trying to listen, to the dull clerical monotone of a clerk's dry voice detailing the wearisome items of certain legal formulæ preliminary to an impending case. Sir Francis had yawned capaciously once or twice, and had played absently with a large ink-stained paperknife,—signs that his mind was wandering somewhat from the point at issue. He was a conscientious man, but he was getting old, and the disputations of obstinate or foolish clients were becoming troublesome to him. Moreover, the case concerning which his clerk was prosing along in the style of a chapel demagogue engaged in extempory prayer, was an extremely uninteresting one, and he thought hazily of his lunch. The hour for that meal was approaching,—a fact for which he was devoutly thankful. For after lunch, he gave himself his own release from work for the rest of the day. He left it all to his subordinates, and to his partner Symonds, who was some eight or ten years his junior. He glanced at the clock, and beat a tattoo with his foot on the floor, conscious of his inward impatience with the reiterated "Whereas the said" and "Witnesseth the so-and-so," which echoed dully on the otherwise unbroken silence. It was a warm, sunshiny morning, but the brightness of the outer air was poorly reflected in the stuffy room, which though comfortably and even luxuriously furnished, conveyed the usual sense of dismal depression common to London precincts of the law. Two or three flies buzzed irritably now and then against the smoke-begrimed windowpanes, and the clerk's dreary preamble went on and on till Sir Francis closed his eyes and wondered whether a small "catnap" would be possible between the sections of the seeming interminable document. Suddenly, to his relief, there came a sharp tap at the door, and an office boy looked in.

"Mr. Helmsley's man, sir," he announced. "Wants to see you personally."

Sir Francis got up from his chair with alacrity.

"All right! Show him in."

The boy retired, and presently reappearing, ushered in a staid-looking personage in black who, saluting Sir Francis respectfully, handed him a letter marked "Confidential."

"Nice day, Benson," remarked the lawyer cheerfully, as he took the missive. "Is your master quite well?"

"Perfectly well, Sir Francis, thank you," replied Benson. "Leastways he was when I saw him off just now."

"Oh! He's gone then?"

"Yes, Sir Francis. He's gone."

Sir Francis broke the seal of the letter,—then bethinking himself of "Whereas the said" and "Witnesseth the so-and-so," turned to his worn and jaded clerk.

"That will do for the present," he said. "You can go."

With pleasing haste the clerk put together the voluminous folios of blue paper from which he had been reading, and quickly made his exit, while Sir Francis, still standing, put on his glasses and unfolded the one sheet of note-paper on which Helmsley's communication was written. Glancing it up and down, he turned it over and over—then addressed himself to the attentively waiting Benson.

"So Mr. Helmsley has started on his trip alone?"

"Yes, Sir Francis. Quite alone."

"Did he say where he was going?"

"He booked for Southhampton, sir."

"Oh!"

"And," proceeded Benson, "he only took one portmanteau."

"Oh!" again exclaimed the lawyer. And, stroking his bearded chin, he thought awhile.

"Are you going to stay at Carlton House Terrace till he comes back?"

"I have a month's holiday, sir. Then I return to my place. The same order applies to all the servants, sir."

"I see! Well!"

And then there came a pause.

"I suppose," said Sir Francis, after some minutes' reflection, "I suppose you know that during Mr. Helmsley's absence you are to apply to me for wages and household expenses—that, in fact, your master has placed me in charge of all his affairs?"

"So I have understood, sir," replied Benson, deferentially. "Mr. Helmsley called us all into his room last night and told us so."

"Oh, he did, did he? But, of course, as a man of business, he would leave nothing incomplete. Now, supposing Mr. Helmsley is away more than a month, I will call or send to the house at stated intervals to see how things are getting on, and arrange any matters that may need arranging"—here he glanced at the letter in his hand—"as your master requests. And—if you want anything—or wish to know any news,—you can always call here and inquire."

"Thank you, Sir Francis."

"I'm sorry,"—and the lawyer's shrewd yet kindly eyes looked somewhat troubled—"I'm very sorry that my old friend hasn't taken you with him, Benson."

Benson caught the ring of sympathetic interest in his voice and at once responded to it.

"Well, sir, so am I!" he said heartily. "For Mr. Helmsley's over seventy, and he isn't as strong as he thinks himself to be by a long way. He ought to have some one with him. But he wouldn't hear of my going. He can be right down obstinate if he likes, you know, sir, though he is one of the best gentlemen to work for that ever lived. But he will have his own way, and, bad or good, he takes it."

"Quite true!" murmured Sir Francis meditatively. "Very true!"

A silence fell between them.

"You say he isn't as strong as he thinks himself to be," began Vesey again, presently. "Surely he's wonderfully alert and active for his time of life?"

"Why, yes, sir, he's active enough, but it's all effort and nerve with him now. He makes up his mind like, and determines to be strong, in spite of being weak. Only six months ago the doctor told him to be careful, as his heart wasn't quite up to the mark."

"Ah!" exclaimed Sir Francis ruefully. "And did the doctor recommend any special treatment?"

"Yes, sir. Change of air and complete rest."

The lawyer's countenance cleared.

"Then you may depend upon it that's why he has gone away by himself, Benson," he said. "He wants change of air, rest, and different surroundings. And as he won't have letters forwarded, and doesn't give any future address, I shouldn't wonder if he starts off yachting somewhere—"

"Oh, no, sir, I don't think so," interposed Benson, "The yacht's in the dry dock, and I know he hasn't given any orders to have her got ready."

"Well, well, if he wants change and rest, he's wise to put a distance between himself and his business affairs"—and Sir Francis here looked round for his hat and walking-stick. "Take me, for example! Why, I'm a different man when I leave this office and go home to lunch! I'm going now. I don't think—I really don't think there is any cause for uneasiness,

Benson. Your master will let us know if there's anything wrong with him."

"Oh, yes, sir, he'll be sure to do that. He said he would telegraph for me if he wanted me."

"Good! Now, if you get any news of him before I do, or if you are anxious that I should attend to any special matter, you'll always find me here till one o'clock. You know my private address?"

"Yes, sir."

"That's all right. And when I go down to my country place for the summer, you can come there whenever your business is urgent. I'll settle all expenses with you."

"Thank you, Sir Francis. Good-day!"

"Good-day! A pleasant holiday to you!"

Benson bowed his respectful thanks again, and retired.

Sir Francis Vesey, left alone, took his hat and gazed abstractedly into its silk-lined crown before putting it on his head. Then setting it aside, he drew Helmsley's letter from his pocket and read it through again. It ran as follows:—

My Dear Vesey,

I had some rather bad news on the night of Miss Lucy Sorrel's birthday party. A certain speculation in which I had an interest has failed, and I have lost on the whole 'gamble.' The matter will not, however, affect my financial position. You have all your instructions in order as given to you when we last met, so I shall leave town with an easy mind. I am likely to be away for some time, and am not yet certain of my destination. Consider me, therefore, for the present as lost. Should I die suddenly, or at sickly leisure, I carry a letter on my person which will be conveyed to you, making you acquainted with the sad (?) event as soon as it occurs. And for all your kindly services in the way of both business and friendship, I owe you a vast debt of thanks, which debt shall be fully and gratefully acknowledged,—*when I make my Will.* I may possibly employ another lawyer than yourself for this purpose. But, for the immediate time, all my affairs are in your hands, as they have been for these twenty years or more. My business goes on as usual, of course; it is a wheel so well accustomed to regular motion that it can very well grind for a while without my personal supervision. And so far as my individual self is concerned, I feel the imperative necessity of rest and freedom. I go to find these, even if I lose myself in the endeavour. So farewell! And as old-fashioned folks used to say—'God be with you!' If there be any meaning in the phrase, it is conveyed to you in all sincerity by your old friend,

DAVID HELMSLEY

"Cryptic, positively cryptic!" murmured Sir Francis, as he folded up the letter and put it by. "There's no clue to anything anywhere. What does he mean by a bad speculation?—a loss 'on the whole gamble'? I know—or at least I thought I knew—every number on which he had put his money. It won't affect his financial position, he says. I should think not! It would take a bigger Colossus than that of Rhodes to overshadow Helmsley in the market! But he's got some queer notion in his mind,—some scheme for finding an heir to his millions,—I'm sure he has! A fit of romance has seized him late in life,—he wants to be loved for himself alone,—which, of course, at his age, is absurd! No one loves old people, except, perhaps (in very rare cases), their children,—if the children are not hopelessly given over to self and the hour, which they generally are." He sighed, and his brows contracted. He had a spendthrift son and a "rapid" daughter, and he knew well enough how little he could depend upon them for either affection or respect.

"Old age is regarded as a sort of crime nowadays," he continued, apostrophising the dingy walls of his office, as he took his walking-stick and prepared to leave the premises—"thanks to the donkey-journalism of the period which brays down everything that is not like itself—mere froth and scum. And unlike our great classic teachers who held that old age was honourable and deserved the highest place in the senate, the present generation affects to consider a man well on the way to dotage after forty. God bless me!—what fools there are in this twentieth century!—what blatant idiots! Imagine national affairs carried on in the country by its young men! The Empire would soon became a mere football for general kicking! However, there's one thing in this Helmsley business that I'm glad of"—and his eyes twinkled—"I believe the Sorrels have lost their game! Positively, I think Miss Lucy has broken her line, and that the fish has gone *without* her hook in its mouth! Old as he is, David is not too old to outwit a woman! I gave him a hint, just the slightest hint in the world,—and I think he's taken it. Anyhow, he's gone,—booked for Southampton. And from Southampton a man can 'ship himself all aboard of a ship,' like Lord Bateman in the ballad, and go anywhere. Anywhere, yes!—but in this case I wonder where he will go? Possibly to America—yet no!—I think not!" And Sir Francis, descending his office stairs, went out into the broad sunshine which flooded the city streets, continuing his inward reverie as he walked,— "I think not. From what he said the other night, I fancy not even the haunting memory of 'ole Virginny' will draw him back *there*. 'Consider me as lost,' he says. An odd notion! David Helmsley, one of the richest men in the whole of two continents, wishes to lose himself! Impossible! He's a marked multi-millionaire,—branded with the golden sign of unlimited wealth, and as well known as a London terminus! If he were 'lost' to-day, he'd be found to-morrow. As matters stand I daresay he'll turn up all right in a month's time and I need not worry my head any more about him!"

With this determination Sir Francis went home to luncheon, and after luncheon duly appeared driving in the Park with Lady Vesey, like the attentive and obliging husband he ever was, despite the boredom which the "Row" and the "Ladies' Mile" invariably inflicted upon him,—yet every now and then before him there rose a mental image of his old friend "King David,"—grey, sad-eyed, and lonely—flitting past like some phantom in a dream, and wandering far away from the crowded vortex of London life, where his name was as honey to a swarm of bees, into some dim unreachable region of shadow and silence, with the brief farewell:

CONSIDER ME AS LOST!

V

Among the many wild and lovely tangles of foliage and flower which Nature and her subject man succeed in working out together after considerable conflict and argument, one of the most beautiful and luxuriant is a Somersetshire lane. Narrow and tortuous, fortified on either side with high banks of rough turf, topped by garlands of climbing wild-rose, bunches of corn-cockles and tufts of meadow-sweet, such a lane in midsummer is one of beauty's ways through the world,—a path, which if it lead to no more important goal than a tiny village or solitary farm, is, to the dreamer and poet, sufficiently entrancing in itself to seem a fairy road to fairyland. Here and there some grand elm or beech tree, whose roots have hugged the soil for more than a century, spreads out broad protecting branches all a-shimmer with green leaves,—between the uneven tufts of grass, the dainty "ragged robin" sprays its rose-pink blossoms contrastingly against masses of snowy star-wort and wild strawberry,—the hedges lean close together, as though accustomed to conceal the shy confidences of young lovers,—and from the fields beyond, the glad singing of countless skylarks, soaring one after the other into the clear pure air, strikes a wave of repeated melody from point to point of the visible sky. All among the delicate or deep indentures of the coast, where the ocean creeps softly inland with a caressing murmur, or scoops out caverns for itself among the rocks with perpetual roar and dash of foam, the glamour of the green extends,—the "lane runs down to meet the sea, carrying with it its garlands of blossoms, its branches of verdure, and all the odour and freshness of the woodlands and meadows, and when at last it drops to a conclusion in some little sandy bay or sparkling weir, it leaves an impression of melody on the soul like the echo of a sweet song just sweetly sung. High up the lanes run;—low down on the shoreline they come to an end,—and the wayfarer, pacing along at the summit of their devious windings, can hear the plash of the sea below him as he walks,—the little tender laughing plash if the winds are calm and the day is fair,—the angry thud and boom of the billows if a storm is rising. These bye-roads, of which there are so many along the Somersetshire coast, are often very lonely,—they are dangerous to traffic, as no two ordinary sized vehicles can pass each other conveniently within so narrow a compass,—and in summer especially they are haunted by gypsies, "pea-pickers," and ill-favoured men and women of the "tramp" species, slouching along across country from Bristol to Minehead, and so over Countisbury Hill into Devon. One such questionable-looking individual there was, who,— in a golden afternoon of July, when the sun was beginning to decline towards the west,—paused in his slow march through the dust, which even in the greenest of hill and woodland ways is bound to accumulate thickly after a fortnight's lack of rain,—and with a sigh of fatigue, sat down at the foot of a tree to rest. He was an old man, with a thin weary face which was rendered more gaunt and haggard-looking by a ragged grey moustache and ugly stubble beard of some ten days' growth, and his attire suggested that he might possibly be a labourer dismissed from farm work for the heinous crime of old age, and therefore "on the tramp" looking out for a job. He wore a soft slouched felt hat, very much out of shape and weather-stained,—and when he had been seated for a few minutes in a kind of apathy of lassitude, he lifted the hat off, passing his hand through his abundant rough white hair in a slow tired way, as though by this movement he sought to soothe some teasing pain.

"I think," he murmured, addressing himself to a tiny brown bird which had alighted on a branch of briar-rose hard by, and was looking at him with bold and lively inquisitiveness,—"I think I have managed the whole thing very well! I have left no clue anywhere. My portmanteau will tell no tales, locked up in the cloak-room at Bristol. If it is ever sold with its contents 'to defray expenses,' nothing will be found in it but some unmarked clothes. And so far as all those who know me are concerned, every trace of me ends at Southampton. Beyond Southampton there is a blank, into which David Helmsley, the millionaire, has vanished. And David Helmsley, the tramp, sits here in his place!"

The little brown bird preened its wing, and glanced at him sideways intelligently, as much as to say: "I quite understand! You have become one of us,—a wanderer, taking no thought for the morrow, but letting to-morrow take thought for the things of itself. There is a bond of sympathy between me, the bird, and you, the man—we are brothers!"

A sudden smile illumined his face. The situation was novel, and to him enjoyable. He was greatly fatigued,—he had over-exerted himself during the past three or four days, walking much further than he had ever been accustomed to, and his limbs ached sorely—nevertheless, with the sense of rest and relief from strain, came a certain exhilaration of spirit, like the vivacious delight of a boy who has run away from school, and is defiantly ready to take all the consequences of his disobedience to the rules of discipline and order. For years he had wanted a "new" experience of life. No one would give him what he sought. To him the "social" round was ever the same dreary, heartless and witless thing, as empty under the sway of one king or queen as another, and as utterly profitless to peace or happiness as it has always been. The world of finance was equally uninteresting so far as he was concerned; he had exhausted it, and found it no more than a monotonous grind of gain which ended in a loathing of the thing gained. Others might and would consume themselves in fevers of avarice, and surfeits of luxury,—but for him such temporary pleasures were past. He desired a complete change,—a change of surroundings, a change of associations—and for this, what could be more excellent or more wholesome than a taste of poverty? In his time he had met men who, worn out with the constant fight of the body's materialism against the soul's idealism, had turned their backs for ever on the world and its glittering shows, and had shut themselves up as monks of "enclosed" or "silent" orders,—others he had known, who, rushing away from what we call civilisation, had encamped in the backwoods of America, or high up among the Rocky Mountains, and had lived the lives of primeval savages in their strong craving to assert a greater manliness than the streets of cities would allow them to enjoy,—and all were moved by the same mainspring of action,—the overpowering spiritual demand within themselves which urged them to break loose from cowardly conventions and escape from Sham. He could not compete with younger men in taking up wild sport and "big game" hunting in far lands, in order to give free play to the natural savage temperament which lies untamed at the root of every man's individual being,—and he had no liking for "monastic" immurements. But he longed for liberty,—liberty to go where he liked without his movements being watched and commented upon by a degraded "personal" press,—liberty to speak as he felt and do as he wished, without being compelled to weigh his words, or to consider his actions. Hence—he had decided on his present course, though how that course was likely to shape itself in its progress he had no very distinct idea. His actual plan was to walk to Cornwall, and there find out the native home of his parents, not so much for sentiment's sake as for the necessity of having a definite object or goal in view. And the reason of his determination to go "on the road," as it were, was simply that he wished to test for himself the actual happiness or misery experienced by the very poor as contrasted with the supposed joys of the very wealthy. This scheme had been working in his brain for the past year or more,— all his business arrangements had been made in such a way as to enable him to carry it out satisfactorily to himself without taking any one else into his confidence. The only thing that might possibly have deterred him from his quixotic undertaking would have been the moral triumph of Lucy Sorrel over the temptation he had held out to her. Had she been honest to her better womanhood,—had she still possessed the "child's heart," with which his remembrance and imagination had endowed her, he would have resigned every other thought save that of so smoothing the path of life for her that she might tread it easily to the end. But now that she had disappointed him, he had, so he told himself, done with fine illusions and fair beliefs for ever. And he had started on a lonely quest,—a search for something vague and intangible, the very nature of which he himself could not tell. Some glimmering ghost of a notion lurked in his mind that perhaps, during his self-imposed solitary ramblings, he might find some new and unexplored channel wherein his vast wealth might flow to good purpose after his death, without the trammels of Committee-ism and Red-Tape-ism. But he expected and formulated nothing,—he was more or less in a state of quiescence, awaiting adventures without either hope or fear. In the meantime, here he sat in the shady Somersetshire lane, resting,—the multi-millionaire whose very name shook the money-markets of the world, but who to all present appearances seemed no more than a tramp, footing it wearily along one of the many winding "short cuts" through the country between Somerset and Devon, and as unlike the actual self of him as known to Lombard Street and the Stock Exchange as a beggar is unlike a king.

"After all, it's quite as interesting as 'big game' shooting!" he said, the smile still lingering in his eyes. "I am after 'sport,'—in a novel fashion! I am on the lookout for new specimens of men and women,—real honest ones! I may find them,—I may not,—but the search will surely prove at least as instructive and profitable as if one went out to the Arctic regions for the purpose of killing innocent polar bears! Change and excitement are what every one craves for nowadays—I'm getting as much as I want—in my own way!"

He thought over the whole situation, and reviewed with a certain sense of interest and amusement his method of action since he left London. Benson, his valet, had packed his portmanteau, according to orders, with everything that was necessary for a short sea trip, and then had seen him off at the station for Southampton,—and to Southampton he had gone. Arrived there, he had proceeded to a hotel, where, under an assumed name, he had stayed the night. The next day he had left Southampton for Salisbury by train, and there staying another night, had left again for Bath and Bristol. On the latter journey he had "tipped" the guard heavily to keep his first-class compartment reserved to himself. This had been done; and the train being an express, stopping at very few stations, he had found leisure and opportunity to unpack his portmanteau and cut away every mark on his linen and other garments which could give the slightest clue to their possessor. When he had removed all possible trace of his identity on or in this one piece of luggage, he packed it up again, and on reaching Bristol, took it to the station's cloak-room, and there deposited it with the stated intention of calling back for it at the hour of the next train to London. This done, he stepped forth untrammelled, a free man. He had with him five hundred pounds in banknotes, and for a day or so was content to remain in Bristol at one of the best hotels, under an assumed name as before, while privately making such other preparations for his intended long "tramp" as he thought necessary. In one of the poorest quarters of the town he purchased a few second-hand garments such as might be worn by an ordinary day-labourer, saying to the dealer that he wanted to "rig out" a man who had just left hospital and who was going in for "field" work. The dealer saw nothing either remarkable or suspicious in this seemingly benevolent act of a kindly-looking well-dressed old gentleman, and sent him the articles he had purchased done up in a neat package and addressed to him at his hotel, by the name he had for the time assumed. When he left the hotel for good, he did so with nothing more than this neat package, which he carried easily in one hand by a loop of string. And so he began his journey, walking steadily for two or three hours,—then pausing to rest awhile,—and after rest, going on again. Once out of Bristol he was glad, and at certain lonely places, when the shadows of night fell, he changed all his garments one by one till he stood transformed as now he was. The clothes he was compelled to discard he got rid of by leaving them in unlikely holes and corners on the road,—as for example, at one place he filled the pockets of his good broadcloth coat with stones and dropped it into the bottom of an old disused well. The curious sense of guilt he felt when he performed this innocent act surprised as well as amused him.

"It is exactly as if I had murdered somebody and had sunk a body into the well instead of a coat!" he said—"and—perhaps I have! Perhaps I am killing my Self,—getting rid of my Self,—which would be a good thing, if I could only find Some one or Some thing better than my Self in my Self's place!"

When he had finally disposed of every article that could suggest any possibility of his ever having been clothed as a gentleman, he unripped the lining of his rough "workman's" vest, and made a layer of the banknotes he had with him between it and the cloth, stitching it securely over and over with coarse needle and thread, being satisfied by this arrangement to carry all his immediate cash hidden upon his person, while for the daily needs of hunger and thirst he had a few loose shillings and coppers in his pocket. He had made up his mind not to touch a single one of the banknotes, unless suddenly overtaken by accident or illness. When his bit of silver and copper came to an end, he meant to beg alms along the road and prove for himself how far it was true that human beings were in the main kind and compassionate, and ready to assist one another in the battle of life. With these ideas and many others in his mind, he started on his "tramp"—and during the first two or three days of it suffered acutely. Many years had passed since he had been accustomed to long sustained bodily exercise, and he was therefore easily fatigued. But by the time he reached the open country between the Quantocks and the Brendon Hills, he had got somewhat into training, and had begun to feel a greater lightness and ease as well as pleasure in walking. He had found it quite easy to live on very simple food,—in fact one of the principal charms of the strange "holiday" he had planned for his own entertainment was to prove for himself beyond all dispute that no very large amount of money is required to sustain a man's life and health. New milk and brown bread had kept him going bravely every day,—fruit was cheap and so was cheese, and all these articles of diet are highly nourishing, so that he had wanted for nothing. At night, the weather keeping steadily fine and warm, he had slept in the open, choosing some quiet nook in the woodland under a tree, or else near a haystack in the fields, and he had benefited greatly by thus breathing the pure air during slumber, and getting for nothing the "cure" prescribed by certain Artful Dodgers of the medical profession who take handfuls of guineas from credulous patients for what Mother Nature willingly gives gratis. And he was beginning to understand the joys of "loafing,"—so much so indeed that he felt a certain sympathy with the lazy varlet who prefers to stroll aimlessly about the country begging his bread rather than do a stroke of honest work. The freedom of such a life is self-evident,—and freedom is the broadest and best way of breathing on earth. To "tramp the road" seems to the well-dressed, conventional human being a sorry life; but it may be questioned whether, after all, he with his social trammels and household cares, is not leading a sorrier one. Never in all his brilliant, successful career till now had David Helmsley, that king of modern finance, realised so intensely the beauty and peace of being alone with Nature,—the joy of feeling the steady pulse of the Spirit of the Universe throbbing through one's own veins and arteries,—the quiet yet exultant sense of knowing instinctively beyond all formulated theory or dogma, that one is a vital part of the immortal Entity, as indestructible as Itself. And a great calm was gradually taking possession of his soul,—a smoothing of all the waves of his emotional and nervous temperament. Under this mystic touch of unseen and uncomprehended heavenly tenderness, all sorrows, all disappointments, all disillusions sank out of sight as though they had never been. It seemed to him that he had put away his former life for ever, and that another life had just begun,—and his brain was ready and eager to rid itself of old impressions in order to prepare for new. Nothing of much moment had occurred to him as yet. A few persons had said "good-day" or "good-night" to him in passing,—a farmer had asked him to hold his horse for a quarter of an hour, which he had done, and had thereby earned threepence,—but he had met with no interesting or exciting incidents which could come under the head of "adventures." Nevertheless he was gathering fresh experiences,—experiences which all tended to show him how the best and brightest part of life is foolishly wasted and squandered by the modern world in a mad rush for gain.

"So very little money really suffices for health, contentment, and harmless pleasure!" he thought. "The secret of our growing social mischief does not lie with the natural order of created things, but solely with ourselves. We will not set any reasonable limit to our desires. If we would, we might live longer and be far happier!"

He stretched out his limbs easefully, and dropped into a reclining posture. The tree he had chosen to rest under was a mighty elm, whose broad branches, thick with leaves, formed a deep green canopy through which the sunbeams filtered in flecks and darts of gold. A constant twittering of birds resounded within this dome of foliage, and a thrush whistled melodious phrases from one of the highest boughs. At his feet was spread a carpet of long soft moss, interspersed with wild thyme and groups of delicate harebells, and the rippling of a tiny stream into a hollow cavity of stones made pleasant and soothing music. Charmed with the tranquillity and loveliness of his surroundings, he determined to stay here for a couple of hours, reading, and perhaps sleeping, before resuming his journey. He had in his pocket a shilling edition of Keats's poems which he had bought in Bristol by way of a silent companion to his thoughts, and he took it out and opened it now, reading and re-reading some of the lines most dear and familiar to him, when, as a boy, he had elected this poet, so wickedly done to death ere his prime by commonplace critics, as one of his chief favourites among the highest Singers. And his lips, half-murmuring, followed the verse which tells of that

> "untrodden region of the mind,
> Where branchèd thoughts, new-grown with pleasant pain,
> Instead of pines, shall murmur in the wind;
> Far, far around shall these dark clustered trees,
> Fledge the wild ridgèd mountains steep by steep,
> And there by zephyrs, streams, and birds and bees,
> The moss-lain Dryads shall be lulled to sleep;
> And in the midst of this wide quietness,
> A rosy sanctuary will I dress
> With the wreathed trellis of a working brain,
> With buds and bells and stars without a name,
> With all the gardener Fancy e'er could feign,
> Who, breeding flowers, will never breed the same;
> And there shall be for thee all soft delight,
> That shadowy thought can win,
> A bright torch and a casement ope at night,
> To let the warm Love in!"

A slight sigh escaped him.

"How perfect is that stanza!" he said. "How I used to believe in all it suggested! And how, when I was a young man, my heart was like that 'casement ope at night, to let the warm Love in!' But Love never came,—only a spurious will-o'-the-wisp imitation of Love. I wonder if many people in this world are not equally deceived with myself in their conceptions of this divine passion? All the poets and romancists may be wrong,—and Lucy Sorrel, with her hard materialism encasing her youth like a suit of steel armour, may be right. Boys and girls 'love,' so they say,—men and women 'love' and marry—and with marriage, the wondrous light that led them on and dazzled them, seems, in nine cases out of ten, to suddenly expire! Taking myself as an example, I cannot say that actual marriage made me happy. It was a great disillusion; a keen disappointment. The birth of my sons certainly gave me some pleasure as well as latent hope, for as little children they were lovable and lovely; but as boys—as men—what bitterness they brought me! Were they the heirs of Love? Nay!—surely Love never generated such callous hearts! They were the double reflex of their mother's nature, grasping all and giving nothing. Is there no such virtue on earth as pure unselfish Love?—love that gives itself freely, unasked, without hope of advantage or reward—and without any personal motive lurking behind its offered tenderness?"

He turned over the pages of the book he held, with a vague idea that some consoling answer to his thoughts would flash out in a stray line or stanza, like a beacon lighting up the darkness of a troubled sea. But no such cheering word met his eyes. Keats is essentially the poet of the young, and for the old he has no comfort. Sensuous, passionate, and almost cloying in the excessive sweetness of his amorous muse, he offers no support to the wearied spirit,—no sense of strength or renewal to the fagged brain. He does not grapple with the hard problems of life; and his mellifluous murmurings of delicious fantasies have no place in the poignant griefs and keen regrets of those who have passed the meridian of earthly hopes, and who see the shadows of the long night closing in. And David Helmsley realised this all suddenly, with something of a pang.

"I am too old for Keats," he said in a half-whisper to the leafy branches that bowed their weight of soft green shelteringly over him. "Too old! Too old for a poet in whose imaginative work I vised to take such deep delight. There is something strange in this, for I cherished a belief that fine poetry would fit every time and every age, and that no matter how heavy the burden of years might be, I should always be able to forget myself and my sorrows in a poet's immortal creations. But I have left Keats behind me. He was with me in the sunshine,—he does not follow me into the shade."

A cloud of melancholy darkened his worn features, and he slowly closed the book. He felt that it was from henceforth a sealed letter. For him the half-sad, half-scornful musings of Omar Khayyám were more fitting, such as the lines that run thus:—

> *"Fair wheel of heaven, silvered with many a star,*
> *Whose sickly arrows strike us from afar,*
> *Never a purpose to my soul was dear,*
> *But heaven crashed down my little dream to mar.*
>
> *Never a bird within my sad heart sings*
> *But heaven a flaming stone of thunder flings;*
> *O valiant wheel! O most courageous heaven,*
> *To leave me lonely with the broken wings!"*

tinging pain, as of tears that rose but would not fall, troubled his eyes. He passed his hand across them, and leaned back against the sturdy trunk of the elm which served him for the moment as a protecting haven of rest. The gentle murmur of the bees among the clover, the soft subdued twittering of the birds, and the laughing ripple of the little stream hard by, all combined to make one sweet monotone of sound which lulled his senses to a drowsiness that gradually deepened into slumber. He made a pathetic figure enough, lying fast asleep there among the wilderness of green,—a frail and apparently very poor old man, adrift and homeless, without a friend in the world. The sun sank, and a crimson after-glow spread across the horizon from west to east, the rich colours flung up from the centre of the golden orb merging by slow degrees into that pure pearl-grey which marks the long and lovely summer twilight of English skies. The air was very still, not so much as the rumble of a distant cart wheel disturbing the silence. Presently, however, the slow shuffle of hesitating footsteps sounded through the muffling thickness of the dust, and a man made his appearance on the top of the little rising where the lane climbed up into a curve of wild-rose hedge and honeysuckle which almost hid the actual road from view. He was not a prepossessing object in the landscape; short and squat, unkempt and dirty, and clad in rough garments which were almost past hanging together, he looked about as uncouth and ugly a customer as one might expect to meet anywhere on a lonely road at nightfall. He carried a large basket on his back, seemingly full of weeds,—the rope which supported it was tied across his chest, and he clasped this rope with both hands crossed in the middle, after the fashion of a praying monk. Smoking a short black pipe, he trudged along, keeping his eyes fixed on the ground with steady and almost surly persistence, till arriving at the tree where Helmsley lay, he paused, and lifting his head stared long and curiously at the sleeping man. Then, unclasping his hands, he lowered his basket to the ground and set it down. Stealthily creeping close up to Helmsley's side, he examined the prone figure from head to foot with quick and eager scrutiny. Spying the little volume of Keats on the grass where it had dropped from the slumberer's relaxed hand, he took it up gingerly, turning over its pages with grimy thumb and finger.

"Portry!" he exclaimed. "Glory be good to me! 'E's a reg'ler noddy none-such! An' measly old enuff to know better!"

He threw the book on the grass again with a sniff of contempt. At that moment Helmsley stirred, and opening his eyes fixed them full and inquiringly on the lowering face above him.

"'Ullo, gaffer! Woke up, 'ave yer?" said the man gruffly. "Off yer lay?"

Helmsley raised himself on one elbow, looking a trifle dazed.

"Off my what?" he murmured. "I didn't quite hear you—?"

"Oh come, stow that!" said the man. "You dunno what I'm talkin' about; that's plain as a pike. *You* aint used to the road! Where d'ye come from?"

"I've walked from Bristol," he answered—"And you're quite right,—I'm not used to the road."

The man looked at him and his hard face softened. Pushing back his tattered cap from his brows he showed his features more openly, and a smile, half shrewd, half kindly, made them suddenly pleasant.

"Av coorse you're not!" he declared. "Glory be good to me! I've tramped this bit o' road for years, an' never come across such a poor old chuckle-headed gammer as you sleepin' under a tree afore! Readin' portry an' droppin' to by-by over it! The larst man as iver I saw a' readin' portry was what they called a 'Serious Sunday' man, an' 'e's doin' time now in Portland."

Helmsley smiled. He was amused;—his "adventures," he thought, were beginning. To be called "a poor old chuckle-headed gammer" was a new and almost delightful experience.

"Portland's an oncommon friendly place," went on his uninvited companion. "Once they gits ye, they likes ye to stop. 'Taint like the fash'nable quality what says to their friends: 'Do-ee come an' stay wi' me, loveys!' wishin' all the while as they wouldn't. Portland takes ye willin', whether ye likes it or not, an' keeps ye so fond that ye can't git away nohow. Oncommon 'ospitable Portland be!"

And he broke into a harsh laugh. Then he glanced at Helmsley again with a more confiding and favourable eye.

"Ye seems a 'spectable sort," he said. "What's wrong wi' ye? Out o' work?"

Helmsley nodded.

"Turned off, eh? Too old?"

"That's about it!" he answered.

"Well, ye do look a bit of a shivery-shake,—a kind o' not-long-for-this-world," said the man. "Howsomiver, we'se be all 'elpless an' 'omeless soon, for the Lord hisself don't stop a man growin' old, an' under the new ways o' the world, it's a reg'lar crime to run past forty. I'm sixty, an' I gits my livin' my own way, axin' nobody for the kind permission. *That's* my fortin!"

And he pointed to the basket of weedy stuff which he had just set down. Helmsley looked at it with some curiosity.

"What's in it?" he asked.

"What's in it? What's *not* in it!" And the man gave a gesture of mingled pride and defiance. "There's all what the doctors makes their guineas out of with their purr-escriptions, for they can't purr-escribe no more than is in that there basket without they goes to minerals. An' minerals is rank poison to ivery 'uman body. But so far as 'erbs an' seeds, an' precious stalks an' flowers is savin' grace for man an' beast, Matthew Peke's got 'em all in there. An' Matthew Peke wouldn't be the man he is, if he didn't know where to find 'em better'n any livin' soul iver born! Ah!—an' there aint a toad in a hole hoppin' out between Quantocks an' Cornwall as hasn't seen Matthew Peke gatherin' the blessin' an' health o' the fields at rise o' sun an' set o' moon, spring, summer, autumn, ay, an' even winter, all the year through!"

Helmsley became interested.

"And you are the man!" he said questioningly—"You are Matthew Peke?"

"I am! An' proud so ter be! An' you—'ave yer got a name for the arskin'?"

"Why, certainly!" And Helmsley's pale face flushed. "My name is David."

"Chrisen name? Surname?"

"Both."

Matthew Peke shook his head.

"'Twon't fadge!" he declared. "It don't sound right. It's like th' owld Bible an' the Book o' Kings where there's nowt but Jews; an' Jews is the devil to pay wheriver you finds 'em!"

"I'm not a Jew," said Helmsley, smiling.

"Mebbe not—mebbe not—but yer name's awsome like it. An' if ye put it short, like D. David, that's just Damn David an' nothin' plainer. Aint it?"

Helmsley laughed.

"Exactly!" he said—"You're right! Damn David suits me down to the ground!"

Peke looked at him dubiously, as one who is not quite sure of his man.

"You're a rum old sort!" he said; "an' I tell ye what it is—you're as tired as a dog limpin' on three legs as has nipped his fourth in a weasel-trap. Wheer are ye goin' on to?"

"I don't know," answered Helmsley—"I'm a stranger to this part of the country. But I mean to tramp it to the nearest village. I slept out in the open yesterday,—I think I'd like a shelter over me to-night."

"Got any o' the King's pictures about ye?" asked Peke.

Helmsley looked, as he felt, bewildered.

"The King's pictures?" he echoed—"You mean—?"

"This!" and Peke drew out of his tattered trouser pocket a dim and blackened sixpence—"'Ere 'e is, as large as life, a bit bald about the top o' 'is blessed old 'ead, Glory be good to 'im, but as useful as if all 'is 'air was still a blowin' an' a growin'! Aint that the King's picture, D. David? Don't it say 'Edwardus VII. D. G. Britt.,' which means Edward the Seventh, thanks be to God Britain? Don't it?"

"It *do*!" replied Helmsley emphatically, taking a fantastic pleasure in the bad grammar of his reply. "I've got a few more pictures of the same kind," and he took out two or three loose shillings and pennies—"Can we get a night's lodging about here for that?"

"Av coorse we can! I'll take ye to a place where ye'll be as welcome as the flowers in May with Matt Peke interroducin' of ye. Two o' them thank-God Britts in silver will set ye up wi' a plate o' wholesome food an' a clean bed at the 'Trusty Man.' It's a pub, but Miss Tranter what keeps it is an old maid, an' she's that proud o' the only 'Trusty Man' she ever 'ad that she calls it an 'Otel!"

He grinned good-humouredly at what he considered his own witticism concerning the little weakness of Miss Tranter, and proceeded to shoulder his basket.

"*You* aint proud, are ye?" he said, as he turned his ferret-brown eyes on Helmsley inquisitively.

Helmsley, who had, quite unconsciously to himself, drawn up his spare figure in his old habitual way of standing very erect, with that composed air of dignity and resolution which those who knew him personally in business were well accustomed to, started at the question.

"Proud!" he exclaimed—"I? What have I to be proud of? I'm the most miserable old fellow in the world, my friend! You may take my word for that! There's not a soul that cares a button whether I live or die! I'm seventy years of age—out of work, and utterly wretched and friendless! Why the devil should *I* be proud?"

"Well, if ye never was proud in yer life, ye can be now," said Peke condescendingly, "for I tell ye plain an' true that if Matt Peke walks with a tramp on this road, every one round the Quantocks knows as how that tramp aint altogether a raskill! I've took ye up on trust as 'twere, likin' yer face for all that it's thin an' mopish,—an' steppin' in wi' me to the 'Trusty Man' will mebbe give ye a character. Anyways, I'll do my best for ye!"

"Thank you," said Helmsley simply.

Again Peke looked at him, and again seemed troubled. Then, stuffing his pipe full of tobacco, he lit it and stuck it sideways between his teeth.

"Now come along!" he said. "You're main old, but ye must put yer best foot foremost all the same. We've more'n an hour's trampin' up hill an' down dale, an' the dew's beginnin' to fall. Keep goin' slow an' steady—I'll give ye a hand."

For a moment Helmsley hesitated. This shaggy, rough, uncouth herb-gatherer evidently regarded him as very feeble and helpless, and, out of a latent kindliness of nature, wished to protect him and see him to some safe shelter for the night. Nevertheless, he hated the position. Old as he knew himself to be, he resented being pitied for his age, while his mind was yet so vigorous and his heart felt still so warm and young. Yet the commonplace fact remained that he was very tired,—very worn out, and conscious that only a good rest would enable him to continue his journey with comfort. Moreover, his experiences at the "Trusty Man" might prove interesting. It was best to take what came in his way, even though some episodes should possibly turn out less pleasing than instructive. So putting aside all scruples, he started to walk beside his ragged comrade of the road, finding, with some secret satisfaction, that after a few paces his own step was light and easy compared to the heavy shuffling movement with which Peke steadily trudged along. Sweet and pungent odours of the field and woodland floated from the basket of herbs as it swung slightly to and fro on its bearer's shoulders, and amid the slowly darkening shadows of evening, a star of sudden silver brilliance sparkled out in the sky.

"Yon's the first twinkler," said Peke, seeing it at once, though his gaze was apparently fixed on the ground. "The love-star's allus up early o' nights to give the men an' maids a chance!"

"Yes,—Venus is the evening star just now," rejoined Helmsley, half-absently.

"Stow Venus! That's a reg'lar fool's name," said Peke surlily. "Where did ye git it from? That aint no Venus,—that's just the love-star, an' it'll be nowt else in these parts till the world-without-end-amen!"

Helmsley made no answer. He walked on patiently, his limbs trembling a little with fatigue and nervous exhaustion. But Peke's words had started the old dream of his life again into being,—the latent hope within him, which though often half-killed, was not yet dead, flamed up like newly kindled vital fire in his mind,—and he moved as in a dream, his eyes fixed on the darkening heavens and the brightening star.

VI

They plodded on together side by side for some time in unbroken silence. At last, after a short but stiff climb up a rough piece of road which terminated in an eminence commanding a wide and uninterrupted view of the surrounding country, they paused. The sea lay far below them, dimly covered by the gathering darkness, and the long swish and roll of the tide could be heard sweeping to and from the shore like the grave and graduated rhythm of organ music.

"We'd best 'ave a bit of a jabber to keep us goin'," said Peke, then— "Jabberin' do pass time, as the wimin can prove t' ye; an' arter such a jumblegut lane as this, it'll seem less lonesome. We're off the main road to towns an' sich like—this is a bye, an' 'ere it stops. We'll 'ave to git over yon stile an' cross the fields—'taint an easy nor clean way, but it's the best goin'. We'll see the lights o' the 'Trusty Man' just over the brow o' the next hill."

Helmsley drew a long breath, and sat down on a stone by the roadside. Peke surveyed him critically.

"Poor old gaffer! Knocked all to pieces, aint ye! Not used to the road? Glory be good to me! I should think ye wornt! Short in yer wind an' weak on yer pins! I'd as soon see my old grandad trampin' it as you. Look 'ere! Will ye take a dram out o' this 'ere bottle?"

He held up the bottle he spoke of,—it was black, and untemptingly dirty. Yet there was such a good-natured expression in the man's eyes, and so much honest solicitude written on his rough bearded face, that Helmsley felt it would be almost like insulting him to refuse his invitation.

"Tell me what's in it first!" he said, smiling.

"'Taint whisky," said Peke. "And 'taint brandy neither. *Nor* rum. *Nor* gin. Nor none o' them vile stuffs which brewers makes as arterwards goes to Parl'ment on the profits of 'avin' poisoned their consti*too*ants. 'Tis nowt but just yerb wine."

"Yerb wine? Wine made of herbs?"

"That's it! 'Erbs or yerbs—I aint pertikler which—I sez both. This,"— and he shook the bottle he held vigorously—"is genuine yerb wine—an' made as I makes it, what do the Wise One say of it? 'E sez:—'It doth strengthen the heart of a man mightily, and refresheth the brain; drunk fasting, it braceth up the sinews and maketh the old feel young; it is of rare virtue to expel all evil humours, and if princes should drink of it oft it would be but an ill service to the world, as they might never die!'"

Peke recited these words slowly and laboriously; it was evident that he had learned them by heart, and that the effort of remembering them correctly was more or less painful to him.

Helmsley laughed, and stretched out his hand.

"Give it over here!" he said. "It's evidently just the stuff for me. How much shall I take at one go?"

Peke uncorked the precious fluid with care, smelt it, and nodded appreciatively.

"Swill it all if ye like," he remarked graciously. "'Twont hurt ye, an' there's more where that came from. It's cheap enuff, too—nature don't keep it back from no man. On'y there aint a many got sense enuff to thank the Lord when it's offered."

As he thus talked, Helmsley took the bottle from him and tasted its contents. The "yerb wine" was delicious. More grateful to his palate than Chambertin or Clos Vougeot, it warmed and invigorated him, and he took a long draught, Matthew Peke watching him drink it with great satisfaction.

"Let the yerbs run through yer veins for two or three minits, an' ye'll step across yon fields as light as a bird 'oppin' to its nest," he declared. "Talk o' tonics,—there's more tonic in a handful o' green stuff growin' as the Lord makes it to grow, than all the purr-escriptions what's sent out o' them big 'ouses in 'Arley Street, London, where the doctors sits from ten to two like spiders waitin' for flies, an' gatherin' in the guineas for lookin' at fools' tongues. Glory be good to me! If all the world were as sick as it's silly, there'd be nowt wantin' to 't but a grave an' a shovel!"

Helmsley smiled, and taking another pull at the black bottle, declared himself much better and ready to go on. He was certainly refreshed, and the weary aching of his limbs which had made every step of the road painful and difficult to him, was gradually passing off.

"You are very good to me," he said, as he returned the remainder of the "yerb wine" to its owner. "I wonder why?"

Peke took a draught of his mixture before replying. Then corking the bottle, he thrust it in his pocket.

"Ye wonders why?" And he uttered a sound between a grunt and a chuckle—"Ye may do that! I wonders myself!"

And, giving his basket a hitch, he resumed his slow trudging movement onward.

"You see," pursued Helmsley, keeping up the pace beside him, and beginning to take pleasure in the conversation—"I may be anything or anybody—"

"Ye may that," agreed Peke, his eyes fixed as usual on the ground. "Ye may be a jail-bird or a missioner,—they'se much of a muchity, an' goes on the road lookin' quite simple like, an' the simpler they seems the deeper they is. White 'airs an' feeble legs 'elps 'em along considerable,—nowt's better stock-in-trade than tremblin' shins. Or ye might be a War-office neglect,—ye looks a bit set that way."

"What's a War-office neglect?" asked Helmsley, laughing.

"One o' them totterin' old chaps as was in the Light Brigade," answered Peke. "There's no end to 'em. They'se all over every road in the country. All of 'em fought wi' Lord Cardigan, an' all o' 'em's driven to starve by an ungrateful Gov'ment. They won't be all dead an' gone till a hundred years 'as rolled away, an' even then I shouldn't wonder if one or two was still left on the tramp a-pipin' his little 'arf-a-league onard tale o' woe to the first softy as forgits the date o' the battle." Here he gave an inquisitive side-glance at his companion. "But you aint quite o' the Balaclava make an' colour. Yer shoulders is millingterry, but yer 'ead is business. Ye might be a gentleman if 'twornt for yer clothes."

Helmsley heard this definition of himself without flinching.

"I might be a thief," he said—"or an escaped convict. You've been kind to me without knowing whether I am one or the other, or both. And I want to know why?"

Peke stopped in his walk. They had come to the stile over which the way lay across the fields, and he rested himself and his basket for a moment against it.

"Why?" he repeated,—then suddenly raising one hand, he whispered, "Listen! Listen to the sea!"

The evening had now almost closed in, and all around them the country lay dark and solitary, broken here and there by tall groups of trees which at night looked like sable plumes, standing stiff and motionless in the stirless summer air. Thousands of stars flashed out across this blackness, throbbing in their orbits with a quick pulsation as of uneasy hearts beating with nameless and ungratified longing. And through the tense silence came floating a long, sweet, passionate cry,—a shivering moan of pain that touched the edge of joy,—a song without words, of pleading and of prayer, as of a lover, who, debarred from the possession of the beloved, murmurs his mingled despair and hope to the unsubstantial dream of his own tortured soul. The sea was calling to the earth,—calling to her in phrases of eloquent and urgent music,—caressing her pebbly shores with winding arms of foam, and showering kisses of wild spray against her rocky bosom. "If I could come to thee! If thou couldst come to me!" was the burden of the waves,—the ceaseless craving of the finite for the infinite, which is, and ever shall be, the great chorale of life. The shuddering sorrow of that low rhythmic boom of the waters rising and falling fathoms deep under cliffs which the darkness veiled from view, awoke echoes from the higher hills around, and David Helmsley, lifting his eyes to the countless planet-worlds sprinkled thick as flowers in the patch of sky immediately above him, suddenly realised with a pang how near he was to death,—how very near to that final drop into the unknown where the soul of man is destined to find All or Nothing! He trembled,—not with fear,—but with a kind of anger at himself for having wasted so much of his life. What had he done, with all his toil and pains? He had gathered a multitude of riches. Well, and then? Then,—why then, and now, he had found riches but vain getting. Life and Death were still, as they have always been, the two supreme Facts of the universe. Life, as ever, asserted itself with an insistence demanding something far more enduring than the mere possession of gold, and the power which gold brings. And Death presented its unwelcome aspect in the same perpetual way as the Last Recorder who, at the end of the day, closes up accounts with a sum-total paid exactly in proportion to the work done. No more, and no less. And with Helmsley these accounts were reaching a figure against which his whole nature fiercely rebelled,—the figure of Nought, showing no value in his life's efforts or its results. And the sound of the sea to-night in his ears was more full of reproach than peace.

"When the water moans like that," said Peke softly, under his breath, "it seems to me as if all the tongues of drowned sailors 'ad got into it an' was beggin' of us not to forget 'em lyin' cold among the shells an' weed. An' not only the tongues o' them seems a-speakin' an' a-cryin', but all the stray bones o' them seems to rattle in the rattle o' the foam. It goes through ye sharp, like a knife cuttin' a sour apple; an' it's made me wonder many a time why we was all put 'ere to git drowned or smashed or choked off or beat down somehows just when we don't expect it. Howsomiver, the Wise One sez it's all right!"

"And who is the Wise One?" asked Helmsley, trying to rouse himself from the heavy thoughts engendered in his mind by the wail of the sea.

"The Wise One was a man what wrote a book a 'underd years ago about 'erbs," said Peke. "'*The Way o' Long Life*,' it's called, an' my father an' grandfather and great-grandfather afore 'em 'ad the book, an' I've got it still, though I shows it to nobody, for nobody but me wouldn't unnerstand it. My father taught me my letters from it, an' I could spell it out when I was a kid—I've growed up on it, an' it's all I ever reads. It's 'ere"—and he touched his ragged vest. "I trusts it to keep me goin' 'ale an' 'arty till I'm ninety,—an' that's drawin' it mild, for my father lived till a 'underd, an' then on'y went through slippin' on a wet stone an' breakin' a bone in 'is back; an' my grandfather saw 'is larst Christmas at a 'underd an' ten, an' was up to kissin' a wench under the mistletoe, 'e was sich a chirpin' old gamecock. 'E didn't look no older'n you do now, an' you're a chicken compared to 'im. You've wore badly like, not knowin' the use o' yerbs."

"That's it!" said Helmsley, now following his companion over the stile and into the dark dewy fields beyond—"I need the advice of the Wise One! Has he any remedy for old age, I wonder?"

"Ay, now there ye treads on my fav'rite corn!" and Peke shook his head with a curious air of petulance. "That's what I'm a-lookin' for day an' night, for the Wise One 'as got a bit in 'is book which 'e's cropped out o' another Wise One's savin's,—a chap called Para-Cel-Sus"—and Peke pronounced this name in three distinct and well-divided syllables. "An this is what it is: 'Take the leaves of the Daura, which prevent those who use it from dying for a hundred and twenty years. In the same way the flower of the *secta croa* brings a hundred years to those who use it, whether they be of lesser or of longer age.' I've been on the 'unt for the 'Daura' iver since I was twenty, an' I've arskt ivery 'yerber I've ivir met for the 'Secta Croa,' an' all I've 'ad sed to me is 'Go 'long wi' ye for a loony jackass! There aint no sich thing.' But jackass or no, I'm of a mind to think there *is* such things as both the 'Daura' an' the 'Secta Croa,' if I on'y knew the English of 'em. An' s'posin' I ivir found 'em—"

"You would become that most envied creature of the present age,—a millionaire," said Helmsley; "you could command your own terms for the wonderful leaves,—you would cease to tramp the road or to gather herbs, and you would live in luxury like a king!"

"Not I!"—and Peke gave a grunt of contempt. "Kings aint my notion of 'appiness nor 'onesty neither. They does things often for which some o' the poor 'ud be put in quod, an' no mercy showed 'em, an' yet 'cos they're kings they gits off. An' I aint great on millionaires neither. They'se mis'able ricketty coves, all gone to pot in their in'ards through grubbin' money an' eatin' of it like, till ivery other kind o' food chokes 'em. There's a chymist in London what pays me five shillings an ounce for a little green yerb I knows on, cos' it's the on'y med'cine as keeps a millionaire customer of 'is a-goin'. I finds the yerb, an' the chymist gits the credit. I gits five shillin', an' the chymist gits a guinea. *That's* all right! *I* don't mind! I on'y gathers,—the chymist, 'e's got to infuse the yerb, distil an' bottle it. I'm paid my price, an 'e's paid 'is. All's fair in love an' war!"

He trudged on, his footsteps now rendered almost noiseless by the thick grass on which he trod. The heavy dew sparkled on every blade, and here and there the pale green twinkle of a glow-worm shone like a jewel dropped from a lady's gown. Helmsley walked beside his companion at an even pace,—the "yerb wine" had undoubtedly put strength in him and he was almost unconscious of his former excessive fatigue. He was interested in Peke's "jabber," and wondered, somewhat enviously, why such a man as this, rough, ragged, and uneducated, should seem to possess a contentment such as he had never known.

"Millionaires is gin'rally fools," continued Peke; "they buys all they wants, an' then they aint got nothin' more to live for. They gits into motor-cars an' scours the country, but they never sees it. They never 'ears the birds singin', an' they misses all the flowers. They never smells the vi'lets nor the mayblossom—they on'y gits their own petrol stench wi' the flavour o' the dust mixed in. Larst May I was a-walkin' in the lanes o' Devon, an' down the 'ill comes a motor-car tearin' an' scorchin' for all it was worth, an' bang went somethin' at the bottom o' the thing, an' it stops suddint. Out jumps a French chauffy, parlyvooin' to hisself, an' out jumps the man what owns it an' takes off his goggles. 'This is Devonshire, my man?' sez 'e to me. 'It is,' I sez to 'im. An' then the cuckoo started callin' away over the trees. 'What's that?' sez 'e lookin' startled like. 'That's the cuckoo,' sez I. An' he takes off 'is 'at an' rubs 'is 'ead, which was a' fast goin' bald. 'Dear, dear me!' sez 'e—'I 'aven't 'eard the cuckoo since I was a boy!' An' he rubs 'is 'ead again, an' laughs to hisself—'Not since I was a boy!' 'e sez. 'An' that's the cuckoo, is it? Dear, dear me!' 'You 'aven't bin much in the country p'r'aps?' sez I. 'I'm always in the country,' 'e sez—'I motor everywhere, but I've missed the cuckoo somehow!' An' then the chauffy puts the machine right, an' he jumps in an' gives me a shillin'. 'Thank-ye, my man!' sez 'e—'I'm glad you told me 'twas a *real* cuckoo!' Hor—er—hor—er—hor—er!" And Peke gave vent to a laugh peculiarly his own. "Mebbe 'e thought I'd got a Swiss clock with a sham cuckoo workin' it in my basket! 'I'm glad,' sez 'e, 'you told me 'twas a *real* cuckoo!' Hor—er—hor—er—hor—er!"

The odd chuckling sounds of merriment which were slowly jerked forth as it were from Peke's husky windpipe, were droll enough in themselves to be somewhat infectious, and Helmsley laughed as he had not done for many days.

"Ay, there's a mighty sight of tringum-trangums an' nonsense i' the world," went on Peke, still occasionally giving vent to a suppressed "Hor—er—hor"—"an' any amount o' Tom Conys what don't know a real cuckoo from a sham un'. Glory be good to me! Think o' the numskulls as goes in for pendlecitis! There's a fine name for ye! Pendlecitis! Hor—er—hor! All the fash'nables 'as got it, an' all the doctors 'as their knives sharpened an' ready to cut off the remains o' the tail we 'ad when we was all 'appy apes together! Hor—er—hor! An' the bit o' tail 's curled up in our in'ards now where it ain't got no business to be. Which shows as 'ow Natur' don't know 'ow to do it, seein' as if we 'adn't wanted a tail, she'd a' took it sheer off an' not left any behind. But the doctors thinks they knows a darn sight better'n Natur', an' they'll soon be givin' lessons in the makin' o' man to the Lord A'mighty hisself! Hor—er—hor! Pendlecitis! That's a precious monkey's tail, that there! In my grandfather's day we didn't 'ear 'bout no monkey's tails,—'twas just a chill an' inflammation o' the in'ards, an' a few yerbs made into a tea an' drunk 'ot fastin', cured it in twenty-four hours. But they've so many new-fangled notions nowadays, they've forgot all the old 'uns. There's the cancer illness,—people goes off all over the country now from cancer as never used to in my father's day, an' why? 'Cos they'se gittin' too wise for Nature's own cure. Nobody thinks o' tryin' agrimony,— water agrimony—some calls it water hemp an' bastard agrimony—'tis a thing that flowers in this month an' the next,—a brown-yellow blossom on a purple stalk, an' ye find it in cold places, in ponds an' ditches an' by runnin' waters. Make a drink of it, an' it'll mend any cancer, if 'taint too far gone. An' a cancer that's outside an' not in, 'ull clean away beautiful wi' the 'elp o' red clover. Even the juice o' nettles, which is common enough, drunk three times a day will kill any germ o' cancer, while it'll set up the blood as fresh an' bright as iver. But who's a-goin' to try common stuff like nettles an' clover an' water hemp, when there's doctors sittin' waitin' wi' knives an' wantin' money for cuttin' up their patients an' 'urryin' 'em into kingdom-come afore their time! Glory be good to me! What wi' doctors an' 'omes an' nusses, an' all the fuss as a sick man makes about hisself in these days, I'd rather be as I am, Matt Peke, a-wanderin' by hill an' dale, an' lyin' down peaceful to die under a tree when my times comes, than take any part wi' the pulin' cowards as is afraid o' cold an' fever an' wet feet an' the like, just as if they was poor little shiverin' mice instead o' men. Take 'em all round, the wimin's the bravest at bearin' pain,—they'll smile while they'se burnin' so as it sha'n't ill-convenience anybody. Wonderful sufferers, is wimin!"

"Yet they are selfish enough sometimes," said Helmsley, quickly.

"Selfish? Wheer was ye born, D. David?" queried Peke—"An' what wimin 'ave ye know'd? Town or country?"

Helmsley was silent.

"Arsk no questions an' ye'll be told no lies!" commented Peke, with a chuckle. "I sees! Ye've bin a gay old chunk in yer time, mebbe! An' it's the wimin as goes in for gay old chunks as ye've made all yer larnin of. But they ain't wimin—not as the country knows 'em. Country wimin works all day an' as often as not dandles a babby all night,—they've not got a minnit but what they aint a-troublin' an' a-worryin' 'bout 'usband or childer, an' their faces is all writ over wi' the curse o' the garden of Eden. Selfish? They aint got the time! Up at cock-crow, scrubbin' the floors, washin' the babies, feedin' the fowls or the pigs, peelin' the taters, makin' the pot boil, an' tryin' to make out 'ow twelve shillin's an' sixpence a week can be made to buy a pound's worth o' food, trapsin' to market, an' wonderin' whether the larst born in the cradle aint somehow got into the fire while mother's away,—'opin' an' prayin' for the Lord's sake as 'usband don't come 'ome blind drunk,—where's the room for any selfishness in sich a life as that?—the life lived by 'undreds o' wimin all over this 'ere blessed free country? Get 'long wi' ye, D. David! Old as y' are, ye 'ad a mother in yer time,—an' I'll take my Gospel oath there was a bit o' good in 'er!"

Helmsley stopped abruptly in his walk.

"You are right, man!" he said, "And I am wrong! You know women better than I do, and—you give me a lesson! One is never too old to learn,"—and he smiled a rather pained smile. "But—I have had a bad experience!"

"Well, if y'ave 'ad it ivir so bad, yer 'xperience aint every one's," retorted Peke. "If one fly gits into the soup, that don't argify that the hull pot's full of 'em. An' there's more good wimin than bad—takin' 'em all round an' includin' 'op pickers, gypsies an' the like. Even Miss Tranter aint wantin' in feelin', though she's a bit sour like, owin' to 'avin missed a 'usband an' all the savin' worrity wear-an-tear a 'usband brings, but she aint arf bad. Yon's the lamp of 'er 'Trusty Man' now."

A gleam of light, not much larger than the glitter of one of the glow-worms in the grass, was just then visible at the end of the long field they were traversing.

"That's an old cart-road down there wheer it stands," continued Peke. "As bad a road as ivir was made, but it runs straight into Devonshire, an' it's a good place for a pub. For many a year 'twornt used, bein' so rough an' ready, but now there's such a crowd o' motors tearin, over Countisbury 'Ill, the carts takes it, keepin' more to theirselves like, an' savin' smashin'. Miss Tranter she knew what she was a-doin' of when she got a licence an' opened 'er bizniss. 'Twas a ramshackle old farm-'ouse, goin' all to pieces when she bought it an' put up 'er sign o' the 'Trusty Man,' an' silly wenches round 'ere do say as 'ow it's 'aunted, owin' to the man as 'ad it afore Miss Tranter, bein' found dead in 'is bed with 'is 'ands a-clutchin' a pack o' cards. An' the ace o' spades—that's death— was turned uppermost. So they goes chatterin' an' chitterin' as 'ow the old chap 'ad been playin' cards wi' the devil, an' got a bad end. But Miss Tranter, she don't listen to maids' gabble,—she's doin' well, devil or no devil—an' if any one was to talk to 'er 'bout ghosteses an' sich-like, she'd wallop 'em out of 'er bar with a broom! Ay, that she would! She's a powerful strong woman Miss Tranter, an' many's the larker what's felt 'er 'and on 'is collar a-chuckin' 'im out o' the 'Trusty Man' neck an' crop for sayin' somethin' what aint ezackly agreeable to 'er feelin's. She don't stand no nonsense, an' though she's lib'ral with 'er pennorths an' pints she don't wait till a man's full boozed 'fore lockin' up the tap-room. 'Git to bed, yer hulkin' fools!' sez she, 'or ye may change my 'Otel for the Sheriff's.' An' they all knuckles down afore 'er as if they was childer gettin' spanked by their mother. Ah, she'd 'a made a grand wife for a man! 'E wouldn't 'ave 'ad no chance to make a pig of hisself if she'd been anywheres round!"

"Perhaps she won't take me in!" suggested Helmsley.

"She will, an' that sartinly!" said Peke. "She'll not refuse bed an' board to any friend o' mine."

"Friend!" Helmsley echoed the word wonderingly.

"Ay, friend! Any one's a friend what trusts to ye on the road, aint 'e? Leastways that's 'ow I take it."

"As I said before, you are very kind to me," murmured Helmsley; "and I have already asked you—Why?"

"There aint no rhyme nor reason in it," answered Peke. "You 'elps a man along if ye sees 'e wants 'elpin', sure-*ly*,—that's nat'ral. 'Tis on'y them as is born bad as don't 'elp nothin' nor nobody. Ye're old an' fagged out, an' yer face speaks a bit o' trouble—that's enuff for me. Hi' y' are!— hi' y' are, old 'Trusty Man!'"

And striding across a dry ditch which formed a kind of entrenchment between the field and the road, Peke guided his companion round a dark corner and brought him in front of a long low building, heavily timbered, with queer little lop-sided gable windows set in the slanting, red-tiled roof. A sign-board swung over the door and a small lamp fixed beneath it showed that it bore the crudely painted portrait of a gentleman in an apron, spreading out both hands palms upwards as one who has nothing to conceal,—the ideal likeness of the "Trusty Man" himself. The door itself stood open, and the sound of male voices evinced the presence of customers within. Peke entered without ceremony, beckoning Helmsley to follow him, and made straight for the bar, where a tall woman with remarkably square shoulders stood severely upright, knitting.

"'Evenin', Miss Tranter!'" said Peke, pulling off his tattered cap. "Any room for poor lodgers?"

Miss Tranter glanced at him, and then at his companion.

"That depends on the lodgers," she answered curtly.

"That's right! That's quite right, Miss!" said Peke with propitiatory deference. "You 'se allus right whatsoever ye does an' sez! But yer knows *me*,—yer knows Matt Peke, don't yer?"

Miss Tranter smiled sourly, and her knitting needles glittered like crossed knives as she finished a particular row of stitches on which she was engaged before condescending to reply. Then she said:—

"Yes, I know *you* right enough, but I don't know your company. I'm not taking up strangers."

"Lord love ye! This aint a stranger!" exclaimed Peke. "This 'ere's old David, a friend o' mine as is out o' work through gittin' more years on 'is back than the British Gov'ment allows, an' 'e's trampin' it to see 'is relations afore 'e gits put to bed wi' a shovel. 'E's as 'armless as they makes 'em, an' I've told 'im as 'ow ye' don't take in nowt but 'spectable folk. Doant 'ee turn out an old gaffer like 'e be, fagged an' footsore, to sleep in open—doant 'ee now, there's a good soul!"

Miss Tranter went on knitting rapidly. Presently she turned her piercing gimlet grey eyes on Helmsley.

"Where do you come from, man?" she demanded.

Helmsley lifted his hat with the gentle courtesy habitual to him.

"From Bristol, ma'am."

"Tramping it?"

"Yes."

"Where are you going?"

"To Cornwall."

"That's a long way and a hard road," commented Miss Tranter; "You'll never get there!"

Helmsley gave a slight deprecatory gesture, but said nothing.

Miss Tranter eyed him more keenly.

"Are you hungry?"

He smiled.

"Not very!"

"That means you're half-starved without knowing it," she said decisively. "Go in yonder," and she pointed with one of her knitting needles to the room beyond the bar whence the hum of male voices proceeded. "I'll send you some hot soup with plenty of stewed meat and bread in it. An old man like you wants more than the road food. Take him in, Peke!"

"Didn't I tell ye!" exclaimed Peke, triumphantly looking round at Helmsley. "She's one that's got 'er 'art in the right place! I say, Miss Tranter, beggin' yer parding, my friend aint a sponger, ye know! 'E can pay ye a shillin' or two for yer trouble!"

Miss Tranter nodded her head carelessly.

"The food's threepence and the bed fourpence," she said. "Breakfast in the morning, threepence,—and twopence for the washing towel. That makes a shilling all told. Ale and liquors extra."

With that she turned her back on them, and Peke, pulling Helmsley by the arm, took him into the common room of the inn, where there were several men seated round a long oak table with "gate-legs" which must have been turned by the handicraftsmen of the time of Henry the Seventh. Here Peke set down his basket of herbs in a corner, and addressed the company generally.

"'Evenin', mates! All well an' 'arty?"

Three or four of the party gave gruff response. The others sat smoking silently. One end of the table was unoccupied, and to this

Peke drew a couple of rush-bottomed chairs with sturdy oak backs, and bade Helmsley sit down beside him.

"It be powerful warm to-night!" he said, taking off his cap, and showing a disordered head of rough dark hair, sprinkled with grey. "Powerful warm it be trampin' the road, from sunrise to sunset, when the dust lies thick and 'eavy, an' all the country's dry for a drop o' rain."

"Wal, *you* aint got no cause to grumble at it," said a fat-faced man in very dirty corduroys. "It's *your* chice, an' *your* livin'! *You* likes the road, an' *you* makes your grub on it! 'Taint no use *you* findin' fault with the gettin' o' *your* victuals!"

"Who's findin' fault, Mister Dubble?" asked Peke soothingly. "I on'y said 'twas powerful warm."

"An' no one but a sawny 'xpects it to be powerful cold in July," growled Dubble—"though some there is an' some there be what cries fur snow in August, but I aint one on 'em."

"No, 'e aint one on 'em," commented a burly farmer, blowing away the foam from the brim of a tankard of ale which was set on the table in front of him. "'E alluz takes just what cooms along easy loike, do Mizter Dubble!"

There followed a silence. It was instinctively felt that the discussion was hardly important enough to be continued. Moreover, every man in the room was conscious of a stranger's presence, and each one cast a furtive glance at Helmsley, who, imitating Peke's example, had taken off his hat, and now sat quietly under the flickering light of the oil lamp which was suspended from the middle of the ceiling. He himself was intensely interested in the turn his wanderings had taken. There was a certain excitement in his present position,—he was experiencing the "new sensation" he had longed for,—and he realised it with the fullest sense of enjoyment. To be one of the richest men in the world, and yet to seem so miserably poor and helpless as to be regarded with suspicion by such a class of fellows as those among whom he was now seated, was decidedly a novel way of acquiring an additional relish for the varying chances and changes of life.

"Brought yer father along wi' ye, Matt?" suddenly asked a wizened little man of about sixty, with a questioning grin on his hard weather-beaten features.

"I aint up to 'awkin' dead bodies out o' their graves yet, Bill Bush," answered Peke. "Unless my old dad's corpsy's turned to yerbs, which is more'n likely, I aint got 'im. This 'ere's a friend o' mine,—Mister

David—e's out o' work through the Lord's speshul dispensation an' rule o' natur—gettin' old!"

A laugh went round, but a more favourable impression towards Peke's companion was at once created by this introduction.

"Sorry for ye!" said the individual called Bill Bush, nodding encouragingly to Helmsley. "I'm a bit that way myself."

He winked, and again the company laughed. Bill was known as one of the most daring and desperate poachers in all the countryside, but as yet he had never been caught in the act, and he was one of Miss Tranter's "respectable" customers. But, truth to tell, Miss Tranter had some very odd ideas of her own. One was that rabbits were vermin, and that it was of no consequence how or by whom they were killed. Another was that "wild game" belonged to everybody, poor and rich. Vainly was it explained to her that rich landowners spent no end of money on breeding and preserving pheasants, grouse, and the like,—she would hear none of it.

"Stuff and nonsense," she said sharply. "The birds breed by themselves quite fast enough if let alone,—and the Lord intended them so to do for every one's use and eating, not for a few mean and selfish money-grubs who'd shoot and sell their own babies if they could get game prices for them!"

And she had a certain sympathy with Bill Bush and his nefarious proceedings. As long as he succeeded in evading the police, so long would he be welcome at the "Trusty Man," but if once he were to be clapped into jail the door of his favourite "public" would be closed to him. Not that Miss Tranter was a woman who "went back," as the saying is, on her friends, but she had to think of her licence, and could not afford to run counter to those authorities who had the power to take it away from her.

"I'm a-shrivellin' away for want o' suthin' to do," proceeded Bill. "My legs aint no show at all to what they once was."

And he looked down at those members complacently. They were encased in brown velveteens much the worse for wear, and in shape resembled a couple of sticks with a crook at the knees.

"I lost my sitivation as gamekeeper to 'is Royal 'Ighness the Dook o' Duncy through bein' too 'onest," he went on with another wink. "'Orful pertikler, the Dook was,—nobuddy was 'llowed to be 'onest wheer 'e was but 'imself! Lord love ye! It don't do to be straight an' square in this world!"

Helmsley listened to this bantering talk, saying nothing. He was pale, and sat very still, thus giving the impression of being too tired to notice what was going on around him. Peke took up the conversation.

"Stow yer gab, Bill!" he said. "When *you* gits straight an' square, it'll be a round 'ole ye'll 'ave to drop into, mark my wurrd! An' no Dook o' Duncy 'ull pull ye out! This 'ere old friend o' mine don't unnerstand ye wi' yer fustian an' yer galligaskins. 'E's kinder eddicated—got a bit o' larnin' as I 'aves myself."

"Eddicated!" echoed Bill. "Eddication's a fine thing, aint it, if it brings an old gaffer like 'im to trampin' the road! Seems to me the more people's eddicated the less they's able to make a livin'."

"That's true! that's *dorned* true!" said the man named Dubble, bringing his great fist down on the table with a force that made the tankards jump. "My darter, she's larned to play the pianner, an' I'm *dorned* if she kin do anythin' else! Just a gillflurt she is, an' as sassy as a magpie. That's what eddication 'as made of 'er an' be *dorned* to 't!"

"'Scuse me," and Bill Bush now addressed himself immediately to Helmsley, "*ef* I may be so bold as to arsk you wheer ye comes from, meanin' no 'arm, an' what's yer purfession?"

Helmsley looked up with a friendly smile.

"I've no profession now," he answered at once. "But in my time— before I got too old—I did a good deal of office work."

"Office work! In a 'ouse of business, ye means? Readin', 'ritin', 'rithmetic, an' mebbe sweepin' the floor at odd times an' runnin' errands?"

"That's it!" answered Helmsley, still smiling.

"An' they won't 'ave ye no more?"

"I am too old," he answered quietly.

Here Dubble turned slowly round and surveyed him.

"How old be ye?"

"Seventy."

Silence ensued. The men glanced at one another. It was plain that the "one touch of nature which makes the whole world kin" was moving them all to kindly and compassionate feeling for the age and frail appearance of their new companion. What are called "rough" and "coarse" types of humanity are seldom without a sense of reverence and even affection for old persons. It is only among ultra-selfish and callous communities where over-luxurious living has blunted all the finer emotions, that age is considered a crime, or what by some individuals is declared worse than a crime, a "bore."

At that moment a short girl, with a very red face and round beady eyes, came into the room carrying on a tray two quaint old pewter tureens full of steaming soup, which emitted very savoury and appetising odours. Setting these down before Matt Peke and Helmsley, with two goodly slices of bread beside them, she held out her podgy hand.

"Threepence each, please!"

They paid her, Peke adding a halfpenny to his threepence for the girl herself, and Helmsley, who judged it safest to imitate Peke's behaviour, doing the same. She giggled.

"'Ope you aint deprivin' yourselves!" she said pertly.

"No, my dear, we aint!" retorted Peke. "We can afford to treat ye like the gentlemen doos! Buy yerself a ribbin to tie up yer bonnie brown 'air!"

She giggled again, and waited to see them begin their meal, then, with a comprehensive roll of her round eyes upon all the company assembled, she retired. The soup she had brought was certainly excellent,—strong, invigorating, and tasty enough to have done credit to a rich man's table, and Peke nodded over it with mingled surprise and appreciation.

"Miss Tranter knows what's good, she do!" he remarked to Helmsley in a low tone. "She's cooked this up speshul! This 'ere broth aint flavoured for *me*,—it's for *you*! Glory be good to me if she aint taken a fancy ter yer!—shouldn't wonder if ye 'ad the best in the 'ouse!"

Helmsley shook his head demurringly, but said nothing. He knew that in the particular position in which he had placed himself, silence was safer than speech.

Meanwhile, the short beady-eyed handmaiden returned to her mistress in the kitchen, and found that lady gazing abstractedly into the fire.

"They've got their soup," she announced, "an' they're eatin' of it up!"

"Is the old man taking it?" asked Miss Tranter.

"Yes'm. An' 'e seems to want it 'orful bad, 'orful bad 'e do, on'y 'e swallers it slower an' more soft like than Matt Peke swallers."

Miss Tranter ceased to stare at the fire, and stared at her domestic instead.

"Prue," she said solemnly, "that old man is a gentleman!"

Prue's round eyes opened a little more roundly.

"Lor', Mis' Tranter!"

"He's a gentleman," repeated the hostess of the "Trusty Man" with emphasis and decision; "and he's fallen on bad times. He may have to beg his bread along the road or earn a shilling here and there as best he can, but nothing"—and here Miss Tranter shook her forefinger defiantly in the air—"nothing will alter the fact that he's a gentleman!"

Prue squeezed her fat red hands together, breathed hard, and not knowing exactly what else to do, grinned. Her mistress looked at her severely.

"You grin like a Cheshire cat," she remarked. "I wish you wouldn't."

Prue at once pursed in her wide mouth to a more serious double line.

"How much did they give you?" pursued Miss Tranter.

"'Apenny each," answered Prue.

"How much have you made for yourself to-day all round!"

"Sevenpence three fardin's," confessed Prue, with an appealing look.

"You know I don't allow you to take tips from my customers," went on Miss Tranter. "You must put those three farthings in my poor-box."

"Yes'm!" sighed Prue meekly.

"And then you may keep the sevenpence."

"Oh thank y' 'm! Thank y', Mis' Tranter!" And Prue hugged herself ecstatically. "You'se 'orful good to me, you is, Mis' Tranter!"

Miss Tranter stood a moment, an upright inflexible figure, surveying her.

"Do you say your prayers every night and morning as I told you to do?"

Prue became abnormally solemn.

"Yes, I allus do, Mis' Tranter, wish I may die right 'ere if I don't!"

"What did I teach you to say to God for the poor travellers who stop at the 'Trusty Man'?"

"'That it may please Thee to succour, help and comfort all that are in danger, necessity and tribulation, we beseech Thee to hear us Good Lord!'" gabbled Prue, shutting her eyes and opening them again with great rapidity.

"That's right!" And Miss Tranter bent her head graciously. "I'm glad you remember it so well! Be sure you say it to-night. And now you may go, Prue."

Prue went accordingly, and Miss Tranter, resuming her knitting, returned to the bar, and took up her watchful position opposite the clock, there to remain patiently till closing time.

VII

The minutes wore on, and though some of the company at the "Trusty Man" went away in due course, others came in to replace them, so that even when it was nearing ten o'clock the common room was still fairly full. Matt Peke was evidently hail-fellow-well-met with many of the loafers of the district, and his desultory talk, with its quaint leaning towards a kind of rustic philosophy intermingled with an assumption of profound scientific wisdom, appeared to exercise considerable fascination over those who had the patience and inclination to listen to it. Helmsley accepted a pipe of tobacco offered to him by the surly-looking Dubble and smoked peacefully, leaning back in his chair and half closing his eyes with a drowsy air, though in truth his senses had never been more alert, or his interest more keenly awakened. He gathered from the general conversation that Bill Bush was an accustomed night lodger at the "Trusty Man," that Dubble had a cottage not far distant, with a scolding wife and an uppish daughter, and that it was because she knew of his home discomforts that Miss Tranter allowed him to pass many of his evenings at her inn, smoking and sipping a mild ale, which without fuddling his brains, assisted him in part to forget for a time his domestic worries. And he also found out that the sturdy farmer sedately sucking his pipe in a corner, and now and then throwing in an unexpected and random comment on whatever happened to be the topic of conversation, was known as "Feathery" Joltram, though why "Feathery" did not seem very clear, unless the term was, as it appeared to be, an adaptation of "father" or "feyther" Joltram. Matt Peke explained that old "Feathery" was a highly respected character in the "Quantocks," and not only rented a large farm, but thoroughly understood the farming business. Moreover, that he had succeeded in making himself somewhat of a terror to certain timorous time-servers, on account of his heterodox and obstinate principles. For example, he had sent his children to school because Government compelled him to do so, but when their schooldays were over, he had informed them that the sooner they forgot all they had ever learned during that period and took to "clean an' 'olesome livin'," the better he should be pleased.

"For it's all rort an' rubbish," he declared, in his broad, soft dialect. "I dozn't keer a tinker's baad 'apenny whether tha knaw 'ow to 'rite tha mizchief or to read it, or whether king o' England is eatin' 'umble pie to the U-nited States top man, or noa,—I keerz nawt aboot it, noben way or t'other. My boys 'as got to laarn draawin' crops out o' fields,—an' my gels must put 'and to milkin' and skimmin' cream an' makin' foinest butter as iver went to market. An' time comin' to wed, the boys 'ull take strong dairy wives, an' the gels 'ull pick men as can thraw through men's wurrk, or they'ze nay gels nor boys o' mine. Tarlk o' Great Britain! Heart alive! Wheer would th' owd country be if 'twere left to pulin' booky clerks what thinks they're gemmen, an' what weds niminy-piminy shop gels, an' breeds nowt but ricketty babes fit for workus' burial! Noa, by the Lord! No school larnin' for me nor mine, thank-ee! Why, the marster of the Board School 'ere doant know more practical business o' life than a suckin' calf! With a bit o' garden ground to 'is cot, e' doant reckon 'ow io till it, an' that's the rakelness o' book larnin'. Noa, noa! Th' owd way o' wurrk's the best way,—brain, 'ands, feet an' good ztrong body all zet on't, an' no meanderin' aff it! Take my wurrd the Lord A'mighty doant 'elp corn to grow if there's a whinin' zany ahint the plough!"

With these distinctly "out-of-date" notions, "Feathery" Joltram had also set himself doggedly against church-going and church people generally. Few dared mention a clergyman in his presence, for his open and successful warfare with the minister of his own parish had been going on for years and had become well-nigh traditional. Looking at him, however, as he sat in his favourite corner of the "Trusty Man's" common room, no one would have given him credit for any particular individuality. His round red face expressed nothing,—his dull fish-like eyes betrayed no intelligence,—he appeared to be nothing more than a particularly large, heavy man, wedged in his chair rather than seated in it, and absorbed in smoking a long pipe after the fashion of an infant sucking a feeding-bottle, with infinite relish that almost suggested gluttony.

The hum of voices grew louder as the hour grew later, and one or two rather noisy disputations brought Miss Tranter to the door. A look of hers was sufficient to silence all contention, and having bent the warning flash of her eyes impressively upon her customers, she retired as promptly and silently as she had appeared. Helmsley was just thinking that he would slip away and get to bed, when, a firm tread sounded in the outer passage, and a tall man, black-haired, black-eyed, and of herculean build, suddenly looked in upon the tavern company with a familiar nod and smile.

"Hullo, my hearties!" he exclaimed. "Is all tankards drained, or is a drop to spare?"

A shout of welcome greeted him:—"Tom!" "Tom o' the Gleam!" "Come in, Tom!" "Drinks all round!"—and there followed a general hustle and scraping of chairs on the floor,—every one seemed eager to make room for the newcomer. Helmsley, startled in a manner by his appearance, looked at him with involuntary and undisguised admiration. Such a picturesque figure of a man he had seldom or never seen, yet the fellow was clad in the roughest, raggedest homespun, the only striking and curious note of colour about him being a knitted crimson waistcoat, which instead of being buttoned was tied together with two or three tags of green ribbon. He stood for a moment watching the men pushing up against one another in order to give him a seat at the table, and a smile, half-amused, half-ironical, lighted up his sun-browned, handsome face.

"Don't put yourselves out, mates!" he said carelessly. "Mind Feathery's toes!—if you tread on his corns there'll be the devil to pay! Hullo, Matt Peke! How are you?"

Matt rose and shook hands.

"All the better for seein' ye again, Tom," he answered, "Wheer d'ye hail from this very present minit?"

"From the caves of Cornwall!" laughed the man. "From picking up drift on the shore and tracking seals to their lair in the hollows of the rocks!" He laughed again, and his great eyes flashed wildly. "All sport, Matt! I live like a gentleman born, keeping or killing at my pleasure!"

Here "Feathery" Joltram looked up and dumbly pointed with the stem of his pipe to a chair left vacant near the middle of the table. Tom o' the Gleam, by which name he seemed to be known to every one present, sat down, and in response to the calls of the company, a wiry pot-boy in shirt-sleeves made his appearance with several fresh tankards of ale, it now being past the hour for the attendance of that coy handmaiden of the "Trusty Man," Miss Prue.

"Any fresh tales to tell, Tom?" inquired Matt Peke then—"Any more harum-scarum pranks o' yours on the road?"

Tom drank off a mug of ale before replying, and took a comprehensive glance around the room.

"You have a stranger here," he said suddenly, in his deep, thrilling voice, "One who is not of our breed,—one who is unfamiliar with our ways. Friend or foe?"

"Friend!" declared Peke emphatically, while Bill Bush and one or two of the men exchanged significant looks and nudged each other. "Now, Tom, none of yer gypsy tantrums! I knows all yer Romany gibberish, an'

I ain't takin' any. Ye've got a good 'art enough, so don't work yer dander up with this 'ere old chap what's a-trampin' it to try and find out all that's left o's fam'ly an' friends 'fore turnin' up 'is toes to the daisies. 'Is name is David, an' 'e's been kickt out o' office work through bein' too old. That's '*is* ticket!"

Tom o' the Gleam listened to this explanation in silence, playing absently with the green tags of ribbon at his waistcoat. Then slowly lifting his eyes he fixed them full on Helmsley, who, despite himself, felt an instant's confusion at the searching intensity of the man's bold bright gaze.

"Old and poor!" he exclaimed. "That's a bad lookout in this world! Aren't you tired of living!"

"Nearly," answered Helmsley quietly—"but not quite."

Their looks met, and Tom's dark features relaxed into a smile.

"You're fairly patient!" he said, "for it's hard enough to be poor, but it's harder still to be old. If I thought I should live to be as old as you are, I'd drown myself in the sea! There's no use in life without body's strength and heart's love."

"Ah, tha be graat on the love business, Tom!" chuckled "Feathery" Joltram, lifting his massive body with a shake out of the depths of his comfortable chair. "Zeems to me tha's zummat like the burd what cozies a new mate ivery zummer!"

Tom o' the Gleam laughed, his strong even white teeth shining like a row of pearls between his black moustaches and short-cropped beard.

"You're a steady-going man, Feathery," he said, "and I'm a wastrel. But I'm ne'er as fickle as you think. I've but one love in the world that's left me—my kiddie."

"Ay, an' 'ow's the kiddie?" asked Matt Peke—"Thrivin' as iver?"

"Fine! As strong a little chap as you'll see between Quantocks and Land's End. He'll be four come Martinmas."

"Zo agein' quick as that!" commented Joltram with a broad grin. "For zure 'e be a man grow'd! Tha'll be puttin' the breechez on 'im an' zendin' 'im to the school—"

"Never!" interrupted Tom defiantly. "They'll never catch my kiddie if I know it! I want him for myself,—others shall have no part in him. He shall grow up wild like a flower of the fields—wild as his mother was—wild as the wild roses growing over her grave—"

He broke off suddenly with an impatient gesture.

"Psha! Why do you drag me over the old rough ground talking of Kiddie!" he exclaimed, almost angrily. "The child's all right. He's safe in camp with the women."

"Anywheres nigh?" asked Bill Bush.

Tom o' the Gleam made no answer, but the fierce look in his eyes showed that he was not disposed to be communicative on this point. Just then the sound of voices raised in some dispute on the threshold of the "Trusty Man," caused all the customers in the common room to pause in their talking and drinking, and to glance expressively at one another. Miss Tranter's emphatic accents rang out sharply on the silence.

"It wants ten minutes to ten, and I never close till half-past ten," she said decisively. "The law does not compel me to do so till eleven, and I resent private interference."

"I am aware that you resent any advice offered for your good," was the reply, delivered in harsh masculine tones. "You are a singularly obstinate woman. But I have my duty to perform, and as minister of this parish I shall perform it."

"Mind your own business first!" said Miss Tranter, with evident vehemence.

"My business is my duty, and my duty is my business,"—and here the male voice grew more rasping and raucous. "I have as much right to use this tavern as any one of the misled men who spend their hard earnings here and neglect their homes and families for the sake of drink. And as you do not close till half-past ten, it is not too late for me to enter."

During this little altercation, the party round the table in the common room sat listening intently. Then Dubble, rousing himself from a pleasant ale-warm lethargy, broke the spell.

"Dorned if it aint old Arbroath!" he said.

"Ay, ay, 'tis old Arbroath zartin zure!" responded "Feathery" Joltram placidly. "Let 'un coom in! Let 'un coom in!"

Tom o' the Gleam gave vent to a loud laugh, and throwing himself back in his chair, crossed his long legs and administered a ferocious twirl to his moustache, humming carelessly under his breath:—

> *"And they called the parson to marry them,*
> *But devil a bit would he—*
> *For they were but a pair of dandy prats*
> *As couldn't pay devil's fee!"*

Helmsley's curiosity was excited. There was a marked stir of expectation among the guests of the "Trusty Man"; they all appeared to be waiting for something about to happen of exceptional interest. He glanced inquiringly at Peke, who returned the glance by one of warning.

"Best sit quiet a while longer," he said. "They won't break up till closin' hour, an' m'appen there'll be a bit o' fun."

"Ay, sit quiet!" said Tom o' the Gleam, catching these words, and turning towards Helmsley with a smile—"There's more than enough time for tramping. Come! Show me if you can smoke *that*!" "That" was a choice Havana cigar which he took out of the pocket of his crimson wool waistcoat. "You've smoked one before now, I'll warrant!"

Helmsley met his flashing eyes without wavering.

"I will not say I have not," he answered quietly, accepting and lighting the fragrant weed, "but it was long ago!"

"Ay, away in the Long, long ago!" said Tom, still regarding him fixedly, but kindly—"where we have all buried such a number of beautiful things,—loves and hopes and beliefs, and dreams and fortunes!—all, all tucked away under the graveyard grass of the Long Ago!"

Here Miss Tranter's voice was heard again outside, saying acidly:—

"It's clear out and lock up at half-past ten, business or no business, duty or no duty. Please remember that!"

"'Ware, mates!" exclaimed Tom,—"Here comes our reverend!"

The door was pushed open as he spoke, and a short, dark man in clerical costume walked in with a would-be imposing air of dignity.

"Good-evening, my friends!" he said, without lifting his hat.

There was no response.

He smiled sourly, and surveyed the assembled company with a curious air of mingled authority and contempt. He looked more like a petty officer of dragoons than a minister of the Christian religion,—one of those exacting small military martinets accustomed to brow-beating and bullying every subordinate without reason or justice.

"So you're there, are you, Bush!" he continued, with a frowning glance levied in the direction of the always suspected but never proved poacher,—"I wonder you're not in jail by this time!"

Bill Bush took up his pewter tankard, and affected to drain it to the last dregs, but made no reply.

"Is that Mr. Dubble!" pursued the clergyman, shading his eyes with one hand from the flickering light of the lamp, and feigning to be doubtful of the actual personality of the individual he questioned.

"Surely not! I should be very much surprised and very sorry to see Mr. Dubble here at such a late hour!"

"Would ye now!" said Dubble. "Wal, I'm allus glad to give ye both a sorrer an' a surprise together, Mr. Arbroath—darned if I aint!"

"You must be keeping your good wife and daughter up waiting for you," proceeded Arbroath, his iron-grey eyebrows drawing together in an ugly line over the bridge of his nose. "Late hours are a mistake, Dubble!"

"So they be, so they be, Mr. Arbroath!" agreed Dubble. "Ef I was oop till midnight naggin' away at my good wife an' darter as they nags away at me, I'd say my keepin' o' late 'ours was a dorned whoppin' mistake an' no doubt o't. But seein' as 'taint arf-past ten yet, an' I aint naggin' nobody nor interferin' with my neighbours nohow, I reckon I'm on the right side o' the night so fur."

A murmur of approving laughter from all the men about him ratified this speech. The Reverend Mr. Arbroath gave a gesture of disdain, and bent his lowering looks on Tom o' the Gleam.

"Aren't you wanted by the police?" he suggested sarcastically.

The handsome gypsy glanced him over indifferently.

"I shouldn't wonder!" he retorted. "Perhaps the police want me as much as the devil wants *you*!"

Arbroath flushed a dark red, and his lips tightened over his teeth vindictively.

"There's a zummat for tha thinkin' on, Pazon Arbroath!" said "Feathery" Joltram, suddenly rising from his chair and showing himself in all his great height and burly build. "Zummat for a zermon on owd Nick, when tha're wantin' to scare the zhoolboys o' Zundays!"

Mr. Arbroath's countenance changed from red to pale.

"I was not aware of your presence, Mr. Joltram," he said stiffly.

"Noa, noa, Pazon, m'appen not, but tha's aweer on it now. Nowt o' me's zo zmall as can thraw to heaven through tha straight and narrer way. I'd 'ave to squeeze for 't!"

He laughed,—a big, slow laugh, husky with good living and good humour. Arbroath shrugged his shoulders.

"I prefer not to speak to you at all, Mr. Joltram," he said. "When people are bound to disagree, as we have disagreed for years, it is best to avoid conversation."

"Zed like the Church all over, Pazon!" chuckled the imperturbable Joltram. "Zeems as if I 'erd the 'Glory be'! But if tha don't want any talk, why does tha coom in 'ere wheer we'se all a-drinkin' steady and talkin' 'arty, an' no quarrellin' nor backbitin' of our neighbours? Tha wants us to go 'ome,—why doezn't tha go 'ome thysen? Tha's a wife a zettin' oop there, an' m'appen she's waitin' with as fine a zermon as iver was preached from a temperance cart in a wasterne field!"

He laughed again; Arbroath turned his back upon him in disgust, and strode up to the shadowed corner where Helmsley sat watching the little scene.

"Now, my man, who are *you*?" demanded the clergyman imperiously. "Where do you come from?"

Matt Peke would have spoken, but Helmsley silenced him by a look and rose to his feet, standing humbly with bent head before his arrogant interlocutor. There were the elements of comedy in the situation, and he was inclined to play his part thoroughly.

"From Bristol," he replied.

"What are you doing here?"

"Getting rest, food, and a night's lodging."

"Why do you leave out drink in the list?" sneered Arbroath. "For, of course, it's your special craving! Where are you going?"

"To Cornwall."

"Tramping it?"

"Yes."

"Begging, I suppose?"

"Sometimes."

"Disgraceful!" And the reverend gentleman snorted offence like a walrus rising from deep waters. "Why don't you work?"

"I'm too old."

"Too old! Too lazy you mean! How old are you?"

"Seventy."

Mr. Arbroath paused, slightly disconcerted. He had entered the "Trusty Man" in the hope of discovering some or even all of its customers in a state of drunkenness. To his disappointment he had found them perfectly sober. He had pounced on the stray man whom he saw was a stranger, in the expectation of proving him, at least, to be intoxicated. Here again he was mistaken. Helmsley's simple straight answers left him no opening for attack.

"You'd better make for the nearest workhouse," he said, at last. "Tramps are not encouraged on these roads."

"Evidently not!" And Helmsley raised his calm eyes and fixed them on the clergyman's lowering countenance with a faintly satiric smile.

"You're not too old to be impudent, I see!" retorted Arbroath, with an unpleasant contortion of his features. "I warn you not to come cadging about anywhere in this neighbourhood, for if you do I shall give you in charge. I have four parishes under my control, and I make it a rule to hand all beggars over to the police."

"That's not very good Christianity, is it?" asked Helmsley quietly.

Matt Peke chuckled. The Reverend Mr. Arbroath started indignantly, and stared so hard that his rat-brown eyes visibly projected from his head.

"Not very good Christianity!" he echoed. "What—what do you mean? How dare you speak to me about Christianity!"

"Ay, 'tis a bit aff!" drawled "Feathery" Joltram, thrusting his great hands deep into his capacious trouser-pockets. "'Tis a bit aff to taalk to Christian parzon 'bout Christianity, zeein' 'tis the one thing i' this warld 'e knaws nawt on!"

Arbroath grew livid, but his inward rage held him speechless.

"That's true!" cried Tom o' the Gleam excitedly—"That's as true as there's a God in heaven! I've read all about the Man that was born a carpenter in Galilee, and so far as I can understand it, He never had a rough word for the worst creatures that crawled, and the worse they were, and the more despised and down-trodden, the gentler He was with them. That's not the way of the men that call themselves His ministers!"

"I 'eerd once," said Mr. Dubble, rising slowly and laying down his pipe, "of a little chap what was makin' a posy for 'is mother's birthday, an' passin' the garden o' the rector o' the parish, 'e spied a bunch o' pink chestnut bloom 'angin' careless over the 'edge, ready to blow to bits wi' the next puff o' wind. The little raskill pulled it down an' put it wi' the rest o' the flowers 'e'd got for 'is mother, but the good an' lovin' rector seed 'im at it, an' 'ad 'im nabbed as a common thief an' sent to prison. 'E wornt but a ten-year-old lad, an' that prison spoilt 'im for life. 'E wor a fust-class Lord's man as did that for a babby boy, an' the hull neighbourhood's powerful obleeged to 'im. So don't ye,"—and here he turned his stolid gaze on Helmsley,—"don't ye, for all that ye're old, an' poor, an' 'elpless, go cadgin' round this 'ere reverend gemmen's property, cos 'e's got a real pityin' Christian 'art o's own, an' ye'd be sent to bed wi' the turnkey." Here he paused with a comprehensive smile round at the company,—then taking up his hat, he put it on. "There's one too many 'ere for pleasantness, an' I'm goin'. Good-den, Tom! Good-den, all!"

And out he strode, whistling as he went. With his departure every one began to move,—the more quickly as the clock in the bar had struck ten a minute or two since. The Reverend Mr. Arbroath stood irresolute for a moment, wishing his chief enemy, "Feathery" Joltram, would go. But Joltram remained where he was, standing erect, and surveying the scene like a heavily caparisoned charger scenting battle.

"Tha's heerd Mizter Dubble's tale afore now, Pazon, hazn't tha?" he inquired. "M'appen tha knaw'd the little chap as Christ's man zent to prizon thysen?"

Arbroath lifted his head haughtily.

"A theft is a theft," he said, "whether it is committed by a young person or an old one, and whether it is for a penny or a hundred pounds makes no difference. Thieves of all classes and all ages should be punished as such. Those are my opinions."

"They were nowt o' the Lord's opinions," said Joltram, "for He told the thief as 'ung beside Him, 'This day shalt thou be with Me in Paradise,' but He didn't say nowt o' the man as got the thief punished!"

"You twist the Bible to suit your own ends, Mr. Joltram," retorted Arbroath contemptuously. "It is the common habit of atheists and blasphemers generally."

"Then, by the Lord!" exclaimed the irrepressible "Feathery," "All th' atheists an' blasphemers must be a-gathered in the fold o' the Church, for if the pazons doan't twist the Bible to suit their own ends, I'm blest if I knaw whaat else they does for a decent livin'!"

Just then a puff of fine odour from the Havana cigar which Helmsley was enjoying floated under the nostrils of Mr. Arbroath, and added a fresh touch of irritation to his temper. He turned at once upon the offending smoker.

"So! You pretend to be poor!" he snarled, "And yet you can smoke a cigar that must have cost a shilling!"

"It was given to me," replied Helmsley gently.

"Given to you! Bah! Who would give an old tramp a cigar like that?"

"I would!" And Tom o' the Gleam sprang lightly up from his chair, his black eyes sparkling with mingled defiance and laughter—"And I did! Here!—will you take another?" And he drew out and opened a handsome case full of the cigars in question.

"Thank you!" and Arbroath's pallid lips trembled with rage. "I decline to share in stolen plunder!"

"Ha—ha—ha! Ha—ha!" laughed Tom hilariously. "Stolen plunder! That's good! D'ye think I'd steal when I can buy! Reverend sir, Tom o' the Gleam is particular as to what he smokes, and he hasn't travelled all over the world for nothing:

> 'Qu'en dictes-vous? Faut-il à ce musier,
> Il n'est trésor que de vivre à son aise!'"

Helmsley listened in wonderment. Here was a vagrant of the highroads and woods, quoting the refrain of Villon's *Contreditz de Franc-Gontier*, and pronouncing the French language with as soft and pure an accent as ever came out of Provence. Meanwhile, Mr. Arbroath, paying no attention whatever to Tom's outburst, looked at his watch.

"It is now a quarter-past ten," he announced dictatorially; "I should advise you all to be going."

"By the law we needn't go till eleven, though Miss Tranter *does* halve it," said Bill Bush sulkily—"and perhaps we won't!"

Mr. Arbroath fixed him with a stern glance.

"Do you know that I am here in the cause of Temperance?" he said.

"Oh, are ye? Then why don't ye call on Squire Evans, as is the brewer wi' the big 'ouse yonder?" queried Bill defiantly. "'E's the man to go to! Arsk 'im to shut up 'is brewery an' sell no more ale wi' pizon in't to the poor! That'll do more for Temp'rance than the early closin' o' the 'Trusty Man.'"

"Ye're right enough," said Matt Peke, who had refrained from taking any part in the conversation, save by now and then whispering a side comment to Helmsley. "There's stuff put i' the beer what the brewers brew, as is enough to knock the strongest man silly. I'm just fair tired o' hearin' o' Temp'rance this an' Temp'rance that, while 'arf the men as goes to Parl'ment takes their livin' out o' the brewin' o' beer an' spiritus liquors. An' they bribes their poor silly voters wi' their drink till they'se like a flock o' sheep runnin' into wotever field o' politics their shepherds drives 'em. The best way to make the temp'rance cause pop'lar is to stop big brewin'. Let every ale'ouse 'ave its own pertikler brew, an' m'appen we'll git some o' the old-fashioned malt an' 'ops agin. That'll be good for the small trader, an' the big brewin' companies can take to somethin' 'onester than the pizonin' bizness."

"You are a would-be wise man, and you talk too much, Matthew Peke!" observed the Reverend Mr. Arbroath, smiling darkly, and still glancing askew at his watch. "I know you of old!"

"Ye knows me an' I knows you," responded Peke placidly. "Yer can't interfere wi' me nohow, an' I dessay it riles ye a bit, for ye loves interferin' with ivery sort o' folk, as all the parsons do. I b'longs to no parish, an' aint under you no more than Tom o' the Gleam be, an' we both thanks the Lord for't! An' I'm earnin' a livin' my own way an' bein' a benefit to the sick an' sorry, which aint so far from proper Christianity. Lor', Parson Arbroath! I wonder ye aint more 'uman like, seein' as yer fav'rite gel in the village was arskin' me t'other day if I 'adn't any yerb for to make a love-charm. 'Love-charm!' sez I—'what does ye want that for, my gel?' An' she up an' she sez—'I'd like to make Parson Arbroath eat it!' Hor—er—hor—er—hor—er! 'I'd like to make Parson Arbroath eat it!' sez she. An' she's a foine strappin' wench, too!—'Ullo, Parson! Goin'?"

The door slammed furiously,—Arbroath had suddenly lost his dignity and temper together. Peke's raillery proved too much for him, and amid the loud guffaws of "Feathery" Joltram, Bill Bush and the rest, he beat a hasty retreat, and they heard his heavy footsteps go hurriedly across the passage of the "Trusty Man," and pass out into the road beyond. Roars of laughter accompanied his departure, and Peke looked round with a smile of triumph.

"It's just like a witch-spell!" he declared. "There's nowt to do but whisper, 'Parson's fav'rite!'—an' Parson hisself melts away like a mist o' the mornin' or a weasel runnin' into its 'ole! Hor—er, hor—er, hor—er!"

And again the laughter pealed out long and loud, "Feathery" Joltram bending himself double with merriment, and slapping the sides of his huge legs in ecstasy. Miss Tranter hearing the continuous uproar, looked in warningly, but there was a glimmering smile on her face.

"We'se goin', Miss Tranter!" announced Bill Bush, his wizened face all one broad grin. "We aint the sort to keep you up, never fear! Your worst customer's just cleared out!"

"So I see!" replied Miss Tranter calmly,—then, nodding towards Helmsley, she said—"Your room's ready."

Helmsley took the hint. He rose from his chair, and held out his hand to Peke.

"Good-night!" he said. "You've been very kind to me, and I shan't forget it!"

The herb-gatherer looked for a moment at the thin, refined white hand extended to him before grasping it in his own horny palm. Then—

"Good-night, old chap!" he responded heartily. "Ef I don't see ye i' the mornin' I'll leave ye a bottle o' yerb wine to take along wi' ye trampin', for the more ye drinks o't the soberer ye'll be an' the better ye'll like it. But ye should give up the idee o' footin' it to Cornwall; ye'll never git there without a liftin'."

"I'll have a good try, anyway," rejoined Helmsley. "Good-night!"

He turned towards Tom o' the Gleam.

"Good-night!"

"Good-night!" And Tom's dark eyes glowed upon him with a sombre intentness. "You know the old proverb which says, 'It's a long lane which has never a turning'?"

Helmsley nodded with a faint smile.

"Your turning's near at hand," said Tom. "Take my word for it!"

"Will it be a pleasant turning?" asked Helmsley, still smiling.

"Pleasant? Ay, and peaceful!" And Tom's mellow voice sank into a softer tone. "Peaceful as the strong love of a pure woman, and as sweet with contentment as is the summer when the harvest is full! Good-night!"

Helmsley looked at him thoughtfully; there was something poetic and fascinating about the man.

"I should like to meet you again," he said impulsively.

"Would you?" Tom o' the Gleam smiled. "So you will, as sure as God's in heaven! But how or when, who can tell!" His handsome face clouded suddenly,—some dark shadow of pain or perplexity contracted his brows,—then he seemed to throw the feeling, whatever it was, aside, and his features cleared. "You are bound to meet me," he continued. "I am as much a part of this country as the woods and hills,—the Quantocks and Brendons know me as well as Exmoor and the Valley of Rocks. But you are safe from me and mine! Not one of our tribe will harm you,—you can pursue your way in peace—and if any one of us can give you help at any time, we will."

"You speak of a community?"

"I speak of a Republic!" answered Tom proudly. "There are thousands of men and women in these islands whom no king governs and no law controls,—free as the air and independent as the birds! They ask nothing at any man's hands—they take and they keep!"

"Like the millionaires!" suggested Bill Bush, with a grin.

"Right you are, Bill!—like the millionaires! None take more than they do, and none keep their takings closer!"

"And very miserable they must surely be sometimes, on both their takings and their keepings," said Helmsley.

"No doubt of it! There'd be no justice in the mind of God if millionaires weren't miserable," declared Tom o' the Gleam. "They've more money than they ought to have,—it's only fair they should have less happiness. Compensation's a natural law that there's no getting away from,—that's why a gypsy's merrier than a king!"

Helmsley smiled assent, and with another friendly good-night all round, left the room. Miss Tranter awaited him, candle in hand, and preceding him up a short flight of ancient and crooked oaken stairs, showed him a small attic room with one narrow bed in it, scrupulously neat and clean.

"You'll be all right here," she said. "There's no lock to your door, but you're out of the truck of house work, and no one will come nigh you."

"Thank you, madam,"—and Helmsley bent his head gently, almost humbly,—"You are very good to me. I am most grateful!"

"Nonsense!" said Miss Tranter, affecting snappishness. "You pay for a bed, and here it is. The lodgers here generally share one room between them, but you are an old man and need rest. It's better you should get your sleep without any chance of disturbance. Good-night!"

"Good-night!"

She set down the candle by his bedside with a "Mind you put it out!" final warning, and descended the stairs to see the rest of her customers cleared off the premises, with the exception of Bill Bush, Matt Peke, and Tom o' the Gleam, who were her frequent night lodgers. She found Tom o' the Gleam standing up and delivering a kind of extemporary oration, while his rough cap, under the pilotage of Bill Bush, was being passed round the table in the fashion of a collecting plate.

"The smallest contribution thankfully received!" he laughed, as he looked and saw her. "Miss Tranter, we're doing a mission! We're Salvationists! Now's your chance! Give us a sixpence!"

"What for?" And setting her arms akimbo, the hostess of the "Trusty Man" surveyed all her lingering guests with a severe face. "What games are you up to now? It's time to clear!"

"So it is, and all the good little boys are going to bed," said Tom. "Don't be cross, Mammy! We want to close our subscription list—that's all! We've raised a few pennies for the old grandfather upstairs. He'll never get to Cornwall, poor chap! He's as white as paper. Office work doesn't fit a man of his age for tramping the road. We've collected two shillings for him among us,—you give sixpence, and there's half-a-crown all told. God bless the total!"

He seized his cap as it was handed back to him, and shook it, to show that it was lined with jingling halfpence, and his eyes sparkled like those of a child enjoying a bit of mischief.

"Come, Miss Tranter! Help the Gospel mission!"

Her features relaxed into a smile, and feeling in her apron pocket, she produced the requested coin.

"There you are!" she said.—"And now you've got it, how are you going to give him the money?"

"Never you mind!" and Tom swept all the coins together, and screwed them up in a piece of newspaper. "We'll surprise the old man as the angels surprise the children!"

Miss Tranter said nothing more, but withdrawing to the passage, stood and watched her customers go out of the door of the "Trusty Man," one by one. Each great hulking fellow doffed his cap to her and bade her a respectful "Good-night" as he passed, "Feathery" Joltram pausing a moment to utter an "aside" in her ear.

"'A fixed oop owd Arbroath for zartin zure!"—and here, with a sly wink, he gave a forcible nudge to her arm,—"An owd larrupin' fox 'e be!—an' Matt Peke giv''im the finish wi's fav'rite! Ha—ha—ha! 'A can't abide a wurrd o' that long-legged wench! Ha—ha—ha! An' look y'ere, Miss Tranter! I'd 'a given a shillin' in Tom's 'at when it went round, but I'm thinkin' as zummat in the face o' the owd gaffer up in bed ain't zet on beggin', an' m'appen a charity'd 'urt 'is feelin's like the poor-'ouse do. But if 'e's wantin' to 'arn a mossel o' victual, I'll find 'im a lightsome job on the farm if he'll reckon to walk oop to me afore noon to-morrer. Tell 'im' that from farmer Joltram, an' good-night t'ye!"

He strode out, and before eleven had struck, the old-fashioned iron bar clamped down across the portal, and the inn was closed. Then Miss Tranter turned into the bar, and before shutting it up paused, and surveyed her three lodgers critically.

"So you pretend to be all miserably poor, and yet you actually collect what you call a 'fund' for the old tramp upstairs who's a perfect stranger to you!" she said—"Rascals that you are!"

Bill Bush looked sheepish.

"Only halfpence, Miss," he explained. "Poor we be as church mice, an' ye knows that, doesn't ye? But we aint gone broken yet, an' Tom 'e started the idee o' doin' a good turn for th' old gaffer, for say what ye like 'e do look a bit feeble for trampin' it."

Miss Tranter sniffed the atmosphere of the bar with a very good assumption of lofty indifference.

"*You* started the idea, did you?" she went on, looking at Tom o' the Gleam. "You're a nice sort of ruffian to start any idea at all, aren't you? I thought you always took, and never gave!"

He smiled, leaning his handsome head back against the white-washed wall of the little entry where he stood, but said nothing. Matt Peke then took up the parable.

"Th' old man be mortal weak an' faint for sure," he said. "I come upon 'im lyin' under a tree wi' a mossel book aside 'im, an' I takes an' looks at the book, an' 'twas all portry an' simpleton stuff like, an' 'e looked old enough to be my dad, an' tired enough to be fast goin' where my dad's gone, so I just took 'im along wi' me, an' giv' 'im my name an' purfession, an' 'e did the same, a-tellin' me as 'ow 'is name was D. David, an' 'ow 'e 'd lost 'is office work through bein' too old an' shaky. 'E's all right,—an office man aint much good on the road, weak on 'is pins an' failin' in 'is sight. M'appen the 'arf-crown we've got 'im 'ull 'elp 'im to a ride part o' the way 'e's goin'."

"Well, don't you men bother about him any more," said Miss Tranter decisively. "You get off early in the morning, as usual. *I'll* look after him!"

"Will ye now?" and Peke's rugged features visibly brightened— "That's just like ye, Miss! Aint it, Tom? Aint it, Bill?"

Both individuals appealed to agreed that it was "Miss Tranter all over."

"Now off to bed with you!" proceeded that lady peremptorily. "And leave your collected 'fund' with me—I'll give it to him."

But Tom o' the Gleam would not hear of this.

"No, Miss Tranter!—with every respect for you, no!" he said gaily. "It's not every night we can play angels! I play angel to my kiddie sometimes, putting a fairing in his little hammock where he sleeps like a bird among the trees all night, but I've never had the chance to do it to an old grandad before! Let me have my way!"

And so it chanced that at about half-past eleven, Helmsley, having lain down with a deep sense of relief and repose on his clean comfortable little bed, was startled out of his first doze by hearing stealthy steps approaching his door. His heart began to beat quickly,—a certain vague misgiving troubled him,—after all, he thought, had he not been very rash to trust himself to the shelter of this strange and lonely inn among the wild moors and hills, among unknown men, who, at any rate by their rough and uncouth appearance, might be members of a gang of thieves? The steps came nearer, and a hand fumbled gently with the door handle. In that tense moment of strained listening he was glad to remember that when undressing, he had carefully placed his vest, lined with the banknotes he carried, under the sheet on which he lay, so that in the event of any one coming to search his clothes, nothing would be found but a few loose coins in his coat pocket. The fumbling at his door continued, and presently it slowly opened, letting in a pale stream of moonlight from a lattice window outside. He just saw the massive figure of Tom o' the Gleam standing on the threshold, clad in shirt and trousers only, and behind him there seemed to be the shadowy outline of Matt Peke's broad shoulders and Bill Bush's bullet head. Uncertain what to expect, he determined to show no sign of consciousness, and half closing his eyes, he breathed heavily and regularly, feigning to be in a sound slumber. But a cold chill ran through his veins as Tom o' the Gleam slowly and cautiously approached the bed, holding something in his right hand, while Matt Peke and Bill Bush tiptoed gently after him half-way into the room.

"Poor old gaffer!" he heard Tom whisper—"Looks all ready laid out and waiting for the winding!"

And the hand that held the something stole gently and ever gentlier towards the pillow. By a supreme effort Helmsley kept quite still. How he controlled his nerves he never knew, for to see through his almost shut eyelids the dark herculean form of the gypsy bending over him with the two other men behind, moved him to a horrible fear. Were they going to murder him? If so, what for? To them he was but an old tramp,—unless—unless somebody had tracked him from London!—unless somebody knew who he really was, and had pointed him out as likely to have money about him. These thoughts ran like lightning through his brain, making his blood burn and his pulses, tingle almost to the verge of a start and cry, when the creeping hand he dreaded quietly laid something on his pillow and withdrew itself with delicate precaution.

"He'll be pleased when he wakes," said Tom o' the Gleam, in the mildest of whispers, retreating softly from the bedside—"Won't he?"

"Ay, that he will!" responded Peke, under his breath;, "aint 'e sleepin' sound?"

"Sound as a babe!"

Slowly and noiselessly they stepped backward,—slowly and noiselessly they closed the door, and the faint echo of their stealthy footsteps creeping away along the outer passage to another part of the house, was hushed at last into silence. After a long pause of intense stillness, some clock below stairs struck midnight with a mellow clang, and Helmsley opening his eyes, lay waiting till the excited beating of his heart subsided, and his quickened breath grew calm. Blaming himself for his nervous terrors, he presently rose from his bed, and struck a match from the box which Miss Tranter had thoughtfully left beside him, and lit his candle. Something had been placed on his pillow, and curiosity moved him to examine it. He looked,—but saw nothing save a mere screw of soiled newspaper. He took it up wonderingly. It was heavy,—and opening it he found it full of pennies, halfpennies, and one odd sixpence. A scrap of writing accompanied this collection, roughly pencilled thus:—"To help you along the road. From friends at the Trusty Man. Good luck!"

For a moment he stood inert, fingering the humble coins,—for a moment he could hardly realise that these rough men of doubtful character and calling, with whom he had passed one evening, were actually humane enough to feel pity for his age, and sympathy for his seeming loneliness and poverty, and that they had sufficient heart and generosity to deprive themselves of money in order to help one whom they judged to be in greater need;—then the pure intention and honest kindness of the little "surprise" gift came upon him all at once, and he was not ashamed to feel his eyes full of tears.

"God forgive me!" he murmured—"God forgive me that I ever judged the poor by the rich!"

With an almost reverential tenderness, he folded the paper and coins together, and put the little packet carefully away, determining never to part with it.

"For its value outweighs every banknote I ever handled!" he said— "And I am prouder of it than of all my millions!"

VIII

The light of the next day's sun, beaming with all the heat and effulgence of full morning, bathed moor and upland in a wide shower of gold, when Miss Tranter, standing on the threshold of her dwelling, and shading her eyes with one hand from the dazzling radiance of the skies, watched a man's tall figure disappear down the rough and precipitous road which led from the higher hills to the seashore. All her night's lodgers had left her save one—and he was still soundly sleeping. Bill Bush had risen as early as five and stolen away,—Matt Peke had broken his fast with a cup of hot milk and a hunch of dry bread, and shouldering his basket, had started for Crowcombe, where he had several customers for his herbal wares.

"Take care o' the old gaffer I brought along wi' me," had been his parting recommendation to the hostess of the "Trusty Man." "Tell 'im I've left a bottle o' yerb wine in the bar for 'im. M'appen ye might find an odd job or two about th' 'ouse an' garden for 'im, just for lettin' 'im rest a while."

Miss Tranter had nodded curtly in response to this suggestion, but had promised nothing.

The last to depart from the inn was Tom o' the Gleam. Tom had risen in what he called his "dark mood." He had eaten no breakfast, and he scarcely spoke at all as he took up his stout ash stick and prepared to fare forth upon his way. Miss Tranter was not inquisitive, but she had rather a liking for Tom, and his melancholy surliness was not lost upon her.

"What's the matter with you?" she asked sharply. "You're like a bear with a sore head this morning!"

He looked at her with sombre eyes in which the flame of strongly restrained passions feverishly smouldered.

"I don't know what's the matter with me," he answered slowly. "Last night I was happy. This morning I am wretched!"

"For no cause?"

"For no cause that I know of,"—and he heaved a sudden sigh. "It is the dark spirit—the warning of an evil hour!"

"Stuff and nonsense!" said Miss Tranter.

He was silent. His mouth compressed itself into a petulant line, like that of a chidden child ready to cry.

"I shall be all right when I have kissed the kiddie," he said.

Miss Tranter sniffed and tossed her head.

"You're just a fool over that kiddie," she declared with emphasis,— "You make too much of him."

"How can I make too much of my all?" he asked.

Her face softened.

"Well, it's a pity you look at it in that way," she said. "You shouldn't set your heart on anything in this world."

"Why not?" he demanded. "Is God a friend that He should grudge us love?"

Her lips trembled a little, but she made no reply.

"What am I to set my heart on?" he continued—"If not on anything in this world, what have I got in the next?"

A faint tinge of colour warmed Miss Tranter's sallow cheeks.

"Your wife's in the next," she answered, quietly.

His face changed—his eyes lightened.

"My wife!" he echoed. "Good woman that you are, you know she was never my wife! No parson ever mocked us wild birds with his blessing! She was my love—my love!—so much more than wife! By Heaven! If prayer and fasting would bring me to the world where *she* is, I'd fast and pray till I turned this body of mine to dust and ashes! But my kiddie is all I have that's left of her; and shall I not love him, nay, worship him for *her* sake?"

Miss Tranter tried to look severe, but could not,—the strong vehemence of the man shook her self-possession.

"Love him, yes!—but don't worship him," she said. "It's a mistake, Tom! He's only a child, after all, and he might be taken from you."

"Don't say that!" and Tom suddenly gripped her by the arm. "For God's sake don't say that! Don't send me away this morning with those words buzzing in my ears!"

Great tears flashed into his eyes,—his face paled and contracted as with acutest agony.

"I'm sorry, Tom," faltered Miss Tranter, herself quite overcome by his fierce emotion—"I didn't mean—"

"Yes—yes!—that's right! Say you didn't mean it!" muttered Tom, with a pained smile—"You didn't—?"

"I didn't mean it!" declared Miss Tranter earnestly. "Upon my word I didn't, Tom!"

He loosened his hold of her arm.

"Thank you! God bless you!" and a shudder ran through his massive frame. "But it's all one with the dark hour!—all one with the wicked tongue of a dream that whispers to me of a coming storm!"

He pulled his rough cap over his brows, and strode forward a step or two. Then he suddenly wheeled round again, and doffed the cap to Miss Tranter.

"It's unlucky to turn back," he said, "yet I'm doing it, because—because—I wouldn't have you think me sullen or ill-tempered with *you*! Nor ungrateful. You're a good woman, for all that you're a bit rough sometimes. If you want to know where we are, we've camped down by Cleeve, and we're on the way to Dunster. I take the short cuts that no one else dare venture by—over the cliffs and through the cave-holes of the sea. When the old man comes down, tell him I'll have a care of him if he passes my way. I like his face! I think he's something more than he seems."

"So do I!" agreed Miss Tranter. "I'd almost swear that he's a gentleman, fallen on hard times."

"A gentleman!" Tom o' the Gleam laughed disdainfully—"What's that? Only a robber grown richer than his neighbours! Better be a plain Man any day than your up-to-date 'gentleman'!"

With another laugh he swung away, and Miss Tranter remained, as already stated, at the door of the inn for many minutes, watching his easy stride over the rough stones and clods of the "by-road" winding down to the sea. His figure, though so powerfully built, was singularly graceful in movement, and commanded the landscape much as that of some chieftain of old might have commanded it in that far back period of time when mountain thieves and marauders were the progenitors of all the British kings and their attendant nobility.

"I wish I knew that man's real history!" she mused, as he at last disappeared from her sight. "The folks about here, such as Mr. Joltram, for instance, say he was never born to the gypsy life,—he speaks too well, and knows too much. Yet he's wild enough—and—yes!—I'm afraid he's bad enough—sometimes—to be anything!"

Her meditations were here interrupted by a touch on her arm, and turning, she beheld her round-eyed handmaiden Prue.

"The old man you sez is a gentleman is down, Mis' Tranter!"

Miss Tranter at once stepped indoors and confronted Helmsley, who, amazed to find it nearly ten o'clock, now proffered humble excuses to his hostess for his late rising. She waived these aside with a good-humoured nod and smile.

"That's all right!" she said. "I wanted you to have a good long rest, and I'm glad you got it. Were you disturbed at all?"

"Only by kindness," answered Helmsley in a rather tremulous voice. "Some one came into my room while I was asleep—and—and—I found a 'surprise packet' on my pillow—"

"Yes, I know all about it," interrupted Miss Tranter, with a touch of embarrassment—"Tom o' the Gleam did that. He's just gone. He's a rough chap, but he's got a heart. He thinks you're not strong enough to tramp it to Cornwall. And all those great babies of men put their heads together last night after you'd gone upstairs, and clubbed up enough among them to give you a ride part of the way—"

"They're very good!" murmured Helmsley. "Why should they trouble about an old fellow like me?"

"Oh well!" said Miss Tranter cheerfully, "it's just because you *are* an old fellow, I suppose! You see you might walk to a station to-day, and take the train as far as Minehead before starting on the road again. Anyhow you've time to think it over. If you'll step into the room yonder, I'll send Prue with your breakfast."

She turned her back upon him, and with a shrill call of "Prue! Prue!" affected to be too busy to continue the conversation. Helmsley, therefore, went as she bade him into the common room, which at this hour was quite empty. A neat white cloth was spread at one end of the table, and on this was set a brown loaf, a pat of butter, a jug of new milk, a basin of sugar, and a brightly polished china cup and saucer. The window was open, and the inflow of the pure fresh morning air had done much to disperse the odours of stale tobacco and beer that subtly clung to the walls as reminders of the drink and smoke of the previous evening.

Just outside, a tangle of climbing roses hung like a delicate pink curtain between Helmsley's eyes and the sunshine, while the busy humming of bees in and out the fragrant hearts of the flowers, made a musical monotony of soothing sound. He sat down and surveyed the simple scene with a quiet sense of pleasure. He contrasted it in his memory with the weary sameness of the breakfasts served to him in his own palatial London residence, when the velvet-footed butler creeping obsequiously round the table, uttered his perpetual "Tea or coffee, sir? 'Am or tongue? Fish or heggs?" in soft sepulchral tones, as though these comestibles had something to do with poison rather than nourishment. With disgust at the luxury which engendered such domestic appurtenances, he thought of the two tall footmen, whose chief duty towards the serving of breakfast appeared to be the taking of covers off dishes and the putting them on again, as if six-footed able-bodied manhood were not equipped for more muscular work than that!

"We do great wrong," he said to himself—"We who are richer than what are called the rich, do infinite wrong to our kind by tolerating so much needless waste and useless extravagance. We merely generate mischief for ourselves and others. The poor are happier, and far kindlier to each other than the moneyed classes, simply because they cannot demand so much self-indulgence. The lazy habits of wealthy men and women who insist on getting an unnecessary number of paid persons to do for them what they could very well do for themselves, are chiefly to blame for all our tiresome and ostentatious social conditions. Servants must, of course, be had in every well-ordered household—but too many of them constitute a veritable hive of discord and worry. Why have huge houses at all? Why have enormous domestic retinues? A small house is always cosiest, and often prettiest, and the fewer servants, the less trouble. Here again comes in the crucial question—Why do we spend all our best years of youth, life, and sentiment in making money, when, so far as the sweetest and highest things are concerned, money can give so little!"

At that moment, Prue entered with a brightly shining old brown "lustre" teapot, and a couple of boiled eggs.

"Mis' Tranter sez you're to eat the eggs cos' they'se new-laid an' incloodid in the bill," she announced glibly—"An' 'opes you've got all ye want."

Helmsley looked at her kindly.

"You're a smart little girl!" he said. "Beginning to earn your own living already, eh?"

"Lor', that aint much!" retorted Prue, putting a knife by the brown loaf, and setting the breakfast things even more straightly on the table than they originally were. "I lives on nothin' scarcely, though I'm turned fifteen an' likes a bit o' fresh pork now an' agen. But I've got a brother as is on'y ten, an' when 'e aint at school 'e's earnin' a bit by gatherin' mussels on the beach, an' 'e do collect a goodish bit too, though 'taint reg'lar biziness, an' 'e gets hisself into such a pickle o' salt water as never was. But he brings mother a shillin' or two."

"And who is your mother?" asked Helmsley, drawing up his chair to the table and sitting down.

"Misses Clodder, up at Blue-bell Cottage, two miles from 'ere across the moor," replied Prue. "She goes out a-charing, but it's 'ard for 'er to be doin' chars now—she's gettin' old an' fat—orful fat she be gettin'. Dunno what we'll do if she goes on fattenin'."

It was difficult not to laugh at this statement, Prue's eyes were so round, her cheeks were so red, and she breathed so spasmodically as she spoke. David Helmsley bit his lips to hide a broad smile, and poured out his tea.

"Have you no father?"

"No, never 'ad," declared Prue, quite jubilantly. "'E droonk 'isself to death an' tumbled over a cliff near 'ere one dark night an' was drowned!" This, with the most thrilling emphasis.

"That's very sad! But you can't say you never had a father," persisted Helmsley. "You had him before he was drowned?"

"No, I 'adn't," said Prue. "'E never comed 'ome at all. When 'e seed me 'e didn't know me, 'e was that blind droonk. When my little brother was born 'e was 'owlin' wild down Watchet way, an' screechin' to all the folks as 'ow the baby wasn't his'n!"

This was a doubtful subject,—a "delicate and burning question," as reviewers for the press say when they want to praise some personal friend's indecent novel and pass it into decent households,—and Helmsley let it drop. He devoted himself to the consideration of his breakfast, which was excellent, and found that he had an appetite to enjoy it thoroughly.

Prue watched him for a minute or two in silence.

"Ye likes yer food?" she demanded, presently.

"Very much!"

"Thought yer did! I'll tell Mis' Tranter."

With that she retired, and shutting the door behind her left Helmsley to himself.

Many and conflicting were the thoughts that chased one another through his brain during the quiet half-hour he gave to his morning meal,—a whole fund of new suggestions and ideas were being generated in him by the various episodes in which he was taking an active yet seemingly passive part. He had voluntarily entered into his present circumstances, and so far, he had nothing to complain of. He had met with friendliness and sympathy from persons who, judged by the world's conventions, were of no social account whatever, and he had seen for himself men in a condition of extreme poverty, who were nevertheless apparently contented with their lot. Of course, as a well-known millionaire, his secretaries had always had to deal with endless cases of real or assumed distress, more often the latter,—and shoals of begging letters from people representing themselves as starving and friendless, formed a large part of the daily correspondence with which his house and office were besieged,—but he had never come into personal contact with these shameless sort of correspondents, shrewdly judging them to be undeserving simply by the very fact that they wrote begging letters. He knew that no really honest or plucky-spirited man or woman would waste so much as a stamp in asking money from a stranger, even if such a stranger were twenty times a millionaire. He had given huge sums away to charitable institutions anonymously; and he remembered with a thrill of pain the "Christian kindness" of some good "Church" people, who, when the news accidentally slipped out that he was the donor of a particularly munificent gift to a certain hospital, remarked that "no doubt Mr. Helmsley had given it anonymously *at first*, in order that it might be made public more effectively *afterwards,* by way of a personal *advertisement!*" Such spiteful comment often repeated, had effectually checked the outflow of his naturally warm and generous spirit, nevertheless he was always ready to relieve any pressing cases of want which were proved genuine, and many a wretched family in the East End of London had cause to bless him for his timely and ungrudging aid. But this present kind of life,—the life of the tramp, the poacher, the gypsy, who is content to be "on the road" rather than submit to the trammels of custom and ordinance, was new to him and full of charm. He took a peculiar pleasure in reflecting as to what he could do to make these men, with whom he had casually foregathered, happier? Did it lie in his power to give them any greater satisfaction than that which they already possessed? He doubted whether a present of money to Matt Peke, for instance, would not offend that rustic philosopher, more than it would gratify him;—while, as for Tom o' the Gleam, that handsome ruffian was more likely to rob a man of gold than accept it as a gift from him. Then involuntarily, his thoughts reverted to the "kiddie." He recalled the look in Tom's wild eyes, and the almost womanish tremble of tenderness in his rough voice, when he had spoken of this little child of his on whom he openly admitted he had set all his love.

"I should like," mused Helmsley, "to see that kiddie! Not that I believe in the apparent promise of a child's life,—for my own sons taught me the folly of indulging in any hopes on that score—and Lucy Sorrel has completed the painful lesson. Who would have ever thought that she,—the little angel creature who seemed too lovely and innocent for this world at ten,—could at twenty have become the extremely commonplace and practical woman she is,—practical enough to wish to marry an old man for his money! But that talk among the men last night about the 'kiddie' touched me somehow,—I fancy it must be a sturdy little lad, with a bright face and a will of its own. I might possibly do something for the child if,—if its father would let me! And that's very doubtful! Besides, should I not be interfering with the wiser and healthier dispensations of nature? The 'kiddie' is no doubt perfectly happy in its wild state of life,—free to roam the woods and fields, with every chance of building up a strong and vigorous constitution in the simple open-air existence to which it has been born and bred. All the riches in the world could not make health or freedom for it,—and thus again I confront myself with my own weary problem—Why have I toiled all my life to make money, merely to find money so useless and comfortless at the end?"

With a sigh he rose from the table. His simple breakfast was finished, and he went to the window to look at the roses that pushed their pretty pink faces up to the sun through a lattice-work of green leaves. There was a small yard outside, roughly paved with cobbles, but clean, and bordered here and there with bright clusters of flowers, and in one particularly sunny corner where the warmth from the skies had made the cobbles quite hot, a tiny white kitten rolled on its back, making the most absurd efforts to catch its own tail between its forepaws,— and a promising brood of fowls were clucking contentedly round some scattered grain lately flung out from the window of the "Trusty Man's" wash-house for their delectation. There was nothing in the scene at all of a character to excite envy in the most morbid and dissatisfied mind;— it was full of the tamest domesticity, and yet—it was a picture such as some thoughtful Dutch artist would have liked to paint as a suggestion of rural simplicity and peace.

"But if one only knew the ins and outs of the life here, it might not prove so inviting," he thought. "I daresay all the little towns and villages in this neighbourhood are full of petty discords, jealousies, envyings and spites,—even Prue's mother, Mrs. Clodder, may have, and probably has, a neighbour whom she hates, and wishes to get the better of, in some way or other, for there is really no such thing as actual peace anywhere except—in the grave! And who knows whether we shall even find it there! Nothing dies which does not immediately begin to live—in another fashion. And every community, whether of insects, birds, wild animals, or men and women, is bound to fight for existence,—therefore those who cry: 'Peace, peace!' only clamour for a vain thing. The very stones and rocks and mountains maintain a perpetual war with destroying elements,—they appear immutable things to our short lives, but they change in their turn even as we do— they die to live again in other forms, even as we do. And what is it all for? What is the sum and substance of so much striving—if merest Nothingness is the end?"

He was disturbed from his reverie by the entrance of Miss Tranter. He turned round and smiled at her.

"Well!" she said—"Enjoyed your breakfast?"

"Very much indeed, thanks to your kindness!" he replied. "I hardly thought I had such a good appetite left to me. I feel quite strong and hearty this morning."

"You look twice the man you were last night, certainly,"—and she eyed him thoughtfully—"Would you like a job here?"

A flush rose to his brows. He hesitated before replying.

"You'd rather not!" snapped out Miss Tranter—"I can see 'No' in your face. Well, please yourself!"

He looked at her. Her lips were compressed in a thin line, and she wore a decidedly vexed expression.

"Ah, you think I don't want to work!" he said—"There you're wrong! But I haven't many years of life in me,—there's not much time left to do what I have to do,—and I must get on."

"Get on, where?"

"To Cornwall."

"Whereabouts in Cornwall?"

"Down by Penzance way."

"You want to start off on the tramp again at once?"

"Yes."

"All right, you must do as you like, I suppose,"—and Miss Tranter sniffed whole volumes of meaning in one sniff—"But Farmer Joltram told me to say that if you wanted a light job up on his place,—that's about a mile from here,—he wouldn't mind giving you a chance. You'd get good victuals there, for he feeds his men well. And I don't mind trusting you with a bit of gardening—you could make a shilling a day easy—so don't say you can't get work. That's the usual whine—but if you say it—"

"I shall be a liar!" said Helmsley, his sunken eyes lighting up with a twinkle of merriment—"And don't you fear, Miss Tranter,—I *won't* say it! I'm grateful to Mr. Joltram—but I've only one object left to me in life, and that is—to get on, and find the person I'm looking for—if I can!"

"Oh, you're looking for a person, are you?" queried Miss Tranter, more amicably—"Some long-lost relative?"

"No,—not a relative, only—a friend."

"I see!" Miss Tranter smoothed down her neatly fitting plain cotton gown with both hands reflectively—"And you'll be all right if you find this friend?"

"I shall never want anything any more," he answered, with an unconsciously pathetic tremor in his voice—"My dearest wish will be granted, and I shall be quite content to die!"

"Well, content or no content, you've got to do it," commented Miss Tranter—"And so have I—and so have all of us. Which I think is a pity. I shouldn't mind living for ever and ever in this world. It's a very comfortable world, though some folks say it isn't. That's mostly liver with them though. People who don't over-eat or over-drink themselves, and who get plenty of fresh air, are generally fairly pleased with the world as they find it. I suppose the friend you're looking for will be glad to see you?"

"The friend I'm looking for will certainly be glad to see me," said Helmsley, gently—"Glad to see me—glad to help me—glad above all things to love me! If this were not so, I should not trouble to search for my friend at all."

Miss Tranter fixed her eyes full upon him while he thus spoke. They were sharp eyes, and just now they were visibly inquisitive.

"You've not been very long used to tramping," she observed.

"No."

"I expect you've seen better days?"

"Some few, perhaps,"—and he smiled gravely—"But it comes harder to a man who has once known comfort to find himself comfortless in his old age."

"That's very true! Well!"—and Miss Tranter gave a short sigh—"I'm sorry you won't stay on here a bit to pick up your strength—but a wilful man must have his way! I hope you'll find your friend!"

"I hope I shall!" said Helmsley earnestly. "And believe me I'm most grateful to you—"

"Tut!" and Miss Tranter tossed her head. "What do you want to be grateful to me for! You've had food and lodging, and you've paid me for it. I've offered you work and you won't take it. That's the long and short of it between us."

And thereupon she marched out of the room, her head very high, her shoulders very square, and her back very straight. Helmsley watched her dignified exit with a curious sense of half-amused contrition.

"What odd creatures some women are!" he thought. "Here's this sharp-tongued, warm-hearted hostess of a roadside inn quite angry because, apparently, an old tramp won't stay and do incompetent work for her! She knows that I should make a mere boggle of her garden,— she is equally aware that I could be no use in any way on 'Feathery' Joltram's farm—and yet she is thoroughly annoyed and disappointed because I won't try to do what she is perfectly confident I can't do, in order that I shall rest well and be fed well for one or two days! Really the kindness of the poor to one another outvalues all the gifts of the rich to the charities they help to support. It is so much more than ordinary 'charity,' for it goes hand in hand with a touch of personal feeling. And that is what few rich men ever get,—except when their pretended 'friends' think they can make something for themselves out of their assumed 'friendship'!"

He put on his hat, and plucked one of the roses clambering in at the window to take with him as a remembrance of the "Trusty Man,"—a place which he felt would henceforward be a kind of landmark for the rest of his life to save him from drowning in utter cynicism, because within its walls he had found unselfish compassion for his age and loneliness, and disinterested sympathy for his seeming need. Then he went to say good-bye to Miss Tranter. She was, as usual, in the bar, standing very erect. She had taken up her knitting, and her needles clicked and glittered busily.

"Matt Peke left a bottle of his herb wine for you," she said. "There it is."

She indicated by a jerk of her head a flat oblong quart flask, neatly corked and tied with string, which lay on the counter. It was of a conveniently portable shape, and Helmsley slipped it into one of his coat pockets with ease.

"Shall you be seeing Peke soon again, Miss Tranter?" he asked.

"I don't know. Maybe so, and maybe not. He's gone on to Crowcombe. I daresay he'll come back this way before the end of the month. He's a pretty regular customer."

"Then, will you thank him for me, and say that I shall never forget his kindness?"

"Never forget is a long time," said Miss Tranter. "Most folks forget their friends directly their backs are turned."

"That's true," said Helmsley, gently; "but I shall not. Good-bye!"

"Good-bye!" Miss Tranter paused in her knitting. "Which road are you going from here?"

Helmsley thought a moment.

"Perhaps," he said at last, "one of the main roads would be best. I'd rather not risk any chance of losing my way."

Miss Tranter stepped out of the bar and came to the open doorway of the inn.

"Take that path across the moor," and she pointed with one of her bright knitting needles to a narrow beaten track between the tufted grass, whitened here and there by clusters of tall daisies, "and follow it as straight as you can. It will bring you out on the highroad to Williton and Watchett. It's a goodish bit of tramping on a hot day like this, but if you keep to it steady you'll be sure to get a lift or so in waggons going along to Dunster. And there are plenty of publics about where I daresay you'd get a night's sixpenny shelter, though whether any of them are as comfortable as the 'Trusty Man,' is open to question."

"I should doubt it very much," said Helmsley, his rare kind smile lighting up his whole face. "The 'Trusty Man' thoroughly deserves trust; and, if I may say so, its kind hostess commands respect."

He raised his cap with the deferential easy grace which was habitual to him, and Miss Tranter's pale cheeks reddened suddenly and violently.

"Oh, I'm only a rough sort!" she said hastily. "But the men like me because I don't give them away. I hold that the poor must get a bit of attention as well as the rich."

"The poor deserve it more," rejoined Helmsley. "The rich get far too much of everything in these days,—they are too much pampered and too much flattered. Yet, with it all, I daresay they are often miserable."

"It must be pretty hard to be miserable on twenty or thirty thousand a year!" said Miss Tranter.

"You think so? Now, I should say it was very easy. For when one has everything, one wants nothing."

"Well, isn't it all right to want nothing?" she queried, looking at him inquisitively.

"All right? No!—rather all wrong! For want stimulates the mind and body to work, and work generates health and energy,—and energy is the pulse of life. Without that pulse, one is a mere husk of a man— as I am!" He doffed his cap again. "Thank you for all your friendliness. Good-bye!"

"Good-bye! Perhaps I shall see you again some time this way?"

"Perhaps—but—"

"With your friend?" she suggested.

"Ay—if I find my friend—then possibly I may return. Meanwhile, all good be with you!"

He turned away, and began to ascend the path indicated across the moor. Once he looked back and waved his hand. Miss Tranter, in response, waved her piece of knitting. Then she went on clicking her needles rapidly through a perfect labyrinth of stitches, her eyes fixed all the while on the tall, thin, frail figure which, with the assistance of a stout stick, moved slowly along between the nodding daisies.

"He's what they call a mystery," she said to herself. "He's as true-born a gentleman as ever lived—with a gentleman's ways, a gentleman's voice, and a gentleman's hands, and yet he's 'on the road' like a tramp! Well! there's many ups and downs in life, certainly, and those that's rich to-day may be poor to-morrow. It's a queer world—and God who made it only knows what it was made for!"

With that, having seen the last of Helmsley's retreating figure, she went indoors, and relieved her feelings by putting Prue through her domestic paces in a fashion that considerably flurried that small damsel and caused her to wonder, "what 'ad come over Miss Tranter suddint, she was that beside 'erself with work and temper!"

IX

It was pleasant walking across the moor. The July sun was powerful, but to ageing men the warmth and vital influences of the orb of day are welcome, precious, and salutary. An English summer is seldom or never too warm for those who are conscious that but few such summers are left to them, and David Helmsley was moved by a devout sense of gratitude that on this fair and tranquil morning he was yet able to enjoy the lovely and loving beneficence of all beautiful and natural things. The scent of the wild thyme growing in prolific patches at his feet,—the more pungent odour of the tall daisies which were of a hardy, free-flowering kind,—the "strong sea-daisies that feast on the sun,"—and the indescribable salty perfume that swept upwards on the faint wind from the unseen ocean, just now hidden by projecting shelves of broken ground fringed with trees,—all combined together to refresh the air and to make the mere act of breathing a delight. After about twenty minutes' walking Helmsley's step grew easier and more springy,—almost he felt young,—almost he pictured himself living for another ten years in health and active mental power. The lassitude and *ennui* inseparable from a life spent for the most part in the business centres of London, had rolled away like a noxious mist from his mind, and he was well-nigh ready to "begin life again," as he told himself, with a smile at his own folly.

"No wonder that the old-world philosophers and scientists sought for the *elixir vitæ*!" he thought. "No wonder they felt that the usual tenure is too short for all that a man might accomplish, did he live well and wisely enough to do justice to all the powers with which nature has endowed him. I am myself inclined to think that the 'Tree of Life' exists,—perhaps its leaves are the 'leaves of the Daura,' for which that excellent fellow Matt Peke is looking. Or it may be the 'Secta Croa'!"

He smiled,—and having arrived at the end of the path which he had followed from the door of the "Trusty Man," he saw before him a descending bank, which sloped into the highroad, a wide track white with thick dust stretching straight away for about a mile and then dipping round a broad curve of land, overarched with trees. He sat down for a few minutes on the warm grass, giving himself up to the idle pleasure of watching the birds skimming through the clear blue sky,—the bees bouncing in and out of the buttercups,—the varicoloured butterflies floating like blown flower-petals on the breeze,—and he heard a distant bell striking the half-hour after eleven. He had noted the time when leaving the "Trusty Man," otherwise he would not have known it so exactly, having left his watch locked up at home in his private desk with other personal trinkets which would have been superfluous and troublesome to him on his self-imposed journey. When the echo of the bell's one stroke had died away it left a great stillness in the air. The heat was increasing as the day veered towards noon, and he decided that it would be as well to get on further down the road and under the shadow of the trees, which were not so very far off, and which looked invitingly cool in their spreading dark soft greenness. So, rising from his brief rest, he started again "on the tramp," and soon felt the full glare of the sun, and the hot sensation of the dust about his feet; but he went on steadily, determining to make light of all the inconveniences and difficulties, to which he was entirely unaccustomed, but to which he had voluntarily exposed himself. For a considerable time he met no living creature; the highroad seemed to be as much his own as though it were part of a private park or landed estate belonging to him only; and it was not till he had nearly accomplished the distance which lay between him and the shelter of the trees, that he met a horse and cart slowly jogging along towards the direction from whence he had come. The man who drove the vehicle was half-asleep, stupefied, no doubt, by the effect of the hot sun following on a possible "glass" at a public-house, but Helmsley called to him just for company's sake.

"Hi! Am I going right for Watchett?"

The man opened his drowsing eyes and yawned expansively.

"Watchett? Ay! Williton comes fust."

"Is it far?"

"Nowt's far to your kind!" said the man, flicking his whip. "An' ye'll meet a bobby or so on the road!"

On he went, and Helmsley without further parley resumed his tramp. Presently, reaching the clump of trees he had seen in the distance, he moved into their refreshing shade. They were broad-branched elms, luxuriantly full of foliage, and the avenue they formed extended for about a quarter of a mile. Cool dells and dingles of mossy green sloped down on one side of the road, breaking into what are sometimes called "coombs" running precipitously towards the sea-coast, and slackening his pace a little he paused, looking through a tangle of shrubs and bracken at the pale suggestion of a glimmer of blue which he realised was the shining of the sunlit ocean. While he thus stood, he fancied he heard a little plaintive whine as of an animal in pain. He listened attentively. The sound was repeated, and, descending the shelving bank a few steps he sought to discover the whereabouts of this piteous cry for help. All at once he spied two bright sparkling eyes and a small silvery grey head perking up at him through the leaves,—the head of a tiny Yorkshire "toy" terrier. It looked at him with eloquent anxiety, and as he approached it, it made an effort to move, but fell back again with a faint moan. Gently he picked it up,—it was a rare and beautiful little creature, but one of its silky forepaws had evidently been caught in some trap, for it was badly mangled and bleeding. Round its neck was a small golden collar, something like a lady's bracelet, bearing the inscription: "I am Charlie. Take care of me!" There was no owner's name or address, and the entreaty "Take care of me!" had certainly not been complied with, or so valuable a pet would not have been left wounded on the highroad. While Helmsley was examining it, it ceased whining, and gently licked his hand. Seeing a trickling stream of water making its way through the moss and ferns close by, he bathed the little dog's wounded paw carefully and tied it up with a strip of material torn from his own coat sleeve.

"So you want to be taken care of, do you, Charlie!" he said, patting the tiny head. "That's what a good many of us want, when we feel hurt and broken by the hard ways of the world!" Charlie blinked a dark eye, cocked a small soft ear, and ventured on another caress of the kind human hand with his warm little tongue. "Well, I won't leave you to starve in the woods, or trust you to the tender mercies of the police,— you shall come along with me! And if I see any advertisement of your loss I'll perhaps take you back to your owner. But in the meantime we'll stay together."

Charlie evidently agreed to this proposition, for when Helmsley tucked him cosily under his arm, he settled down comfortably as though well accustomed to the position. He was certainly nothing of a weight to carry, and his new owner was conscious of a certain pleasure in feeling the warm, silky little body nestling against his breast. He was not quite alone any more,—this little creature was a companion,—a something to talk to, to caress and to protect. He ascended the bank, and regaining the highroad resumed his vagrant way. Noon was now at the full, and the sun's heat seemed to create a silence that was both oppressive and stifling. He walked slowly, and began to feel that perhaps after all he had miscalculated his staying powers, and that the burden of old age would, in the end, take vengeance upon him for running risks of fatigue and exhaustion which, in his case, were wholly unnecessary.

"Yet if I were really poor," he argued with himself, "if I were in very truth a tramp, I should have to do exactly what I am doing now. If one man can stand 'life on the road,' so can another."

And he would not allow his mind to dwell on the fact that a temperament which has become accustomed to every kind of comfort and luxury is seldom fitted to endure privation. On he jogged steadily, and by and by began to be entertained by his own thoughts as pleasantly as a poet or romancist is entertained by the fancies which come and go in the brain with all the vividness of dramatic reality. Yet always he found himself harking back to what he sometimes called the "incurability" of life. Over and over again he asked himself the old eternal question: Why so much Product to end in Waste? Why are thousands of millions of worlds, swarming with life-organisms, created to revolve in space, if there is no other fate for them but final destruction?

"There *must* be an Afterwards!" he said. "Otherwise Creation would not only be a senseless joke, but a wicked one! Nay, it would almost be a crime. To cause creatures to be born into existence without their own consent, merely to destroy them utterly in a few years and make the fact of their having lived purposeless, would be worse than the dreams of madmen. For what is the use of bringing human creatures into the world to suffer pain, sickness, and sorrow, if mere life-torture is all we can give them, and death is the only end?"

Here his meditations were broken in upon by the sound of a horse's hoofs trotting briskly behind him, and pausing, he saw a neat little cart and pony coming along, driven by a buxom-looking woman with a brown sun-hat tied on in the old-fashioned manner under her chin.

"Would ye like a lift?" she asked. "It's mighty warm walkin'."

Helmsley raised his eyes to the sun-bonnet, and smiled at the cheerful freckled face beneath its brim.

"You're very kind—" he began.

"Jump in!" said the woman. "I'm taking cream and cheeses into Watchett, but it's a light load, an' Jim an' me can do with ye that far. This is Jim."

She flicked the pony's ears with her whip by way of introducing the animal, and Helmsley clambered up into the cart beside her.

"That's a nice little dog you've got," she remarked, as Charlie perked his small black nose out from under his protector's arm to sniff the subtle atmosphere of what was going to happen next. "He's a real beauty!"

"Yes," replied Helmsley, without volunteering any information as to how he had found the tiny creature, whom he now had no inclination to part with. "He got his paw caught in a trap, so I'm obliged to carry him."

"Poor little soul! There's a-many traps all about 'ere, lots o' the land bein' private property. Go on, Jim!" And she shook the reins on her pony's neck, thereby causing that intelligent animal to start off at a pleasantly regular pace. "I allus sez that if the rich ladies and gentlemen as eats up every bit o' land in Great Britain could put traps in the air to catch the noses of everything but themselves as dares to breathe it, they'd do it, singin' glory all the time. For they goes to church reg'lar."

"Ah, it's a wise thing to be seen *looking* good in public!" said Helmsley.

The woman laughed.

"That's right! You can do a lot o' humbuggin' if you're friends with the parson, what more often than not humbugs everybody hisself. I'm no church-goer, but I turn out the best cheese an' butter in these parts, an' I never tells no lies nor cheats any one of a penny, so I aint worryin' about my soul, seein' it's straight with my neighbours."

"Are there many rich people living about here?" inquired Helmsley.

"Not enough to do the place real good. The owners of the big houses are here to-day and gone to-morrow, and they don't trouble much over their tenantry. Still we rub on fairly well. None of us can ever put by for a rainy day,—and some folk as is as hard-working as ever they can be, are bound to come on the parish when they can't work no more—no doubt o' that. You're a stranger to these parts?"

"Yes, I've tramped from Bristol."

The woman opened her eyes widely.

"That's a long way! You must be fairly strong for your age. Where are ye wantin' to get to?"

"Cornwall."

"My word! You've got a goodish bit to go. All Devon lies before you."

"I know that. But I shall rest here and there, and perhaps get a lift or two if I meet any more such kind-hearted folk as yourself."

She looked at him sharply.

"That's what we may call a bit o' soft soap," she said, "and I'd advise ye to keep that kind o' thing to yourself, old man! It don't go down with Meg Ross, I can tell ye!"

"Are you Meg Ross?" he asked, amused at her manner.

"That's me! I'm known all over the countryside for the sharpest tongue as ever wagged in a woman's head. So you'd better look out!"

"I'm not afraid of you!" he said smiling.

"Well, you might be if you knew me!" and she whipped up her pony smartly. "Howsomever, you're old enough to be past hurtin' or bein' hurt."

"That's true!" he responded gently.

She was silent after this, and not till Watchett was reached did she again begin conversation. Rattling quickly through the little watering-place, which at this hour seemed altogether deserted or asleep, she pulled up at an inn in the middle of the principal street.

"I've got an order to deliver here," she said. "What are *you* going to do with yourself?"

"Nothing in particular," he answered, with a smile. "I shall just take my little dog to a chemist's and get its paw dressed, and then I shall walk on."

"Don't you want any dinner?"

"Not yet. I had a good breakfast, I daresay I'll have a glass of milk presently."

"Well, if you come back here in half an hour I can drive you on a little further. How would you like that?"

"Very much! But I'm afraid of troubling you—"

"Oh, you won't do that!" said Meg with a defiant air. "No man, young or old, has ever troubled *me*! I'm not married, thank the Lord!"

And jumping from the cart, she began to pull out sundry cans, jars, and boxes, while Helmsley standing by with the small Charlie under his arm, wished he could help her, but felt sure she would resent assistance even if he offered it. Glancing at him, she gave him a kindly nod.

"Off you go with your little dog! You'll find me ready here in half an hour."

With that she turned from him into the open doorway of the inn, and Helmsley made his way slowly along the silent, sun-baked little street till he found a small chemist's shop, where he took his lately found canine companion to have its wounded paw examined and attended to. No bones were broken, and the chemist, a lean, pale, kindly man, assured him that in a few days the little animal would be quite well.

"It's a pretty creature," he said. "And valuable too."

"Yes. I found it on the highroad," said Helmsley; "and of course if I see any advertisement out for it, I'll return it to its owner. But if no one claims it I'll keep it."

"Perhaps it fell out of a motor-car," said the chemist. "It looks as if it might have belonged to some fine lady who was too wrapped up in herself to take proper care of it. There are many of that kind who come this way touring through Somerset and Devon."

"I daresay you're right," and Helmsley gently stroked the tiny dog's soft silky coat. "Rich women will pay any amount of money for such toy creatures out of mere caprice, and will then lose them out of sheer laziness, forgetting that they are living beings, with feelings and sentiments of trust and affection greater sometimes than our own. However, this little chap will be safe with me till he is rightfully claimed, if ever that happens. I don't want to steal him; I only want to take care of him."

"I should never part with him if I were you," said the chemist. "Those who were careless enough to lose him deserve their loss."

Helmsley agreed, and left the shop. Finding a confectioner's near by, he bought a few biscuits for his new pet, an attention which that small animal highly appreciated. "Charlie" was hungry, and cracked and munched the biscuits with exceeding relish, his absurd little nose becoming quite moist with excitement and appetite. Returning presently to the inn where he had left Meg Ross, Helmsley found that lady quite ready to start.

"Oh, here you are, are you?" she said, smiling pleasantly, "Well, I'm just on the move. Jump in!"

Helmsley hesitated a moment, standing beside the pony-cart.

"May I pay for my ride?" he said.

"Pay?" Meg stuck her stout arms akimbo, and glanced him all over. "Well, I never! How much 'ave ye got?"

"Two or three shillings," he answered.

Meg laughed, showing a very sound row of even white teeth.

"All right! You can keep 'em!" she said. "Mebbe you want 'em. *I* don't! Now don't stand haverin' there,—get in the cart quick, or Jim'll be runnin' away."

Jim showed no sign of this desperate intention, but, on the contrary, stood very patiently waiting till his passengers were safely seated, when he trotted off at a great pace, with such a clatter of hoofs and rattle of wheels as rendered conversation impossible. But Helmsley was very content to sit in silence, holding the little dog "Charlie" warmly against his breast, and watching the beauties of the scenery expand before him like a fairy panorama, ever broadening into fresh glimpses of loveliness. It was a very quiet coastline which the windings of the road now followed,—a fair and placid sea shining at wide intervals between a lavish flow of equally fair and placid fields. The drive seemed all too short, when at the corner of a lane embowered in trees, Meg Ross pulled up short.

"The best of friends must part!" she said. "I'm right sorry I can't take ye any further. But down 'ere's a farm where I put up for the afternoon an' 'elps 'em through with their butter-makin', for there's a lot o' skeery gals in the fam'ly as thinks more o' doin' their 'air than churnin', an' doin' the 'air don't bring no money in, though mebbe it might catch a 'usband as wasn't worth 'avin'. An' Jim gets his food 'ere too. Howsomever, I'm real put about that I can't drive ye a bit towards Cleeve Abbey, for that's rare an' fine at this time o' year,—but mebbe ye're wantin' to push on quickly?"

"Yes, I must push on," rejoined Helmsley, as he got out of the cart; then, standing in the road, he raised his cap to her. "And I'm very grateful to you for helping me along so far, at the hottest time of the day too. It's most kind of you!"

"Oh, I don't want any thanks!" said Meg, smiling. "I'm rather sweet on old men, seein' old age aint their fault even if trampin' the road is. You'd best keep on the straight line now, till you come to Blue Anchor. That's a nice little village, and you'll find an inn there where you can get a night's lodging cheap. I wouldn't advise you to stay much round Cleeve after sundown, for there's a big camp of gypsies about there, an' they're a rough lot, pertikly a man they calls Tom o' the Gleam."

Helmsley smiled.

"I know Tom o' the Gleam," he said. "He's a friend of mine."

Meg Ross opened her round, bright brown eyes.

"Is he? Dear life, if I'd known that, I mightn't 'ave been so ready to give you a ride with me!" she said, and laughed. "Not that I'm afraid of Tom, though he's a queer customer. I've given a good many glasses of new milk to his 'kiddie,' as he calls that little lad of his, so I expect I'm fairly in his favour."

"I've never seen his 'kiddie,'" said Helmsley. "What is the boy like?"

"A real fine little chap!" said Meg, with heartiness and feeling. "I'm not a crank on children, seein' most o' them's muckers an' trouble from mornin' to night, but if it 'ad pleased the Lord as I should wed, I shouldn't 'a wished for a better specimen of a babe than Tom's kiddie. Pity the mother died!"

"When the child was born?" queried Helmsley gently.

"No—oh no!"—and Meg's eyes grew thoughtful. "She got through her trouble all right, but 'twas about a year or eighteen months arterwards that she took to pinin' like, an' droopin' down just like the poppies droops in the corn when the sun's too fierce upon 'em. She used to sit by the roadside o' Sundays, with a little red handkerchief tied across her shoulders, and all her dark 'air tumblin' about 'er face, an' she used to look up with her great big black eyes an' smile at the finicky fine church misses as come mincin' an' smirkin' along, an' say: 'Tell your fortune, lady?' She was the prettiest creature I ever saw—not a good lass—no!—nobody could say she was a good lass, for she went to Tom without church or priest, but she loved him an' was faithful. An' she just worshipped her baby." Here Meg paused a moment. "Tom was a real danger to the country when she died," she presently went on. "He used to run about the woods like a madman, calling her to come back to 'im, an' threatenin' to murder any one who came nigh 'im;—then, by and by, he took to the kiddie, an' he's steadier now."

There was something in the narration of this little history that touched Helmsley too deeply for comment, and he was silent.

"Well!"—and Meg gave her pony's reins a shake—"I must be off! Sorry to leave ye standin' in the middle o' the road like, but it can't be helped. Mind you keep the little dog safe!—and take a woman's advice—don't walk too far or too fast in one day. Good luck t' ye!"

Another shake of the reins, and "Jim" turned briskly down the lane. Once Meg looked back and waved her hand,—then the green trees closed in upon her disappearing vehicle, and Helmsley was again alone, save for "Charlie," who, instinctively aware that some friend had left them, licked his master's hand confidentially, as much as to say "I am still with you." The air was cooler now, and Helmsley walked on with comparative ease and pleasure. His thoughts were very busy. He was drawing comparisons between the conduct of the poor and the rich to one another, greatly to the disadvantage of the latter class.

"If a wealthy man has a carriage," he soliloquised, "how seldom will he offer it or think of offering its use to any one of his acquaintances who may be less fortunate! How rarely will he even say a kind word to any man who is 'down'! Do I not know this myself! I remember well on one occasion when I wished to send my carriage for the use of a poor fellow who had once been employed in my office, but who had been compelled to give up work, owing to illness, my secretary advised me not to show him this mark of sympathy and attention. 'He will only take it as his right,' I was assured,—'these sort of men are always ungrateful.' And I listened to my secretary's advice—more fool I! For it should have been nothing to me whether the man was ungrateful or not; the thing was to do the good, and let the result be what it might. Now this poor Meg Ross has no carriage, but such vehicle as she possesses she shares with one whom she imagines to be in need. No other motive has moved her save womanly pity for lonely age and infirmity. She has taught me a lesson by simply offering a kindness without caring how it might be received or rewarded. Is not that a lovely trait in human nature?—one which I have never as yet discovered in what is called 'swagger society'! When I was in the hey-dey of my career, and money was pouring in from all my business 'deals' like water from a never-ending main, I had a young Scotsman for a secretary, as close-fisted a fellow as ever was, who managed to lose me the chance of doing a great many kind actions. More than that, whenever I was likely to have any real friends whom I could confidently trust, and who wanted nothing from me but affection and sincerity, he succeeded in shaking off the hold they had upon me. Of course I know now why he did this,—it was in order that he himself might have his grip of me more securely, but at that time I was unsuspicious, and believed the best of every one. Yes! I honestly thought people were honest,—I trusted their good faith, with the result that I found out the utter falsity of their pretensions. And here I am,— old and nearing the end of my tether—more friendless than when I first began to make my fortune, with the certain knowledge that not a soul has ever cared or cares for me except for what can be got out of me in the way of hard cash! I have met with more real kindness from the rough fellows at the 'Trusty Man,' and from the 'Trusty Man's' hostess, Miss Tranter, and now from this good woman Meg Ross, than has ever been offered to me by those who know I am rich, and who have 'used' me accordingly."

Here, coming to a place where two cross-roads met, he paused, looking about him. The afternoon was declining, and the loveliness of the landscape was intensified by a mellow softness in the sunshine, which deepened the rich green of the trees and wakened an opaline iridescence in the sea. A sign-post on one hand bore the direction "To

Cleeve Abbey," and the road thus indicated wound upward somewhat steeply, disappearing amid luxuriant verdure which everywhere crowned the higher summits of the hills. While he yet stood, looking at the exquisitely shaded masses of foliage which, like festal garlands, adorned and over-hung this ascent, the discordant "hoot" of a motor-horn sounded on the stillness, and sheer down the winding way came at a tearing pace the motor vehicle itself. It was a large, luxurious car, and pounded along with tremendous speed, swerving at the bottom of the declivity with so sharp a curve as to threaten an instant overturn, but, escaping this imminent peril by almost a hairsbreadth, it dashed onward straight ahead in a cloud of dust that for two or three minutes entirely blurred and darkened the air. Half-blinded and choked by the rush of its furious passage past him, Helmsley could only just barely discern that the car was occupied by two men, the one driving, the other sitting beside the driver,—and shading his eyes from the sun, he strove to track its way as it flew down the road, but in less than a minute it was out of sight.

"There's not much 'speed limit' in that concern!" he said, half-aloud, still gazing after it. "I call such driving recklessly wicked! If I could have seen the number of that car, I'd have given information to the police. But numbers on motors are no use when such a pace is kept up, and the thick dust of a dry summer is whirled up by the wheels. It's fortunate the road is clear. Yes, Charlie!"—this, as he saw his canine foundling's head perk out from under his arm, with a little black nose all a-quiver with anxiety,—"it's just as well for you that you've got a wounded paw and can't run too far for the present! If you had been in the way of that car just now, your little life would have been ended!"

Charlie pricked his pretty ears, and listened, or appeared to listen, but had evidently no forebodings about himself or his future. He was quite at home, and, after the fashion of dogs, who are often so much wiser than men, argued that being safe and comfortable now, there was no reason why he should not be safe and comfortable always. And Helmsley presently bent himself to steady walking, and got on well, only pausing to get some tea and bread and butter at a cottage by the roadside, where a placard on the gate intimated that such refreshments were to be had within. Nevertheless, he was a slow pedestrian, and what with lingering here and there for brief rests by the way, the sun had sunk fully an hour before he managed to reach Blue Anchor, the village of which Meg Ross had told him. It was a pretty, peaceful place, set among wide stretches of beach, extending for miles along the margin of the waters, and the mellow summer twilight showed little white wreaths of foam crawling lazily up on the sand in glittering curves that gleamed like snow for a moment and then melted softly away into the deepening darkness. He stopped at the first ale-house, a low-roofed, cottage-like structure embowered in clambering flowers. It had a side entrance which led into a big, rambling stableyard, and happening to glance that way he perceived a vehicle standing there, which he at once recognised as the large luxurious motor-car that had dashed past him at such a tearing pace near Cleeve. The inn door was open, and the bar faced the road, exhibiting a brave show of glittering brass taps, pewter tankards, polished glasses and many-coloured bottles, all these things being presided over by a buxom matron, who was not only an agreeable person to look at in herself, but who was assisted by two pretty daughters. These young women, wearing spotless white cuffs and aprons, dispensed the beer to the customers, now and then relieving the monotony of this occupation by carrying trays of bread and cheese and meat sandwiches round the wide room of which the bar was a part, evidently bent on making the general company stay as long as possible, if fascinating manners and smiling eyes could work any detaining influence. Helmsley asked for a glass of ale and a plate of bread and cheese, and on being supplied with these refreshments, sat down at a small table in a corner well removed from the light, where he could see without being seen. He did not intend to inquire for a night's lodging yet. He wished first to ascertain for himself the kind of people who frequented the place. The fear of discovery always haunted him, and the sight of that costly motor-car standing in the stableyard had caused him to feel a certain misgiving lest any one of marked wealth or position should turn out to be its owner. In such a case, the world being proverbially small, and rich men being in the minority, it was just possible that he, David Helmsley, even clad as he was in workman's clothes and partially disguised in features by the growth of a beard, might be recognised. With this idea, he kept himself well back in the shadow, listening attentively to the scraps of desultory talk among the dozen or so of men in the room, while carefully maintaining an air of such utter fatigue as to appear indifferent to all that passed around him. Nobody noticed him, for which he was thankful. And presently, when he became accustomed to the various contending voices, which in their changing tones of gruff or gentle, quick or slow, made a confused din upon his ears, he found out that the general conversation was chiefly centred on one subject, that of the very motor-car whose occupants he desired to shun.

"Serve 'em right!" growled one man. "Serve 'em right to 'ave broke down! 'Ope the darned thing's broke altogether!"

"You shouldn't say that,—'taint Christian," expostulated his neighbour at the same table. "Them cars cost a heap o' money, from eight 'undred to two thousand pounds, I've 'eerd tell."

"Who cares!" retorted the other. "Them as can pay a fortin on a car to swish 'emselves about in, should be made to keep on payin' till they're cleaned out o' money for good an' all. The road's a reg'lar hell since them engines started along cuttin' everything to pieces. There aint a man, woman, nor child what's safe from the moneyed murderers."

"Oh come, I say!" exclaimed a big, burly young fellow in corduroys. "Moneyed murderers is going a bit too strong!"

"No 'taint!" said the first man who had spoken. "That's what the motor-car folks are—no more nor less. Only t' other day in Taunton, a woman as was the life an' soul of 'er 'usband an' childern, was knocked down by a car as big as a railway truck. It just swept 'er off the curb like a bundle o' rags. She picked 'erself up again an' walked 'ome, tremblin' a little, an' not knowin' rightly what 'ad chanced to 'er, an' in less than an hour she was dead. An' what did they say at the inquest? Just 'death from shock'—an' no more. For them as owned the murderin' car was proprietors o' a big brewery, and the coroner hisself 'ad shares in it. That's 'ow justice is done nowadays!"

"Yes, we's an obligin' lot, we poor folks," observed a little man in the rough garb of a cattle-driver, drawing his pipe from his mouth as he spoke. "We lets the rich ride over us on rubber tyres an' never sez a word on our own parts, but trusts to the law for doin' the same to a millionaire as 'twould to a beggar,—but, Lord!—don't we see every day as 'ow the millionaire gets off easy while the beggar goes to prison? There used to be justice in old England, but the time for that's gone past."

"There's as much justice in England as you'll ever get anywheres else!" interrupted the hostess at the bar, nodding cheerfully at the men, and smiling,—"And as for the motor-cars, they bring custom to my house, and I don't grumble at anything which does me and mine a good turn. If it hadn't been for a break-down in that big motor standing outside in the stableyard, I shouldn't have had two gentlemen staying in my best rooms to-night. I never find fault with money!"

She laughed and nodded again in the pleasantest manner. A slow smile went round among the men,—it was impossible not to smile in response to the gay good-humour expressed on such a beaming countenance.

"One of them's a lord, too," she added. "Quite a young fellow, just come into his title, I suppose." And referring to her day-book, she ran her plump finger down the various entries. "I've got his name here— Wrotham,—Lord Reginald Wrotham."

"Wrotham? That aint a name known in these parts," said the man in corduroys. "Wheer does 'e come from?"

"I don't know," she replied. "And I don't very much care. It's enough for me that he's here and spending money!"

"Where's his chauffy?" inquired a lad, lounging near the bar.

"He hasn't got one. He drives his car himself. He's got a friend with him—a Mr. James Brookfield."

There was a moment's silence. Helmsley drew further back into the corner where he sat, and restrained the little dog Charlie from perking its inquisitive head out too far, lest its beauty should attract undesirable attention. His nervous misgivings concerning the owner of the motor-car had not been entirely without foundation, for both Reginald Wrotham and James Brookfield were well known to him. Wrotham's career had been a sufficiently disgraceful one ever since he had entered his teens,—he was a modern degenerate of the worst type, and though his coming-of-age and the assumption of his family title had caused certain time-servers to enrol themselves among his flatterers and friends, there were very few decent houses where so soiled a member of the aristocracy as he was could find even a semblance of toleration. James Brookfield was a proprietor of newspapers as well as a "something in the City," and if Helmsley had been asked to qualify that "something" by a name, he would have found a term by no means complimentary to the individual in question. Wrotham and Brookfield were always seen together,—they were brothers in every sort of social iniquity and licentiousness, and an attempt on Brookfield's part to borrow some thousands of pounds for his "lordly" patron from Helmsley, had resulted in the latter giving the would-be borrower's go-between such a strong piece of his mind as he was not likely to forget. And now Helmsley was naturally annoyed to find that these two abandoned rascals were staying at the very inn where he, in his character of a penniless wayfarer, had hoped to pass a peaceful night; however, he resolved to avoid all danger and embarrassment by leaving the place directly he had finished his supper, and going in search of some more suitable lodgment. Meanwhile, the hum of conversation grew louder around him, and opinion ran high on the subject of "the right of the road."

"The roads are made for the people, sure-*ly*!" said one of a group of men standing near the largest table in the room—"And the people 'as the right to 'xpect safety to life an' limb when they uses 'em."

"Well, the motors can put forward the same claim," retorted another. "Motor folks are people too, an' they can say, if they likes, that if roads is made for people, they're made for *them* as well as t' others, and they expects to be safe on 'em with their motors at whatever pace they travels."

"Go 'long!" exclaimed the cattle-driver, who had before taken part in the discussion—"Aint we got to take cows an' sheep an' 'osses by the road? An' if a car comes along at the rate o' forty or fifty miles an hour, what's to be done wi' the animals? An' if they're not to be on the road, which way is they to be took?"

"Them motors ought to have roads o' their own like the railways," said a quiet-looking grey-haired man, who was the carrier of the district. "When the steam-engine was invented it wasn't allowed to go tearin' along the public highway. They 'ad to make roads for it, an' lay tracks, and they should do the same for motors which is gettin' just as fast an' as dangerous as steam-engines."

"Yes, an' with makin' new roads an' layin' tracks, spoil the country for good an' all!" said the man in corduroys—"An' alter it so that there aint a bit o' peace or comfort left in the land! Level the hills an' cut down the trees—pull up the hedges an' scare away all the singin' birds, till the hull place looks like a football field!—all to please a few selfish rich men who'd be better dead than livin'! A fine thing for England that would be!"

At that moment, there was the noise of an opening door, and the hostess, with an expressive glance at her customers, held up her finger warningly.

"Hush, please!" she said. "The gentlemen are coming out."

A sudden pause ensued. The men looked round upon one another, half sheepishly, half sullenly, and their growling voices subsided into a murmur. The hostess settled the bow at her collar more becomingly, and her two pretty daughters feigned to be deeply occupied with some drawn thread work. David Helmsley, noting everything that was going on from his coign of vantage, recognised at once the dissipated, effeminate-looking young man, who, stepping out of a private room which opened on a corridor apparently leading to the inner part of the house, sauntered lazily up to the bar and, resting his arm upon its oaken counter, smiled condescendingly, not to say insolently, upon the women who stood behind it. There was no mistaking him,—it was the same Reginald Wrotham whose scandals in society had broken his worthy father's heart, and who now, succeeding to a hitherto unblemished title, was doing his best to load it with dishonour. He was followed by his friend Brookfield,—a heavily-built, lurching sort of man, with a nose reddened by strong drink, and small lascivious eyes which glittered dully in his head like the eyes of poisonous tropical beetle. The hush among the "lower" class of company at the inn deepened into the usual stupid awe which at times so curiously affects untutored rustics who are made conscious of the presence of a "lord." Said a friend of the present writer's to a waiter in a country hotel where one of these "lords" was staying for a few days: "I want a letter to catch to-night's post, but I'm afraid the mail has gone from the hotel. Could you send some one to the post-office with it?" "Oh yes, sir!" replied the waiter grandiloquently. "The servant of the Lord will take it!" Pitiful beyond most piteous things is the grovelling tendency of that section of human nature which has not yet been educated sufficiently to lift itself up above temporary trappings and ornaments; pitiful it is to see men, gifted in intellect, or distinguished for bravery, flinch and cringe before one of their own flesh and blood, who, having neither cleverness nor courage, but only a Title, presumes upon that foolish appendage so far as to consider himself superior to both valour and ability. As well might a stuffed boar's head assume a superiority to other comestibles because decorated by the cook with a paper frill and bow of ribbon! The atmosphere which Lord Reginald Wrotham brought with him into the common-room of the bar was redolent of tobacco-smoke and whisky, yet, judging from the various propitiatory, timid, anxious, or servile looks cast upon him by all and sundry, it might have been fragrant and sacred incense wafted from the altars of the goddess Fortune to her waiting votaries. Helmsley's spirit rose up in contempt against the effete dandy as he watched him leaning carelessly against the counter, twirling his thin sandy moustache, and talking to his hostess merely for the sake of offensively ogling her two daughters.

"Charming old place you have here!—charming!" drawled his lordship. "Perfect dream! Love to pass all my days in such a delightful spot! 'Pon my life! Awful luck for us, the motor breaking down, or we never should have stopped at such a jolly place, don't-cher-know. Should we, Brookfield?"

Brookfield, gently scratching a pimple on his fat, clean-shaven face, smiled knowingly.

"*Couldn't* have stopped!" he declared. "We were doing a record run. But we should have missed a great deal,—a great deal!" And he emitted a soft chuckle. "Not only the place,—but—!"

He waved his hand explanatorily, with a slight bow, which implied an unspoken compliment to the looks of the mistress of the inn and her family. One of the young women blushed and peeped slyly up at him. He returned the glance with interest.

"May I ask," pursued Lord Wrotham, with an amicable leer, "the names of your two daughters, Madam? They've been awfully kind to us broken-down-travellers—should just like to know the difference between them. Like two roses on one stalk, don't-cher-know! Can't tell which is which!"

The mother of the girls hesitated a moment. She was not quite sure that she liked the "tone" of his lordship's speech. Finally she replied somewhat stiffly:—

"My eldest daughter is named Elizabeth, my lord, and her sister is Grace."

"Elizabeth and Grace! Charming!" murmured Wrotham, leaning a little more confidentially over the counter—"Now which—which is Grace?"

At that moment a tall, shadowy form darkened the open doorway of the inn, and a man entered, carrying in his arms a small oblong bundle covered with a piece of rough horse-cloth. Placing his burden down on a vacant bench, he pushed his cap from his brows and stared wildly about him. Every one looked at him,—some with recognition, others in alarm,—and Helmsley, compelled as he was to keep himself out of the general notice in his corner, almost started to his feet with an involuntary cry of amazement. For it was Tom o' the Gleam.

X

Tom o' the Gleam,—Tom, with his clothes torn and covered with dust,—Tom, changed suddenly to a haggard and terrible unlikeness of himself, his face drawn and withered, its healthy bronze colour whitened to a sickly livid hue,—Tom, with such an expression of dazed and stupid horror in his eyes as to give the impression that he was heavily in drink, and dangerous.

"Well, mates!" he said thickly—"A fine night and a clear moon!"

No one answered him. He staggered up to the bar. The hostess looked at him severely.

"Now, Tom, what's the matter?" she said.

He straightened himself, and, throwing back his shoulders as though parrying a blow, forced a smile.

"Nothing! A touch of the sun!" A strong shudder ran through his limbs, and his teeth chattered,—then suddenly leaning forward on the counter, he whispered: "I'm not drunk, mother!—for God's sake don't think it!—I'm ill. Don't you see I'm ill?—I'll be all right in a minute,— give me a drop of brandy!"

She fixed her candid gaze full upon him. She had known him well for years, and not only did she know him, but, rough character as he was, she liked and respected him. Looking him squarely in the face she saw at once that he was speaking the truth. He was not drunk. He was ill,—very ill. The strained anguish on his features proved it.

"Hadn't you better come inside the bar and sit down?" she suggested, in a low tone.

"No, thanks—I'd rather not. I'll stand just here."

She gave him the brandy he had asked for. He sipped it slowly, and, pushing his cap further off his brows, turned his dark eyes, full of smouldering fire, upon Lord Wrotham and his friend, both of whom had succeeded in getting up a little conversation with the hostess's younger daughter, the girl named Grace. Her sister, Elizabeth, put down her needlework, and watched Tom with sudden solicitude. An instinctive dislike of Lord Wrotham and his companion caused her to avoid looking their way, though she heard every word they were saying,—and her interest became centred on the handsome gypsy, whose pallid features and terrible expression filled her with a vague alarm.

"It would be awfully jolly of you if you'd come for a spin in my motor," said his lordship, twirling his sandy moustache and conveying a would-be amorous twinkle into his small brown-green eyes for the benefit of the girl he was ogling. "Beastly bore having a break-down, but it's nothing serious—half a day's work will put it all right, and if you and your sister would like a turn before we go on from here, I shall be charmed. We can't do the record business now—not this time,—so it doesn't matter how long we linger in this delightful spot."

"Especially in such delightful company!" added his friend, Brookfield. "I'm going to take a photograph of this house to-morrow, and perhaps"— here he smiled complacently—"perhaps Miss Grace and Miss Elizabeth will consent to come into the picture?"

"Ya-as—ya-as!—oh do!" drawled Wrotham. "Of course they will! *You* will, I'm sure, Miss Grace! This gentleman, Mr. Brookfield, has got nearly all the pictorials under his thumb, and he'll put your portrait in them as 'The Beauty of Somerset,' won't you, Brookfield?"

Brookfield laughed, a pleased laugh of conscious power.

"Of course I will," he said. "You have only to express the wish and the thing is done!"

Wrotham twirled his moustache again.

"Awful fun having a friend on the press, don't-cher-know!" he went on. "I get all my lady acquaintances into the papers,—makes 'em famous in a day! The women I like are made to look beautiful, and those I don't like are turned into frights—positive old horrors, give you my life! Easily done, you know!—touch up a negative whichever way you fancy, and there you are!"

The girl Grace lifted her eyes,—very pretty sparkling eyes they were,—and regarded him with a mutinous air of contempt.

"It must be 'awfully' amusing!" she said sarcastically.

"It is!—give you my life!" And his lordship played with a charm in the shape of an enamelled pig which dangled at his watch-chain. "It pleases all parties except those whom I want to rub up the wrong way. I've made many a woman's hair curl, I can tell you! You'll be my 'Somersetshire beauty,' won't you, Miss Grace?"

"I think not!" she replied, with a cool glance. "My hair curls quite enough already. I never use tongs!"

Brookfield burst into a laugh, and the laugh was echoed murmurously by the other men in the room. Wrotham flushed and bit his lip.

"That's a one—er for me," he said lazily. "Pretty kitten as you are, Miss Grace, you can scratch! That's always the worst of women,—they've got such infernally sharp tongues—"

"Grace!" interrupted her mother, at this juncture—"You are wanted in the kitchen."

Grace took the maternal hint and retired at once. At that instant Tom o' the Gleam stirred slightly from his hitherto rigid attitude. He had only taken half his glass of brandy, but that small amount had brought back a tinge of colour to his face and deepened the sparkle of fire in his eyes.

"Good roads for motoring about here!" he said.

Lord Wrotham looked up,—then measuring the great height, muscular build, and commanding appearance of the speaker, nodded affably.

"First-rate!" he replied. "We had a splendid run from Cleeve Abbey."

"Magnificent!" echoed Brookfield. "Not half a second's stop all the way. We should have been far beyond Minehead by this time, if it hadn't been for the break-down. We were racing from London to the Land's End,—but we took a wrong turning just before we came to Cleeve—"

"Oh! Took a wrong turning, did you?" And Tom leaned a little forward as though to hear more accurately. His face had grown deadly pale again, and he breathed quickly.

"Yes. We found ourselves quite close to Cleeve Abbey, but we didn't stop to see old ruins this time, you bet! We just tore down the first lane we saw running back into the highroad,—a pretty steep bit of ground too—and, by Jove!—didn't we whizz round the corner at the bottom! That was a near shave, I can tell you!"

"Ay, ay!" said Tom slowly, listening with an air of profound interest. "You've got a smart chauffeur, no doubt!"

"No chauffeur at all!" declared Brookfield, emphatically. "His lordship drives his car himself."

There followed an odd silence. All the customers in the room, drinking and eating as many of them were, seemed to be under a dumb spell. Tom o' the Gleam's presence was at all times more or less of a terror to the timorous, and that he, who as a rule avoided strangers, should on his own initiative enter into conversation with the two motorists, was of itself a circumstance that awakened considerable wonder and interest. David Helmsley, sitting apart in the shadow, could not take his eyes off the gypsy's face and figure,—a kind of fascination impelled him to watch with strained attention the dark shape, moulded with such herculean symmetry, which seemed to command and subdue the very air that gave it force and sustenance.

"His lordship drives his car himself!" echoed Tom, and a curious smile parted his lips, showing an almost sinister gleam of white teeth between his full black moustache and beard,—then, bringing his sombre glance to bear slowly down on Wrotham's insignificant form, he continued,—"Are you his lordship?"

Wrotham nodded with a careless condescension, and, lighting a cigar, began to smoke it.

"And you drive your car yourself!" proceeded Tom,—"you must have good nerve and a keen eye!"

"Oh well!" And Wrotham laughed airily—"Pretty much so!—but I won't boast!"

"How many miles an hour?" went on Tom, pursuing his inquiries with an almost morbid eagerness.

"Forty or fifty, I suppose—sometimes more. I always run at the highest speed. Of course that kind of thing knocks the motor to pieces rather soon, but one can always buy another."

"True!" said Tom. "Very true! One can always buy another!" He paused, and seemed to collect his thoughts with an effort,—then noticing the half-glass of brandy he had left on the counter, he took it up and drank it all off at a gulp. "Have you ever had any accidents on the road?"

"Accidents?" Lord Wrotham put up an eyeglass. "Accidents? What do you mean?"

"Why, what should I mean except what I say!" And Tom gave a sudden loud laugh,—a laugh which made the hostess at the bar start nervously, while many of the men seated round the various tables exchanged uneasy glances. "Accidents are accidents all the world over! Haven't you ever been thrown out, upset, shaken in body, broken in bone, or otherwise involved in mischief?"

Lord Wrotham smiled, and let his eyeglass fall with a click against his top waistcoat button.

"Never!" he said, taking his cigar from his mouth, looking at it, and then replacing it with a relish—"I'm too fond of my own life to run any risk of losing it. Other people's lives don't matter so much, but mine is precious! Eh, Brookfield?"

Brookfield chuckled himself purple in the face over this pleasantry, and declared that his lordship's wit grew sharper with every day of his existence. Meanwhile Tom o' the Gleam moved a step or two nearer to Wrotham.

"You're a lucky lord!" he said, and again he laughed discordantly. "Very lucky! But you don't mean to tell me that while you're pounding along at full speed, you've never upset anything in your way?—never knocked down an old man or woman,—never run over a dog,—or a child?"

"Oh, well, if you mean that kind of thing!" murmured Wrotham, puffing placidly at his cigar—"Of course! That's quite common! We're always running over something or other, aren't we, Brookie?"

"Always!" declared that gentleman pleasantly. "Really it's half the fun!"

"Positively it is, don't-cher-know!" and his lordship played again with his enamelled pig—"But it's not our fault. If things will get into our way, we can't wait till they get out. We're bound to ride over them. Do you remember that old hen, Brookie?"

Brookfield spluttered into a laugh, and nodded in the affirmative.

"There it was skipping over the road in front of us in as great a hurry as ever hen was," went on Wrotham. "Going back to its family of eggs per express waddle! Whiz! Pst—and all its eggs and waddles were over! By Jove, how we screamed! Ha—ha—ha!—he—he—he!"

Lord Wrotham's laugh resembled that laugh peculiar to "society" folk,—the laugh civil-sniggering, which is just a tone between the sheep's bleat and the peewit's cry. But no one laughed in response, and no one spoke. Some heavy spell was in the air like a cloud shadowing a landscape, and an imaginative onlooker would have been inclined to think that this imperceptible mystic darkness had come in with Tom o' the Gleam and was centralising itself round him alone. Brookfield, seeing that his lordly patron was inclined to talk, and that he was evidently anxious to narrate various "car" incidents, similar to the hen episode, took up the conversation and led it on.

"It is really quite absurd," he said, "for any one of common sense to argue that a motorist can, could, or should pull up every moment for the sake of a few stray animals, or even people, when they don't seem to know or care where they are going. Now think of that child to-day! What an absolute little idiot! Gathering wild thyme and holding it out to the car going full speed! No wonder we knocked it over!"

The hostess of the inn looked up quickly.

"I hope it was not hurt?" she said.

"Oh dear no!" answered Lord Wrotham lightly. "It just fell back and turned a somersault in the grass,—evidently enjoying itself. It had a narrow escape though!"

Tom o' the Gleam stared fixedly at him. Once or twice he essayed to speak, but no sound came from his twitching lips. Presently, with an effort, he found his voice.

"Did you—did you stop the car and go back to see—to see if—if it was all right?" he asked, in curiously harsh, monotonous accents.

"Stop the car? Go back? By Jove, I should think not indeed! I'd lost too much time already through taking a wrong turning. The child was all right enough."

"Are you sure?" muttered Tom thickly. "Are you—quite—sure?"

"Sure?" And Wrotham again had recourse to his eyeglass, which he stuck in one eye, while he fixed his interlocutor with a supercilious glance. "Of course I'm sure! What the devil d' ye take me for? It was a mere beggar's brat anyhow—there are too many of such little wretches running loose about the roads—regular nuisances—a few might be run over with advantage—Hullo! What now? What's the matter? Keep your distance, please!" For Tom suddenly threw up his clenched fists with an inarticulate cry of rage, and now leaped towards Wrotham in the attitude of a wild beast springing on its prey. "Hands off! Hands off, I say! Damn you, leave me alone! Brookfield! Here! Some one get a hold of this fellow! He's mad!"

But before Brookfield or any other man could move to his assistance, Tom had pounced upon him with all the fury of a famished tiger.

"God curse you!" he panted, between the gasps of his labouring breath—"God burn you for ever in Hell!"

Down on the ground he hurled him, clutching him round the neck, and choking every attempt at a cry. Then falling himself in all his huge height, breadth, and weight, upon Wrotham's prone body he crushed it under and held it beneath him, while, with appalling swiftness and vehemence, he plunged a drawn claspknife deep in his victim's throat, hacking the flesh from left to right, from right to left with reckless ferocity, till the blood spurted about him in horrid crimson jets, and gushed in a dark pool on the floor.

Piercing screams from the women, groans and cries from the men, filled the air, and the lately peaceful scene was changed to one of maddening confusion. Brookfield rushed wildly through the open door of the inn into the village street, yelling: "Help! Help! Murder! Help!" and in less than five minutes the place was filled with an excited crowd. "Tom!" "Tom o' the Gleam!" ran in frightened whispers from mouth to mouth. David Helmsley, giddy with the sudden shock of terror, rose shuddering from his place with a vague idea of instant flight in his mind, but remained standing inert, half paralysed by sheer panic, while several men surrounded Tom, and dragged him forcibly up from the ground where he lay, still grasping his murdered man. As they wrenched the gypsy's grappling arms away, Wrotham fell back on the floor, stone dead. Life had been thrust out of him with the first blow dealt him by Tom's claspknife, which had been aimed at his throat as a butcher aims at the throat of a swine. His bleeding corpse presented a frightful spectacle, the head being nearly severed from the body.

Brookfield, shaking all over, turned his back upon the awful sight, and kept on running to and fro and up and down the street, clamouring like a madman for the police. Two sturdy constables presently came, their appearance restoring something like order. To them Tom o' the Gleam advanced, extending his blood-stained hands.

"I am ready!" he said, in a quiet voice. "I am the murderer!"

They looked at him. Then, by way of precaution, one of them clasped a pair of manacles on his wrists. The other, turning his eyes to the corpse on the floor, recoiled in horror.

"Throw something over it!" he commanded.

He was obeyed, and the dreadful remains of what had once been human, were quickly shrouded from view.

"How did this happen?" was the next question put by the officer of the law who had already spoken, opening his notebook.

A chorus of eager tongues answered him, Brookfield's excited explanation echoing above them all. His dear friend, his great, noble, good friend had been brutally murdered! His friend was Lord Wrotham, of Wrotham Hall, Blankshire! A break-down had occurred within half a mile of Blue Anchor, and Lord Wrotham had taken rooms at the present inn for the night. His lordship had condescended to enter into a friendly conversation with the ruffian now under arrest, who, without the slightest cause or provocation whatsoever, had suddenly attacked and overthrown his lordship, and plunged a knife into his lordship's throat! He himself was James Brookfield, proprietor of the *Daily Post-Bag*, the *Pictorial Pie*, and the *Illustrated Invoice*, and he should make this outrageous, this awful crime a warning to motorists throughout the world—!"

"That will do, thank you," said the officer briefly—then he gave a sharp glance around him—"Where's the landlady?"

She had fled in terror from the scene, and some one went in search of her, returning with the poor woman and her two daughters, all of them deathly pale and shivering with dread.

"Don't be frightened, mother!" said one of the constables kindly—"No harm will come to you. Just tell us what you saw of this affair—that's all."

Whereat the poor hostess, her narrative interrupted by tears, explained that Tom o' the Gleam was a frequent customer of hers, and that she had never thought badly of him.

"He was a bit excited to-night, but he wasn't drunk," she said. "He told me he was ill, and asked for a glass of brandy. He looked as if he were in great pain, and I gave him the brandy at once and asked him to step inside the bar. But he wouldn't do that,—he just stood talking with the gentlemen about motoring, and then something was said about a child being knocked over by the motor,—and all of a sudden—"

Here her voice broke, and she sank on a seat half swooning, while Elizabeth, her eldest girl, finished the story in low, trembling tones. Tom o' the Gleam meanwhile stood rigidly upright and silent. To him the chief officer of the law finally turned.

"Will you come with us quietly?" he asked, "or do you mean to give us trouble?"

Tom lifted his dark eyes.

"I shall give no man any more trouble," he answered. "I shall go nowhere save where I am taken. You need fear nothing from me now. But I must speak."

The officer frowned warningly.

"You'd better not!" he said.

"I must!" repeated Tom. "You think,—all of you,—that I had no cause—no provocation—to kill the man who lies there"—and he turned a fierce glance upon the covered corpse, from which a dark stream of blood was trickling slowly along the floor—"I swear before God that I *had* cause!—and that my cause was just! I *had* provocation!—the bitterest and worst! That man was a murderer as surely as I am. Look yonder!" And lifting his manacled hands he extended them towards the bench where lay the bundle covered with horse-cloth, which he had carried in his arms and set down when he had first entered the inn. "Look, I say!—and then tell me I had no cause!"

With an uneasy glance one of the officers went up to the spot indicated, and hurriedly, yet fearfully, lifted the horse-cloth and looked under it. Then uttering an exclamation of horror and pity, he drew away the covering altogether, and disclosed to view the dead body of a child,—a little curly-headed lad,—lying as if it were asleep, a smile on its pretty mouth, and a bunch of wild thyme clasped in the clenched fingers of its small right hand.

"My God! It's Kiddie!"

The exclamation was uttered almost simultaneously by every one in the room, and the girl Elizabeth sprang forward.

"Oh, not Kiddie!" she cried—"Oh, surely not Kiddie! Oh, the poor little darling!—the pretty little man!"

And she fell on her knees beside the tiny corpse and gave way to a wild fit of weeping.

There was an awful silence, broken only by her sobbing. Men turned away and covered their eyes—Brookfield edged himself stealthily through the little crowd and sneaked out into the open air— and the officers of the law stood inactive. Helmsley felt the room whirling about him in a sickening blackness, and sat down to steady himself, the stinging tears rising involuntarily in his throat and almost choking him.

"Oh, Kiddie!" wailed Elizabeth again, looking up in plaintive appeal—"Oh, mother, mother, see! Grace come here! Kiddie's dead! The poor innocent little child!" They came at her call, and knelt with her, crying bitterly, and smoothing back with tender hands the thickly tangled dark curls of the smiling dead thing, with the fragrance of wild thyme clinging about it, as though it were a broken flower torn from the woods where it had blossomed. Tom o' the Gleam watched them, and his broad chest heaved with a sudden gasping sigh.

"You all know now," he said slowly, staring with strained piteous eyes at the little lifeless body—"you understand,—the motor killed my Kiddie! He was playing on the road—I was close by among the trees—I saw the cursed car coming full speed downhill—I rushed to take the boy, but was too late—he cried once—and then—silence! All the laughter gone out of him—all the life and love—" He paused with a shudder.—"I carried him all the way, and followed the car," he went on—"I would have followed it to the world's end! I ran by a short cut down near the sea,—and then—I saw the thing break down. I thanked God for that! I tracked the murderers here,—I meant to kill the man who killed my child!—and I have done it!" He paused again. Then he held out his hands and looked at the constable.

"May I—before I go—take him in my arms—and kiss him?" he asked.

The chief officer nodded. He could not speak, but he unfastened Tom's manacles and threw them on the floor. Then Tom himself moved feebly and unsteadily to where the women knelt beside his dead child. They rose as he approached, but did not turn away.

"You have hearts, you women!" he said faintly. "You know what it is to love a child! And Kiddie,—Kiddie was such a happy little fellow!—so strong and hearty!—so full of life! And now—now he's stiff and cold! Only this morning he was jumping and laughing in my arms—" He broke off, trembling violently, then with an effort he raised his head and turned his eyes with a wild stare upon all around him. "We are only poor folk!" he went on, in a firmer voice. "Only gypsies, tinkers, road-menders, labourers, and the like! We cannot fight against the rich who ride us down! There's no law for us, because we can't pay for it. We can't fee the counsel or dine the judge! The rich can pay. They can trample us down under their devilish motor-cars, and obliging juries will declare our wrongs and injuries and deaths to be mere 'accident' or 'misadventure'! But if *they* can kill, by God!—so can *we*! And if the law lets them off for murdering our children, we must take the law into our own hands and murder *them* in turn—ay! even if we swing for it!"

No one spoke. The women still sobbed convulsively, but otherwise there was a great silence. Tom o' the Gleam stretched forth his hands with an eloquent gesture of passion.

"Look at him lying there!" he cried—"Only a child—a little child! So pretty and playful!—all his joy was in the birds and flowers! The robins knew him and would perch on his shoulder,—he would call to the cuckoo,—he would race the swallow,—he would lie in the grass and sing with the skylark and talk to the daisies. He was happy with the simplest things—and when we put him to bed in his little hammock under the trees, he would smile up at the stars and say: 'Mother's up there! Good-night, mother!' Oh, the lonely trees, and the empty hammock! Oh, my lad!—my little pretty lad! Murdered! Murdered! Gone from me for ever! For ever! God! God!"

Reeling heavily forward, he sank in a crouching heap beside the child's dead body and snatched it into his embrace, kissing the little cold lips and cheeks and eyelids again and again, and pressing it with frantic fervour against his breast.

"The dark hour!" he muttered—"the dark hour! To-day when I came away over the moors I felt it creeping upon me! Last night it whispered to me, and I felt its cold breath hissing against my ears! When I climbed down the rocks to the seashore, I heard it wailing in the waves!—and through the hollows of the rocks it shrieked an unknown horror at me! Who was it that said to-day—'He is only a child after all, and he might be taken from you'? I remember!—it was Miss Tranter who spoke— and she was sorry afterwards—ah, yes!—she was sorry!—but it was the spirit of the hour that moved her to the utterance of a warning—she could not help herself,—and I—I should have been more careful!—I should not have left my little one for a moment,—but I never thought any harm could come to him—no, never to *him*! I was always sure God was too good for that!"

Moaning drearily, he rocked the dead boy to and fro.

"Kiddie—my Kiddie!" he murmured—"Little one with my love's eyes!—heart's darling with my love's face! Don't go to sleep, Kiddie!— not just yet!—wake up and kiss me once!—only once again, Kiddie!"

"Oh, Tom!" sobbed Elizabeth,—"Oh, poor, poor Tom!"

At the sound of her voice he raised his head and looked up at her. There was a strange expression on his face,—a fixed and terrible stare in his eyes. Suddenly he broke into a wild laugh.

"Ha-ha!" he cried. "Poor Tom! Tom o' the Gleam! That's me!—the me that was not always me! Not always me—no!—not always Tom o' the Gleam! It was a bold life I led in the woods long ago!—a life full of sunshine and laughter—a life for a man with man's blood in his veins! Away out in the land that once was old Provence, we jested and sang the hours away,—the women with their guitars and mandolines—the men with their wild dances and tambourines,—and love was the keynote of the music—love!—always love! Love in the sunshine!—love under the moonbeams!—bright eyes in which to drown one's soul,—red lips on which to crush one's heart!—Ah, God!—such days when we were young!

> *'Ah! Craignons de perdre un seul jour,*
> *De la belle saison de l'amour!'"*

He sang these lines in a rich baritone, clear and thrilling with passion, and the men grouped about him, not understanding what he sang, glanced at one another with an uneasy sense of fear. All at once he struggled to his feet without assistance, and stood upright, still clasping the body of his child in his arms.

"Come, come!" he said thickly—"It's time we were off, Kiddie! We must get across the moor and into camp. It's time for all lambs to be in the fold;—time to go to bed, my little lad! Good-night, mates! Good-night! I know you all,—and you all know me—you like fair play! Fair play all round, eh? Not one law for the rich and another for the poor! Even justice, boys! Justice! Justice!"

Here his voice broke in a great and awful cry,—blood sprang from his lips—his face grew darkly purple,—and like a huge tree snapped asunder by a storm, he reeled heavily to the ground. One of the constables caught him as he fell.

"Hold up, Tom!" he said tremulously, the thick tears standing in his eyes. "Don't give way! Be a man! Hold up! Steady! Here, let me take the poor Kiddie!"

For a ghastly pallor was stealing over Tom's features, and his lips were widely parted in a gasping struggle for breath.

"No—no!—don't take my boy!" he muttered feebly. "Let me—keep him—with me! God is good—good after all!—we shall not—be parted!"

A strong convulsion shook his sinewy frame from head to foot, and he writhed in desperate agony. The officer put an arm under his head, and made an expressive sign to the awed witnesses of the scene. Helmsley, startled at this, came hurriedly forward, trembling and scarcely able to speak in the extremity of his fear and pity.

"What—what is it?" he stammered. "Not—not—?"

"Death! That's what it is!" said the officer, gently. "His heart's broken!"

One rough fellow here pushed his way to the side of the fallen man,—it was the cattle-driver who had taken part in the previous conversation among the customers at the inn before the occurrence of the tragedy. He knelt down, sobbing like a child.

"Tom!" he faltered, "Tom, old chap! Hearten up a bit! Don't leave us! There's not one of us us'll think ill of ye!—no, not if the law was to shut ye up for life! You was allus good to us poor folk—an' poor folk aint as forgittin' o' kindness as rich. Stay an' help us along, Tom!—you was allus brave an' strong an' hearty—an' there's many of us wantin' comfort an' cheer, eh Tom?"

Tom's splendid dark eyes opened, and a smile, very wan and wistful, gleamed across his lips.

"Is that you, Jim?" he muttered feebly. "It's all dark and cold!—I can't see!—there'll be a frost to-night, and the lambs must be watched a bit—I'm afraid I can't help you, Jim—not to-night! Wanting comfort, did you say? Ay!—plenty wanting that, but I'm past giving it, my boy! I'm done."

He drew a struggling breath with pain and difficulty.

"You see, Jim, I've killed a man!" he went on, gaspingly—"And—and—I've no money—we all share and share alike in camp—it won't be worth any one's while to find excuses for me. They'd shut me up in prison if I lived—but now—God's my judge! And He's merciful—He's giving me my liberty!"

His eyelids fell wearily, and a shadow, dark at first, and then lightening into an ivory pallor, began to cover his features like a fine mask, at sight of which the girls, Elizabeth and Grace, with their mother, knelt down and hid their faces. Every one in the room knelt too, and there was a profound stillness. Tom's breathing grew heavier and more laboured,—once they made an attempt to lift the weight of his child's dead body from his breast, but his hands were clenched upon it convulsively and they could not loosen his hold. All at once Elizabeth lifted her head and prayed aloud—

"O God, have mercy on our poor friend Tom, and help him through the Valley of the Shadow! Grant him Thy forgiveness for all his sins, and let him find—" here she broke down and sobbed pitifully,—then between her tears she finished her petition—"Let him find his little child with Thee!"

A low and solemn "Amen" was the response to her prayer from all present, and suddenly Tom opened his eyes with a surprised bright look.

"Is Kiddie all right?" he asked.

"Yes, Tom!" It was Elizabeth who answered, bending over him—"Kiddie's all right! He's fast asleep in your arms."

"So he is!" And the brilliancy in Tom's eyes grew still more radiant, while with one hand he caressed the thick dark curls that clustered on the head of his dead boy—"Poor little chap! Tired out, and so am I! It's very cold surely!"

"Yes, Tom, it is. Very cold!"

"I thought so! I—I must keep the child warm. They'll be worried in camp over all this—Kiddie never stays out so late. He's such a little fellow—only four!—and he goes to bed early always. And when—when he's asleep—why then—then—the day's over for me,—and night begins—night begins!"

The smile lingered on his lips, and settled there at last in coldest gravity,—the fine mask of death covered his features with an impenetrable waxen stillness—all was over! Tom o' the Gleam had gone with his slain child, and the victim he had sacrificed to his revenge, into the presence of that Supreme Recorder who chronicles all deeds both good and evil, and who, in the character of Divine Justice, may, perchance, find that the sheer brutal selfishness of the modern social world is more utterly to be condemned, and more criminal even than murder.

XI

S ick at heart, and utterly overcome by the sudden and awful tragedy
to which he had been an enforced silent witness, David Helmsley
had now but one idea, and that was at once to leave the scene of horror
which, like a ghastly nightmare, scarred his vision and dizzied his brain.
Stumbling feebly along, and seeming to those who by chance noticed
him, no more than a poor old tramp terrified out of his wits by the grief
and confusion which prevailed, he made his way gradually through
the crowd now pressing closely round the dead, and went forth into
the village street. He held the little dog Charlie nestled under his coat,
where he had kept it hidden all the evening,—the tiny creature was
shivering violently with that strange consciousness of the atmosphere
of death which is instinctive to so many animals,—and a vague wish
to soothe its fears helped him for the moment to forget his own
feelings. He would not trust himself to look again at Tom o' the Gleam,
stretched lifeless on the ground with his slaughtered child clasped in his
arms; he could not speak to any one of the terrified people. He heard
the constables giving hurried orders for the removal of the bodies, and
he saw two more police officers arrive and go into the stableyard of the
inn, there to take the number of the motor-car and write down the full
deposition of that potentate of the pictorial press, James Brookfield.
And he knew, without any explanation, that the whole affair would
probably be served up the next day in the cheaper newspapers as a
"sensational" crime, so worded as to lay all the blame on Tom o' the
Gleam, and to exonerate the act, and deplore the violent death of
the "lordly" brute who, out of his selfish and wicked recklessness, had
snatched away the life of an only child from its father without care or
compunction. But it was the fearful swiftness of the catastrophe that
affected Helmsley most,—that, and what seemed to him, the needless
cruelty of fate. Only last night he had seen Tom o' the Gleam for the
first time—only last night he had admired the physical symmetry and
grace of the man,—his handsome head, his rich voice, and the curious
refinement, suggestive of some past culture and education, which gave
such a charm to his manner,—only last night he had experienced that
little proof of human sympathy and kindliness which had shown itself
in the gift of the few coins which Tom had collected and placed on his
pillow,—only last night he had been touched by the herculean fellow's

tenderness for his little "Kiddie,"—and now,—within the space of twenty-four hours, both father and child had gone out of life at a rush as fierce and relentless as the speed of the motor-car which had crushed a world of happiness under its merciless wheels. Was it right—was it just that such things should be? Could one believe in the goodness of God, in such a world of wanton wickedness? Moving along in a blind haze of bewilderment, Helmsley's thoughts were all disordered and his mind in a whirl,—what consciousness he had left to him was centred in an effort to get away—away!—far away from the scene of murder and death,—away from the scent and trail of blood which seemed to infect and poison the very air!

It was a calm and lovely night. The moon rode high, and there was a soft wind blowing in from the sea. Out over the waste of heaving water, where the moonbeams turned the small rippling waves to the resemblance of netted links of silver or steel, the horizon stretched sharply clear and definite, like a line drawn under the finished chapter of vision. There was a gentle murmur of the inflowing tide among the loose stones and pebbles fringing the beach,—but to Helmsley's ears it sounded like the miserable moaning of a broken heart,—the wail of a sorrowful spirit in torture. He went on and on, with no very distinct idea of where he was going,—he simply continued to walk automatically like one in a dream. He did not know the time, but guessed it must be somewhere about midnight. The road was quite deserted, and its loneliness was to him, in his present over-wrought condition, appalling. Desolation seemed to involve the whole earth in gloom,—the trees stood out in the white shine of the moon like dark shrouded ghosts waving their cerements to and fro,—the fields and hills on either side of him were bare and solitary, and the gleam of the ocean was cold and cheerless as a "Dead Man's Pool." Slowly he plodded along, with a thousand disjointed fragments of thought and memory teasing his brain, all part and parcel of his recent experiences,—he seemed to have lived through a whole history of strange events since the herb-gatherer, Matt Peke, had befriended him on the road,—and the most curious impression of all was that he had somehow lost his own identity for ever. It was impossible and ridiculous to think of himself as David Helmsley, the millionaire,—there was, there could be no such person! David Helmsley,—the real David Helmsley,—was very old, very tired, very poor,—there was nothing left for him in this world save death. He had no children, no friends,—no one who cared for him or who wanted to know what had become of him. He was absolutely alone,—and in the hush of the summer night he fancied that the very moon looked down upon him with a chill stare as though wondering why he burdened the earth with his presence when it was surely time for him to die!

It was not till he found that he was leaving the shore line, and that one or two gas lamps twinkled faintly ahead of him, that he realized he was entering the outskirts of a small town. Pausing a moment, he looked about him. A high-walled castle, majestically enthroned on a steep wooded height, was the first object that met his view,—every line of its frowning battlements and turrets was seen clearly against the sky as though etched out on a dark background with a pencil of light. A sign-post at the corner of a winding road gave the direction "To Dunster Castle." Reading this by the glimmer of the moon, Helmsley stood irresolute for a minute or so, and then resumed his tramp, proceeding through the streets of what he knew must be Dunster itself. He had no intention of stopping in the town,—an inward nervousness pushed him on, on, in spite of fatigue, and Dunster was not far enough away from Blue Anchor to satisfy him. The scene of Tom o' the Gleam's revenge and death surrounded him with a horrible environment,—an atmosphere from which he sought to free himself by sheer distance, and he resolved to walk till morning rather than remain anywhere near the place which was now associated in his mind with one of the darkest episodes of human guilt and suffering that he had ever known. Passing by the old inn known as "The Luttrell Arms," now fast closed for the night, a policeman on his beat stopped in his marching to and fro, and spoke to him.

"Hillo! Which way do you come from?"

"From Watchett."

"Oh! We've just had news of a murder up at Blue Anchor. Have you heard anything of it?"

"Yes." And Helmsley looked his questioner squarely in the face. "It's a terrible business! But the murderer's caught!"

"Caught is he? Who's got him?"

"Death!" And Helmsley, lifting his cap, stood bareheaded in the moonlight. "He'll never escape again!"

The constable looked amazed and a little awed.

"Death? Why, I heard it was that wild gypsy, Tom o' the Gleam—"

"So it was,"—said Helmsley, gently,—"and Tom o' the Gleam is dead!"

"No! Don't say that!" exclaimed the constable with real concern. "There's a lot of good in Tom! I shouldn't like to think he's gone!"

"You'll find it's true," said Helmsley. "And perhaps, when you get all the details, you'll think it for the best. Good-night!"

"Are you staying in Dunster?" queried the officer with a keen glance.

"No. I'm moving on." And Helmsley smiled wearily as he again said—"Good-night!"

He walked steadily, though slowly, through the sleeping town, and passed out of it. Ascending a winding bit of road he found himself once more in the open country, and presently came to a field where part of the fence had been broken through by the cattle. Just behind the damaged palings there was a covered shed, open in front, with a few bundles of straw packed within it. This place suggested itself as a fairly comfortable shelter for an hour's rest, and becoming conscious of the intense aching of his limbs, he took possession of it, setting the small "Charlie" down to gambol on the grass at pleasure. He was far more tired than he knew, and remembering the "yerb wine" which Matt Peke had provided him with, he took a long draught of it, grateful for its reviving warmth and tonic power. Then, half-dreamily, he watched the little dog whom he had rescued and befriended, and presently found himself vaguely entertained by the graceful antics of the tiny creature which, despite its wounded paw, capered limpingly after its own shadow flung by the moonlight on the greensward, and attempted in its own playful way to attract the attention of its new master and wile him away from his mood of utter misery. Involuntarily he thought of the frenzied cry of Shakespeare's "Lear" over the dead body of Cordelia:—

> *"What! Shall a dog, a horse, a rat, have life*
> *And thou no breath at all!"*

What curious caprice of destiny was it that saved the life of a dog, yet robbed a father of his child? Who could explain it? Why should a happy innocent little lad like Tom o' the Gleam's "Kiddie" have been hurled out of existence in a moment as it were by the mad speed of a motor's wheels,—and a fragile "toy" terrier, the mere whim of dog-breeders and plaything for fanciful women, be plucked from starvation and death as though the great forces of creation deemed it more worth cherishing than a human being! For the murder of Lord Wrotham, Helmsley found excuse,—for the death of Tom there was ample natural cause,—but for the wanton killing of a little child no reason could justly be assigned. Propping his elbows on his knees, and resting his aching head on his hands, he thought and thought,—till Thought became almost as a fire in his brain. What was the use of life? he asked himself. What definite plan or object could there possibly be in the perpetuation of the human race?

> "To pace the same dull round
> On each recurring day,
> For seventy years or more
> Till strength and hope decay,—
> To trust,—and be deceived,—
> And standing,—fear to fall!
> To find no resting-place—
> Can this be all?"

Beginning with hope and eagerness, and having confidence in the good faith of his fellow-men, had he not himself fought a hard fight in the world, setting before him a certain goal,—a goal which he had won and passed,—to what purpose? In youth he had been very poor,—and poverty had served him as a spur to ambition. In middle life he had become one of the richest men in the world. He had done all that rich and ambitious men set themselves out to do. He might have said with the Preacher:

"Whatsoever mine eyes desired I kept not from them,—I withheld not my heart from any joy, for my heart rejoiced in all my labour, and this was my portion of all my labour. Then I looked on all the works that my hands had wrought, and on the labour that I had laboured to do, and behold, all was vanity and vexation of spirit, and there was no profit under the sun."

He had loved,—or rather, he had imagined he loved,—he had married, and his wife had dishonoured him. Sons had been born to him, who, with their mother's treacherous blood in their veins, had brought him to shame by their conduct,—and now all the kith and kin he had sought to surround himself with were dead, and he was alone—as alone as he had ever been at the very commencement of his career. Had his long life of toil led him only to this? With a sense of dull disappointment, his mind reverted to the plan he had half entertained of benefiting Tom o' the Gleam in some way and making him happy by prospering the fortunes of the child he loved so well,—though he was fully aware that perhaps he could not have done much in that direction, as it was more than likely that Tom would have resented the slightest hint of a rich man's patronage. Death, however, in its fiercest shape, had now put an abrupt end to any such benevolent scheme, whether or not it might have been feasible,—and, absorbed in a kind of lethargic reverie, he again and again asked himself what use he was in the world?—what could he do with the brief remaining portion of his life?—and how he could dispose, to his own satisfaction, of the vast wealth which, like a huge golden mill-stone, hung round his neck, dragging him down to the grave? Such poor people as he had met with during his tramp seemed fairly contented with their lot; he, at any rate, had heard no complaints of poverty from them. On the contrary, they had shown an independence of thought and freedom of life which was wholly incompatible with the mere desire of money. He could put a five-pound note in an envelope and post it anonymously to Matt Peke at the "Trusty Man" as a slight return for his kindness, but he was quite sure that though Matt might be pleased enough with the money he would equally be puzzled, and not entirely satisfied in his mind as to whether he was doing right to accept and use it. It would probably be put in a savings bank for a "rainy day."

"It is the hardest thing in the world to do good with money!" he mused, sorrowfully. "Of course if I were to say this to the unthinking majority, they would gape upon me and exclaim—'Hard to do good! Why, there's nothing so easy! There are thousands of poor,—there are the hospitals—the churches!' True,—but the thousands of *real* poor are not so easily found! There are thousands, ay, millions of 'sham' poor. But the *real* poor, who never ask for anything,—who would not know how to write a begging letter, and who would shrink from writing it even if they did know—who starve patiently, suffer uncomplainingly, and die resignedly—these are as difficult to meet with as diamonds in a coal mine. As for hospitals, do I not know how many of them pander to the barbarous inhumanity of vivisection!—and have I not experienced to the utmost dregs of bitterness, the melting of cash through the hands of secretaries and under-secretaries, and general Committee-ism, and Red Tape-ism, while every hundred thousand pounds bestowed on these necessary institutions turns out in the end to be a mere drop in the sea of incessant demand, though the donors may possibly purchase a knighthood, a baronetcy, or even a peerage, in return for their gifts!

And the churches!—my God!—as Madame Roland said of Liberty, what crimes are committed in Thy Name!"

He looked up at the sky through the square opening of the shed, and saw the moon, now changed in appearance and surrounded by a curious luminous halo like the nimbus with which painters encircle the head of a saint. It was a delicate aureole of prismatic radiance, and seemed to have swept suddenly round the silver planet in companionship with a light mist from the sea,—a mist which was now creeping slowly upwards and covering the land with a glistening wetness as of dew. A few fleecy clouds, pale grey and white, were floating aloft in the western half of the heavens, evoked by some magic touch of the wind.

"It will soon be morning,"—thought Helmsley—"The sun will rise in its same old glorious way—with as measured and monotonous a circuit as it has made from the beginning. The Garden of Eden, the Deluge, the building of the Pyramids, the rise and fall of Rome, the conquests of Alexander, the death of Socrates, the murder of Cæsar, the crucifixion of Christ,—the sun has shone on all these things of beauty, triumph or horror with the same even radiance, always the generator of life and fruitfulness, itself indifferent as to what becomes of the atoms germinated under its prolific heat and vitality. The sun takes no heed whether a man dies or lives—neither does God!"

Yet with this idea came a sudden revulsion. Surely in the history of human events, there was ample proof that God, or the invisible Power we call by that name, did care? Crime was, and is, always followed by punishment, sooner or later. Who ordained,—who ordains that this shall be? Who is it that distinguishes between Right and Wrong, and adjusts the balance accordingly? Not Man,—for Man in a barbarous state is often incapable of understanding moral law, till he is trained to it by the evolution of his being and the ever-progressive working of the unseen spiritual forces. And the first process of his evolution is the awakening of conscience, and the struggle to rise from his mere Self to a higher ideal of life,—from material needs to intellectual development. Why is he thus invariably moved towards this higher ideal? If the instinct were a mistaken one, foredoomed to disappointment, it would not be allowed to exist. Nature does not endow us with any sense of which we do not stand in need, or any attribute which is useless to us in the shaping and unfolding of our destinies. True it is that we see many a man and woman who appear to have no souls, but we dare not infer from these exceptions that the soul does not exist. Soulless beings simply have no need of spirituality, just as the night-owl has no need of the sun,—they are bodies merely, and as bodies perish. As the angel said to the prophet Esdras:—"The Most High hath made this world for many, but the world to come for few. I will tell thee a similitude, Esdras; As when thou askest the earth, it shall say unto thee that it giveth much mould whereof earthern vessels are made, but little dust that gold cometh of, even so is the course of this present world!"

Weary of arguing with himself, Helmsley tried to reflect back on certain incidents of his youth, which now in his age came out like prominent pictures in the gallery of his brain. He remembered the pure and simple piety which distinguished his mother, who lived her life out as sweetly as a flower blooms,—thanking God every morning and night for His goodness to her, even at times when she was most sorrowful,—he thought of his little sister, dead in the springtime of her girlhood, who never had a doubt of the unfailing goodness and beneficence of her Creator, and who, when dying, smiled radiantly, and whispered with her last breath, "I wish you would not cry for me, Davie dear!—the next world is so beautiful!" Was this "next world" in her imagination, or was it a fact? Materialists would, of course, say it was imagination. But, in the light of present-day science and discovery, who can pin one's faith on Materialism?

"I have missed the talisman that would have made all the darkness of life clear to me," he said at last, half aloud; "and missing it, I have missed everything of real value. Pain, loss, old age, and death would have been nothing to me, if I had only won that magic glory of the world—Love!"

His eyes again wandered to the sky, and he noticed that the grey-and-white clouds in the west were rising still higher in fleecy pyramids, and were spreading with a wool-like thickness gradually over the whole heavens. The wind, too, had grown stronger, and its sighing sound had changed to a more strenuous moaning. The little dog, Charlie, tired of its master's gloomy absorption, jumped on his knee, and intimated by eloquent looks and wagging tail a readiness to be again nestled into some cosy corner. The shed was warm and comfortable, and after some brief consideration, he decided to try and sleep for an hour or so before again starting on his way. With this object in view, he arranged the packages of straw which filled one side of the shed into the form of an extemporary couch, which proved comfortable enough when he lay down with Charlie curled up beside him. He could not help thinking of the previous night, when he had seen the tall figure of Tom o' the Gleam approaching his bedside at the "Trusty Man," with the little "surprise" gift he had so stealthily laid upon his pillow,—and it was difficult to realise or to believe that the warm, impulsive heart had ceased to beat, and that all that splendid manhood was now but lifeless clay. He tried not to see the horribly haunting vision of the murdered Wrotham, with that terrible gash in his throat, and the blood pouring from it,—he strove to forget the pitiful picture of the little dead "Kiddie" in the arms of its maddened and broken-hearted father—but the impression was too recent and too ghastly for forgetfulness.

"And yet with it all," he mused, "Tom o' the Gleam had what I have never possessed—love! And perhaps it is better to die—even in the awful way he died—in the very strength and frenzy of love—rather than live loveless!"

Here Charlie heaved a small sigh, and nestled a soft silky head close against his breast. "I love you!" the little creature seemed to say—"I am only a dog—but I want to comfort you if I can!" And he murmured—"Poor Charlie! Poor wee Charlie!" and, patting the flossy coat of his foundling, was conscious of a certain consolation in the mere companionship of an animal that trusted to him for protection.

Presently he closed his eyes and tried to sleep. His brain was somewhat confused, and scraps of old songs and verses he had known in boyhood, were jumbled together without cause or sequence, varying in their turn with the events of his business, his financial "deals" and the general results of his life's work. He remembered quite suddenly and for no particular reason, a battle he had engaged in with certain directors of a company who had attempted to "better" him in a particularly important international trade transaction, and he recalled his own sweeping victory over them with a curious sense of disgust. What did it matter—now?—whether he had so many extra millions, or so many more degrees of power? Certain lines of Tennyson's seemed to contain greater truths than all the money-markets of the world could supply:—

> *"O let the solid earth*
> *Not fail beneath my feet,*
> *Before my life has found*
> *What some have found so sweet—*
> *Then let come what come may,*
> *What matter if I go mad,*
> *I shall have had my day!*

> *"Let the sweet heavens endure*
> *Not close and darken above me,*
> *Before I am quite, quite sure*
> *That there is one to love me;*
> *Then let come what come may*
> *To a life that has been so sad,*
> *I shall have had my day!"*

He murmured this last verse over and over again till it made mere monotony in his mind, and till at last exhausted nature had its way and lulled his senses into a profound slumber. Strange to say, as soon as he was fast asleep, Charlie woke up. Perking his little ears sharply, he sat briskly erect on his tiny haunches, his forepaws well placed on his master's breast, his bright eyes watchfully fixed on the opening of the shed, and his whole attitude expressing that he considered himself "on guard." It was evident that had the least human footfall broken the stillness, he would have made the air ring with as much noise as he was capable of. He had a vibrating bark of his own, worthy of a much larger animal, and he appeared to be anxiously waiting for an opportunity to show off this special accomplishment. No such chance, however, offered itself; the minutes and hours went by in undisturbed order. Now and then a rabbit scampered across the field, or an owl flew through the trees with a plaintive cry,—otherwise, so far as the immediate surroundings of the visible land were concerned, everything was perfectly calm. But up in the sky there were signs of gathering trouble. The clouds had formed into woollier masses,—their grey had changed to black, their white to grey, and the moon, half hidden, appeared to be hurrying downward to the west in a flying scud of etheric foam. Some disturbance was brewing in the higher altitudes of air, and a low snarling murmur from the sea responded to what was, perchance, the outward gust of a fire-tempest in the sun. The small Charlie was, no doubt, quite ignorant of meteorological portents, nevertheless he kept himself wide awake, sniffing at empty space in a highly suspicious manner, his tiny black nose moist with aggressive excitement, and his whole miniature being prepared to make "much ado about nothing" on the smallest provocation.

The morning broke sullenly, in a dull haze, though here and there pale patches of blue, and flushes of rose-pink, showed how fair the day would willingly have made itself, had only the elements been propitious. Helmsley slept well on through the gradual unfolding of the dawn, and it was fully seven o'clock when he awoke with a start, scarcely knowing where he was. Charlie hailed his return to consciousness with marked enthusiasm, and dropping the sentry "Who goes there?" attitude, gambolled about him delightedly. Presently remembering his environment and the events which were a part of it, he quickly aroused himself, and carefully packing up all the bundles of straw in the shed, exactly as he had found them, he again went forth upon what he was disposed to consider now a penitential pilgrimage.

"In old times," he said to himself, as he bathed his face and hands in a little running stream by the roadside—"kings, when they found themselves miserable and did not know why they were so, went to the church for consolation, and were told by the priests that they had sinned—and that it was their sins that made them wretched. And a journey taken with fasting was prescribed—much in the way that our fashionable physicians prescribe change of air, a limited diet and plenty of exercise to the luxurious feeders of our social hive. And the weary potentates took off their crowns and their royal robes, and trudged along as they were told—became tramps for the nonce, like me. But I need no priest to command what I myself ordain!"

He resumed his onward way ploddingly and determinedly, though he was beginning to be conscious of an increasing weariness and lassitude which seemed to threaten him with a break-down ere long. But he would not think of this.

"Other men have no doubt felt just as weak," he thought. "There are many on the road as old as I am and even older. I ought to be able to do of my own choice what others do from necessity. And if the worst comes to the worst, and I am compelled to give up my project, I can always get back to London in a few hours!"

He was soon at Minehead, and found that quaint little watering-place fully astir; for so far as it could have a "season," that season was now on. A considerable number of tourists were about, and coaches and brakes were getting ready in the streets for those who were inclined to undertake the twenty miles drive from Minehead to Lynton. Seeing a baker's shop open he went in and asked the cheery-looking woman behind the counter if she would make him a cup of coffee, and let him have a saucer of milk for his little dog. She consented willingly, and showed him a little inner room, where she spread a clean white cloth on the table and asked him to sit down. He looked at her in some surprise.

"I'm only 'on the road,'" he said—"Don't put yourself out too much for me."

She smiled.

"You'll pay for what you've ordered, I suppose?"

"Certainly!"

"Then you'll get just what everybody gets for their money,"—and her smile broadened kindly—"We don't make any difference between poor and rich."

She retired, and he dropped into a chair, wearily. "We don't make any difference between poor and rich!" said this simple woman. How very simple she was! No difference between poor and rich! Where would "society" be if this axiom were followed! He almost laughed to think of it. A girl came in and brought his coffee with a plate of fresh bread-and-butter, a dish of Devonshire cream, a pot of jam, and a small round basket full of rosy apples,—also a saucer of milk which she set down on the floor for Charlie, patting him kindly as she did so, with many admiring comments on his beauty.

"You've brought me quite a breakfast!" said Helmsley. "How much?"

"Sixpence, please."

"Only sixpence?"

"That's all. It's a shilling with ham and eggs."

Helmsley paid the humble coin demanded, and wondered where the "starving poor" came in, at any rate in Somersetshire. Any beggar on the road, making sixpence a day, might consider himself well fed with such a meal. Just as he drew up his chair to the table, a sudden gust of wind swept round the house, shaking the whole building, and apparently hurling the weight of its fury on the roof, for it sounded as if a whole stack of chimney-pots had fallen.

"It's a squall,"—said the girl—"Father said there was a storm coming. It often blows pretty hard up this way."

She went out, and left Helmsley to himself. He ate his meal, and fed Charlie with as much bread and milk as that canine epicure could consume,—and then sat for a while, listening to the curious hissing of the wind, which was like a suppressed angry whisper in his ears.

"It will be rough weather,"—he thought—"Now shall I stay in Minehead, or go on?"

Somehow, his experience of vagabondage had bred in him a certain restlessness, and he did not care to linger in any one place. An inexplicable force urged him on. He was conscious that he entertained a most foolish, most forlorn secret hope,—that of finding some yet unknown consolation,—of receiving some yet unobtained heavenly benediction. And he repeated again the lines:—

"Let the sweet heavens endure,
Not close and darken above me,
Before I am quite, quite sure
That there is one to love me!"

Surely a Divine Providence there was who could read his heart's desire, and who could see how sincerely in earnest he was to find some channel wherein the current of his accumulated wealth might flow after his own death, to fruitfulness and blessing for those who truly deserved it.

"Is it so much to ask of destiny—just one honest heart?" he inwardly demanded—"Is it so large a return to want from the world in which I have toiled so long—just one unselfish love? People would tell me I am too old to expect such a thing,—but I am not seeking the love of a lover,—that I know is impossible. But Love,—that most god-like of all emotions, has many phases, and a merely sexual attraction is the least and worst part of the divine passion. There is a higher form,—one far more lasting and perfect, in which Self has very little part,—and though I cannot give it a name, I am certain of its existence!"

Another gust of wind, more furious than the last, whistled overhead and through the crannies of the door. He rose, and tucking Charlie warmly under his coat as before, he went out, pausing on his way to thank the mistress of the little bakery for the excellent meal he had enjoyed.

"Well, you won't hurt on it," she said, smilingly; "it's plain, but it's wholesome. That's all we claim for it. Are you going on far?"

"Yes, I'm bound for a pretty long tramp,"—he replied. "I'm walking to find friends in Cornwall."

She opened her eyes in unfeigned wonder and compassion.

"Deary me!" she exclaimed—"You've a stiff road before you. And to-day I'm afraid you'll be in for a storm."

He glanced out through the shop-window.

"It's not raining,"—he said.

"Not yet,—but it's blowing hard,"—she replied—"And it's like to blow harder."

"Never mind, I must risk it!" And he lifted his cap; "Good-day!"

"Good-day! A safe journey to you!"

"Thank you!"

And, gratefully acknowledging the kindly woman's parting nod and smile, he stepped out of the shop into the street. There he found the wind had risen indeed. Showers of blinding dust were circling in the air, blotting out the view,—the sky was covered with masses of murky cloud drifting against each other in threatening confusion—and there was a dashing sound of the sea on the beach which seemed to be steadily increasing in volume and intensity. He paused for a moment under the shelter of an arched doorway, to place Charlie more comfortably under his arm and button his coat more securely, the while he watched the people in the principal thoroughfare struggling with the capricious attacks of the blast, which tore their hats off and sent them spinning across the road, and played mischievous havoc with women's skirts, blowing them up to the knees, and making a great exhibition of feet, few of which were worth looking at from any point of beauty or fitness. And then, all at once, amid the whirling of the gale, he heard a hoarse stentorian shouting—"Awful Murder! Local Crime! Murder of a Nobleman! Murder at Blue Anchor! Latest details!" and he started precipitately forward, walking hurriedly along with as much nervous horror as though he had been guiltily concerned in the deed with which the town was ringing. Two or three boys ran past him, with printed placards in their hands, which they waved in front of them, and on which in thick black letters could be seen:—"Murder of Lord Wrotham! Death of the Murderer! Appalling Tragedy at Blue Anchor!" And, for a few seconds, amid the confusion caused by the wind, and the wild clamour of the news-vendors, he felt as if every one were reeling pell-mell around him like persons on a ship at sea,—men with hats blown off,—women and children running aslant against the gale with hair streaming,—all eager to purchase the first papers which contained the account of a tragedy, enacted, as it were, at their very doors. Outside a little glass and china shop at the top of a rather hilly street a group of workingmen were standing, with the papers they had just bought in their hands, and Helmsley, as he trudged by, with stooping figure and bent head set against the wind, lingered near them a moment to hear them discuss the news.

"Ah, poor Tom!" exclaimed one—"Gone at last! I mind me well how he used to say he'd die a bad death!"

"What's a bad death?" queried another, gruffly—"And what's the truth about this here business anyhow? Newspapers is allus full o' lies. There's a lot about a lord that's killed, but precious little about Tom!"

"That's so!" said an old farmer, who with spectacles on was leaning his back against the wall of the shop near which they stood, to shelter himself a little from the force of the gale, while he read the paper he held—"See here,—this lord was driving his motor along by Cleeve, and ran over Tom's child,—why, that's the poor Kiddie we used to see Tom carrying for miles on his shoulder—"

"Ah, the poor lamb!" And a commiserating groan ran through the little group of attentive listeners.

"And then,"—continued the farmer—"from what I can make out of this paper, Tom picked up his baby quite dead. Then he started to run all the way after the fellow whose motor car had killed it. That's nat'ral enough!"

"Of course it is!" "I'd a' done it myself!" "Damn them motors!" muttered the chorus, fiercely.

"If so be the motor 'ad gone on, Tom couldn't never 'ave caught up with it, even if he'd run till he dropped," went on the farmer—"but as luck would 'ave it, the thing broke down nigh to Blue Anchor, and Tom got his chance. Which he took. And—he killed this Lord Wrotham, whoever he is,—stuck him in the throat with a knife as though he were a pig!"

There was a moment's horrified silence.

"So he wor!" said one man, emphatically—"A right-down reg'lar road-hog!"

"Then,"—proceeded the farmer, carefully studying the paper again—"Tom, 'avin' done all his best an' worst in this world, gives himself up to the police, but just 'afore goin' off, asks if he may kiss his dead baby,—"

A long pause here ensued. Tears stood in many of the men's eyes.

"And," continued the farmer, with a husky and trembling voice—"he takes the child in his arms, an' all sudden like falls down dead. God rest him!"

Another pause.

"And what does the paper say about it all?" enquired one of the group.

"It says—wait a minute!—it says—'Society will be plunged into mourning for Lord Wrotham, who was one of the most promising of our younger peers, and whose sporting tendencies made him a great favourite in Court circles.'"

"That's a bit o' bunkum paid for by the fam'ly!" said a great hulking drayman who had joined the little knot of bystanders, flicking his whip as he spoke,—"Sassiety plunged into mourning for the death of a precious raskill, is it? I 'xpect it's often got to mourn that way! Rort an' rubbish! Tell ye what!—Tom o' the Gleam was worth a dozen o' your motorin' lords!—an' the hull countryside through Quantocks, ay, an' even across Exmoor, 'ull 'ave tears for 'im an' 'is pretty little Kiddie what didn't do no 'arm to anybody more'n a lamb skippin' in the fields. Tom worn't known in their blessed 'Court circles,'—but, by the Lord!—he'd got a grip o' the people's heart about here, an' the people don't forget their friends in a hurry! Who the devil cares for Lord Wrotham!"

"Who indeed!" murmured the chorus.

"An' who'll say a bad word for Tom o' the Gleam?"

"Nobody!" "He wor a rare fine chap!" "We'll all miss him!" eagerly answered the chorus.

With a curious gesture, half of grief, half of defiance, the drayman tore a scrap of black lining from his coat, and tied it to his whip.

"Tom was pretty well known to be a terror to some folk,—specially liars an' raskills,"—he said—"An' I aint excusin' murder. But all the same I'm in mourning for Tom an' 'is little Kiddie, an' I don't care who knows it!"

He went off, and the group dispersed, partly driven asunder by the increasing fury of the wind, which was now sweeping through the streets in strong, steady gusts, hurling everything before it. But Helmsley set his face to the storm and toiled on. He must get out of Minehead. This he felt to be imperative. He could not stay in a town which now for many days would talk of nothing else but the tragic death of Tom o' the Gleam. His nerves were shaken, and he felt himself to be mentally, as well as physically, distressed by the strange chance which had associated him against his will with such a grim drama of passion and revenge. He remembered seeing the fateful motor swing down that precipitous road near Cleeve,—he recalled its narrow escape from a complete upset at the end of the declivity when it had swerved round the corner and rushed on,—how little he had dreamed that a child's life had just been torn away by its reckless wheels!—and that child the all-in-the-world to Tom o' the Gleam! Tom must have tracked the motor by following some side-lane or short cut known only to himself, otherwise Helmsley thought he would hardly have escaped seeing him. But, in any case, the slow and trudging movements of an old man must have lagged far, far behind those of the strong, fleet-footed gypsy to whom the wildest hills and dales, cliffs and sea caves were all familiar ground. Like a voice from the grave, the reply Tom had given to Matt Peke at the "Trusty Man," when Matt asked him where he had come from, rang back upon his ears—"From the caves of Cornwall! From picking up drift on the shore and tracking seals to their lair in the hollows of the rocks! All sport, Matt! I live like a gentleman born, keeping or killing at my pleasure!"

Shuddering at this recollection, Helmsley pressed on in the teeth of the blast, and a sudden shower of rain scudded by, stinging him in the face with the sharpness of needlepoints. The gale was so high, and the blown dust so thick on all sides, that he could scarcely see where he was going, but his chief effort was to get out of Minehead and away from all contact with human beings—for the time. In this he succeeded very soon. Once well beyond the town, he did not pause to make a choice of roads. He only sought to avoid the coast line, rightly judging that way to lie most open and exposed to the storm,—moreover the wind swooped in so fiercely from the sea, and the rising waves made such a terrific roaring, that, for the mere sake of greater quietness, he turned aside and followed a path which appeared to lead invitingly into some deep hollow of the hills. There seemed a slight chance of the weather clearing at noon, for though the wind was so high, the clouds were whitening under passing gleams of sunlight, and the scud of rain had passed. As he walked further and further he found himself entering a deep green valley—a cleft between high hills,—and though he had no idea which way it led him, he was pleased to have reached a comparatively sheltered spot where the force of the hurricane was not so fiercely felt, and where the angry argument of the sea was deadened by distance. There was a lovely perfume everywhere,—the dash of rain on the herbs and field flowers had brought out their scent, and the freshness of the stormy atmosphere was bracing and exhilarating. He put Charlie down on the grass, and was amused to see how obediently the tiny creature trotted after him, close at his heels, in the manner of a well-trained, well-taught lady's favourite. There was no danger of wheeled or motor traffic in this peaceful little glen, which appeared to be used solely by pedestrians. He rather wondered now and then whither it led, but was not very greatly concerned on the subject. What pleased him most was that he did not see a single human being anywhere or a sign of human habitation.

Presently the path began to ascend, and he followed it upward. The climb became gradually steep and wearisome, and the track grew smaller, almost vanishing altogether among masses of loose stones, which had rolled down from the summits of the hills, and he had again to carry Charlie, who very strenuously objected to the contact of sharp flints against his dainty little feet. The boisterous wind now met him full-faced,—but, struggling against it, he finally reached a wide plateau, commanding a view of the surrounding country and the sea. Not a house was in sight;—all around him extended a chain of hills, like a fortress set against invading ocean,—and straight away before his eyes ocean itself rose and fell in a chaos of billowy blackness. What a sight it was! Here, from this point, he could take some measure and form some idea of the storm, which so far from abating as he had imagined it might, when passing through the protected seclusion of the valley he had just left, was evidently gathering itself together for a still fiercer onslaught.

Breathless with his climbing exertions he stood watching the huge walls of water, built up almost solidly as it seemed, by one force and dashed down again by another,—it was as though great mountains lifted themselves over each other to peer at the sky and were driven back again to shapelessness and destruction. The spectacle was all the more grand and impressive to him, because where he now was he could not hear the full clamour of the rolling and retreating billows. The thunder of the surf was diminished to a sullen moan, which came along with the wind and clung to it like a concordant note in music, forming one sustained chord of wrath and desolation. Darkening steadily over the sea and densely over-spreading the whole sky, there were flying clouds of singular shape,—clouds tossed up into the momentary similitude of Titanesque human figures with threatening arms outstretched,—anon, to the filmy outlines of fabulous birds swooping downwards with jagged wings and ravenous beaks,—or twisting into columns and pyramids of vapour as though the showers of foam flung up by the waves had been caught in mid-air and suddenly frozen. Several sea-gulls were flying inland; two or three soared right over Helmsley's head with a plaintive cry. He turned to watch their graceful flight, and saw another phalanx of clouds coming up behind to meet and cope with those already hurrying in with the wind from the sea. The darkness of the sky was deepening every minute, and he began to feel a little uneasy. He realised that he had lost his way, and he looked on all sides for some glimpse of a main road, but could see none, and the path he had followed evidently terminated at the summit where he stood. To return to the valley he had left seemed futile, as it was only a way back to Minehead, which place he wished to avoid. There was a small sheep track winding down on the other side of the hill, and he thought it possible that this might lead to a farm-road, which again might take him out on some more direct highway. He therefore started to follow it. He could scarcely walk against the wind; it blew with such increasing fury. Charlie shivered away from its fierce breath and snuggled his tiny body more warmly under his protector's arm, withdrawing himself entirely from view. And now with a sudden hissing whirl, down came the rain. The two opposing forces of cloud met with a sudden rush, and emptied their pent-up torrents on the earth, while a low muttering noise, not of the wind, betokened thunder. The prolonged heat of the last month had been very great all over the country, and a suppressed volcano was smouldering in the heart of the heavens, ready to shoot forth fire. The roaring of the sea grew more distinct as Helmsley descended from the height and came nearer to the coast line,—and the mingled scream of the angry surf on the shore and the sword-like sweep of the rain, rang in his ears deafeningly, with a kind of monotonous horror. His head began to swim, and his eyes were half blinded by the sharp showers that whipped his face with blown drops as hard and cold as hail. On he went, however, more like a struggling dreamer in a dream, than with actual consciousness,—and darker and wilder grew the storm. A forked flash of lightning, running suddenly like melted lava down the sky, flung half a second's lurid blue glare athwart the deepening blackness,—and in less than two minutes it was followed by the first decisive peal of thunder rolling in deep reverberations from sea to land, from land to sea again. The war of the elements had begun in earnest. Amid their increasing giant wrath, Helmsley stumbled almost unseeingly along,— keeping his head down and leaning more heavily than was his usual wont upon the stout ash stick which was part of the workman's outfit he had purchased for himself in Bristol, and which now served him as his best support. In the gathering gloom, with his stooping thin figure, he looked more like a faded leaf fluttering in the gale than a man, and he was beginning now to realise with keen disappointment that his strength was not equal to the strain he had been putting upon it. The weight of his seventy years was pressing him down,—and a sudden thrill of nervous terror ran through him lest his whim for wandering should cost him his life.

"And if I were to die of exhaustion out here on the hills, what would be said of me?" he thought—"They would find my body—perhaps—after some days;—they would discover the money I carry in my vest lining, and a letter to Vesey which would declare my actual identity. Then I should be called a fool or a madman—most probably the latter. No one would know,—no one would guess—except Vesey—the real object with which I started on this wild goose chase after the impossible. It is a foolish quest! Perhaps after all I had better give it up, and return to the old wearisome life of luxury,—the old ways!—and die in my bed in the usual 'respectable' style of the rich, with expensive doctors, nurses and medicines set in order round me, and all arrangements getting ready for a 'first-class funeral'!"

He laughed drearily. Another flash of lightning, followed almost instantaneously by a terrific crash of thunder, brought him to a pause. He was now at the bottom of the hill which he had ascended from the other side, and perceived a distinct and well-trodden path which appeared to lead in a circuitous direction towards the sea. Here there seemed some chance of getting out of the labyrinth of hills into which he had incautiously wandered, and, summoning up his scattered forces, he pressed on. The path proved to be an interminable winding way,—first up—then down,—now showing glimpses of the raging ocean, now dipping over bare and desolate lengths of land,—and presently it turned abruptly into a deep thicket of trees. Drenched with rain and tired of fighting against the boisterous wind which almost tore his breath away, he entered this dark wood with a vague sense of relief,—it offered some sort of shelter, and if the trees attracted the lightning and he were struck dead beneath them, what did it matter after all! One way of dying was as good (or as bad) as another!

The over-arching boughs dripping with wet, closed over him and drew him, as it were, into their dense shadows,—the wind shrieked after him like a scolding fury, but its raging tone grew softer as he penetrated more deeply into the sable-green depths of heavily foliaged solitude. His weary feet trod gratefully on a thick carpet of pine needles and masses of the last year's fallen leaves,—and a strong sweet scent of mingled elderflower and sweetbriar was tossed to him on every gust of rain. Here the storm turned itself to music and revelled in a glorious symphony of sound.

"Oh ye Winds of God, bless ye the Lord; praise Him and magnify Him for ever!

"Oh ye Lightnings and Clouds, bless ye the Lord; praise Him and magnify Him for ever!"

In full chords of passionate praise the hurricane swept its grand anthem through the rustling, swaying trees, as though these were the strings of a giant harp on which some great Archangel played,—and the dash and roar of the sea came with it, rolling in the track of another mighty peal of thunder. Helmsley stopped and listened, seized by an overpowering enchantment and awe.

"This—this is Life!" he said, half aloud—"Our miserable human vanities—our petty schemes—our poor ambitions—what are they? Motes in a sunbeam!—gone as soon as realised! But Life,—the deep, self-contained divine Life of Nature—this is the only life that lives for ever, the Immortality of which we are a part!"

A fierce gust of wind here snapped asunder a great branch from a tree, and flung it straight across his path. Had he been a few inches nearer, it would have probably struck him down with it. Charlie peeped out from under his arm with a pitiful little whimper, and Helmsley's heart smote him.

"Poor wee Charlie!" he said, fondling the tiny head; "I know what you would say to me! You would say that if I want to risk my own life, I needn't risk yours! Is that it? Well!—I'll try to get you out of this if I can! I wish I I could see some sign of a house anywhere! I'd make for it and ask for shelter."

He trudged patiently onwards,—but he was beginning to feel unsteady in his limbs,—and every now and then he had to stop, overcome by a sickening sensation of giddiness. The tempest had now fully developed into a heavy thunderstorm, and the lightning quivered and gleamed through the trees incessantly, followed by huge claps of thunder which clashed down without a second's warning, afterwards rolling away in long thudding detonations echoing for miles and miles. It was difficult to walk at all in such a storm,—the youngest and strongest pedestrian might have given way under the combined onslaught of rain, wind, and the pattering shower of leaves which were literally torn, fresh and green, from their parent boughs and cast forth to whirl confusedly amid the troubled spaces of the air. And if the young and strong would have found it hard to brave such an uproar of the elements, how much harder was it for an old man, who, deeming himself stronger than he actually was, and buoyed up by sheer nerve and mental obstinacy, had, of his own choice, brought himself into this needless plight and danger. For now, in utter weariness of body and spirit, Helmsley began to reproach himself bitterly for his rashness. A mere caprice of the imagination,—a fancy that, perhaps, among the poor and lowly he might find a love or a friendship he had never met with among the rich and powerful, was all that had led him forth on this strange journey of which the end could but be disappointment and failure;—and at the present moment he felt so thoroughly conscious of his own folly, that he almost resolved on abandoning his enterprise as soon as he found himself once more on the main road.

"I will take the first vehicle that comes by,"—he said, "and make for the nearest railway station. And I'll end my days with a character for being 'hard as nails!'—that's the only way in which one can win the respectful consideration of one's fellows as a thoroughly 'sane and sensible' man!"

Just then, the path he was following started sharply up a steep acclivity, and there was no other choice left to him but still to continue in it, as the trees were closing in blindly intricate tangles about him, and the brushwood was becoming so thick that he could not have possibly forced a passage through it. His footing grew more difficult, for now, instead of soft pine-needles and leaves to tread upon, there were only loose stones, and the rain was blowing in downward squalls that almost by their very fury threw him backward on the ground. Up, still up, he went, however, panting painfully as he climbed,—his breath was short and uneasy—and all his body ached and shivered as with strong ague. At last,—dizzy and half fainting,—he arrived at the top of the tedious and troublesome ascent, and uttered an involuntary cry at the scene of beauty and grandeur stretched in front of him. How far he had walked he had no idea,—nor did he know how many hours he had taken in walking,—but he had somehow found his way to the summit of a rocky wooded height, from which he could survey the whole troubled expanse of wild sky and wilder sea,—while just below him the hills were split asunder into a huge cleft, or "coombe," running straight down to the very lip of ocean, with rampant foliage hanging about it on either side in lavish garlands of green, and big boulders piled up about it, from whose smooth surfaces the rain swept off in sleety sheets, leaving them shining like polished silver. What a wild Paradise was here disclosed!—what a matchless picture, called into shape and colour with all the forceful ease and perfection of Nature's handiwork! No glimpse of human habitation was anywhere visible; man seemed to have found no dwelling here;

there was nothing—nothing, but Earth the Beautiful, and her Lover the Sea! Over these twain the lightnings leaped, and the thunder played in the sanctuary of heaven,—this hour of storm was all their own, and humanity was no more counted in their passionate intermingling of life than the insects on a leaf, or the grains of sand on the shore. For a moment or two Helmsley's eyes, straining and dim, gazed out on the marvellously bewitching landscape thus suddenly unrolled before him,—then all at once a sharp pain running through his heart caused him to flinch and tremble. It was a keen stab of anguish, as though a knife had been plunged into his body.

"My God!" he muttered—"What—what is this?"

Walking feebly to a great stone hard by, he sat down upon it, breathing with difficulty. The rain beat full upon him, but he did not heed it; he sought to recover from the shock of that horrible pain,—to overcome the creeping sick sensation of numbness which seemed to be slowly freezing him to death. With a violent effort he tried to shake the illness off;—he looked up at the sky—and was met by a blinding flash which tore the clouds asunder and revealed a white blaze of palpitating fire in the centre of the blackness—and at this he made some inarticulate sound, putting both his hands before his face to hide the angry mass of flame. In so doing he let the little Charlie escape, who, finding himself out of his warm shelter and on the wet grass, stood amazed, and shivering pitifully under the torrents of rain. But Helmsley was not conscious of his canine friend's distress. Another pang, cruel and prolonged, convulsed him,—a blood-red mist swam before his eyes, and he lost all hold on sense and memory. With a dull groan he fell forward, slipping from the stone on which he had been seated, in a helpless heap on the ground,—involuntarily he threw up his arms as a drowning man might do among great waves overwhelming him,—and so went down—down!—into silence and unconsciousness.

XII

The storm raged till sunset; and then exhausted by its own stress of fury, began to roll away in angry sobs across the sea. The wind sank suddenly; the rain as suddenly ceased. A wonderful flush of burning orange light cut the sky asunder, spreading gradually upward and paling into fairest rose. The sullen clouds caught brightness at their summits, and took upon themselves the semblance of Alpine heights touched by the mystic glory of the dawn, and a clear silver radiance flashed across the ocean for a second and then vanished, as though a flaming torch had just flared up to show the troublous heaving of the waters, and had then been instantly quenched. As the evening came on the weather steadily cleared;—and presently a pure, calm, dark-blue expanse of ether stretched balmily across the whole width of the waves, with the evening star—the Star of Love—glimmering faintly aloft like a delicate jewel hanging on the very heart of the air. Far away down in the depths of the "coombe," a church bell rang softly for some holy service,—and when David Helmsley awoke at last from his death-like swoon he found himself no longer alone. A woman knelt beside him, supporting him in her arms,—and when he looked up at her wonderingly, he saw two eyes bent upon him with such watchful tenderness that in his weak, half-conscious state he fancied he must be wandering somewhere through heaven if the stars were so near. He tried to speak—to move,—but was checked by a gentle pressure of the protecting arms about him.

"Better now, dearie?" murmured a low anxious voice. "That's right! Don't try to get up just yet—take time! Let the strength come back to you first!"

Who was it—who could it be, that spoke to him with such affectionate solicitude? He gazed and gazed and marvelled,—but it was too dark to see the features of his rescuer. As consciousness grew more vivid, he realised that he was leaning against her bosom like a helpless child,—that the wet grass was all about him,—and that he was cold,— very cold, with a coldness as of some enclosing grave. Sense and memory returned to him slowly with sharp stabs of physical pain, and presently he found utterance.

"You are very kind!" he muttered, feebly—"I begin to recollect now—I had walked a long way—and I was caught in the storm—I felt ill,—very ill!—I suppose I must have fallen down here—"

"That's it!" said the woman, gently—"Don't try to think about it! You'll be better presently."

He closed his eyes wearily,—then opened them again, struck by a sudden self-reproach and anxiety.

"The little dog?" he asked, trembling—"The little dog I had with me—?"

He saw, or thought he saw, a smile on the face in the darkness.

"The little dog's all right,—don't you worry about him!" said the woman—"He knows how to take care of himself and you too! It was just him that brought me along here where I found you. Bless the little soul! He made noise enough for six of his size!"

Helmsley gave a faint sigh of pleasure.

"Poor little Charlie! Where is he?"

"Oh, he's close by! He was almost drowned with the rain, like a poor mouse in a pail of water, but he went on barking all the same! I dried him as well as I could in my apron, and then wrapped him up in my cloak,—he's sitting right in it just now watching me."

"If—if I die,—please take care of him!" murmured Helmsley.

"Nonsense, dearie! I'm not going to let you die out here on the hills,—don't think it!" said the woman, cheerily,—"I want to get you up, and take you home with me. The storm's well overpast,—if you could manage to move—"

He raised himself a little, and tried to see her more closer.

"Do you live far from here?" he asked.

"Only just on the upper edge of the 'coombe'—not in the village,"— she answered—"It's quite a short way, but a bit steep going. If you lean on me, I won't let you slip,—I'm as strong as a man, and as men go nowadays, stronger than most!"

He struggled to rise, and she assisted him. By dint of sheer mental force and determination he got himself on his feet, but his limbs shook violently, and his head swam.

"I'm afraid"—he faltered—"I'm afraid I am very ill. I shall only be a trouble to you—"

"Don't talk of trouble? Wait till I fetch the doggie!" And, turning from him a moment, she ran to pick up Charlie, who, as she had said, was snugly ensconced in the folds of her cloak, which she had put for him under the shelter of a projecting boulder,—"Could you carry him, do you think?"

He nodded assent, and put the little animal under his coat as before, touched almost to weak tears to feel it trying to lick his hand.

Meanwhile his unknown and scarcely visible protectress put an arm round him, holding him up as carefully as though he were a tottering infant.

"Don't hurry—just take an easy step at a time,"—she said—"The moon rises a bit late, and we'll have to see our way as best we can with the stars." And she gave a glance upward. "That's a bright one just over the coombe,—the girls about here call it 'Light o' Love.'"

Moving stiffly, and with great pain, Helmsley was nevertheless impelled, despite his suffering, to look, as she was looking, towards the heavens. There he saw the same star that had peered at him through the window of his study at Carlton House Terrace,—the same that had sparkled out in the sky the night that he and Matt Peke had trudged the road together, and which Matt had described as "the love-star, an' it'll be nowt else in these parts till the world-without-end-amen!" And she whose eyes were upturned to its silvery glory,—who was she? His sight was very dim, and in the deepening shadows he could only discern a figure of medium womanly height,—an uncovered head with the hair loosely knotted in a thick coil at the nape of the neck,—and the outline of a face which might be fair or plain,—he could not tell. He was conscious of the warm strength of the arm that supported him, for when he slipped once or twice, he was caught up tenderly, without hurt or haste, and held even more securely than before. Gradually, and by halting degrees, he made the descent of the hill, and, as his guide helped him carefully over a few loose stones in the path, he saw through a dark clump of foliage the glimmer of twinkling lights, and heard the rush of water. He paused, vaguely bewildered.

"Nearly home now!" said his guide, encouragingly; "Just a few steps more and we'll be there. My cottage is the last and the highest in the coombe. The other houses are all down closer to the sea."

Still he stood inert.

"The sea!" he echoed, faintly—"Where is it?"

With her disengaged hand she pointed outwards.

"Yonder! By and by, when the moon comes over the hill, it will be shining like a silver field with big daisies blowing and growing all over it. That's the way it often looks after a storm. The tops of the waves are just like great white flowers."

He glanced at her as she said this, and caught a closer glimpse of her face. Some faint mystical light in the sky illumined the outlines of her features, and showed him a calm and noble profile, such as may be found in early Greek sculpture, and which silently expresses the lines:

> *"Beauty is truth, truth beauty,—that is all*
> *Ye know on earth, and all ye need to know!"*

He moved on with a quicker step, touched by a keen sense of expectation. Ill as he knew himself to be, he was eager to reach this woman's dwelling and to see her more closely. A soft laugh of pleasure broke from her lips as he tried to accelerate his pace.

"Oh, we're getting quite strong and bold now, aren't we!" she exclaimed, gaily—"But take care not to go too fast! There's a rough bit of bog and boulder coming."

This was true. They had arrived at the upper edge of a bank overlooking a hill stream which was pouring noisily down in a flood made turgid by the rain, and the "rough bit of bog and boulder" was a sort of natural bridge across the torrent, formed by heaps of earth and rock, out of which masses of wet fern and plumy meadow-sweet sprang in tall tufts and garlands, which though beautiful to the eyes in day-time, were apt to entangle the feet in walking, especially when there was only the uncertain glimmer of the stars by which to grope one's way. Helmsley's age and over-wrought condition made his movements nervous and faltering at this point, and nothing could exceed the firm care and delicate solicitude with which his guide helped him over this last difficulty of the road. She was indeed strong, as she had said,—she seemed capable of lifting him bodily, if need were—yet she was not a woman of large or robust frame. On the contrary, she appeared slightly built, and carried herself with that careless grace which betokens perfect form. Once safely across the bridge and on the other side of the coombe, she pointed to a tiny lattice window with a light behind it which gleamed out through the surrounding foliage like a glow-worm in the darkness.

"Here we are at home," she said,—"Just along this path—it's quite easy!—now under this tree—it's a big chestnut,—you'll love it!—now here's the garden gate—wait till I lift the latch—that's right!—the garden's quite small you see,—it goes straight up to the cottage—and here's the door! Come in!"

As in a dream, Helmsley was dimly conscious of the swishing rustle of wet leaves, and the fragrance of mignonette and roses mingling with the salty scent of the sea,—then he found himself in a small, low, oak-raftered kitchen, with a wide old-fashioned hearth and ingle-nook, warm with the glow of a sparkling fire. A quaintly carved comfortably cushioned armchair was set in the corner, and to this his guide conducted him, and gently made him sit down.

"Now give me the doggie!" she said, taking that little personage from his arms—"He'll be glad of his supper and a warm bed, poor little soul! And so will you!"

With a kindly caress she set Charlie down in front of the hearth, and proceeded to shut the cottage door, which had been left open as they entered,—and locking it, dropped an iron bar across it for the night. Then she threw off her cloak, and hung it up on a nail in the wall, and bending over a lamp which was burning low on the table, turned up its wick a little higher. Helmsley watched her in a kind of stupefied wonderment. As the lamplight flashed up on her features, he saw that she was not a girl, but a woman who seemed to have thought and suffered. Her face was pale, and the lines of her mouth were serious, though very sweet. He could hardly judge whether she had beauty or not, because he saw her at a disadvantage. He was too ill to appreciate details, and he could only gaze at her in the dim and troubled weariness of an old and helpless man, who for the time being was dependent on any kindly aid that might be offered to him. Once or twice the vague idea crossed his mind that he would tell her who he was, and assure her that he had plenty of money about him to reward her for her care and pains,—but he could not bring himself to the point of this confession. The surprise and sweetness of being received thus unquestioningly under the shelter of her roof as merely the poor way-worn tramp he seemed to be, were too great for him to relinquish. She, meanwhile, having trimmed the lamp, hurried into a neighboring room, and came in again with a bundle of woollen garments, and a thick flannel dressing gown on her arm.

"This was my father's," she said, as she brought it to him—"It's soft and cosy. Get off your wet clothes and slip into it, while I go and make your bed ready."

She spread the dressing gown before the fire to warm it, and was about to turn away again, when Helmsley laid a detaining hand on her arm.

"Wait—wait!" he said—"Do you know what you are doing?"

She laughed.

"Well, now that *is* a question! Do I seem crazy?"

"Almost you do—to me!" And stirred into a sudden flicker of animation, he held her fast as he spoke—"Do you live alone here?"

"Yes,—quite alone."

"Then don't you see how foolish you are? You are taking into your house a mere tramp,—a beggar who is more likely to die than live! Do you realise how dangerous this is for you? I may be an escaped convict,—a thief—even a murderer! You cannot tell!"

She smiled and nodded at him as a nurse might nod and smile at a fanciful or querulous patient.

"I can't tell, certainly, and don't want to know!" she replied—"I go by what I see."

"And what do you see?"

She patted his thin cold hand kindly.

"I see a very old man—older than my own dear father was when he died—and I know he is too old and feeble to be out at night in the wet and stormy weather. I know that he is ill and weak, and suffering from exhaustion, and that he must rest and be well nourished for a few days till he gets strong again. And I am going to take care of him,"—here she gave a consoling little pressure to the hand she held. "I am indeed! And he must do as he is told, and take off his wet clothes and get ready for bed!"

Something in Helmsley's throat tightened like the contraction of a rising sob.

"You will risk all this trouble,"—he faltered—"for a stranger—who—who—cannot repay you—?—"

"Now, now! You mustn't hurt me!" she said, with a touch of reproach in her soft tones—"I don't want to be repaid in any way. You know Who it was that said 'I was a stranger and ye took me in'? Well, He would wish me to take care of you."

She spoke quite simply, without any affectation of religious sentiment. Helmsley looked at her steadily.

"Is that why you shelter me?"

She smiled very sweetly, and he saw that her eyes were beautiful.

"That is one reason, certainly!"—she answered; "But there is another,—quite a selfish one! I loved my father, and when he died, I lost everything I cared for in the world. You remind me of him—just a little. Now will you do as I ask you, and take off your wet things?"

He let go her hand gently.

"I will,"—he said, unsteadily—for there were tears in his eyes—"I will do anything you wish. Only tell me your name!"

"My name? My name is Mary,—Mary Deane."

"Mary Deane!" he repeated softly—and yet again—"Mary Deane! A pretty name! Shall I tell you mine!"

"Not unless you like,"—she replied, quickly—"It doesn't matter!"

"Oh, you'd better know it!" he said—"I'm only old David—a man 'on the road' tramping it to Cornwall."

"That's a long way!" she murmured compassionately, as she took his weather-beaten hat and shook the wet from it—"And why do you want to tramp so far, you poor old David?"

"I'm looking for a friend,"—he answered—"And maybe it's no use trying,—but I should like to find that friend before I die."

"And so you will, I'm sure!" she declared, smiling at him, but with something of an anxious expression in her eyes, for Helmsley's face was very pinched and pallid, and every now and then he shivered violently as with an ague fit—"But you must pick up your strength first. Then you'll get on better and quicker. Now I'm going to leave you while you change. You'll find plenty of warm things with the dressing gown."

She went out as before into the next room, and Helmsley managed, though with considerable difficulty, to divest himself of his drenched clothes and get on the comfortable woollen garments she had put ready for him. When he took off his coat and vest, he spread them in front of the fire to dry instead of the dressing-gown which he now wore, and as soon as she returned he specially pointed out the vest to her.

"I should like you to put that away somewhere in your own safe keeping,"—he said. "It has a few letters and—and papers in it which I value,—and I don't want any stranger to see them. Will you take care of it for me?"

"Of course I will! Nobody shall touch it, be sure! Not a soul ever comes nigh me unless I ask for company!—so you can be quite easy in your mind. Now I'm going to give you a cup of hot soup, and then you'll go to bed, won't you?—and, please God, you'll be better in the morning!"

He nodded feebly, and forced a smile. He had sunk back in the armchair and his eyes were fixed on the warm-hearth, where the tiny dog, Charlie, whom he had rescued, and who in turn had rescued him, was curled up and snoozing peacefully. Now that the long physical and nervous strain of his journey and of his ghastly experience at Blue Anchor was past, he felt almost too weak to lift a hand, and the sudden change from the fierce buffetings of the storm to the homely tranquillity of this little cottage into which he had been welcomed just as though he had every right to be there, affected him with a strange sensation which he could not analyse. And once he murmured half unconsciously:

"Mary! Mary Deane!"

"Yes,—that's me!" she responded cheerfully, coming to his side at once—"I'm here!"

He lifted his head and looked at her.

"Yes, I know you are here,—Mary!" he said, his voice trembling a little as he uttered her name—"And I thank God for sending you to me in time! But how—how was it that you found me?"

"I was watching the storm,"—she replied—"I love wild weather!—I love to hear the wind among the trees and the pouring of the rain! I was standing at my door listening to the waves thudding into the hollow of the coombe, and all at once I heard the sharp barking of a dog on the hill just above here—and sometimes the bark changed to a pitiful little howl, as if the animal were in pain. So I put on my cloak and crossed the coombe up the bank—it's only a few minutes' scramble, though to you it seemed ever such a long way to-night,—and there I saw you lying on the grass with the little doggie running round and round you, and making all the noise he could to bring help. Wise little beastie!" And she stooped to pat the tiny object of her praise, who sighed comfortably and stretched his dainty paws out a little more luxuriously—"If it hadn't been for him you might have died!"

He said nothing, but watched her in a kind of morbid fascination as she went to the fire and removed a saucepan which she had set there some minutes previously. Taking a large old-fashioned Delft bowl from a cupboard at one side of the fire-place, she filled it with steaming soup which smelt deliciously savoury and appetising, and brought it to him with some daintily cut morsels of bread. He was too ill to feel much hunger, but to please her, he managed to sip it by slow degrees, talking to her between-whiles.

"You say you live alone here,"—he murmured—"But are you always alone?"

"Always,—ever since father died."

"How long is that ago?"

"Five years."

"You are not—you have not been—married?"

She laughed.

"No indeed! I'm an old maid!"

"Old?" And he raised his eyes to her face. "You are not old!"

"Well, I'm not young, as young people go,"—she declared—"I'm thirty-four. I was never married for myself in my youth,—and I shall certainly never be married for my money in my age!" Again her pretty laugh rang softly on the silence. "But I'm quite happy, all the same!"

He still looked at her intently,—and all suddenly it dawned upon him that she was a beautiful woman. He saw, as for the first time, the clear transparency of her skin, the soft brilliancy of her eyes, and the wonderful masses of her warm bronze brown hair. He noted the perfect poise of her figure, clad as it was in a cheap print gown,—the slimness of her waist, the fulness of her bosom, the white roundness of her throat. Then he smiled.

"So you are an old maid!" he said—"That's very strange!"

"Oh, I don't think so!" and she shook her head deprecatingly— "Many women are old maids by choice as well as by necessity. Marriage isn't always bliss, you know! And unless a woman loves a man very very much—so much that she can't possibly live her life without him, she'd better keep single. At least that's *my* opinion. Now Mr. David, you must go to bed!"

He rose obediently—but trembled as he rose, and could scarcely stand from sheer weakness. Mary Deane put her arm through his to support him.

"I'm afraid,"—he faltered—"I'm afraid I shall be a burden to you! I don't think I shall be well enough to start again on my way to-morrow."

"You won't be allowed to do any such foolish thing!" she answered, with quick decision—"So you can just make up your mind on *that* score! You must stay here as my guest."

"Not a paying one, I fear!" he said, with a pained smile, and a quick glance at her.

She gave a slight gesture of gentle reproach.

"I wouldn't have you on paying terms,"—she answered; "I don't take in lodgers."

"But—but—how do you live?"

He put the question hesitatingly, yet with keen curiosity.

"How do I live? You mean how do I work for a living? I am a lace mender, and a bit of a laundress too. I wash fine muslin gowns, and mend and clean valuable old lace. It's pretty work and pleasant enough in its way."

"Does it pay you well?"

"Oh, quite sufficiently for all my needs. I don't cost much to keep!" And she laughed—"I'm all by myself, and I was never money-hungry! Now come!—you mustn't talk any more. You know who I am and what I am,—and we'll have a good long chat to-morrow. It's bed-time!"

She led him, as though he were a child, into a little room,—one of the quaintest and prettiest he had ever seen,—with a sloping raftered ceiling, and one rather wide latticed window set in a deep embrasure and curtained with spotless white dimity. Here there was a plain old-fashioned oak bedstead, trimmed with the same white hangings, the bed itself being covered with a neat quilt of diamond-patterned silk patchwork. Everything was delicately clean, and fragrant with the odour of dried rose-leaves and lavender,—and it was with all the zealous care of an anxious housewife that Mary Deane assured her "guest" that the sheets were well-aired, and that there was not "a speck of damp" anywhere. A kind of instinct told him that this dainty little sleeping chamber, so fresh and pure, with not even a picture on its white-washed walls, and only a plain wooden cross hung up just opposite to the bed, must be Mary's own room, and he looked at her questioningly.

"Where do you sleep yourself?" he asked.

"Upstairs,"—she answered, at once—"Just above you. This is a two-storied cottage—quite large really! I have a parlour besides the kitchen,—oh, the parlour's very sweet!—it has a big window which my father built himself, and it looks out on a lovely view of the orchard and the stream,—then I have three more rooms, and a wash-house and cellar. It's almost too big a cottage for me, but father loved it, and he died here,—that's why I keep all his things about me and stay on in it. He planted all the roses in the orchard,—and I couldn't leave them!"

Helmsley said nothing in answer to this. She put an armchair for him near the bed.

"Now as soon as you're in bed, just call to me and I'll put out the light in the kitchen and go to bed myself,"—she said—"And I'll take the little doggie with me, and make him comfortable for the night. I'm leaving you a candle and matches, and if you feel badly at all, there's a handbell close by,—mind you ring it, and I'll come to you at once and do all I can for you."

He bent his eyes searchingly upon her in his old suspicious "business" way, his fuzzy grey eyebrows almost meeting in the intensity of his gaze.

"Tell me—why are you so good to me?" he asked.

She smiled.

"Don't ask nonsense questions, please, Mr. David! Haven't I told you already?—not why I am 'good,' because that's rubbish—but why I am trying to take care of you?"

"Yes—because I am old!" he said, with a sudden pang of self-contempt—"and—useless!"

"Good-night!" she answered, cheerfully—"Call to me when you are ready!"

She was gone before he could speak another word and he heard her talking to Charlie in petting playful terms of endearment. Judging from the sounds in the kitchen, he concluded, and rightly, that she was getting her own supper and that of the dog at the same time. For two or three minutes he sat inert, considering his strange and unique position. What would this present adventure lead to? Unless his new friend, Mary Deane, examined the vest he had asked her to take care of for him, she would not discover who he was or from whence he came. Would she examine it?—would she unrip the lining, just out of feminine curiosity, and sew it up again, pretending that she had not touched it, after the "usual way of women"? No! He was sure,—absolutely sure—of her integrity. What? In less than an hour's acquaintance with her, would he swear to her honesty? Yes, he would! Never could such eyes as hers, so softly, darkly blue and steadfast, mirror a falsehood, or deflect the fragment of a broken promise! And so, for the time being, in utter fatigue of both body and mind, he put away all thought, all care for the future, and resigned himself to the circumstances by which he was now surrounded. Undressing as quickly as he could in his weak and trembling condition, he got into the bed so comfortably prepared for him, and lay down in utter lassitude, thankful for rest. After he had lain so for a few minutes he called:

"Mary Deane!"

She came at once, and looked in, smiling.

"All cosy and comfortable?" she queried—"That's right!" Then entering the room, she showed him the very vest, the possible fate of which he had been considering.

"This is quite dry now,"—she said—"I've been thinking that perhaps as there are letters and papers inside, you'd like to have it near you,—so I'm just going to put it in here—see?" And she opened a small cupboard in the wall close to the bed—"There! Now I'll lock it up"—and she suited the action to the word—"Where shall I put the key?"

"Please keep it for me yourself!" he answered, earnestly,—"It will be safest with you!"

"Well, perhaps it will,"—she agreed. "Anyhow no one can get at your letters without *my* consent! Now, are you quite easy?"

And, as she spoke, she came and smoothed the bedclothes over him, and patted one of his thin, worn hands which lay, almost unconsciously to himself, outside the quilt.

"Quite!" he said, faintly, "God bless you!"

"And you too!" she responded—"Good-night—David!"

"Good-night—Mary!"

She went away with a light step, softly closing the door behind her. Returning to the kitchen she took up the little dog Charlie in her arms, and nestled him against her bosom, where he was very well content to be, and stood for a moment looking meditatively into the fire.

"Poor old man!" she murmured—"I'm so glad I found him before it was too late! He would have died out there on the hills, I'm sure! He's very ill—and so worn out and feeble!"

Involuntarily her glance wandered to a framed photograph which stood on the mantelshelf, showing the likeness of a white-haired man standing among a group of full-flowering roses, with a smile upon his wrinkled face,—a smile expressing the quaintest and most complete satisfaction, as though he sought to illustrate the fact that though he was old, he was still a part of the youthful blossoming of the earth in summer-time.

"What would you have done, father dear, if you had been here to-night?"—she queried, addressing the portrait—"Ah, I need not ask! I know! You would have brought your suffering brother home, to share all you had;—you would have said to him 'Rest, and be thankful!' For you never turned the needy from your door, my dear old dad!—never!—no matter how much you were in need yourself!"

She wafted a kiss to the venerable face among the roses,—and then turning, extinguished the lamp on the table. The dying glow of the fire shone upon her for a moment, setting a red sparkle in her hair, and a silvery one on the silky head of the little dog she carried, and outlining her fine profile so that it gleamed with a pure soft pallor against the surrounding darkness,—and with one final look round to see that all was clear for the night, she went away noiselessly like a lovely ghost and disappeared, her step making no sound on the short wooden stairs that led to the upper room which she had hastily arranged for her own accommodation, in place of the one now occupied by the homeless wayfarer she had rescued.

There was no return of the storm. The heavens, with their mighty burden of stars, remained clear and tranquil,—the raging voice of ocean was gradually sinking into a gentle crooning song of sweet content,— and within the little cottage complete silence reigned, unbroken save for the dash of the stream outside, rushing down through the "coombe" to the sea.

XIII

The next morning Helmsley was too ill to move from his bed, or to be conscious of his surroundings. And there followed a long period which to him was well-nigh a blank. For weeks he lay helpless in the grasp of a fever which over and over again threatened to cut the last frail thread of his life asunder. Pain tortured every nerve and sinew in his body, and there were times of terrible collapse,—when he was conscious of nothing save an intense longing to sink into the grave and have done with all the sharp and cruel torment which kept him on the rack of existence. In a semi-delirious condition he tossed and moaned the hours away, hardly aware of his own identity. In certain brief pauses of the nights and days, when pain was momentarily dulled by stupor, he saw, or fancied he saw a woman always near him, with anxiety in her eyes and words of soothing consolation on her lips;—and then he found himself muttering, "Mary! Mary! God bless you!" over and over again. Once or twice he dimly realised that a small dark man came to his bedside and felt his pulse and looked at him very doubtfully, and that she, Mary, called this personage "doctor," and asked him questions in a whisper. But all within his own being was pain and bewilderment,— sometimes he felt as though he were one drop in a burning whirlpool of madness—and sometimes he seemed to himself to be spinning round and round in a haze of blinding rain, of which the drops were scalding hot, and heavy as lead,—and occasionally he found that he was trying to get out of bed, uttering cries of inexplicable anguish, while at such moments, something cool was placed on his forehead, and a gentle arm was passed round him till the paroxysm abated, and he fell down again among his pillows exhausted. Slowly, and as it were grudgingly, after many days, the crisis of the illness passed and ebbed away in dull throbs of agony,—and he sank into a weak lethargy that was almost like the comatose condition preceding death. He lay staring at the ceiling for hours, heedless as to whether he ever moved or spoke again. Some-one came and put spoonfuls of liquid nourishment between his lips, and he swallowed it mechanically without any sign of conscious appreciation. White as white marble, and aged by many years, he remained stretched in his rigid corpse-like attitude, his eyes always fixedly upturned, till one day he was roused from his deepening torpor by the sound of sobbing. With a violent effort he brought his gaze down from the ceiling, and saw a figure kneeling by his bed, and a mass of bronze brown hair falling over a face concealed by two shapely white hands through which the tears were falling. Feebly astonished, he stretched out his thin, trembling fingers to touch that wonderful bright mesh of waving tresses, and asked—

"What is this? Who—who is crying?"

The hidden face was uplifted, and two soft eyes, wet with weeping, looked up hopefully.

"It's Mary!" said a trembling voice—"You know me, don't you? Oh, dearie, if you would but try to rouse yourself, you'd get well even now!"

He gazed at her in a kind of childish admiration.

"It's Mary!" he echoed, faintly—"And who is Mary?"

"Don't you remember?" And rising from her knees, she dashed away her tears and smiled at him—"Or is it too hard for you to think at all about it just now? Didn't I find you out on the hills in the storm, and bring you home here?—and didn't I tell you that my name was Mary?"

He kept his eyes upon her wistful face,—and presently a wan smile crossed his lips.

"Yes!—so you did!" he answered—"I know you now, Mary! I've been ill, haven't I?"

She nodded at him—the tears were still wet on her lashes.

"Very ill!"

"Ill all night, I suppose?"

She nodded again.

"It's morning now?"

"Yes, it's morning!"

"I shall get up presently,"—he said, in his old gentle courteous way—"I am sorry to have given you so much trouble! I must not burden your hospitality—your kindness—"

His voice trailed away into silence,—his eyelids drooped—and fell into a sound slumber,—the first refreshing sleep he had enjoyed for many weary nights and days.

Mary Deane stood looking at him thoughtfully. The turn had come for the better, and she silently thanked God. Night after night, day after day, she had nursed him with unwearying patience and devotion, having no other help or guidance save her own womanly instinct, and the occasional advice of the village doctor, who, however, was not a qualified medical man, but merely a herbalist who prepared his own simples. This humble Gamaliel diagnosed Helmsley's case as one of rheumatic fever, complicated by heart trouble, as well as by the natural weakness of decaying vitality. Mary had explained to him Helmsley's presence in her cottage by a pious falsehood, which Heaven surely forgave her as soon as it was uttered. She had said that he was a friend of her late father's, who had sought her out in the hope that she might help him to find some light employment in his old age, and that not knowing the country at all, he had lost his way across the hills during the blinding fury of the storm. This story quickly ran through the little village, of which Mary's house was the last, at the summit of the "coombe," and many of its inhabitants came to inquire after "Mr. David," while he lay tossing and moaning between life and death, most of them seriously commiserating Mary herself for the "sight o' trouble" she had been put to,—"all for a trampin' stranger like!"

"Though,"—observed one rustic sage—"Bein' a lone woman as y' are, Mis' Deane, m'appen if he knew yer father 'twould be pleasant to talk to him when 'is 'ed comes clear, if clear it iver do come. For when we've put our owd folk under the daisies, it do cheer the 'art a bit to talk of 'em to those as knew 'em when they was a standin' upright, bold an' strong, for all they lays so low till last trumpet."

Mary smiled a grave assent, and with wise tact and careful forethought for the comfort and well-being of her unknown guest, quietly accepted the position she had brought upon herself as having given shelter and lodging to her "father's friend," thus smoothing all difficulties away for him, whether he recovered from his illness or not. Had he died, she would have borne the expenses of his burial without a word of other explanation than that which she had offered by way of appeasing the always greedy curiosity of any community of human beings who are gathered in one small town or village,—and if he recovered, she was prepared to treat him in very truth as her "father's friend."

"For,"—she argued with herself, quite simply—"I am sure father would have been kind to him, and when once *he* was kind, it was impossible not to be his friend."

And, little by little, Helmsley struggled back to life,—life that was very weak and frail indeed, but still, life that contained the whole essence and elixir of being,—a new and growing interest. Little by little his brain cleared and recovered its poise,—once more he found himself thinking of things that had been done, and of things that were yet worth doing. Watching Mary Deane as she went softly to and fro in constant attendance on his needs, he was divided in his mind between admiration, gratitude, and—a lurking suspicion, of which he was ashamed. As a business man, he had been taught to look for interested motives lying at the back of every action, bad or good,—and as his health improved, and calm reason again asserted its sway, he found it difficult and well-nigh impossible to realise or to believe that this woman, to whom he was a perfect stranger, no more than a vagrant on the road, could have given him so much of her time, attention, and care, unless she had dimly supposed him to be something other than he had represented himself. Unable yet to leave his bed, he lay, to all appearances, quietly contented, acknowledging her gentle ministrations with equally gentle words of thanks, while all the time he was mentally tormenting himself with doubts and fears. He knew that during his illness he had been delirious,—surely in that delirium he might have raved and talked of many things that would have yielded the entire secret of his identity. This thought made him restless,—and one afternoon when Mary came in with the deliciously prepared cup of tea which she always gave him about four o'clock, he turned his eyes upon her with a sudden keen look which rather startled her by its piercing brightness suggesting, as it did, some return of fever.

"Tell me,"—he said—"Have I been ill long? More than a week?"

She smiled.

"A little more than a week,"—she answered, gently—"Don't worry!"

"I'm not worrying. Please tell me what day it is!"

"What day it is? Well, to-day is Sunday."

"Sunday! Yes—but what is the date of the month?"

She laughed softly, patting his hand.

"Oh, never mind! What does it matter?"

"It does matter,"—he protested, with a touch of petulance—"I know it is July, but what time of July?"

She laughed again.

"It's not July," she said.

"Not July!"

"No. Nor August!"

He raised himself on his pillow and stared at her in questioning amazement.

"Not July? Not August? Then—?"

She took his hand between her own kind warm palms, stroking it soothingly up and down.

"It's not July, and it's not August!" she repeated, nodding at him as though he were a worried and fractious child—"It's the second week in September. There!"

His eyes turned from right to left in utter bewilderment. "But how—" he murmured—

Then he suddenly caught her hands in the one she was holding.

"You mean to say that I have been ill all those weeks—a burden upon you?"

"You've been ill all those weeks—yes!" she answered "But you haven't been a burden. Don't you think it! You've—you've been a pleasure!" And her blue eyes filled with soft tears, which she quickly mastered and sent back to the tender source from which they sprang; "You have, really!"

He let go her hand and sank back on his pillows with a smothered groan.

"A pleasure!" he muttered—"I!" And his fuzzy eyebrows met in almost a frown as he again looked at her with one of the keen glances which those who knew him in business had learned to dread. "Mary Deane, do not tell me what is not and what cannot be true! A sick man—an old man—can be no 'pleasure' to anyone;—he is nothing but a bore and a trouble, and the sooner he dies the better!"

The smiling softness still lingered in her eyes.

"Ah well!"—she said—"You talk like that because you're not strong yet, and you just feel a bit cross and worried! You'll be better in another few days—"

"Another few days!" he interrupted her—"No—no—that cannot be—I must be up and tramping it again—I must not stay on here—I have already stayed too long."

A slight shadow crossed her face, but she was silent. He watched her narrowly.

"I've been off my head, haven't I?" he queried, affecting a certain brusqueness in his tone—"Talking a lot of nonsense, I suppose?"

"Yes—sometimes,"—she replied—"But only when you were *very* bad."

"And what did I say?"

She hesitated a moment, and he grew impatient.

"Come, come!" he demanded, irritably—"What did I say?"

She looked at him candidly.

"You talked mostly about 'Tom o' the Gleam,'"—she answered—"That was a poor gypsy well known in these parts. He had just one little child left to him in the world—its mother was dead. Some rich lord driving a motor car down by Cleeve ran over the poor baby and killed it—and Tom—"

"Tom tracked the car to Blue Anchor, where he found the man who had run over his child and killed *him*!" said Helmsley, with grim satisfaction—"I saw it done!"

Mary shuddered.

"I saw it done!" repeated Helmsley—"And I think it was rightly done! But—I saw Tom himself die of grief and madness—with his dead child in his arms—and *that!*—that broke something in my heart and brain and made me think God was cruel!"

She bent over him, and arranged his pillows more comfortably.

"I knew Tom,"—she said, presently, in a soft voice—"He was a wild creature, but very kind and good for all that. Some folks said he had been born a gentleman, and that a quarrel with his family had made him take to the gypsy life—but that's only a story. Anyway his little child—'kiddie'—as it used to be called, was the dearest little fellow in the world—so playful and affectionate!—I don't wonder Tom went mad when his one joy was killed! And you saw it all, you say?"

"Yes, I saw it all!" And Helmsley, with a faint sigh half closed his eyes as he spoke—"I was tramping from Watchett,—and the motor passed me on my way, but I did not see the child run over. I meant to get a lodging at Blue Anchor—and while I was having my supper at the public house Tom came in,—and—and it was all over in less than fifteen minutes! A horrible sight—a horrible, horrible sight! I see it now!—I shall never forget it!"

"Enough to make you ill, poor dear!" said Mary, gently—"Don't think of it now! Try and sleep a little. You mustn't talk too much. Poor Tom is dead and buried now, and his little child with him—God rest them both! It's better he should have died than lived without anyone to love him in the world."

"That's true!" And opening his eyes widely again, he gazed full at her—"That's the worst fate of all—to live in the world without anyone to love you! Tell me—when I was delirious did I only talk of Tom o' the Gleam?"

"That's the only person whose name you seemed to have on your mind,"—she answered, smiling a little—"But you *did* make a great noise about money!"

"Money?" he echoed—"I—I made a noise about money?"

"Yes!" And her smile deepened—"Often at night you quite startled me by shouting 'Money! Money!' I'm sure you've wanted it very badly!"

He moved restlessly and avoided her gaze. Presently he asked querulously:

"Where is my old vest with all my papers?"

"It's just where I put it the night you came,"—she answered—"I haven't touched it. Don't you remember you told me to keep the key of the cupboard which is right here close to your bed? I've got it quite safe."

He turned his head round on the pillow and looked at her with a sudden smile.

"Thank you! You are very kind to me, Mary! But you must let me work off all I owe you as soon as I'm well."

She put one finger meditatively on her lips and surveyed him with a whimsically indulgent air.

"Let you work it off? Well, I don't mind that at all! But a minute ago you were saying you must get up and go on the tramp again. Now, if you want to work for me, you must stay—"

"I will stay till I have paid you my debt somehow!" he said—"I'm old—but I can do a few useful things yet."

"I'm sure you can!" And she nodded cheerfully—"And you shall! Now rest a while, and don't fret!"

She went away from him then to fetch the little dog, Charlie, who, now that his master was on the fair road to complete recovery, was always brought in to amuse him after tea. Charlie was full of exuberant life, and his gambols over the bed where Helmsley lay, his comic interest in the feathery end of his own tail, and his general intense delight in the fact of his own existence, made him a merry and affectionate little playmate. He had taken immensely to his new home, and had attached himself to Mary Deane with singular devotion, trotting after her everywhere as close to her heels as possible. The fame of his beauty had gone through the village, and many a small boy and girl came timidly to the cottage door to try and "have a peep" at the smallest dog ever seen in the neighbourhood, and certainly the prettiest.

"That little dawg be wurth twenty pun!"—said one of the rustics to Mary, on one occasion when she was sitting in her little garden, carefully brushing and combing the silky coat of the little "toy"— "Th'owd man thee's been a' nussin' ought to give 'im to thee as a thank-offerin'."

"I wouldn't take him,"—Mary answered—"He's perhaps the only friend the poor old fellow has got in the world. It would be just selfish of me to want him."

And so the time went on till it was past mid-September, and there came a day, mild, warm, and full of the soft subdued light of deepening autumn, when Mary told her patient that he might get up, and sit in an armchair for a few hours in the kitchen. She gave him this news when she brought him his breakfast, and added—

"I'll wrap you up in father's dressing gown, and you'll be quite cosy and safe from chill. And after another week you'll be so strong that you'll be able to dress yourself and do without me altogether!"

This phrase struck curiously on his ears. "Do without her altogether!" That would be strange indeed—almost impossible! It was quite early in the morning when she thus spoke—about seven o'clock,—and he was not to get up till noon, "when the air was at its warmest," said Mary—so he lay very quietly, thinking over every detail of the position in which he found himself. He was now perfectly aware that it was a position which opened up great possibilities. His dream,— the vague indefinable longing which possessed him for love—pure, disinterested, unselfish love,—seemed on the verge of coming true. Yet he would not allow himself to hope too much,—he preferred to look on the darker side of probable disillusion. Meanwhile, he was conscious of a sweetness and comfort in his life such as he had never yet experienced. His thoughts dwelt with secret pleasure on the open frankness and calm beauty of the face that had bent over him with the watchfulness of a guardian angel through so many days and nights of pain, delirium, and dread of death,—and he noted with critically observant eyes the noiseless graceful movement of this humbly-born woman, whose instincts were so delicate and tender, whose voice was so gentle, and whose whole bearing expressed such unaffected dignity and purity of mind. On this particular morning she was busy ironing;—and she had left the door open between his bedroom and the kitchen, so that he might benefit by the inflow of fresh air from the garden, the cottage door itself being likewise thrown back to allow a full entrance of the invigorating influences of the light breeze from the sea and the odours of the flowers. From his bed he could see her slim back bent over the fine muslin frills she was pressing out with such patient precision, and he caught the glint of the sun on the rich twist of her bronze brown hair. Presently he heard some one talking to her,—a woman evidently, whose voice was pitched in a plaintive and almost querulous key.

"Well, Mis' Deane, say 'ow ye will an' what ye will,—there's a spider this very blessed instant a' crawlin' on the bottom of the ironin' blanket, which is a sure sign as 'ow yer washin' won't come to no good try iver so 'ard, for as we all knows—'See a spider at morn, An' ye'll wish ye wornt born: See a spider at night, An' yer wrongs'll come right!'"

Mary laughed; and Helmsley listened with a smile on his own lips. She had such a pretty laugh,—so low and soft and musical.

"Oh, never mind the poor spider, Mrs. Twitt!"—she said—"Let it climb up the ironing blanket if it likes! I see dozens of spiders 'at morn,' and I've never in my life wished I wasn't born! Why, if you go out in the garden early, you're bound to see spiders!"

"That's true—that's Testymen true!" And the individual addressed as Mrs. Twitt, heaved a profound sigh which was loud enough to flutter through the open door to Helmsley's ears—"Which, as I sez to Twitt often, shows as 'ow we shouldn't iver tempt Providence. Spiders there is, an' spiders there will be 'angin' on boughs an' 'edges, frequent too in September, but we aint called upon to look at 'em, only when the devil puts 'em out speshul to catch the hi, an' then they means mischief. An' that' just what 'as 'appened this present minit, Mis' Deane,—that spider on yer ironin' blanket 'as caught my hi."

"I'm so sorry!" said Mary, sweetly—"But as long as the spider doesn't bring *you* any ill-luck, Mrs. Twitt, I don't mind for myself—I don't, really!"

Mrs. Twitt emitted an odd sound, much like the grunt of a small and discontented pig.

"It's a reckless foot as don't mind precipeges,"—she remarked, solemnly—"'Owsomever, I've given ye fair warnin'. An' 'ow's yer father's friend?"

"He's much better,—quite out of danger now,"—replied Mary—"He's going to get up to-day."

"David's 'is name, so I 'ears,"—continued Mrs. Twitt; "I've never myself knowed anyone called David, but it's a common name in some parts, speshul in Scripter. Is 'e older than yer father would 'a bin if so be the Lord 'ad carried 'im upright to this present?"

"He seems a little older than father was when he died,"—answered Mary, in slow, thoughtful accents—"But perhaps it is only trouble and illness that makes him look so. He's very gentle and kind. Indeed,"—

here she paused for a second—then went on—"I don't know whether it's because I've been nursing him so long and have got accustomed to watch him and take care of him—but I've really grown quite fond of him!"

Mrs. Twitt gave a short laugh.

"That's nat'ral, seein' as ye're lone in life without 'usband or childer,"—she said—"There's a many wimmin as 'ud grow fond of an Aunt Sally on a pea-stick if they'd nothin' else to set their 'arts on. An' as the old chap was yer father's friend, there's bin a bit o' feelin' like in lookin' arter 'im. But I wouldn't take 'im on my back as a burgin, Mis' Deane, if I were you. Ye're far better off by yerself with the washin' an' lace-mendin' business."

Mary was silent.

"It's all very well,"—proceeded Mrs. Twitt—"for 'im to say 'e knew yer father, but arter all *that* mayn't be true. The Lord knows whether 'e aint a 'scaped convick, or a man as is grown 'oary-'edded with 'is own wickedness. An' though 'e's feeble now an' wants all ye can give 'im, the day may come when, bein' strong again, 'e'll take a knife an' slit yer throat. Bein' a tramp like, it 'ud come easy to 'im an' not to be blamed, if we may go by what they sez in the 'a'penny noospapers. I mind me well on the night o' the storm, the very night ye went out on the 'ills an' found 'im, I was settin' at my door down shorewards watchin' the waves an' hearin' the wind cryin' like a babe for its mother, an' if ye'll believe me, there was a sea-gull as came and flopped down on a stone just in front o' me!—a thing no sea-gull ever did to me all the time I've lived 'ere, which is thirty years since I married Twitt. There it sat, drenched wi' the rain, an' Twitt came out in that slow, silly way 'e 'as, an' 'e sez—'Poor bird!' 'Ungry, are ye? an' throws it a reg'lar full meal, which, if you believe me, it ate all up as cool as a cowcumber. An' then—"

"And then?" queried Mary, with a mirthful quiver in her voice.

"Then,—oh, well, then it flew away,"—and Mrs. Twitt seemed rather sorry for this commonplace end to what she imagined was a thrilling incident—"But the way that bird looked at me was somethin' awful! An' when I 'eerd as 'ow you'd found a friend o' yer father's a' trampin' an' wanderin' an' 'ad took 'im in to board an' lodge on trust, I sez to Twitt—'There you've got the meanin' o' that sea-gull! A stranger in the village bringin' no good to the 'and as feeds 'im!'"

Mary's laughter rang out now like a little peal of bells.

"Dear Mrs. Twitt!" she said—"I know how good and kind you are—

but you mustn't have any of your presentiments about me! I'm sure the poor sea-gull meant no harm! And I'm sure that poor old David won't ever hurt me—" Here she suddenly gave an exclamation—"Why, I forgot! The door of his room has been open all this time! He must have heard us talking!"

She made a hurried movement, and Helmsley diplomatically closed his eyes. She entered, and came softly up to his bedside, and he felt that she stood there looking at him intently. He could hardly forbear a smile;—but he managed to keep up a very creditable appearance of being fast asleep, and she stole away again, drawing the door to behind her. Thus, for the time being, he heard no more,—but he had gathered quite enough to know exactly how matters stood with regard to his presence in her little home.

"She has given out that I am an old friend of her father's!" he mused—"And she has done that in order to silence both inquiry and advice as to the propriety of her having taken me under her shelter and protection. Kind heart! Gentle soul! And—what else did she say? That she had 'really grown quite fond' of me! Can I—dare I—believe that? No!—it is a mere feminine phrase—spoken out of compassionate impulse. Fond of me! In my apparent condition of utter poverty,—old, ill and useless, who could or would be 'fond' of me!"

Yet he dwelt on the words with a kind of hope that nerved and invigorated him, and when at noon Mary came and assisted him to get up out of bed, he showed greater evidence of strength than she had imagined would be possible. True, his limbs ached sorely, and he was very feeble, for even with the aid of a stick and the careful support of her strong arm, his movements were tottering and uncertain, and the few steps between his bedroom and the kitchen seemed nearly a mile of exhausting distance. But the effort to walk did him good, and when he sank into the armchair which had been placed ready for him near the fire, he looked up with a smile and patted the gentle hand that had guided him along so surely and firmly.

"I'm an old bag of bones!" he said—"Not much good to myself or to any one else! You'd better bundle me out on the doorstep!"

For an answer she brought him a little cup of nourishing broth tastily prepared and bade him drink it—"every drop, mind!"—she told him with a little commanding nod. He obeyed her,—and when he gave her back the cup empty he said, with a keen glance:

"So I am your father's friend, am I, Mary?"

The blood rushed to her cheeks in a crimson tide,—she looked at him appealingly, and her lips trembled a little.

"You were so very ill!" she murmured—"I was afraid you might die,—and I had to send for the only doctor we have in the village—Mr. Bunce,—the boys call him Mr. Dunce, but that's their mischief, for he's really quite clever,—and I was bound to tell him something by way of introducing you and making him take care of you—even—even if what I said wasn't quite true! And—and—I made it out to myself this way—that if father had lived he would have done just all he could for you, and then you *would* have been his friend—you couldn't have helped yourself!"

He kept his eyes upon her as she spoke. He liked to see the soft flitting of the colour to-and-fro in her face,—her skin was so clear and transparent,—a physical reflection, he thought, of the clear transparency of her mind.

"And who was your father, Mary?" he asked, gently.

"He was a gardener and florist,"—she answered, and taking from the mantelshelf the photograph of the old man smiling serenely amid a collection of dwarf and standard roses, she showed it to him—"Here he is, just as he was taken after an exhibition where he won a prize. He was so proud when he heard that the first prize for a dwarf red rose had been awarded to James Deane of Barnstaple. My dear old dad! He was a good, good man—he was indeed! He loved the flowers—he used to say that they thought and dreamed and hoped, just as we do—and that they had their wishes and loves and ambitions just as we have. He had a very good business once in Barnstaple, and every one respected him, but somehow he could not keep up with the demands for new things—'social sensations in the way of flowers,' he used to call them, and he failed at last, through no fault of his own. We sold all we had to pay the creditors, and then we came away from Barnstaple into Somerset, and took this cottage. Father did a little business in the village, and for some of the big houses round about,—not much, of course—but I was always handy with my needle, and by degrees I got a number of customers for lace-mending and getting up ladies' fine lawn and muslin gowns. So between us we made quite enough to live on—till he died." Her voice sank—and she paused—then she added—"I've lived alone here ever since."

He listened attentively.

"And that is all your history, Mary? What of your mother?" he asked.

Mary's eyes softened and grew wistful.

"Mother died when I was ten,"—she said—"But though I was so little, I remember her well. She was pretty—oh, so very pretty! Her hair was quite gold like the sun,—and her eyes were blue—like the sea. Dad worshipped her, and he never would say that she was dead. He liked to think that she was always with him,—and I daresay she was. Indeed, I am sure she was, if true love can keep souls together."

He was silent.

"Are you tired, David?" she asked, with sudden anxiety,—"I'm afraid I'm talking too much!"

He raised a hand in protest.

"No—no! I—I love to hear you talk, Mary! You have been so good to me—so more than kind—that I'd like to know all about you. But I've no right to ask you any questions—you see I'm only an old, poor man, and I'm afraid I shall never be able to do much in the way of paying you back for all you've done for me. I used to be clever at office work—reading and writing and casting up accounts, but my sight is failing and my hands tremble,—so I'm no good in that line. But whatever I *can* do for you, as soon as I'm able, I will!—you may depend upon that!"

She leaned towards him, smiling.

"I'll teach you basket-making,"—she said—"Shall I?"

His eyes lit up with a humorous sparkle.

"If I could learn it, should I be useful to you?" he asked.

"Why, of course you would! Ever so useful! Useful to me and useful to yourself at the same time!" And she clapped her hands with pleasure at having thought of something easy upon which he could try his energies; "Basket-making pays well here,—the farmers want baskets for their fruit, and the fishermen want baskets for their fish,—and its really quite easy work. As soon as you're a bit stronger, you shall begin—and you'll be able to earn quite a nice little penny!"

He looked stedfastly into her radiant face.

"I'd like to earn enough to pay you back all the expense you've been put to with me,"—he said, and his voice trembled—"But your patience and goodness—that—I can never hope to pay for—that's heavenly!—that's beyond all money's worth—"

He broke off and put his hand over his eyes. Mary feigned not to notice his profound emotion, and, taking up a paper parcel on the table, opened it, and unrolled a long piece of wonderful old lace, yellow with age, and fine as a cobweb.

"Do you mind my going on with my work?" she asked, cheerily— "I'm mending this for a Queen!" And as he took away his hand from his eyes, which were suspiciously moist, and looked at her wonderingly, she nodded at him in the most emphatic way. "Yes, truly, David!—for a Queen! Oh, it's not a Queen who is my direct employer—no Queen ever knows anything about me! It's a great firm in London that sends this to me to mend for a Queen—they trust me with it, because they know me. I've had lace worth thousands of pounds in my hands,—this piece is valued at eight hundred, apart from its history—it belonged to Marie Louise, second wife of Napoleon the First. It's a lovely bit!—but there are some cruel holes in it. Ah, dear me!" And, sitting down near the door, she bent her head closely over the costly fabric—"Queens don't think of the eyes that have gone out in blindness doing this beautiful work!—or the hands that have tired and the hearts that have broken over it! They would never run pins into it if they did!"

He watched her sitting as she now was in the sunlight that flooded the doorway, and tried to overcome the emotional weakness that moved him to stretch out his arms to her as though she were his daughter, to call her to his side, and lay his hands on her head in blessing, and to beg her to let him stay with her now and always until the end of his days,— an end which he instinctively felt could not be very long in coming. But he realised enough of her character to know that were he to give himself away, and declare his real identity and position in the world of men, she would probably not allow him to remain in her cottage for another twenty-four hours. She would look at him with her candid eyes, and express her honest regret that he had deceived her, but he was certain that she would not accept a penny of payment at his hands for anything she had done for him,—her simple familiar manner and way of speech would change—and he should lose her—lose her altogether. And he was nervously afraid just now to think of what her loss might mean to him. He mastered his thoughts by an effort, and presently, forcing a smile, said:

"You were ironing lace this morning, instead of mending it, weren't you, Mary?"

She looked up quickly.

"No, I wasn't ironing lace—lace must never be ironed, David! It must all be pulled out carefully with the fingers, and the pattern must be pricked out on a frame or a cushion, with fine steel pins, just as if it were in the making. I was ironing a beautiful muslin gown for a lady who buys all her washing dresses in Paris. She couldn't get any one in England to wash them properly till she found me. She used to send them all away to a woman in Brittany before. The French are wonderful washers,—we're not a patch on them over here. So you saw me ironing?"

"I could just catch a glimpse of you at work through the door," he answered—"and I heard you talking as well—"

"To Mrs. Twitt? Ah, I thought you did!" And she laughed. "Well, I wish you could have seen her, as well as heard her! She is the quaintest old soul! She's the wife of a stonemason who lives at the bottom of the village, near the shore. Almost everything that happens in the day or the night is a sign of good or bad luck with her. I expect it's because her husband makes so many tombstones that she gets morbid,—but, oh dear!—if God managed the world according to Mrs. Twitt's notions, what a funny world it would be!"

She laughed again,—then shook her finger archly at him.

"You *pretended* to be asleep, then, when I came in to see if you heard us talking?"

He nodded a smiling assent.

"That was very wrong of you! You should never pretend to be what you are not!" He started nervously at this, and to cover his confusion called to the little dog, Charlie, who at once jumped up on his knees;—"You shouldn't, really! Should he, Charlie?" Charlie sat upright, and lolled a small red tongue out between two rows of tiny white teeth, by way of a laugh at the suggestion—"People—even dogs—are always found out when they do that!"

"What are those bright flowers out in your garden just beyond the door where you are sitting?" Helmsley asked, to change the conversation.

"Phloxes,"—she answered—"I've got all kinds and colours—crimson, white, mauve, pink, and magenta. Those which you can see from where you sit are the crimson ones—father's favourites. I wish you could get out and look at the Virginian creeper—it's lovely just now—quite a blaze of scarlet all over the cottage. And the Michaelmas daisies are coming on finely."

"Michaelmas!" he echoed—"How late in the year it is growing!"

"Ay, that's true!" she replied—"Michaelmas means that summer's past."

"And it was full summer when I started on my tramp to Cornwall!" he murmured.

"Never mind thinking about that just now," she said quickly—"You mustn't worry your head. Mr. Bunce says you mustn't on any account worry your head."

"Mr. Bunce!" he repeated wearily—"What does Mr. Bunce care?"

"Mr. Bunce *does* care," averred Mary, warmly—"Mr. Bunce is a very good little man, and he says you are a very gentle patient to deal with. He's done all he possibly could for you, and he knows you've got no money to pay him, and that I'm a poor woman, too—but he's been in to see you nearly every day—so you must really think well of Mr. Bunce."

"I do think well of him—I am most grateful to him," said David humbly—"But all the same it's *you*, Mary! You even got me the attention of Mr. Bunce!"

She smiled happily.

"You're feeling better, David!" she declared—"There's a nice bright sparkle in your eyes! I should think you were quite a cheerful old boy when you're well!"

This suggestion amused him, and he laughed.

"I have tried to be cheerful in my time,"—he said—"though I've not had much to be cheerful about."

"Oh, that doesn't matter!" she replied!—"Dad used to say that whatever little we had to be thankful for, we ought to make the most of it. It's easy to be glad when everything is gladness,—but when you've only got just a tiny bit of joy in a whole wilderness of trouble, then we can't be too grateful for that tiny bit of joy. At least, so I take it."

"Where did you learn your philosophy, Mary?" he asked, half whimsically—"I mean, who taught you to think?"

She paused in her lace-mending, needle in hand.

"Who taught me to think! Well, I don't know!—it come natural to me. But I'm not what is called 'educated' at all."

"Are you not?"

"No. I never learnt very much at school. I got the lessons into my head as long as I had to patter them off by heart like a parrot,—but the teachers were all so dull and prosy, and never took any real pains to explain things to me,—indeed, now when I come to think of it, I don't believe they *could* explain!—they needed teaching themselves. Anyhow, as soon as I came away I forgot everything but reading and writing and sums—and began to learn all over again with Dad. Dad made me read to him every night—all sorts of books."

"Had you a Free Library at Barnstaple?"

"I don't know—I never asked,"—she said—"Father hated 'lent' books. He had a savings-box—he used to call it his 'book-box'—and he would always drop in every spare penny he had for books till he'd got a few shillings, and then he would buy what he called 'classics.' They're all so cheap, you see. And by degrees we got Shakespeare and Carlyle, and Emerson and Scott and Dickens, and nearly all the poets; when you go into the parlour you'll see quite a nice bookcase there, full of books. It's much better to have them like that for one's own, than wait turns at a Free Library. I've read all Shakespeare at least twenty times over." The garden-gate suddenly clicked open and she turned her head. "Here's Mr. Bunce come to see you."

Helmsley drew himself up a little in his chair as the village doctor entered, and after exchanging a brief "Good-morning!" with Mary, approached him. The situation was curious;—here was he,—a multi-millionaire, who could have paid the greatest specialists in the world for their medical skill and attendance,—under the supervision and scrutiny of this simple herbalist, who, standing opposite to him, bent a pair of kindly brown eyes enquiringly upon his face.

"Up to-day, are we?" said Mr. Bunce—"That is well; that's very well! Better in ourselves, too, are we? Better in ourselves?"

"I am much better,"—replied Helmsley—"Very much better!—thanks to you and Miss Deane. You—you have both been very good to me."

"That's well—that's very well!" And Mr. Bunce appeared to ruminate, while Helmsley studied his face and figure with greater appreciation than he had yet been able to do. He had often seen this small dark man in the pauses of his feverish delirium,—often he had tried to answer his gentle questions,—often in the dim light of early morning or late evening he had sought to discern his features, and yet could make nothing clear as to their actual form, save that their expression was kind. Now, as it seemed for the first time, he saw Mr. Bunce as he was,—small and wiry, with a thin, clean-shaven face, deeply furrowed, broad brows, and a pleasant look,—the eyes especially, deep sunk in the head though they were, had a steady tenderness in them such as one sees in the eyes of a brave St. Bernard dog who has saved many lives.

"We must,"—said Mr. Bunce, after a long pause—"be careful. We have got out of bed, but we must not walk much. The heart is weak— we must avoid any strain upon it. We must sit quiet."

Mary was listening attentively, and nodded her agreement to this pronouncement.

"We must,"—proceeded Mr. Bunce, laboriously—"sit quiet. We may get up every day now,—a little earlier each time, remaining up a little later each time,—but we must sit quiet."

Again Mary nodded gravely. Helmsley looked quickly from one to the other. A close observer might have seen the glimmer of a smile through his fuzzy grey-white beard,—for his thoughts were very busy. He saw in Bunce another subject whose disinterested honesty might be worth dissecting.

"But, doctor—" he began.

Mr. Bunce raised a hand.

"I'm not 'doctor,' my man!" he said—"have no degree—no qualification—no diploma—no anything whatever but just a little, a very little common sense,—yes! And I am simply Bunce,"—and here a smile spread out all the furrows in his face and lit up his eyes; "Or, as the small boys call me, Dunce!"

"That's all very well, but you're a doctor to me," said Helmsley—"And you've been as much as any other doctor could possibly be, I'm sure. But you tell me I must sit quiet—I don't see how I can do that. I was on the tramp till I broke down,—and I must go on the tramp again,—I can't be a burden on—on—"

He broke off, unable to find words to express himself. But his inward eagerness to test the character and attributes of the two human beings who had for the present constituted themselves as his guardians, made him tremble violently. And Mr. Bunce looked at him with the scrutinising air of a connoisseur in the ailments of all and sundry.

"We are nervous,"—he pronounced—"We are highly nervous. And we are therefore not sure of ourselves. We must be entirely sure of ourselves, unless we again wish to lose ourselves. Now we presume that when 'on the tramp' as we put it, we were looking for a friend. Is that not so?"

Helmsley nodded.

"We were trying to find the house of the late Mr. James Deane?"

Mary uttered a little sound that was half a sob and half a sigh. Helmsley glanced at her with a reassuring smile, and then replied steadily,—

"That was so!"

"Our friend, Mr. Deane, unfortunately died some five years since,"—proceeded Mr. Bunce,—"And we found his daughter, or rather, his daughter found us, instead. This we may put down to an act of Providence.

Now the only thing we can do under the present circumstances is to remain with our late old friend's daughter, till we get well."

"But, doctor,"—exclaimed Helmsley, determined, if possible, to shake something selfish, commercial and commonplace out of this odd little man with the faithful canine eyes—"I can't be a burden on her! I've got no money—I can't pay you for all your care! What you do for me, you do for absolutely nothing—nothing—nothing! Don't you understand?"

His voice rang out with an almost rasping harshness, and Mr. Bunce tapped his own forehead gently, but significantly.

"We worry ourselves,"—he observed, placidly—"We imagine what does not exist. We think that Bunce is sending in his bill. We should wait till the bill comes, should we not, Miss Deane?" He smiled, and Mary gave a soft laugh of agreement—"And while we wait for Bunce's bill, we will also wait for Miss Deane's. And, in the meantime, we must sit quiet."

There was a moment's silence. Helmsley felt a smarting moisture at the back of his eyes. He longed to pour out all his history to these two simple unworldly souls,—to tell them that he was rich,—rich beyond the furthest dreams of their imagining,—rich enough to weigh down the light-hearted contentment of their lives with a burden of gold,— and yet—yet he knew that if he spoke thus and confessed himself, all the sweetness of the friendship which was now so disinterested would be embittered and lost. He thought, with a latent self-contempt and remorse, of certain moods in which he had sometimes indulged,— moods in which he had cynically presumed that he could buy everything in the world for money. Kings, thrones, governments, might be had for money, he knew, for he had often purchased their good-will—but Love was a jewel he had never found in any market—unpurchasable as God! And while he yet inwardly mused on his position, Bunce bent over him, and taking his thin wrinkled hand, patted it gently.

"Good-bye for the present, David!" he said, kindly—"We are on the mend—we are certainly on the mend! We hope the ways of nature will be remedial—and that we shall pick up our strength before the winter fairly sets in—yes, we hope—we certainly may hope for that—"

"Mr. Bunce," said Helmsley, with sudden energy—"God bless you!"

XIV

The time now went on peacefully, one day very much like another, and Helmsley steadily improved in health and strength, so far recovering some of his old vigour and alertness as to be able to take a slow and halting daily walk through the village, which, for present purposes shall be called Weircombe. The more he saw of the place, the more he loved it, and the more he was enchanted with its picturesque position. In itself it was a mere cluster of little houses, dotted about on either side of a great cleft in the rocks through which a clear mountain stream tumbled to the sea,—but the houses were covered from basement to roof with clambering plants and flowers, especially the wild fuschia, which, with one or two later kinds of clematis and "morning glory" convolvolus, were still in brilliant bloom when the mellow days of October began to close in to the month's end. All the cottages in the "coombe" were pretty, but to Helmsley's mind Mary Deane's was the prettiest, perched as it was on a height overlooking the whole village and near to the tiny church, which crowned the hill with a little tower rising heavenward. The view of the ocean from Weircombe was very wide and grand,—on sunny days it was like an endless plain of quivering turquoise-blue, with white foam-roses climbing up here and there to fall and vanish again,—and when the wind was high, it was like an onward sweeping array of Titanic shapes clothed in silver armour and crested with snowy plumes, all rushing in a wild charge against the shore, with such a clatter and roar as often echoed for miles inland. To make his way gradually down through the one little roughly cobbled street to the very edge of the sea, was one of Helmsley's greatest pleasures, and he soon got to know most of the Weircombe folk, while they in their turn, grew accustomed to seeing him about among them, and treated him with a kindly familiarity, almost as if he were one of themselves. And his new lease of life was, to himself, singularly happy. He enjoyed every moment of it,—every little incident was a novel experience, and he was never tired of studying the different characters he met,—especially and above all the character of the woman whose house was, for the time being, his home, and who treated with him all the care and solicitude that a daughter might show to her father. And—he was learning what might be called a trade or a craft,—which fact interested and amused him. He who had moved the great wheel of many trades at a mere touch of his finger, was now docilely studying the art of basket-making, and training his unaccustomed hands to the bending of withes and osiers,—he whose deftly-laid financial schemes had held the money-markets of the world in suspense, was now patiently mastering the technical business of forming a "slath," and fathoming the mysteries of "scalluming." Like an obedient child at school he implicitly followed the instructions of his teacher, Mary, who with the first basket he completed went out and effected a sale as she said "for fourpence," though really for twopence.

"And good pay, too!" she said, cheerfully—"It's not often one gets so much for a first make."

"That fourpence is yours," said Helmsley, smiling at her—"You've the right to all my earnings!"

She looked serious.

"Would you like me to keep it?" she asked—"I mean, would it please you if I did,—would you feel more content?"

"I should—you know I should!" he replied earnestly.

"All right, then! I'll check it off your account!" And laughing merrily, she patted his head as he sat bending over another specimen of his basket manufacture—"At any rate, you're not getting bald over your work, David! I never saw such beautiful white hair as yours!"

He glanced up at her.

"May I say, in answer to that, that I never saw such beautiful brown hair as yours?"

She nodded.

"Oh, yes, you may say it, because I know it's true. My hair is my one beauty,—see!"

And pulling out two small curved combs, she let the whole wealth of her tresses unwind and fall. Her hair dropped below her knees in a glorious mass of colour like that of a brown autumn leaf with the sun just glistening on it. She caught it up in one hand and knotted it all again at the back of her head in a minute.

"It's lovely, isn't it?"—she said, quite simply—"I should think it lovely if I saw it on anybody else's head, or cut off hanging in a hair-dresser's shop window. I don't admire it because it's mine, you know! I admire it as hair merely."

"Hair merely—yes, I see!" And he bent and twisted the osiers in his hands with a sudden vigour that almost snapped them. He was thinking of certain women he had known in London—women whose tresses, dyed, waved, crimped and rolled over fantastically shaped "frames," had moved him to positive repulsion,—so much so that he would rather have touched the skin of a dead rat than laid a finger on the tinted stuff called "hair" by these feminine hypocrites of fashion. He had so long been accustomed to shams that the open sincerity of the Weircombe villagers was almost confusing to his mind. Nobody seemed to have anything to conceal. Everybody knew, or seemed to know, all about everybody else's business. There were no bye-roads or corners in Weircombe. There was only one way out,—to the sea. Height at the one end,—width and depth at the other. It seemed useless to have any secrets. He, David Helmsley, felt himself to be singular and apart, in that he had his own hidden mystery. He often found himself getting restless under the quiet observation of Mr. Bunce's eye, yet Mr. Bunce had no suspicions of him whatever. Mr. Bunce merely watched him "professionally," and with the kindest intention. In fact, he and Bunce became great friends. Bunce had entirely accepted the story he told about himself to the effect that he had once been "in an office in the city," and looked upon him as a superannuated bank clerk, too old to be kept on in his former line of business. Questions that were put to him respecting his "late friend, James Deane," he answered with apparent good faith by saying that it was a long time since he had seen him, and that it was only as a "last forlorn hope" that he had set out to try and find him, "as he had always been helpful to those in need." Mary herself wished that this little fiction of her "father's friend" should be taken as fact by all the village, and a curious part of her character was that she never sought to ask Helmsley privately, for her own enlightenment, anything of his history. She seemed content to accept him as an old and infirm man, who must be taken care of simply because he was old and infirm, without further question or argument. Bunce was always very stedfast in his praise of her.

"She ought—yes—she ought possibly to have married,—" he said, in his slow, reflective way—"She would have made a good wife, and a still better mother. But an all-wise Providence has a remarkable habit—yes, I think we may call it quite a remarkable habit!—of persuading men generally to choose thriftless and flighty women for their wives, and to leave the capable ones single. That is so. Or in Miss Deane's case it may be an illustration of the statement that 'Mary hath chosen the better part.' Certainly when either men or women are happy in a state of single blessedness, a reference to the Seventh Chapter of the

Epistle of St. Paul to the Corinthians, will strengthen their minds and considerably assist them to remain in that condition."

Thus Bunce would express himself, with a weighty air as of having given some vastly important and legal pronouncement. And when Helmsley suggested that it was possible Mary might yet marry, he shook his head in a strongly expressed negative.

"No, David—no!" he said—"She is what we call—yes, I think we call it—an old maid. This is not a kind term, perhaps, but it is a true one. She is, I believe, in her thirty-fifth year,—a settled and mature woman. No man would take her unless she had a little money—enough, let us say, to help him set up a farm. For if a man takes youth to his bosom, he does not always mind poverty,—but if he cannot have youth he always wants money. Always! There is no middle course. Now our good Miss Deane will never have any money. And, even if she had, we may take it—yes, I certainly *think* we may take it—that she would not care to *buy* a husband. No—no! Her marrying days are past."

"She is a beautiful woman!" said Helmsley, quietly.

"You think so? Well, well, David! We have got used to her in Weircombe,—she seems to be a part of the village. When one is familiar with a person, one often fails to perceive the beauty that is apparent to a stranger. I believe this to be so—I believe, in general, we may take it to be so."

And such was the impression that most of the Weircombe folks had about Mary—that she was just "a part of the village." During his slow ramblings about the little sequestered place, Helmsley talked to many of the cottagers, who all treated him with that good-humour and tolerance which they considered due to his age and feebleness. Young men gave him a ready hand if they saw him inclined to falter or to stumble over rough places in the stony street,—little children ran up to him with the flowers they had gathered on the hills, or the shells they had collected from the drift on the shore—women smiled at him from their open doors and windows—girls called to him the "Good morning!" or "Good-night!"—and by and by he was almost affectionately known as "Old David, who makes baskets up at Miss Deane's." One of his favourite haunts was the very end of the "coombe," which,—sharply cutting down to the shore,—seemed there to have split asunder with volcanic force, hurling itself apart to right and left in two great castellated rocks, which were piled up, fortress-like, to an altitude of about four hundred or more feet, and looked sheer down over the sea. When the tide was high the waves rushed swirlingly round the base of these natural towers, forming a deep blackish-purple pool in which the wash to and fro of pale rose and deep magenta seaweed, flecked with trails of pale grassy green, were like the colours of a stormy sunset reflected in a prism. The sounds made here by the inflowing and outgoing of the waves were curiously musical,—like the thudding of a great organ, with harp melodies floating above the stronger bass, while every now and then a sweet sonorous call, like that of a silver trumpet, swung from the cavernous depths into clear space and echoed high up in the air, dying lingeringly away across the hills. Near this split of the "coombe" stood the very last house at the bottom of the village, built of white stone and neatly thatched, with a garden running to the edge of the mountain stream, which at this point rattled its way down to the sea with that usual tendency to haste exhibited by everything in life and nature when coming to an end. A small square board nailed above the door bore the inscription legibly painted in plain black letters:—

ABEL TWITT,
Stone Mason,
N. B. Good Grave-Work Guaranteed.

The author of this device, and the owner of the dwelling, was a round, rosy-faced little man, with shrewd sparkling grey eyes, a pleasant smile, and a very sociable manner. He was the great "gossip" of the place; no old woman at a wash-tub or behind a tea-tray ever wagged her tongue more persistently over the concerns of he and she and you and they, than Abel Twitt. He had a leisurely way of talking,—a "slow and silly way" his wife called it,—but he managed to convey a good deal of information concerning everybody and everything, whether right or wrong, in a very few sentences. He was renowned in the village for his wonderful ability in the composition of epitaphs, and by some of his friends he was called "Weircombe's Pote Lorit." One of his most celebrated couplets was the following:—

"This Life while I lived it, was Painful and seldom Victorious,
I trust in the Lord that the next will be Pleasant and Glorious!"

Everybody said that no one but Abel Twitt could have thought of such grand words and good rhymes. Abel himself was not altogether without a certain gentle consciousness that in this particular effort he had done well. But he had no literary vanity.

"It comes nat'ral to me,"—he modestly declared—"It's a God's gift which I takes thankful without pride."

Helmsley had become very intimate with both Mr. and Mrs. Twitt. In his every-day ramble down to the ocean end of the "coombe" he often took a rest of ten minutes or a quarter of an hour at Twitt's house before climbing up the stony street again to Mary Deane's cottage, and Mrs. Twitt, in her turn, was a constant caller on Mary, to whom she brought all the news of the village, all the latest remedies for every sort of ailment, and all the oddest superstitions and omens which she could either remember or invent concerning every incident that had occurred to her or to her neighbours within the last twenty-four hours. There was no real morbidity of character in Mrs. Twitt; she only had that peculiar turn of mind which is found quite as frequently in the educated as in the ignorant, and which perceives a divine or a devilish meaning in almost every trifling occurrence of daily life. A pin on the ground which was not picked up at the very instant it was perceived, meant terrible ill-luck to Mrs. Twitt,—if a cat sneezed, it was a sign that there was going to be sickness in the village,—and she always carried in her pocket "a bit of coffin" to keep away the cramp. She also had a limitless faith in the power of cursing, and she believed most implicitly in the fiendish abilities of a certain person, (whether male or female, she did not explain) whose address she gave vaguely as, "out on the hills," and who, if requested, and paid for the trouble, would put a stick into the ground, muttering a mysterious malison on any man or woman you chose to name as an enemy, with the pronounced guarantee:—

"As this stick rotteth to decay,
So shall (Mr. Miss or Mrs. So-and-so) rot away!"

But with the exception of these little weaknesses, Mrs. Twitt was a good sort of motherly old body, warm-hearted and cheerful, too, despite her belief in omens. She had taken quite a liking to "old David" as she called him, and used to watch his thin frail figure, now since his illness sadly bent, jogging slowly down the street towards the sea, with much kindly solicitude. For despite Mr. Bunce's recommendation that he should "sit quiet," Helmsley could not bring himself to the passively restful condition of weak and resigned old age. He had too much on his mind for that. He worked patiently every morning at basket-making, in which he was quickly becoming an adept; but in the afternoon he grew restless, and Mary, seeing it was better for him to walk as long as walking was possible to him, let him go out when he fancied it, though always with a little anxiety for him lest he should meet with some accident. In this anxiety, however, all the neighbours took a share, so that he was well watched, and more carefully guarded than he knew, on his way down to the shore and back again, Abel Twitt himself often giving him an arm on the upward climb home.

"You'll have to do some of that for me soon!" said Helmsley on one of these occasions, pointing up with his stick at the board over Twitt's door, which said "Good Grave-Work Guaranteed:"

Twitt rolled his eyes slowly up in the direction indicated, smiled, and rolled them down again.

"So I will,—so I will!" he replied cheerfully—"An I'll charge ye nothin' either. I'll make ye as pretty a little stone as iver ye saw—what'll last too!—ay, last till th' Almighty comes a' tearin' down in clouds o' glory. A stone well bedded in, ye unnerstan'?—one as'll stay upright—no slop work. An' if ye can't think of a hepitaph for yerself I'll write one for ye—there now! Bible texes is goin' out o' fashion—it's best to 'ave somethin' orig'nal—an' for originality I don't think I can be beat in these parts. I'll do ye yer hepitaph with pleasure!"

"That will be kind!" And Helmsley smiled a little sadly—"What will you say of me when I'm gone?"

Twitt looked at him thoughtfully, with his head very much on one side.

"Well, ye see, I don't know yer history,"—he said—"But I considers ye 'armless an' unfortunate. I'd 'ave to make it out in my own mind like. Now Timbs, the grocer an' 'aberdashery man, when 'is wife died, he wouldn't let me 'ave my own way about the moniment at all. 'Put 'er down,' sez 'e—'Put 'er down as the Dearly-Beloved Wife of Samuel Timbs.' 'Now, Timbs,' sez I—'don't ye go foolin' with 'ell-fire! Ye know she wor'nt yer Dearly Beloved, forbye that she used to throw wet dish-clouts at yer 'ed, screechin' at ye for all she was wuth, an' there ain't no Dearly Beloved in that. Why do ye want to put a lie on a stone for the Lord to read?' But 'e was as obst'nate as pigs. 'Dish-clouts or no dish-clouts,' sez 'e, 'I'll 'ave 'er fixed up proper as my Dearly-Beloved Wife for sight o' parson an' neighbours.' 'Ah, Sam!' sez I—'I've got ye! It's for parson an' neighbours ye want the hepitaph, an' not for the Lord at all!

Well, I'll do it if so be yer wish it, but I won't take the 'sponsibility of it at the Day o' Judgment.' 'I don't want ye to'—sez 'e, quite peart. 'I'll take it myself.' An' if ye'll believe me, David, 'e sits down an' writes me what 'e calls a 'Memo' of what 'e wants put on the grave stone, an' it's the biggest whopper I've iver seen out o' the noospapers. I've got it 'ere—" And, referring to a much worn and battered old leather pocket-book, Twitt drew from it a soiled piece of paper, and read as follows—

Here lies
All that is Mortal
of
CATHERINE TIMBS
The Dearly Beloved Wife
of
Samuel Timbs of Weircombe.
She Died
At the Early Age of Forty-Nine
Full of Virtues and Excellencies
Which those who knew Her
Deeply Deplore
and
Now is in Heaven.

"And the only true thing about that hepitaph,"—continued Twitt, folding up the paper again and returning it to its former receptacle,— "is the words 'Here Lies.'"

Helmsley laughed, and Twitt laughed with him.

"Some folks 'as the curiousest ways o' wantin' theirselves remembered arter they're gone"—he went on—"An' others seems as if they don't care for no mem'ry at all 'cept in the 'arts o' their friends. Now there was Tom o' the Gleam, a kind o' gypsy rover in these parts, 'im as murdered a lord down at Blue Anchor this very year's July—"

Helmsley drew a quick breath.

"I know!" he said—"I was there!"

"So I've 'eerd say,"—responded Twitt sympathetically—"An' an awsome sight it must a' bin for ye! Mary Deane told us as 'ow ye'd bin ravin' about Tom—an' m'appen likely it give ye a turn towards yer long sickness."

"I was there,"—said Helmsley, shuddering at the recollection—"I had stopped on the road to try and get a cheap night's lodging at the very inn where the murder took place—but—but there were two murders that day, and the *first* one was the worst!"

"That's what I said at the time, an' that's what I've allus thought!"—declared Twitt—"Why that little 'Kiddie' child o' Tom's was the playfullest, prettiest little rogue ye'd see in a hundred mile or more! 'Oldin' out a posy o' flowers to a motor-car, poor little innercent! It might as well 'ave 'eld out flowers to the devil!—though my own opinion is as the devil 'imself wouldn't 'a ridden down a child. But a motorin' lord o' these days is neither man nor beast nor devil,—'e's a somethin' altogether *on*human—*on*human out an' out,—a thing wi' goggles over his eyes an' no 'art in his body, which we aint iver seen in this poor old world afore. Thanks be to the Lord no motors can ever come into Weircombe,—they tears round an' round by another road, an' we neither sees, 'ears, nor smells 'em, for which I often sez to my wife—'O be joyful in the Lord all ye lands; serve the Lord with gladness an' come before His presence with a song!' An' she ups an' sez—'Don't be blaspheemous, Twitt,—I'll tell parson'—an' I sez—'Tell 'im, old 'ooman, if ye likes!' An' when she tells 'im, 'e smiles nice an' kind, an' sez—'It's quite lawful, Mrs. Twitt, to quote Scriptural thanksgiving on all *necessary* occasions!' E's a good little chap, our parson, but 'e's that weak on his chest an' ailing that 'e's goin' away this year to Madeira for rest and warm—an' a blessid old Timp'rance raskill's coming to take dooty in 'is place. Ah!—none of us Weircombe folk 'ill be very reg'lar church-goers while Mr. Arbroath's here."

Helmsley started slightly.

"Arbroath? I've seen that man."

"'Ave ye? Well, ye 'aven't seen no beauty!" And Twitt gave vent to a chuckling laugh—"'E'll be startin' is 'Igh Jink purcessions an' vestiments in our plain little church up yonder, an' by the Lord, 'e'll 'ave to purcess an' vestiment by 'isself, for Weircombe wont 'elp 'im. We aint none of us 'Igh Jink folks."

"Is that your name for High Church?" asked Helmsley, amused.

"It is so, an' a very good name it be," declared Twitt, stoutly—"For if all the bobbins' an' scrapins' an' crosses an' banners aint a sort o' jinkin' Lord Mayor's show, then what be they? It's fair oaffish to bob to the east as them 'Igh Jinkers does, for we aint never told in the Gospels that th' Almighty 'olds that partikler quarter o' the wind as a place o' residence. The Lord's everywhere,—east, west, north, south,—why he's with us at this very minute!"—and Twitt raised his eyes piously to the heavens—

"He's 'elpin' you an' me to draw the breath through our lungs—for if He didn't 'elp, we couldn't do it, that's certain. An' if He makes the sun to rise in the east, He makes it to sink in the west, an' there's no choice either way, an' we sez our prayers simple both times o' day, not to the sun at all, but to the Maker o' the sun, an' of everything else as we sees. No, no!—no 'Igh Jinks for me!—I don't want to bow to no East when I sees the Lord's no more east than He's west, an' no more in either place than He is here, close to me an' doin' more for me than I could iver do for myself. 'Igh Jinks is unchristin,—as unchristin as cremation, an' nothin's more unchristin than that!"

"Why, what makes you think so?" asked Helmsley, surprised.

"What makes me think so?" And Twitt drew himself up with a kind of reproachful dignity—"Now, old David, don't go for to say as *you* don't think so too?"

"Cremation unchristian? Well, I can't say I've ever thought of it in that light,—it's supposed to be the cleanest way of getting rid of the dead—"

"Gettin' rid of the dead!"—echoed Twitt, almost scornfully—"That's what ye can never do! They'se everywhere, all about us, if we only had strong eyes enough to see 'em. An' cremation aint Christin. I'll tell ye for why,"—here he bent forward and tapped his two middle fingers slowly on Helmsley's chest to give weight to his words—"Look y'ere! Supposin' our Lord's body 'ad been cremated, where would us all a' bin? Where would a' bin our 'sure an' certain 'ope' o' the resurrection?"

Helmsley was quite taken aback by this sudden proposition, which presented cremation in an entirely new light. But a moment's thought restored to him his old love of argument, and he at once replied:—

"Why, it would have been just the same as it is now, surely! If Christ was divine, he could have risen from burnt ashes as well as from a tomb."

"Out of a hurn?" demanded Twitt, persistently—"If our Lord's body 'ad bin burnt an' put in a hurn, an' the hurn 'ad bin took into the 'ouse o' Pontis Pilate, an' sealed, an' *kept till now*? Eh? What d'ye say to that? I tell ye, David, there wouldn't a bin no savin' grace o' Christ'anity at all! An' that's why I sez cremation is unchristin,—it's blaspheemous an' 'eethen. For our Lord plainly said to 'is disciples arter he came out o' the tomb—'Behold my hands and my feet,—handle me and see,'—an' to the doubtin' Thomas He said—'Reach hither thy hand and thrust it into my side, and be not faithless but believing.' David, you mark my words!—them as 'as their bodies burnt in crematorums is just as dirty in their souls as they can be, an' they 'opes to burn all the blackness o' theirselves into nothingness an' never to rise no more, 'cos they'se afraid! They don't want to be laid in good old mother earth, which is the warm forcin' place o' the Lord for raisin' up 'uman souls as He raises up the blossoms in spring, an' all other things which do give Him grateful praise an' thanksgivin'! They gits theirselves burnt to ashes 'cos they don't *want* to be raised up,—they'se never praised the Lord 'ere, an' they wouldn't know 'ow to do it *there*! But, mercy me!" concluded Twitt ruminatingly,—"I've seen orful queer things bred out of ashes!—beetles an' sich like reptiles,—an' I wouldn't much care to see the spechul stock as raises itself from the burnt bits of a liar!"

Helmsley hardly knew whether to smile or to look serious,—such quaint propositions as this old stonemason put forward on the subject of cremation were utterly novel to his experience. And while he yet stood under the little porch of Twitt's cottage, there came shivering up through the quiet autumnal air a slow thud of breaking waves.

"Tide's comin' in,"—said Twitt, after listening a minute or two—"An' that minds me o' what I was goin' to tell ye about Tom o' the Gleam. After the inkwist, the gypsies came forward an' claimed the bodies o' Tom an' 'is Kiddie,—an' they was buried accordin' to Tom's own wish, which it seems 'e'd told one of 'is gypsy pals to see as was carried out whenever an' wheresoever 'e died. An' what sort of a buryin' d'ye think 'e 'ad?"

Helmsley shook his head in an expressed inability to imagine.

"'Twas out there,"—and Twitt pointed with one hand to the shining expanse of the ocean—"The gypsies put 'im an' is Kiddie in a basket coffin which they made theirselves, an' covered it all over wi' garlands o' flowers an' green boughs, an' then fastened four great lumps o' lead to the four corners, an' rowed it out in a boat to about four or five miles from the shore, right near to the place where the moon at full 'makes a hole in the middle o' the sea,' as the children sez, and there they dropped it into the water. Then they sang a funeral song—an' by the Lord!—the sound o' that song crept into yer veins an' made yer blood run cold!—'twas enough to break a man's 'art, let alone a woman's, to 'ear them gypsy voices all in a chorus wailin' a farewell to the man an' the child in the sea,—an' the song floated up an' about, 'ere an' there an' everywhere, all over the land from Cleeve Abbey onnards, an' at Blue Anchor, so they sez, it was so awsome an' eerie that the people got out o' their beds, shiverin', an' opened their windows to listen, an' when they listened they all fell a cryin' like children. An' it's no wonder the inn where poor Tom did his bad deed and died his bad death, is shut up for good, an' the people as kept it gone away—no one couldn't stay there arter that. Ay, ay!" and Twitt sighed profoundly—"Poor wild ne'er-do-weel Tom! He lies deep down enough now with the waves flowin' over 'im an' 'is little 'Kiddie' clasped tight in 'is arms. For they never separated 'em,—death 'ad locked 'em up too fast together for that. An' they're sleepin' peaceful,—an' there they'll sleep till—till 'the sea gives up its dead.'"

Helmsley could not speak,—he was too deeply moved. The sound of the in-coming tide grew fuller and more sonorous, and Twitt presently turned to look critically at the heaving waters.

"There's a cry in the sea to-day,"—he said,—"M'appen it'll be rough to-night."

They were silent again, till presently Helmsley roused himself from the brief melancholy abstraction into which he had been plunged by the story of Tom o' the Gleam's funeral.

"I think I'll go down on the shore for a bit,"—he said; "I like to get as close to the waves as I can when they're rolling in."

"Well, don't get too close,"—said Twitt, kindly—"We'll be havin' ye washed away if ye don't take care! There's onny an hour to tea-time, an' Mary Deane's a punctooal 'ooman!"

"I shall not keep her waiting—never fear!" and Helmsley smiled as he said good-day, and jogged slowly along his favourite accustomed path to the beach. The way though rough, was not very steep, and it was becoming quite easy and familiar to him. He soon found himself on the firm brown sand sprinkled with a fringe of seaweed and shells, and further adorned in various places with great rough boulders, picturesquely set up on end, like the naturally hewn memorials of great heroes passed away. Here, the ground being level, he could walk more quickly and with greater comfort than in the one little precipitous street of Weircombe, and he paced up and down, looking at the rising and falling hollows of the sea with wistful eyes that in their growing age and dimness had an intensely pathetic expression,—the expression one sometimes sees in the eyes of a dog who knows that its master is leaving it for an indefinite period.

"What a strange chaos of brain must be that of the suicide!" he thought—"Who, that can breathe the fresh air and watch the lights and shadows in the sky and on the waves, would really wish to leave the world, unless the mind had completely lost its balance! We have never seen anything more beautiful than this planet upon which we are born,—though there is a sub-consciousness in us which prophesies of yet greater beauty awaiting higher vision. The subconscious self! That is the scientist's new name for the Soul,—but the Soul is a better term. Now my subconscious self—my Soul,—is lamenting the fact that it must leave life when it has just begun to learn how to live! I should like to be here and see what Mary will do when—when I am gone! Yet how do I know but that in very truth I shall be here?—or in some way be made aware of her actions? She has a character such as I never thought to find in any mortal woman,—strong, pure, tender,—and sincere!—ah, that sincerity of hers is like the very sunlight!—so bright and warm, and clean of all ulterior motive! And measured by a worldly estimate only—what is she? The daughter of a humble florist,—herself a mere mender of lace, and laundress of fine ladies' linen! And her sweet and honest eyes have never looked upon that rag-fair of nonsense we call 'society';—she never thinks of riches;—and yet she has refined and artistic taste enough to love the lace she mends, just for pure admiration of its beauty,—not because she herself desires to wear it, but because it represents the work and lives of others, and because it is in itself a miracle of design. I wonder if she ever notices how closely I watch her! I could draw from memory the shapely outline of her hand,—a white, smooth, well-kept hand, never allowed to remain soiled by all her various forms of domestic labour,—an expressive hand, indicating health and sanity, with that deep curve at the wrist, and the delicately shaped fingers which hold the needle so lightly and guide it so deftly through the intricacies of the riven lace, weaving a web of such fairy-like stitches that the original texture seems never to have been broken. I have sat quiet for an hour or more studying her when she has thought me asleep in my chair by the fire,—and I have fancied that my life is something like the damaged fabric she is so carefully repairing,—holes and rents everywhere,—all the symmetry of design dropping to pieces,—the little garlands of roses and laurels snapped asunder,—and she, with her beautiful white hands is gently drawing the threads together and mending it,—for what purpose?—to what end?"

And here the involuntary action of some little brain-cell gave him the memory of certain lines in Browning's "Rabbi Ben Ezra":—

> "Therefore I summon age
> To grant youth's heritage

Life's struggle having so far reached its term;
Thence shall I pass, approved
A man, for aye removed
From the developed brute; a god, though in the germ.
And I shall thereupon
Take rest ere I be gone
Once more on my adventures brave and new—
Fearless—and unperplexed
When I wage battle next,
What weapons to select, what armour to indue!"

HE TURNED HIS EYES AGAIN to the sea just as a lovely light, pale golden and clear as topaz, opened suddenly in the sky, shedding a shower of luminant reflections on the waves. He drew a deep breath, and unconsciously straightened himself.

"When death comes it shall find me ready!" he said, half aloud;— and then stood, confronting the ethereal glory. The waves rolled in slowly and majestically one after the other, and broke at his feet in long wreaths of creamy foam,—and presently one or two light gusts of a rather chill wind warned him that he had best be returning homeward. While he yet hesitated, a leaf of paper blew towards him, and danced about like a large erratic butterfly, finally dropping just where the stick on which he leaned made a hole in the sand. He stooped and picked it up. It was covered with fine small handwriting, and before he could make any attempt to read it, a man sprang up from behind one of the rocky boulders close by, and hurried forward, raising his cap as he came.

"That's mine!" he said, quickly, with a pleasant smile—"It's a loose page from my notebook. Thank-you so much for saving it!"

Helmsley gave him the paper at once, with a courteous inclination of the head.

"I've been scribbling down here all day,"—proceeded the new comer—"And there's not been much wind till now. But"—and he glanced up and about him critically; "I think we shall have a puff of sou'wester to-night."

Helmsley looked at him with interest. He was a man of distinctive appearance,—tall, well-knit, and muscular, with a fine intellectual face and keen clear grey eyes. Not a very young man;—he seemed about thirty-eight or forty, perhaps more, for his dark hair was fairly sprinkled with silver. But his manner was irresistibly bright and genial, and it was impossible to meet his frank, open, almost boyish gaze, without a desire to know more of him, and an inclination to like him.

"Do you make the seashore your study?" asked Helmsley, with a slight gesture towards the notebook into which the stranger was now carefully putting the strayed leaflet.

"Pretty much so!" and he laughed—"I've only got one room to live in—and it has to serve for both sleeping and eating—so I come out here to breathe and expand a bit." He paused, and then added gently—"May I give you my arm up to Miss Deane's cottage?"

"Why, how do you know I live there?" and Helmsley smiled as he put the question.

"Oh, well, all the village knows that!—and though I'm quite new to the village—I've only been here a week—I know it too. You're old David, the basket-maker, aren't you?"

"Yes." And Helmsley nodded emphatically—"That's me!"

"Then I know all about you! My name's Angus Reay. I'm a Scotchman,—I am, or rather, I *was* a journalist, and as poor as Job! That's *me*! Come along!"

The cheery magnetism of his voice and look attracted Helmsley, and almost before he knew it he was leaning on this new friend's arm, chatting with him concerning the village, the scenery, and the weather, in the easiest way possible.

"I came on here from Minehead,"—said Reay—"That was too expensive a place for me!" And a bright smile flashed from lips to eyes with an irresistible sunny effect; "I've got just twenty pounds in the world, and I must make it last me a year. For room, food, fuel, clothes, drink and smoke! I've promptly cut off the last two!"

"And you're none the worse for it, I daresay!" rejoined Helmsley.

"Not a bit! A good deal the better. In Fleet Street the men drank and smoked pretty heavily, and I had to drink and smoke with them, if I wanted to keep in with the lot. I did want to keep in with them, and yet I didn't. It was a case of 'needs must when the devil drives!'"

"You say you were a journalist. Aren't you one now?"

"No. I'm 'kicked off'!" And Reay threw back his head and laughed joyously. "'Off you go!' said my editor, one fine morning, after I had slaved away for him for nearly two years—'We don't want any canting truth-tellers here!' Now mind that stone! You nearly slipped. Hold my arm tighter!"

Helmsley did as he was told, quite meekly, looking up with a good deal of curiosity at this tall athletic creature, with the handsome head and masterful manner. Reay caught his enquiring glance and laughed again.

"You look as if you wanted to know more about me, old David!" he said gaily—"So you shall! I've nothing to conceal! As I tell you I was 'kicked off' out of journalism—my fault being that I published a leaderette exposing a mean 'deal' on the part of a certain city plutocrat. I didn't know the rascal had shares in the paper. But he *had*—under an 'alias.' And he made the devil's own row about it with the editor, who nearly died of it, being inclined to apoplexy—and between the two of them I was 'dropped.' Then the word ran along the press wires that I was an 'unsafe' man. I could not get any post worth having—I had saved just twenty pounds—so I took it all and walked away from London— literally *walked* away! I haven't spent a penny in other locomotion than my own legs since I left Fleet Street."

Helmsley listened with eager interest. Here was a man who had done the very thing which he himself had started to do;—"tramped" the road. But—with what a difference! Full manhood, physical strength, and activity on the one side,—decaying power, feebleness of limb and weariness on the other. They had entered the village street by this time, and were slowly walking up it together.

"You see,"—went on Reay,—"of course I could have taken the train— but twenty pounds is only twenty pounds—and it must last me twelve solid months. By that time I shall have finished my work."

"And what's that?" asked Helmsley.

"It's a book. A novel. And"—here he set his teeth hard—"I intend that it shall make me—famous!"

"The intention is good,"—said Helmsley, slowly—"But—there are so many novels!"

"No, there are not!" declared Reay, decisively—"There are plenty of rag-books *called* novels—but they are not real 'novels.' There's nothing 'new' in them. There's no touch of real, suffering, palpitating humanity in them! The humanity of to-day is infinitely more complex than it was in the days of Scott or Dickens, but there's no Scott or Dickens to epitomise its character or delineate its temperament. I want to be the twentieth century Scott and Dickens rolled into one stupendous literary Titan!"

His mellow laughter was hearty and robust. Helmsley caught its infection and laughed too.

"But why,"—he asked—"do you want to write a novel? Why not write a real *book*?"

"What do you call a real book, old David?" demanded Reay, looking down upon him with a sudden piercing glance.

Helmsley was for a moment confused. He was thinking of such books as Carlyle's "Past and Present"—Emerson's "Essays" and the works of Ruskin. But he remembered in good time that for an old "basket-maker" to be familiar with such literary masterpieces might seem strange to a wide-awake "journalist," therefore he checked himself in time.

"Oh, I don't know! I believe I was thinking of 'Pilgrim's Progress'!" he said.

"'Pilgrim's Progress'? Ah! A fine book—a grand book! Twelve years and a half of imprisonment in Bedford Jail turned Bunyan out immortal! And here am I—*not* in jail—but free to roam where I choose,—with twenty pounds! By Jove! I ought to be greater than Bunyan! Now 'Pilgrim's Progress' was a 'novel,' if you like!"

"I thought,"—submitted Helmsley, with the well-assumed air of a man who was not very conversant with literature—"that it was a religious book?"

"So it is. A religious novel. And a splendid one! But humanity's gone past that now—it wants a wider view—a bigger, broader outlook. Do you know—" and here he stopped in the middle of the rugged winding street, and looked earnestly at his companion—"do you know what I see men doing at the present day?—I see them rushing towards the verge—the very extreme edge of what they imagine to be the Actual—and from that edge getting ready to plunge—into Nothingness!"

Something thrilling in his voice touched a responsive chord in Helmsley's own heart.

"Why—that is where we all tend!" he said, with a quick sigh—"That is where *I* am tending!—where *you*, in your time, must also tend—nothingness—or death!"

"No!" said Reay, almost loudly—"That's not true! That's just what I deny! For me there is no 'Nothingness'—no 'death'! Space is full of creative organisms. Dissolution means re-birth. It is all life—life:—glorious life! We live—we have always lived—we *shall* always live!" He paused, flushing a little as though half ashamed of his own enthusiasm—then, dropping his voice to its normal tone he said—"You've got me on my hobby horse—I must come off it, or I shall gallop too far! We're just at the top of the street now. Shall I leave you here?"

"Please come on to the cottage,"—said Helmsley—"I'm sure Mary—Miss Deane—will give you a cup of tea."

Angus Reay smiled.

"I don't allow myself that luxury,"—he said.

"Not when you're invited to share it with others?"

"Oh yes, in that way I do—but I'm not overburdened with friends just now. A man must have more than twenty pounds to be 'asked out' anywhere!"

"Well, *I* ask you out!"—said Helmsley, smiling—"Or rather, I ask you *in*. I'm sure Miss Deane will be glad to talk to you. She is very fond of books."

"I've seen her just once in the village,"—remarked Reay—"She seems to be very much respected here. And what a beautiful woman she is!"

"You think so?" and Helmsley's eyes lighted with pleasure—"Well, I think so, too—but they tell me that it's only because I'm old, and apt to see everyone beautiful who is kind to me. There's a good deal in that!—there's certainly a good deal in that!"

They could now see the garden gate of Mary's cottage through the boughs of the great chestnut tree, which at this season was nearly stripped of all its leaves, and which stood like a lonely forest king with some scanty red and yellow rags of woodland royalty about him, in solitary grandeur at the bending summit of the hill. And while they were yet walking the few steps which remained of the intervening distance, Mary herself came out to the gate, and, leaning one arm lightly across it, watched them approaching. She wore a pale lilac print gown, high to the neck and tidily finished off by a plain little muslin collar fastened with a coquettish knot of black velvet,—her head was uncovered, and the fitful gleams of the sinking sun shed a russet glow on her shining hair and reddened the pale clear transparency of her skin. In that restful waiting attitude, with a smile on her face, she made a perfect picture, and Helmsley stole a side-glance at his companion, to see if he seemed to be in any way impressed by her appearance. Angus Reay was certainly looking at her, but what he thought could hardly be guessed by his outward expression. They reached the gate, and she opened it.

"I was getting anxious about you, David!"—she said; "you aren't quite strong enough to be out in such a cold wind." Then she turned her eyes enquiringly on Reay, who lifted his cap while Helmsley explained his presence.

"This is a gentleman who is staying in the village—Mr. Reay,"—he said—"He's been very kind in helping me up the hill—and I said you would give him a cup of tea."

"Why, of course!"—and Mary smiled—"Please come in, sir!"

She led the way, and in another few minutes, all three of them were seated in her little kitchen round the table and Mary was busy pouring out the tea and dispensing the usual good things that are always found in the simplest Somersetshire cottage,—cream, preserved fruit, scones, home-made bread and fresh butter.

"So you met David on the seashore?" she said, turning her soft dark-blue eyes enquiringly on Reay, while gently checking with one hand the excited gambols of Charlie, who, as an epicurean dog, always gave himself up to the wildest enthusiasms at tea-time, owing to his partiality for a small saucer of cream which came to him at that hour— "I sometimes think he must expect to pick up a fortune down among the shells and seaweed, he's so fond of walking about there!"—And she smiled as she put Helmsley's cup of tea before him, and gently patted his wrinkled hand in the caressing fashion a daughter might show to a father whose health gave cause for anxiety.

"Well, *I* certainly don't go down to the shore in any such expectation!" said Reay, laughing—"Fortunes are not so easily picked up, are they, David?"

"No, indeed!" replied Helmsley, and his old eyes sparkled up humorously under their cavernous brows; "fortunes take some time to make, and one doesn't meet millionaires every day!"

"Millionaires!" exclaimed Reay—"Don't speak of them! I hate them!"

Helmsley looked at him stedfastly.

"It's best not to hate anybody,"—he said—"Millionaires are often the loneliest and most miserable of men."

"They deserve to be!" declared Reay, hotly—"It isn't right—it isn't just that two or three, or let us say four or five men should be able to control the money-markets of the world. They generally get their wealth through some unscrupulous 'deal,' or through 'sweating' labour. I hate all 'cornering' systems. I believe in having enough to live upon, but not too much."

"It depends on what you call enough,"—said Helmsley, slowly— "We're told that some people never know when they *have* enough."

"Why *this* is enough!" said Reay, looking admiringly round the little kitchen in which they sat—"This sweet little cottage with this oak raftered ceiling, and all the dear old-fashioned crockery, and the ingle-nook over there,—who on earth wants more?"

Mary laughed.

"Oh dear me!" she murmured, gently—"You praise it too much!—it's only a very poor place, sir,—"

He interrupted her, the colour rushing to his brows.

"Please don't!"

She glanced at him in surprise.

"Don't—what?"

"Don't call me 'sir'! I'm only a poor chap,—my father was a shepherd, and I began life as a cowherd—I don't want any titles of courtesy."

She still kept her eyes upon him thoughtfully.

"But you're a gentleman, aren't you?" she asked.

"I hope so!" And he laughed. "Just as David is! But we neither of us wish the fact emphasised, do we, David? It goes without saying!"

Helmsley smiled. This Angus Reay was a man after his own heart.

"Of course it does!"—he said—"In the way you look at it! But you should tell Miss Deane all about yourself—she'll be interested."

"Would you really care to hear?" enquired Reay, suddenly, turning his clear grey eyes full on Mary's face.

"Why certainly I should!" she answered, frankly meeting his glance,—and then, from some sudden and inexplicable embarrassment, she blushed crimson, and her eyelids fell. And Reay thought what a clear, healthy skin she had, and how warmly the blood flowed under it.

"Well, after tea I'll hold forth!" he said—"But there isn't much to tell. Such as there is, you shall know, for I've no mysteries about me. Some fellows love a mystery—I cannot bear it! Everything must be fair, open and above board with me,—else I can't breathe! Pouf!" And he expanded his broad chest and took a great gulp of air in as he spoke—"I hate a man who tries to hide his own identity, don't you, David?"

"Yes—yes—certainly!" murmured Helmsley, absently, feigning to be absorbed in buttering a scone for his own eating—"It is often very awkward—for the man."

"I always say, and I always will maintain,"—went on Reay—"let a man be a man—a something or a nothing. If he is a criminal, let him say he is a criminal, and not pretend to be virtuous—if he is an atheist, let him say he is an atheist, and not pretend to be religious—if he's a beggar and can't help himself, let him admit the fact—if he's a millionaire, don't let him skulk round pretending he's as poor as Job—always let him be himself and no other!—eh?—what is it, David?"

For Helmsley was looking at him intently with eyes that were almost young in their sudden animation and brilliancy.

"Did you ever meet a millionaire who skulked round pretending he was as poor as Job?" he enquired, with a whimsical air—"*I* never did!"

"Well no, I never did, either!" And Reay's mellow laughter was so loud and long that Mary was quite infected by it, and laughed with him—"But you see millionaires are all marked men. Everybody knows them. Their portraits are in all the newspapers—horrid-looking rascals most of them!—Nature doesn't seem to endow them with handsome features anyway. 'Keep your gold, and never mind your face,'—she seems to say—'*I'll* take care of that!' And she does take care of it! O Lord! The only millionaire I ever saw in my life was ugly enough to frighten a baby into convulsions!"

"What was his name?" asked Helmsley.

"Well, it wouldn't be fair to tell his name now, after what I've said!" laughed Reay—"Besides, he lives in America, thank God! He's one of the few who have spared the old country his patronage!"

Here a diversion was created by the necessity of serving the tiny but autocratic Charlie with his usual "dish of cream," of which he partook on Mary's knee, while listening (as was evident from the attentive cocking of his silky ears) to the various compliments he was accustomed to receive on his beauty. This business over, they rose from the tea-table. The afternoon had darkened into twilight, and the autumnal wind was sighing through the crannies of the door. Mary stirred the fire into a brighter blaze, and drawing Helmsley's armchair close to its warm glow, stood by him till he was comfortably seated—then she placed another chair opposite for Reay, and sat down herself on a low oaken settle between the two.

"This is the pleasantest time of the day just now,"—she said—"And the best time for talking! I love the gloaming. My father loved it too."

"So did *my* father!" and Reay's eyes softened as he bent them on the sparkling fire—"In winter evenings when the darkness fell down upon our wild Highland hills, he would come home to our shieling on the edge of the moor, shaking all the freshness of the wind and the scent of the dying heather out of his plaid as he threw it from his shoulders,— and he would toss fresh peat on the fire till it blazed red and golden, and he would lay his hand on my head and say to me: 'Come awa' bairnie!

Now for a bogle story in the gloamin'!' Ah, those bogle stories! They are answerable for a good deal in my life! They made me want to write bogle stories myself!"

"And *do* you write them?" asked Mary.

"Not exactly. Though perhaps all human life is only a bogle tale! Invented to amuse the angels!"

She smiled, and taking up a delicate piece of crochet lace, which she called her "spare time work," began to ply the glittering needle in and out fine intricacies of thread, her shapely hands gleaming like alabaster in the fire-light reflections.

"Well, now tell us your own bogle tale!" she said—"And David and I will play the angels!"

XV

He watched her working for a few minutes before he spoke again. And shading his eyes with one hand from the red glow of the fire, David Helmsley watched them both.

"Well, it's rather cool of me to take up your time talking about my own affairs,"—began Reay, at last—"But I've been pretty much by myself for a good while, and it's pleasant to have a chat with friendly people—man wasn't made to live alone, you know! In fact, neither man nor beast nor bird can stand it. Even a sea cormorant croaks to the wind!"

Mary laughed.

"But not for company's sake,"—she said—"It croaks when it's hungry."

"Oh, I've often croaked for that reason!" and Reay pushed from his forehead a wayward tuft of hair which threatened to drop over his eye in a thick silvery brown curl—"But it's wonderful how little a fellow can live upon in the way of what is called food. I know all sorts of dodges wherewith to satisfy the greedy cravings of the vulgar part of me."

Helmsley took his hand from his eyes, and fixed a keenly observant look upon the speaker. Mary said nothing, but her crochet needle moved more slowly.

"You see," went on Reay, "I've always been rather fortunate in having had very little to eat."

"You call it 'fortunate'?" queried Helmsley, abruptly.

"Why, of course! I've never had what the doctors call an 'overloaded system'—therefore I've no lading bill to pay. The million or so of cells of which I am composed are not at all anxious to throw any extra nourishment off,—sometimes they intimate a strong desire to take some extra nourishment in—but that is an uneducated tendency in them which I sternly repress. I tell all those small grovelling cells that extra nourishment would not be good for them. And they shrink back from my moral reproof ashamed of themselves—and become wiry instead of fatty. Which is as it should be."

"You're a queer chap!" said Helmsley, with a laugh.

"Think so? Well, I daresay I am—all Scotsmen are. There's always the buzzing of the bee in our bonnets. I come of an ancient Highland stock who were certainly 'queer' as modern ways go,—for they were famous for their pride, and still more famous for their poverty all the way through. As far back as I can go in the history of my family, and that's a pretty long way, we were always at our wit's end to live. From the days of the founder of our house, a glorious old chieftain who used to pillage his neighbour chieftain in the usual style of those glorious old times, we never had more than just enough for the bare necessities of life. My father, as I told you, was a shepherd—a strong, fine-looking man over six feet in height, and as broad-chested as a Hercules—he herded sheep on the mountains for a Glasgow dealer, as low-down a rascal as ever lived, a man who, so far as race and lineage went, wasn't fit to scrape mud off my father's boots. But we often see gentlemen of birth obliged to work for knaves of cash. That was the way it was with my father. As soon as I was old enough—about ten,—I helped him in his work—I used to tramp backwards and forwards to school in the nearest village, but after school hours I got an evening job of a shilling a week for bringing home eight Highland bull-heifers from pasture. The man who owned them valued them highly, but was afraid of them—wouldn't go near them for his life—and before I'd been with them a fortnight they all knew me. I was only a wee laddie, but they answered to my call like friendly dogs rather than the great powerful splendid beasts they were, with their rough coats shining like floss silk in the sunset, when I went to drive them home, singing as I came. And my father said to me one night—'Laddie, tell me the truth—are ye ever scared at the bulls!' 'No, father!' said I—'It's a bonnie boy I am to the bulls!' And he laughed— by Jove!—how he laughed! 'Ye're a wee raskell!' he said—'An' as full o' conceit as an egg's full o' meat!' I expect that was true too, for I always thought well of myself. You see, if I hadn't thought well of myself, no one would ever have thought well of *me*!"

"There's something in that!" said Helmsley, the smile still lingering in his eyes—"Courage and self-reliance have often conquered more than eight bulls!"

"Oh, I don't call it either courage or self-reliance—it was just that I thought myself of too much importance to be hurt by bulls or anything else,"—and Angus laughed,—then with a sudden knitting of his brows as though his thoughts were making hard knots in his brain, he added—"Even as a laddie I had an idea—and I have it now—that there was something in me which God had put there for a purpose of His own,—something that he would not and *could* not destroy till His purpose had been fulfilled!"

Mary stopped working and looked at him earnestly. Her breath came and went quickly—her eyes shone dewily like stars in a summer haze,—she was deeply interested.

"That was—and *is*—a conceited notion, of course,"—went on Angus, reflectively—"And I don't excuse it. But I'm not one of the 'meek who shall inherit the earth.' I'm a robustious combustious sort of chap—if a fellow knocks me down, I jump up and give it him back with as jolly good interest as I can—and if anyone plays me a dirty trick I'll move all the mental and elemental forces of the universe to expose him. That's my way—unfortunately—"

"Why 'unfortunately'?" asked Helmsley.

Reay threw back his head and indulged in one of his mellow peals of laughter.

"Can you ask why? Oh David, good old David!—it's easy to see you don't know much of the world! If you did, you'd realise that the best way to 'get on' in the usual way of worldly progress, is to make up to all sorts of social villains and double-dyed millionaire-scoundrels, find out all their tricks and their miserable little vices and pamper them, David!—pamper them and flatter them up to the top of their bent till you've got them in your power—and then—then *use* them—use them for everything you want. For once you know what blackguards they are, they'll give you anything not to tell!"

"I should be sorry to think that's true,"—murmured Mary.

"Don't think it, then,"—said Angus—"You needn't,—because millionaires are not likely to come in your way. Nor in mine—now. I've cut myself adrift from all chance of ever meeting them. But only a year ago I was on the road to making a good thing out of one or two of the so-called 'kings of finance'—then I suddenly took a 'scunner' as we Scots say, at the whole lot, and hated and despised myself for ever so much as thinking that it might serve my own ends to become their tool. So I just cast off ropes like a ship, and steamed out of harbour."

"Into the wide sea!" said Mary, looking at him with a smile that was lovely in its radiance and sympathy.

"Into the wide sea—yes!" he answered—"And sea that was pretty rough at first. But one can get accustomed to anything—even to the high rock-a-bye tossing of great billows that really don't want to put you to sleep so much as to knock you to pieces. But I'm galloping along too fast. From the time I made friends with young bulls to the time I began to scrape acquaintance with newspaper editors is a far cry—and in the interim my father died. I should have told you that I lost my mother when I was born—and I don't think that the great wound her death left in my father's heart ever really healed. He never seemed quite at one with the things of life—and his 'bogle tales' of which I was so fond, all turned on the spirits of the dead coming again to visit those whom they had loved, and from whom they had been taken—and he used to tell them with such passionate conviction that sometimes I trembled and wondered if any spirit were standing near us in the light of the peat fire, or if the shriek of the wind over our sheiling were the cry of some unhappy soul in torment. Well! When his time came, he was not allowed to suffer—one day in a great storm he was struck by lightning on the side of the mountain where he was herding in his flocks—and there he was found lying as though he were peacefully asleep. Death must have been swift and painless—and I always thank God for that!" He paused a moment—then went on—"When I found myself quite alone in the world, I hired myself out to a farmer for five years—and worked faithfully for him—worked so well that he raised my wages and would willingly have kept me on—but I had the 'bogle tales' in my head and could not rest. It was in the days before Andrew Carnegie started trying to rub out the memory of his 'Homestead' cruelty by planting 'free' libraries, (for which taxpayers are rated) all over the country—and pauperising Scottish University education by grants of money—I suppose he is a sort of little Pontiff unto himself, and thinks that money can pacify Heaven, and silence the cry of brothers' blood rising from the Homestead ground. In my boyhood a Scottish University education had to be earned by the would-be student himself—earned by hard work, hard living, patience, perseverance and *grit*. That's the one quality I had—grit—and it served me well in all I wanted. I entered at St. Andrews—graduated, and came out an M.A. That helped to give me my first chance with the press. But I'm sure I'm boring you by all this chatter about myself! David, *you* stop me when you think Miss Deane has had enough!"

Helmsley looked at Mary's figure in its pale lilac gown touched here and there by the red sparkle of the fire, and noted the attentive poise of her head, and the passive quietude of her generally busy hands which now lay in her lap loosely folded over her lace work.

"Have we had enough, Mary, do you think?" he asked, with the glimmering of a tender little smile under his white moustache.

She glanced at him quickly in a startled way, as though she had been suddenly wakened from a reverie.

"Oh no!" she answered—"I love to hear of a brave man's fight with the world—it's the finest story anyone can listen to."

Reay coloured like a boy.

"I'm not a brave man,"—he said—"I hope I haven't given you that idea. I'm an awful funk at times."

"When are those times?" and Mary smiled demurely, as she put the question.

Again the warm blood rushed up to his brows.

"Well,—please don't laugh! I'm afraid—horribly afraid—of women!"

Helmsley's old eyes sparkled.

"Upon my word!" he exclaimed—"That's a funny thing for you to say!"

"It is, rather,"—and Angus looked meditatively into the fire—"It's not that I'm bashful, at all—no—I'm quite the other way, really,—only—only—ever since I was a lad I've made such an ideal of woman that I'm afraid of her when I meet her,—afraid lest she shouldn't come up to my ideal, and equally afraid lest I shouldn't come up to hers! It's all conceit again! Fear of anything or anybody is always born of self-consciousness. But I've been disappointed once—"

"In your ideal?" questioned Mary, raising her eyes and letting them rest observantly upon his face.

"Yes. I'll come to that presently. I was telling you how I graduated at St. Andrews, and came out with M.A. tacked to my name, but with no other fortune than those two letters. I had made a few friends, however, and one of them, a worthy old professor, gave me a letter of recommendation to a man in Glasgow, who was the proprietor of one of the newspapers there. He was a warm-hearted, kindly fellow, and gave me a berth at once. It was hard work for little pay, but I got into thorough harness, and learnt all the ins and outs of journalism. I can't say that I ever admired the general mechanism set up for gulling the public, but I had to learn how it was done, and I set myself to master the whole business. I had rather a happy time of it in Glasgow, for though it's the dirtiest, dingiest and most depressing city in the world, with its innumerable drunkards and low Scoto-Irish ne'er-do-weels loafing about the streets on Saturday nights, it has one great charm—you get away from it into some of the loveliest scenery in the world. All my spare time was spent in taking the steamer up the Clyde, and sometimes going as far as Crinan and beyond it—or what I loved best of all, taking a trip to Arran, and there roaming about the hills to my heart's content. Glorious Arran! It was there I first began to feel my wings growing!"

"Was it a pleasant feeling?" enquired Helmsley, jocosely.

"Yes—it *was*!" replied Angus, clenching his right hand and bringing it down on his knee with emphasis; "whether they were goose wings or eagle wings didn't matter—the pricking of the budding quills was an *alive* sensation! The mountains, the burns, the glens, all had something to say to me—or I thought they had—something new, vital and urgent. God Himself seemed to have some great command to impose upon me—and I was ready to hear and obey. I began to write—first verse—then prose—and by and by I got one or two things accepted here and there—not very much, but still enough to fire me to further endeavours. Then one summer, when I was taking a holiday at a little village near Loch Lomond, I got the final dig of the spur of fate—I fell in love."

Mary raised her eyes again and looked at him. A slow smile parted her lips.

"And did the girl fall in love with you?" she asked.

"For a time I believe she did,"—said Reay, and there was an under-tone of whimsical amusement in his voice as he spoke—"She was spending the summer in Scotland with her mother and father, and there wasn't anything for her to do. She didn't care for scenery very much—and I just came in as a sort of handy man to amuse her. She was a lovely creature in her teens,—I thought she was an angel—till—till I found her out."

"And then?" queried Helmsley.

"Oh well, then of course I was disillusioned. When I told her that I loved her more than anything else in the world, she laughed ever so sweetly, and said, 'I'm sure you do!' But when I asked her if she loved *me*, she laughed again, and said she didn't know what I was talking about— she didn't believe in love. 'What do you believe in?' I asked her. And she looked at me in the prettiest and most innocent way possible, and said quite calmly and slowly—'A rich marriage.' And my heart gave a great dunt in my side, for I knew it was all over. 'Then you won't marry *me*?'—I said—'for I'm only a poor journalist. But I mean to be famous some day!' 'Do you?' she said, and again that little laugh of hers rippled out like the tinkle of cold water—'Don't you think famous men are very tiresome? And they're always dreadfully poor!' Then I took hold of her hands, like the desperate fool I was, and kissed them, and said, 'Lucy, wait for me just a few years! Wait for me! You're so young'—for she was only seventeen, and still at school in Brighton somewhere—'You can afford to wait,—give me a chance!' And she looked down at the water—we were 'on the bonnie banks of Loch Lomond,' as the song says—in quite a picturesque little attitude of reflection, and sighed ever so prettily, and said—'I can't, Angus! You're very nice and kind!—and I like you very much!—but I am going to marry a millionaire!' Now you know why I hate millionaires."

"Did you say her name was Lucy?" asked Helmsley.

"Yes. Lucy Sorrel."

A bright flame leaped up in the fire and showed all three faces to one another—Mary's face, with its quietly absorbed expression of attentive interest—Reay's strongly moulded features, just now somewhat sternly shadowed by bitter memories—and Helmsley's thin, worn, delicately intellectual countenance, which in the brilliant rosy light flung upon it by the fire-glow, was like a fine waxen mask, impenetrable in its unmoved austerity and calm. Not so much as the faintest flicker of emotion crossed it at the mention of the name of the woman he knew so well,—the surprise he felt inwardly was not apparent outwardly, and he heard the remainder of Reay's narration with the most perfectly controlled imperturbability of demeanour.

"She told me then," proceeded Reay—"that her parents had spent nearly all they had upon her education, in order to fit her for a position as the wife of a rich man—and that she would have to do her best to 'catch'—that's the way she put it—to 'catch' this rich man as soon as she got a good opportunity. He was quite an old man, she said—old enough to be her grandfather. And when I asked her how she could reconcile it to her conscience to marry such a hoary-headed rascal—"

Here Helmsley interrupted him.

"Was he a hoary-headed rascal?"

"He must have been," replied Angus, warmly—"Don't you see he must?"

Helmsley smiled.

"Well—not exactly!" he submitted, with a gentle air of deference—"I think—perhaps—he might deserve a little pity for having to be 'caught' as you say just for his money's sake."

"Not a bit of it!" declared Reay—"Any old man who would marry a young girl like that condemns himself as a villain. An out-an-out, golden-dusted villain!"

"But *has* he married her?" asked Mary.

Angus was rather taken aback at this question,—and rubbed his forehead perplexedly.

"Well, no, he hasn't—not yet—not that I know of, and I've watched the papers carefully too. Such a marriage couldn't take place without columns and columns of twaddle about it—all the dressmakers who made gowns for the bride would want a mention—and if they paid for it of course they'd get it. No—it hasn't come off yet—but it will. The venerable bridegroom that is to be has just gone abroad somewhere—so I see by one of the 'Society' rags,—probably to the States to make some more 'deals' in cash before his wedding."

"You know his name, then?"

"Oh yes! Everybody knows it, and knows him too! David Helmsley's too rich to hide his light under a bushel! They call him 'King David' in the city. Now your name's David—but, by Jove, what a difference in Davids!" And he laughed, adding quickly—"I prefer the David I see before me now, to the David I never saw!"

"Oh! You never saw the old rascal then?" murmured Helmsley, putting up one hand to stroke his moustache slowly down over the smile which he could not repress.

"Never—and don't want to! If I become famous—which I *will* do,"—and here Angus set his teeth hard—"I'll make my bow at one of Mrs. Millionaire Helmsley's receptions one day! And how will she look then!"

"I should say she would look much the same as usual,"—said Helmsley, drily—"If she is the kind of young woman you describe, she is not likely to be overcome by the sight of a merely 'famous' man. You would have to be twice or three times as wealthy as herself to move her to any sense of respect for you. That is, if we are to judge by what our newspapers tell us of 'society' people. The newspapers are all we poor folk have got to go by."

"Yes—I've often thought of that!" and Angus rubbed his forehead again in a vigorous way as though he were trying to rub ideas out of it—"And I've pitied the poor folks from the bottom of my heart! They get pretty often misled—and on serious matters too."

"Oh, we're not all such fools as we seem,"—said Helmsley—"We can read between the lines as well as anyone—and we understand pretty clearly that it's only money which 'makes' the news. We read of 'society ladies' doing this, that and t' other thing, and we laugh at their doings—

and when we read of a great lady conducting herself like an outcast, we feel a contempt for her such as we never visit on her poor sister of the streets. The newspapers may praise these women, but we 'common people' estimate them at their true worth—and that is—nothing! Now the girl you made an ideal of—"

"She was to be bought and sold,"—interrupted Reay; "I know that now. But I didn't know it then. She looked a sweet innocent angel,—with a pretty face and beautiful eyes—just the kind of creature we men fall in love with at first sight—"

"The kind of creature who, if you had married her, would have made you wretched for life,"—said Helmsley. "Be thankful you escaped her!"

"Oh, I'm thankful enough now!" and Reay pushed back his rebellious lock of hair again—"For when one has a great ambition in view, freedom is better than love—"

Helmsley raised his wrinkled, trembling hand.

"No, don't say that!" he murmured, gently—"Nothing—nothing in all the world is better than love!"

Involuntarily his eyes turned towards Mary with a strange wistfulness. There was an unspoken yearning in his face that was almost pain. Her quick instinctive sympathy responded to his thought, and rising, she went to him on the pretext of re-arranging the cushion in his chair, so that he might lean back more comfortably. Then she took his hand and patted it kindly.

"You're a sentimental old boy, aren't you, David!" she said, playfully—"You like being taken care of and fussed over! Of course you do! Was there ever a man that didn't!"

He was silent, but he pressed her caressing hand gratefully.

"No one has ever taken care of or fussed over *me*," said Reay—"I should rather like to try the experiment!"

Mary laughed good-humouredly.

"You must find yourself a wife,"—she said—"And then you'll see how you like it."

"But wives don't make any fuss over their husbands it seems to me," replied Reay—"At any rate in London, where I have lived for the past five years—husbands seem to be the last persons in the world whom their wives consider. I don't think I shall ever marry."

"I'm sure *I* shan't,"—said Mary, smiling—and as she spoke, she bent over the fire, and threw a fresh log of wood on to keep up the bright glow which was all that illuminated the room, from which almost every pale glimmer of the twilight had now departed—"I'm an old maid. But I was an engaged girl once!"

Helmsley lifted up his head with sudden and animated interest.

"Were you, Mary?"

"Oh, yes!" And the smile deepened round her expressive mouth and played softly in her eyes—"Yes, David, really! I was engaged to a very good-looking young man in the electrical engineering business. And I was very fond of him. But when my father lost every penny, my good-looking young man went too. He said he couldn't possibly marry a girl with nothing but the clothes on her back. I cried very much at the time, and thought my heart was broken. But—it wasn't!"

"I should hope it wouldn't break for such a selfish rascal!" said Reay, warmly.

"Do you think he was more selfish than most?" queried Mary, thoughtfully—"There's a good many who would do as he did."

A silence followed. She sat down and resumed her work.

"Have you finished your story?" she asked Reay—"It has interested me so much that I'm hoping there's some more to tell."

As she spoke to him he started as if from a dream. He had been watching her so earnestly that he had almost forgotten what he had previously been talking about. He found himself studying the beautiful outline of her figure, and wondering why he had never before seen such gracious curves of neck and shoulder, waist and bosom as gave symmetrical perfection of shape to this simple woman born of the "common" people.

"More to tell?" he echoed, hastily,—"Well, there's a little—but not much. My love affair at Loch Lomond did one thing for me,—it made me work hard. I had a sort of desperate idea that I might wrest a fortune out of journalism by dint of sheer grinding at it—but I soon found out my mistake there. I toiled away so steadily and got such a firm hold of all the affairs of the newspaper office where I was employed, that one fine morning I was dismissed. My proprietor, genial and kindly as ever, said he found 'no fault'—but that he wanted 'a change.' I quite understood that. The fact is I knew too much—that's all. I had saved a bit, and so, with a few good letters of introduction, went on from Glasgow to London. There, in that great black ant-hill full of crawling sooty human life, I knocked about for a time from one newspaper office to another, doing any sort of work that turned up, just to keep body and soul together,—and at last I got a fairly good berth in the London branch of a big press syndicate. It was composed of three or four proprietors, ever so many editors, and an army of shareholders representing almost every class in Great Britain. Ah, those shareholders! There's the whole mischief of the press nowadays!"

"I suppose it's money again!" said Helmsley.

"Of course it is. Here's how the matter stands. A newspaper syndicate is like any other trading company, composed for the sole end and object of making as much profit out of the public as possible. The lion's portion naturally goes to the heads of the concern—then come the shareholders' dividends. The actual workers in the business, such as the 'editors,' are paid as little as their self-respect will allow them to take, and as for the other fellows *under* the editors—well!—you can just imagine they get much less than the little their self-respect would claim, if they were not, most of them, so desperately poor, and so anxious for a foothold somewhere as to be ready to take anything. I took the first chance I could get, and hung on to it, not for the wretched pay, but for the experience, and for the insight it gave me into men and things. I witnessed the whole business;—the 'doctoring up' of social scandals,—the tampering with the news in order that certain items might not affect certain shares on the Stock Exchange,—the way 'discussions' of the most idiotic kind were started in the office just to fill up space, such as what was best to make the hair grow; what a baby ought to weigh at six months; what food authors write best on; and whether modern girls make as good wives as their mothers did, and so on. These things were generally got up by 'the fool of the office' as we called him—a man with a perpetual grin and an undyingly good opinion of himself. He was always put into harness when for some state or financial reason the actual facts had to be euphonised or even suppressed and the public 'let down gently.' For a time I was drafted off on the 'social' business—ugh?—how I hated it?"

"What did you have to do?" asked Mary, amused.

"Oh, I had to deal with a motley crowd of court flunkeys, Jews, tailors and dressmakers, and fearful-looking women catering for 'fashion,' who came with what they called 'news,' which was generally that 'Mrs. "Bunny" Bumpkin looked sweet in grey'—or that 'Miss "Toby" Tosspot was among the loveliest of the débutantes at Court.' Sometimes a son of Israel came along, all in a mortal funk, and said he 'didn't want it mentioned' that Mrs. So-and-So had dined with him at a certain public restaurant last night. Generally, he was a shareholder, and his orders had to be obeyed. The shareholders in fact had most to do with the 'society' news,—and they bored me nearly to death. The trifles they wanted 'mentioned' were innumerable—the other trifles they didn't want mentioned, were quite as endless. One day there was a regular row—a sort of earthquake in the place. Somebody had presumed to mention that the beautiful Mrs. Mushroom Ketchup had smoked several cigarettes with infinite gusto at a certain garden party,—now what are you laughing at, Miss Deane?"

"At the beautiful Mrs. Mushroom Ketchup!" and Mary's clear laughter rippled out in a silvery peal of purest merriment—"That's not her name surely!"

"Oh no, that's not her name!" and Angus laughed too—"It wouldn't do to give her real name!—but Ketchup's quite as good and high-sounding as the one she's got. And as I tell you, the whole 'staff' was convulsed. Three shareholders came down post haste to the office—one at full speed in a motor,—and said how *dare* I mention Mrs. Mushroom Ketchup at all? It was like my presumption to notice that she had smoked! Mrs. Mushroom Ketchup's name must be kept out of the papers—she was a 'lady'! Oh, by Jove!—how I laughed!—I couldn't help myself! I just roared with laughter in the very faces of those shareholders! 'A lady!' said I—'Why, she's— ' But I wasn't allowed to say what she was, for the shareholder who had arrived in the motor, fixed a deadly glance upon me and said—'If you value your po-seetion'—he was a Lowland Scot, with the Lowland accent—'if you value your po-seetion on this paper, you'll hold your tongue!' So I did hold my tongue then—but only because I meant to wag it more violently afterwards. I always devote Mrs. Mushroom Ketchup to the blue blazes, because I'm sure it was through her I lost my post. You see a shareholder in a paper has a good deal of influence, especially if he has as much as a hundred thousand shares. You'd be surprised if I told you the real names of some of the fellows who control newspaper syndicates!—you wouldn't believe it! Or at any rate, if you *did* believe it, you'd never believe the newspapers!"

"I don't believe them now,"—said Helmsley—"They say one thing to-day and contradict it to-morrow."

"Oh, but that's like all news!" said Mary, placidly—"Even in our little village here, you never know quite what to believe. One morning you are told that Mrs. Badge's baby has fallen downstairs and broken its neck, and you've scarcely done being sorry for Mrs. Badge, when in comes Mrs. Badge herself, baby and all, quite well and smiling, and she says she 'never did hear such tales as there are in Wiercombe'!"

They all laughed.

"Well, there's the end of my story,"—said Angus—"I worked on the syndicate for two years, and then was given the sack. The cause of my dismissal was, as I told you, that I published a leading article exposing a mean and dirty financial trick on the part of a man who publicly assumed to be a world's benefactor—and he turned out to be a shareholder in the paper under an 'alias.' There was no hope for me after that—it was a worse affair than that of Mrs. Mushroom Ketchup. So I marched out of the office, and out of London—I meant to make for Exmoor, which is wild and solitary, because I thought I might find some cheap room in a cottage there, where I might live quietly on almost nothing and write my book—but I stumbled by chance on this place instead—and I rather like being so close to the sea."

"You are writing a book?" said Mary, her eyes resting upon him thoughtfully.

"Yes. I've got a room in the village for half-a-crown a week and 'board myself' as the good woman of the house says. And I'm perfectly happy!"

A long pause followed. The fire was dying down from a flame to a dull red glow, and a rush of wind against the kitchen window was accompanied by the light pattering of rain. Angus Reay rose.

"I must be going,"—he said—"I've made you quite a visitation! Old David is nearly asleep!"

Helmsley looked up.

"Not I!" and he smiled—"I'm very wide awake: I like your story, and I like *you*! Perhaps you'll come in again sometimes and have a chat with us?"

Reay glanced enquiringly at Mary, who had also risen from her chair, and was now lighting the lamp on the table.

"May I?" he asked hesitatingly.

"Why, of course!" And her eyes met his with hospitable frankness— "Come whenever you feel lonely!"

"I often do that!" he said.

"All the better!—then we shall often see you!"—she answered—"And you'll always be welcome!"

"Thank-you! I believe you mean it!"

Mary smiled.

"Why of course I do! I'm not a newspaper syndicate!"

"Nor a Mrs. Mushroom Ketchup!" put in Helmsley.

Angus threw back his head and gave one of his big joyous laughs.

"No! You're a long way off that!" he said—"Good-evening, David!"

And going up to the armchair where Helmsley sat he shook hands with him.

"Good-evening, Mr. Reay!" rejoined Helmsley, cheerily; "I'm very glad we met this afternoon!"

"So am I!" declared Angus, with energy—"I don't feel quite so much of a solitary bear as I did. I'm in a better temper altogether with the world in general!"

"That's right!" said Mary—"Whatever happens to you it's never the fault of the world, remember!—it's only the trying little ways of the people in it!"

She held out her hand in farewell, and he pressed it gently. Then he threw on his cap, and she opened her cottage door for him to pass out. A soft shower of rain blew full in their faces as they stood on the threshold.

"You'll get wet, I'm afraid!" said Mary.

"Oh, that's nothing!" And he buttoned his coat across his chest— "What's that lovely scent in the garden here, just close to the door?"

"It's the old sweetbriar bush,"—she replied—"It lasts in leaf till nearly Christmas and always smells so delicious. Shall I give you a bit of it?"

"It's too dark to find it now, surely!" said Angus.

"Oh, no! I can feel it!"

And stretching out her white hand into the raining darkness, she brought it back holding a delicate spray of odorous leaves.

"Isn't it sweet?" she said, as she gave it to him.

"It is indeed!" he placed the little sprig in his buttonhole. "Thank-you! Good-night!"

"Good-night!"

He lifted his hat and smiled into her eyes—then walked quickly through the tiny garden, opened the gate, shut it carefully behind him, and disappeared. Mary listened for a moment to the swish of the falling rain among the leaves, and the noise of the tumbling hill-torrent over its stony bed. Then she closed and barred the door.

"It's going to be a wet night, David!" she said, as she came back towards the fire—"And a bit rough, too, by the sound of the sea."

He did not answer immediately, but watched her attentively as she made up the fire, and cleared the table of the tea things, packing up the cups and plates and saucers in the neat and noiseless manner which was particularly her own, preparatory to carrying them all on a tray out to the little scullery adjoining the kitchen, which with its well polished saucepans, kettles, and crockery was quite a smart feature of her small establishment. Then—

"What do you think of him, Mary?" he asked suddenly.

"Of Mr. Reay?"

"Yes."

She hesitated a moment, looking intently at a small crack in one of the plates she was putting by.

"Well, I don't know, David!—it's rather difficult to say on such a short acquaintance—but he seems to me quite a good fellow."

"Quite a good fellow, yes!" repeated Helmsley, nodding gravely— "That's how he seems to me, too."

"I think,"—went on Mary, slowly—"that he's a thoroughly manly man,—don't you?" He nodded gravely again, and echoed her words—

"A thoroughly manly man!"

"And perhaps," she continued—"it would be pleasant for you, David, to have a chat with him now and then especially in the long winter evenings—wouldn't it?"

She had moved to his side, and now stood looking down upon him with such a wistful sweetness of expression, that he was content to merely watch her, without answering her question.

"Because those long winter evenings are sometimes very dull, you know!" she went on—"And I'm afraid I'm not very good company when I'm at work mending the lace—I have to take all my stitches so carefully that I dare not talk much lest I make a false knot."

He smiled.

"*You* make a false knot!" he said—"You couldn't do it, if you tried! You'll never make a false knot—never!"—and his voice sank to an almost inaudible murmur—"Neither in your lace nor in your life!"

She looked at him a little anxiously.

"Are you tired, David?"

"No, my dear! Not tired—only thinking!"

"Well, you mustn't think too much,"—she said—"Thinking is weary work, sometimes!"

He raised his eyes and looked at her steadily.

"Mr. Reay was very frank and open in telling us all about himself, wasn't he, Mary?"

"Oh yes!" and she laughed—"But I think he is one of those men who couldn't possibly be anything else but frank and open."

"Oh, you do?"

"Yes."

"Don't you sometimes wonder,"—went on Helmsley slowly, keeping his gaze fixed on the fire—"why *I* haven't told you all about myself?"

She met his eyes with a candid smile.

"No—I haven't thought about it!" she said.

"Why haven't you thought about it?" he persisted.

She laughed outright.

"Simply because I haven't! That's all!"

"Mary,"—he said, seriously—"You know I was not your 'father's friend'! You know I never saw your father!"

The smile still lingered in her eyes.

"Yes—I know that!"

"And yet you never ask me to give an account of myself!"

She thought he was worrying his mind needlessly, and bending over him took his hand in hers.

"No, David, I never ask impertinent questions!" she said—"I don't want to know anything more about you than you choose to tell. You seem to me like my dear father—not quite so strong as he was, perhaps—but I have taken care of you for so many weeks, that I almost feel as if you belonged to me! And I want to take care of you still, because I know you *must* be taken care of. And I'm so well accustomed to you now that I shouldn't like to lose you, David—I shouldn't really! Because you've been so patient and gentle and grateful for the little I have been able to do for you, that I've got fond of you, David! Yes!—actually fond of you! What do you say to that?"

"Say to it!" he murmured, pressing the hand he held. "I don't know what to say to it, Mary!—except—God bless you!"

She was silent a minute—then she went on in a cheerfully rallying tone—

"So I don't want to know anything about you, you see! Now, as to Mr. Reay—"

"Ah, yes!" and Helmsley gave her a quick observant glance which she herself did not notice—"What about Mr. Reay?"

"Well it would be nice if we could cheer him up a little and make him bear his poor and lonely life more easily. Wouldn't it?"

"Cheer him up a little and make him bear his poor and lonely life more easily!" repeated Helmsley, slowly, "Yes. And do you think we can do that, Mary?"

"We can try!" she said, smiling—"At any rate, while he's living in Wiercombe, we can be friendly to him, and give him a bit of dinner now and then!"

"So we can!" agreed Helmsley—"Or rather, so *you* can!"

"*We!*" corrected Mary—"*You're* helping me to keep house now, David,—remember that!"

"Why I haven't paid half or a quarter of my debt to you yet!" he exclaimed.

"But you're paying it off every day,"—she answered; "Don't you fear! I mean to have every penny out of you that I can!"

She laughed gaily, and taking up the tray upon which she had packed all the tea-things, carried it out of the kitchen. Helmsley heard her singing softly to herself in the scullery, as she set to work to wash the cups and saucers. And bending his old eyes on the fire, he smiled,— and an indomitable expression of energetic resolve strengthened every line of his features.

"You mean to have every penny out of me that you can, my dear, do you!" he said, softly—"And so—if Love can find out the way—you will!"

XVI

The winter now closed in apace,—and though the foliage all about Weircombe was reluctant to fall, and kept its green, russet and gold tints well on into December, the high gales which blew in from the sea played havoc with the trembling leaves at last and brought them to the ground like the painted fragments of Summer's ruined temple. All the fishermen's boats were hauled up high and dry, and great stretches of coarse net like black webs, were spread out on the beach for drying and mending,—while through the tunnels scooped out of the tall castellated rocks which guarded either side of the little port, or "weir," the great billows dashed with a thunderous roar of melody, oftentimes throwing aloft fountains of spray well-nigh a hundred feet in height—spray which the wild wind caught and blew in pellets of salty foam far up the little village street. Helmsley was now kept a prisoner indoors,—he had not sufficient strength to buffet with a gale, or to stand any unusually sharp nip of cold,—so he remained very comfortably by the side of the fire, making baskets, which he was now able to turn out quickly with quite an admirable finish, owing to the zeal and earnestness with which he set himself to the work. Mary's business in the winter months was entirely confined to the lace-mending—she had no fine laundry work to do, and her time was passed in such household duties as kept her little cottage sweet and clean, in attentive guardianship and care of her "father's friend"—and in the delicate weaving of threads whereby the fine fabric which had once perchance been damaged and spoilt by flaunting pride, was made whole and beautiful again by simple patience. Helmsley was never tired of watching her. Whether she knelt down with a pail of suds, and scrubbed her cottage doorstep—or whether she sat quietly opposite to him, with the small "Charlie" snuggled on a rug between them, while she mended her lace, his eyes always rested upon her with deepening interest and tenderness. And he grew daily more conscious of a great peace and happiness—peace and happiness such as he had never known since his boyhood's days. He, who had found the ways of modern society dull to the last point of excruciating boredom, was not aware of any monotony in the daily round of the hours, which, laden with simple duties and pleasures, came and went softly and slowly like angel messengers stepping gently from one heaven to another. The world—or that which is called the world,—had receded from him altogether. Here, where he had found a shelter, there was no talk of finance—the claims of the perpetual "bridge" party had vanished like the misty confusion of a bad dream from the brain—the unutterably vulgar intrigues common to the so-called "better" class of twentieth century humanity could not intrude any claim on his attention or his time—the perpetual lending of money to perpetually dishonest borrowers was, for the present, a finished task—and he felt himself to be a free man—far freer than he had been for many years. And, to add to the interest of his days, he became engrossed in a scheme—a strange scheme which built itself up in his head like a fairy palace, wherein everything beautiful, graceful, noble, helpful and precious, found place and position, and grew from promise to fulfilment as easily as a perfect rosebud ripens to a perfect rose. But he said nothing of his thoughts. He hugged them, as it were, to himself, and toyed with them as though they were jewels,—precious jewels selected specially to be set in a crown of inestimable worth. Meanwhile his health kept fairly equable, though he was well aware within his own consciousness that he did not get stronger. But he was strong enough to be merry at times—and his kindly temper and cheery conversation made him a great favourite with the Weircombe folk, who were never tired of "looking in" as they termed it, on Mary, and "'avin' a bit of a jaw with old David."

Sociable evenings they had too, during that winter—evenings when Angus Reay came in to tea and stayed to supper, and after supper entertained them by singing in a deep baritone voice as soft as honey, the old Scotch songs now so hopelessly "out of fashion"— such as "My Nannie O"—"Ae fond kiss"—and "Highland Mary," in which last exquisite ballad he was always at his best. And Mary sang also, accompanying herself on a quaint old Hungarian zither, which she said had been left with her father as guarantee for ten shillings which he had lent to a street musician wandering about Barnstaple. The street musician disappeared and the ten shillings were never returned, so Mary took possession of the zither, and with the aid of a cheap instruction book, managed to learn enough of its somewhat puzzling technique to accompany her own voice with a few full, rich, plaintive chords. And it was in this fashion that Angus heard her first sing what she called "A song of the sea," running thus:

> *I heard the sea cry out in the night*
> *Like a fretful child—*

Moaning under the pale moonlight
In a passion wild—
And my heart cried out with the sea, in tears,
For the sweet lost joys of my vanished years!

I heard the sea laugh out in the noon
Like a girl at play—
All forgot was the mournful moon
In the dawn of day!
And my heart laughed out with the sea, in gladness,
And I thought no more of bygone sadness.

I think the sea is a part of me
With its gloom and glory—
What Has Been, and what yet Shall Be
Is all its story;
Rise up, O Heart, with the tidal flow,
And drown the sorrows of Long Ago!

Something eerie and mystical there was in these words, sung as she sang them in a low, soft, contralto, sustained by the pathetic quiver of the zither strings throbbing under the pressure of her white fingers, and Angus asked her where she had learned the song.

"I found it,"—she answered, somewhat evasively.

"Did you compose it yourself?"

She flushed a little.

"How can you imagine such a thing?"

He was silent, but "imagined" the more. And after this he began to show her certain scenes and passages in the book he was writing, sometimes reading them aloud to her with all that eager eloquence which an author who loves and feels his work is bound to convey into the pronounced expression of it. And she listened, absorbed and often entranced, for there was no gain-saying the fact that Angus Reay was a man of genius. He was inclined to underrate rather than overestimate his own abilities, and often showed quite a pathetic mistrust of himself in his very best and most original conceptions.

"When I read to you,"—he said to her, one day—"You must tell me the instant you feel bored. That's a great point! Because if *you* feel bored, other people who read the book will feel bored exactly as you do and at the very same passage. And you must criticise me mercilessly! Rend me to pieces—tear my sentences to rags, and pick holes in every detail, if you like! That will do me a world of good!"

Mary laughed.

"But why?" she asked, "Why do you want me to be so unkind to you?"

"It won't be unkind,"—he declared—"It will be very helpful. And I'll tell you why. There's no longer any real 'criticism' of literary work in the papers nowadays. There's only extravagant eulogium written up by an author's personal friends and wormed somehow into the press—or equally extravagant abuse, written and insinuated in similar fashion by an author's personal enemies. Well now, you can't live without having both friends and enemies—you generally have more of the latter than the former, particularly if you are successful. There's nothing a lazy man won't do to 'down' an industrious one,—nothing an unknown scrub won't attempt in the way of trying to injure a great fame. It's a delightful world for that sort of thing!—so truly 'Christian,' pleasant and charitable! But the consequence of all these mean and petty 'personal' views of life is, that sound, unbiased, honest literary criticism is a dead art. You can't get it anywhere. And yet if you could, there's nothing that would be so helpful, or so strengthening to a man's work. It would make him put his best foot foremost. I should like to think that my book when it comes out, would be 'reviewed' by a man who had no prejudices, no 'party' politics, no personal feeling for or against me,—but who simply and solely considered it from an impartial, thoughtful, just and generous point of view—taking it as a piece of work done honestly and from a deep sense of conviction. Criticism from fellows who just turn over the pages of a book to find fault casually wherever they can—(I've seen them at it in newspaper offices!) or to quote unfairly mere scraps of sentences without context,—or to fly off into a whirlwind of personal and scurrilous calumnies against an author whom they don't know, and perhaps never will know,—that sort of thing is quite useless to me. It neither encourages nor angers me. It is a mere flabby exhibition of incompetency—much as if a jelly-fish should try to fight a sea-gull! Now you,—if you criticise me,—your criticism will be valuable, because it will be quite honest—there will be no 'personal' feeling in it—"

She raised her eyes to his and smiled.

"No?"

Something warm and radiant in her glance flashed into his soul and thrilled it strangely. Vaguely startled by an impression which he did not try to analyse, he went on hastily—"No—because you see you are neither my friend nor my enemy, are you?"

She was quite silent.

"I mean,"—he continued, blundering along somewhat lamely,—"You don't hate me very much, and you don't like me very much. I'm just an ordinary man to you. Therefore you're bound to be perfectly impartial, because what I do is a matter of 'personal' indifference to you. That's why your criticism will be so helpful and valuable."

She bent her head closely over the lace she was mending for a minute or two, as though she were making a very intricate knot. Then she looked up again.

"Well, if you wish it, I'll tell you just what I think," she said, quietly—"But you mustn't call it criticism. I'm not clever enough to judge a book. I only know what pleases *me*,—and what pleases me may not please the world. I know very little about authors, and I've taught myself all that I do know. I love Shakespeare,—but I could not explain to you why I love him, because I'm not clever enough. I only feel his work,—I feel that it's all right and beautiful and wonderful—but I couldn't criticise it."

"No one can,—no one should!" said Reay, warmly—"Shakespeare is above all criticism!"

"But is he not always being criticised?" she asked.

"Yes. By little men who cannot understand greatness,"—he answered—"It gives a kind of 'scholarly importance' to the little men, but it leaves the great one unscathed."

This talk led to many others of a similar nature between them, and Reay's visits to Mary's cottage became more and more frequent. David Helmsley, weaving his baskets day by day, began to weave something more delicate and uncommon than the withes of willow,—a weaving which went on in his mind far more actively than the twisting and plaiting of the osiers in his hands. Sometimes in the evenings, when work was done, and he sat in his comfortable easy chair by the fire watching Mary at her sewing and Angus talking earnestly to her, he became so absorbed in his own thoughts that he scarcely heard their voices, and often when they spoke to him, he started from a profound reverie, unconscious of their words. But it was not the feebleness or weariness of age that made him seem at times indifferent to what was going on around him—it was the intensity and fervour of a great and growing idea of happiness in his soul,—an idea which he cherished so fondly and in such close secrecy, as to be almost afraid to whisper it to himself lest by some unhappy chance it should elude his grasp and vanish into nothingness.

And so the time went on to Christmas and New Year. Weircombe kept these festivals very quietly, yet not without cheerfulness. There was plenty of holly about, and the children, plunging into the thick of the woods at the summit of the "coombe" found mistletoe enough for the common need. The tiny Church was prettily decorated by the rector's wife and daughters, assisted by some of the girls of the village, and everybody attended service on Christmas morning, not only because it was Christmas, but because it was the last time their own parson would preach to them, before he went away for three months or more to a warm climate for the benefit of his health. But Helmsley did not join the little crowd of affectionate parishioners—he stayed at home while Mary went, as she said "to pray for him." He watched her from the open cottage door, as she ascended the higher part of the "coombe," dressed in a simple stuff gown of darkest blue, with a prim little "old maid's" bonnet, as she called it, tied neatly under her rounded white chin—and carrying in her hand a much worn "Book of Common Prayer" which she held with a certain delicate reverence not often shown to holy things by the church-going women of the time. Weircombe Church had a small but musical chime of bells, presented to it by a former rector—and the silvery sweetness of the peal just now ringing was intensified by the close proximity of the mountain stream, which, rendered somewhat turbulent by recent rains, swept along in a deep swift current, carrying the melody of the chimes along with it down to the sea and across the waves in broken pulsation, till they touched with a faint mysterious echo the masts of home-returning ships, and brought a smile to the faces of sailors on board who, recognising the sound, said "Weircombe bells, sure-*ly*!"

Helmsley stood listening, lost in meditation. To anyone who could have seen him then, a bent frail figure just within the cottage door, with his white hair, white beard, and general appearance of gentle and resigned old age, he would have seemed nothing more than a venerable peasant, quietly satisfied with his simple surroundings, and as far apart from every association of wealth, as the daisy in the grass is from the star in the sky. Yet, in actual fact, his brain was busy weighing millions of money,—the fate of an accumulated mass of wealth hung on the balance of his decision,—and he was mentally arranging his plans with all the clearness, precision and practicality which had distinguished him in his biggest financial schemes,—schemes which had from time to time amazed and convulsed the speculating world. A certain wistful sadness touched him as he looked on the quiet country landscape in the wintry sunlight of this Christmas morn,—some secret instinctive foreboding told him that it might be the last Christmas he should ever see. And a sudden wave of regret swept over his soul,—regret that he had not appreciated the sweet things of life more keenly when he had been able to enjoy their worth. So many simple joys missed!—so many gracious and helpful sentiments discarded!—all the best of his years given over to eager pursuit of gold,—not because he cared for gold really, but because, owing to a false social system which perverted the moral sense, it seemed necessary to happiness. Yet he had proved it to be the very last thing that could make a man happy. The more money, the less enjoyment of it—the greater the wealth, the less the content. Was this according to law?—the spiritual law of compensation, which works steadily behind every incident which we may elect to call good or evil? He thought it must be so. This very festival—Christmas—how thoroughly he had been accustomed by an effete and degenerate "social set" to regard it as a "bore,"—an exploded superstition—a saturnalia of beef and pudding—a something which merely served as an excuse for throwing away good money on mere stupid sentiment. "Stupid" sentiment? Had he ever thought true, tender, homely sentiment "stupid"? Yes,—perhaps he had, when in the bold carelessness of full manhood he had assumed that the race was to the swift and the battle to the strong—but now, when the shadows were falling—when, perhaps, he would never hear the Christmas bells again, or be troubled by the "silly superstitions" of loving, praying, hoping, believing humanity, he would have given much could he have gone back in fancy to every Christmas of his life and seen each one spent cheerily amid the warm associations of such "sentiments" as make friendship valuable and lasting. He looked up half vaguely at the sky, clear blue on this still frosty morning, and was conscious of tears that crept smartingly behind his eyes and for a moment dimmed his sight. And he murmured dreamily—

"Behold we know not anything;
I can but trust that good shall fall
At last—far off—at last, to all—
And every winter change to spring!"

A tall, athletic figure came between him and the light, and Angus Reay's voice addressed him—

"Hullo, David! A merry Christmas to you! Do you know you are standing out in the cold? What would Miss Mary say?"

"Miss Mary" was the compromise Angus hit upon between "Miss Deane" and "Mary,"—considering the first term too formal, and the last too familiar.

Helmsley smiled.

"Miss Mary has gone to church,"—he replied—"I thought you had gone too."

Reay gave a slight gesture of mingled regret and annoyance.

"No—I never go to church,"—he said—"But don't you think I despise the going. Not I. I wish I could go to church! I'd give anything to go as I used to do with my father every Sunday."

"And why can't you?"

"Because the church is not what it used to be,"—declared Reay—"Don't get me on that argument, David, or I shall never cease talking! Now, see here!—if you stand any longer at that open door you'll get a chill! You go inside the house and imitate Charlie's example—look at him!" And he pointed to the tiny toy terrier snuggled up as usual in a ball of silky comfort on the warm hearth—"Small epicure! Come back to your chair, David, and sit by the fire—your hands are quite cold."

Helmsley yielded to the persuasion, not because he felt cold, but because he was rather inclined to be alone with Reay for a little. They entered the house and shut the door.

"Doesn't it look a different place without her!" said Angus, glancing round the trim little kitchen—"As neat as a pin, of course, but all the life gone from it."

Helmsley smiled, but did not answer. Seating himself in his armchair, he spread out his thin old hands to the bright fire, and watched Reay as he stood near the hearth, leaning one arm easily against a rough beam which ran across the chimney piece.

"She is a wonderful woman!" went on Reay, musingly; "She has a power of which she is scarcely conscious."

"And what is that?" asked Helmsley, slowly rubbing his hands with quite an abstracted air.

Angus laughed lightly, though a touch of colour reddened his bronzed cheeks.

"The power that the old alchemists sought and never could find!" he answered—"The touch that transmutes common metals to fine gold, and changes the every-day prose of life to poetry."

Helmsley went on rubbing his hands slowly.

"It's so extraordinary, don't you think, David,"—he continued—"that there should be such a woman as Miss Mary alive at all?"

Helmsley looked up at him questioningly, but said nothing.

"I mean,"—and Angus threw out his hand with an impetuous gesture—"that considering all the abominable, farcical tricks women play nowadays, it is simply amazing to find one who is contented with a simple life like this, and who manages to make that simple life so gracious and beautiful!"

Still Helmsley was silent.

"Now, just think of that girl I've told you about—Lucy Sorrel,"—proceeded Angus—"Nothing would have contented her in all this world!"

"Not even her old millionaire?" suggested Helmsley, placidly.

"No, certainly not! Poor old devil! He'll soon find himself put on the shelf if he marries her. He won't be able to call his soul his own! If he gives her diamonds, she'll want more diamonds—if he covers her and stuffs her with money, she'll never have enough! She'll want all she can get out of him while he lives and everything he has ever possessed when he's dead."

Helmsley rubbed his hands more vigorously together.

"A very nice young lady," he murmured. "Very nice indeed! But if you judge her in this way now, why did you ever fall in love with her?"

"She was pretty, David!" and Reay smiled—"That's all! My passion for her was skin-deep! And hers for me didn't even touch the cuticle! She was pretty—as pretty as a wax-doll,—perfect eyes, perfect hair, perfect figure, perfect complexion—ugh! how I hate perfection!"

And taking up the poker, he gave a vigorous blow to a hard lump of coal in the grate, and split it into a blaze.

"I hate perfection!" he resumed—"Or rather, I hate what passes for perfection, for, as a matter of fact, there's nothing perfect. And I specially and emphatically hate the woman that considers herself a 'beauty,' that gets herself photographed as a 'beauty,' that the press reporter speaks of as a 'beauty,'—and that affronts you with her 'beauty' whenever you look at her, as though she were some sort of first-class goods for sale. Now Miss Mary is a beautiful woman—and she doesn't seem to know it."

"Her time for vanity is past,"—said Helmsley, sententiously—"She is an old maid."

"Old maid be shot!" exclaimed Angus, impetuously—"By Jove! Any man might be proud to marry her!"

A keen, sharp glance, as incisive as any that ever flashed up and down the lines of a business ledger, gleamed from under Helmsley's fuzzy brows.

"Would you?" he asked.

"Would I marry her?" And Angus reddened suddenly like a boy—"Dear old David, bless you! That's just what I want you to help me to do!"

For a moment such a great wave of triumph swept over Helmsley's soul that he could not speak. But he mastered his emotion by an effort.

"I'm afraid,"—he said—"I'm afraid I should be no use to you in such a business,—you'd much better speak to her yourself—"

"Why, of course I mean to speak to her myself,"—interrupted Reay, warmly—"Don't be dense, David! You don't suppose I want *you* to speak for me, do you? Not a bit of it! Only before I speak, I do wish you could find out whether she likes me a little—because—because—I'm afraid she doesn't look upon me at all in *that* light—"

"In what light?" queried Helmsley, gently.

"As a lover,"—replied Angus—"She's given up thinking of lovers."

Helmsley leaned back in his chair, and clasping his hands together so that the tips of his fingers met, looked over them in almost the same meditative businesslike way as he had looked at Lucy Sorrel when he had questioned her as to her ideas of her future.

"Well, naturally she has,"—he answered—"Lovers have given up thinking of *her*!"

"I hope they have!" said Angus, fervently—"I hope I have no rivals! For my love for her is a jealous love, David! I must be all in all to her, or nothing! I must be the very breath of her breath, the life of her life! I must!—or I am no use to her. And I want to be of use. I want to work for her, to look upon her as the central point of all my actions—the very core of ambition and endeavour,—so that everything I do may be well done enough to meet with her praise. If she does not like it, it will be worthless. For her soul is as pure as the sunlight and as full of great depths as the sea! Simplest and sweetest of women as she is, she has enough of God in her to make a man live up to the best that is in him!"

His voice thrilled with passion as he spoke—and Helmsley felt a strange contraction at his heart—a pang of sharp memory, desire and regret all in one, which moved him to a sense of yearning for this love which he had never known—this divine and wonderful emotion whose power could so transform a man as to make him seem a very king among men. For so Angus Reay looked just now, with his eyes flashing unutterable tenderness, and his whole aspect expressive of a great hope born of a great ideal. But he restrained the feeling that threatened to over-master him, and merely said very quietly, and with a smile—

"I see you are very much in love with her, Mr. Reay!"

"In love?" Angus laughed—"No, my dear old David! I'm not a bit 'in love.' I love her! That's love with a difference. But you know how it is with me. I haven't a penny in the world but just what I told you must last me for a year—and I don't know when I shall make any more. So that I wouldn't be such a cad as to speak to her about it yet. But—if I could only get a little hope,—if I could just find out whether she liked me a little, that would give me more energy in my work, don't you see? And that's where you could help me, David!"

Helmsley smiled ever so slightly.

"Tell me how,"—he said.

"Well, you might talk to her sometimes and ask her if she ever thinks of getting married—"

"I have done that,"—interrupted Helmsley—"and she has always said 'No.'"

"Never mind what she *has* said—ask her again, David,"—persisted Angus—"And then lead her on little by little to talk about me—"

"Lead her on to talk about you—yes!" and Helmsley nodded his head sagaciously.

"David, my dear old man, you *will* interrupt me,"—and Angus laughed like a boy—"Lead her on, I say,—and find out whether she likes me ever so little—and then—"

"And then?" queried Helmsley, his old eyes beginning to sparkle—"Must I sing your praises to her?"

"Sing my praises! No, by Jove!—there's nothing to praise in me. I don't want you to say a word, David. Let *her* speak—hear what *she* says—and then—and then tell *me*!"

"Then tell *you*—yes—yes, I see!" And Helmsley nodded again in a fashion that was somewhat trying to Reay's patience. "But, suppose she finds fault with you, and says you are not at all the style of man she likes—what then?"

"Then,"—said Reay, gloomily—"my book will never be finished!"

"Dear, dear!" Helmsley raised his hands with a very well acted gesture of timid concern—"So bad as all that!"

"So bad as all that!" echoed Reay, with a quick sigh; "Or rather so good as all that. I don't know how it has happened, David, but she has quite suddenly become the very life of my work. I don't think I could get on with a single page of it, if I didn't feel that I could go to her and ask her what she thinks of it."

"But,"—said Helmsley, in a gentle, argumentative way—"all this is very strange! She is not an educated woman."

Reay laughed lightly.

"No? What do you call an educated woman, David?"

Helmsley thought a moment. The situation was a little difficult, for he had to be careful not to say too much.

"Well, I mean,"—he said, at last—"She is not a lady."

Reay's eyes flashed sudden indignation.

"Not a lady!" he exclaimed—"Good God! Who is a lady then?"

Helmsley glanced at him covertly. How fine the man looked, with his tall, upright figure, strong, thoughtful face, and air of absolute determination!

"I'm afraid,"—he murmured, humbly—"I'm afraid I don't know how to express myself,—but what I want to say is that she is not what the world would call a lady,—just a simple lace-mender,—real 'ladies' would not ask her to their houses, or make a friend of her, perhaps—"

"She's a simple lace-mender,—I was a common cowherd,"—said Angus, grimly—"Do you think those whom the world calls 'ladies' would make a friend of *me*?"

Helmsley smiled.

"You're a man—and to women it doesn't matter what a man *was*, so long as he *is* something. You were a cowherd, as you say—but you educated yourself at a University and got a degree. In that way you've raised yourself to the rank of a gentleman—"

"I was always that,"—declared Angus, boldly, "even as a cowherd! Your arguments won't hold with me, David! A gentleman is not made by a frock coat and top hat. And a lady is not a lady because she wears fine clothes and speaks one or two foreign languages very badly. For that's about all a 'lady's' education amounts to nowadays. According to Victorian annals, 'ladies' used to be fairly accomplished—they played and sang music well, and knew that it was necessary to keep up intelligent conversation and maintain graceful manners—but they've gone back to sheer barbarism in the frantic ugliness of their performances at hockey—and they've taken to the repulsive vices of Charles the Second's time in gambling and other immoralities. No, David! I don't take kindly to the 'ladies' who disport themselves under the benevolent dispensation of King Edward the Seventh."

Helmsley was silent. After a pause, Reay went on—

"You see, David, I'm a poor chap—poorer than Mary is. If I could get a hundred, or say, two hundred pounds for my book when it is finished, I could ask her to marry me then, because I could bring that money to her and do something to keep up the home. I never want anything sweeter or prettier than this little cottage to live in. If she would let me share it with her as her husband, we should live a perfectly happy life—a life that thousands would envy us! That is, of course, if she loved me."

"Ay!—that's a very important 'if,'" said Helmsley.

"I know it is. That's why I want you to help me to find out her mind, David—will you? Because, if you should discover that I am objectionable to her in any way, it would be better for me, I think, to go straight away from Weircombe, and fight my trouble out by myself. Then, you see, she would never know that I wanted to bother her with my life-long presence. Because she's very happy as she is,—her face has all the lovely beauty of perfect content—and I'd rather do anything than trouble her peace."

There followed a pause. The fire crackled and burned with a warm Christmas glow, and Charlie, uncurling his soft silky body, stretched out each one of his tiny paws separately, with slow movements expressive of intense comfort. If ever that little dog had known what it was to lie in the lap of luxury amid aristocratic surroundings, it was certain that he was conscious of being as well off in a poor cottage as in a palace of a king. And after a minute or two, Helmsley raised himself in his chair and held out his hand to Angus Reay, who grasped it warmly.

"I'll do my best,"—he said, quietly—"I know what you mean—and I think your feeling does you honour. Of course you know I'm only a kind of stranger here—just a poor old lonely man, very dependent on Miss Deane for her care of me, and trying my best to show that I'm not ungrateful to her for all her goodness—and I mustn't presume too far—but—I'll do my best. And I hope—I hope all will be well!" He paused—and pressed Reay's hand again—then glanced up at the quaint sheep-faced clock that ticked monotonously against the kitchen

wall. "She will be coming back from church directly,"—he continued—
"Won't you go and meet her?"

"Shall I?" And Reay's face brightened.

"Do!"

Another moment, and Helmsley was alone—save for the silent
company of the little dog stretched out upon the hearth. And he lost
himself in a profound reverie, the while he built a castle in the air of
his own designing, in which Self had no part. How many airy fabrics of
beauty and joy had he not raised one after the other in his mind, only
to see them crumble into dust!—but this one, as he planned it in his
thoughts, nobly uplifted above all petty limits, with all the light of a
broad beneficence shining upon it, and a grand obliteration of his own
personality serving as the very cornerstone of its foundation, seemed
likely to be something resembling the house spoken of by Christ, which
was built upon a rock—against which neither winds, nor rains, nor
floods could prevail. And when Mary came back from Church, with
Reay accompanying her, she found him looking very happy. In fact, she
told him he had quite "a Christmas face."

"What is a Christmas face, Mary?" he asked, smiling.

"Don't you know? A face that looks glad because other people are
glad,"—she replied, simply.

An expressive glance flashed from Reay's eyes,—a glance which
Helmsley caught and understood in all its eloquent meaning.

"We had quite a touching little sermon this morning," she went
on, untying her bonnet strings, and taking off that unassuming head-
gear—"It was just a homely simple, kind talk. Our parson's sorry to be
going away, but he hopes to be back with us at the beginning of April,
fit and well again. He's looking badly, poor soul! I felt a bit like crying
when he wished us all a bright Christmas and happy New Year, and said
he hoped God would allow him to see us all again."

"Who is going to take charge of the parish in his absence?" asked
Reay.

"A Mr. Arbroath. He isn't a very popular man in these parts, and I
can't think why he has volunteered to come here, seeing he's got several
parishes of his own on the other side of Dunster to attend to. But I'm
told he also wants a change—so he's got some one to take his duties,
and he is coming along to us. Of course, it's well known that he likes to
try a new parish whenever he can."

"Has he any reason for that special taste?" enquired Reay.

"Oh yes!" answered Mary, quietly—"He's a great High Churchman, and he wants to introduce Mass vestments and the confessional whenever he can. Some people say that he receives an annual payment from Rome for doing this kind of work."

"Another form of the Papal secret service!" commented Reay, drily—"I understand! I've seen enough of it!"

Mary had taken a clean tablecloth from an oaken press, and was spreading it out for dinner.

"Well," she said, smilingly, "he won't find it very advantageous to him to take the duties here. For every man and woman in the village intends to keep away from Church altogether if he does not give us our services exactly as we have always been accustomed to them. And it won't be pleasant for him to read prayers and preach to empty seats, will it?"

"Scarcely!"

And Angus, standing near the fire, bent his brows with meditative sternness on the glowing flames. Then suddenly addressing Helmsley, he said—"You asked me a while ago, David, why I didn't go to Church. I told you I wished I could go, as I used to do with my father every Sunday. For, when I was a boy, our Sundays were real devotional days—our preachers *felt* what they preached, and when they told us to worship the great Creator 'in spirit and in truth,' we knew they were in earnest about it. Now, religion is made a mere 'party' system—a form of struggle as to which sect can get the most money for its own purposes. Christ,—the grand, patient, long-suffering Ideal of all goodness, is gone from it! How can He remain with it while it is such a Sham! Our bishops in England truckle to Rome—and, Rome itself is employing every possible means to tamper with the integrity of the British constitution. The spies and emissaries of Rome are everywhere—both in our so-called 'national' Church and in our most distinctly *un*-national Press!"

Helmsley listened with keen interest. As a man of business, education, observation, and discernment, he knew that what Reay said was true,—but in his assumed rôle of a poor and superannuated old office clerk, who had been turned adrift from work by reason of age and infirmities, he had always to be on his guard against expressing his opinion too openly or frankly.

"I don't know much about the newspapers,"—he said, mildly—"I read those I can get, just for the news—but there isn't much news, it appears to me—"

"And what there is may be contradicted in an hour's time,"—said Angus—"I tell you, David, when I started working in journalism, I thought it was the finest profession going. It seemed to me to have all the responsibilities of the world on its back. I considered it a force with which to educate, help, and refine all peoples, and all classes. But I found it was only a money speculation after all. How much profit could be made out of it? That was the chief point of action. That was the mainspring of every political discussion—and in election times, one side had orders to abuse the other, merely to keep up the popular excitement. By Jove! I should like to take a select body of electors 'behind the scenes' of a newspaper office and show them how the whole business is run!"

"You know too much, evidently!" said Mary smiling—"I don't wonder you were dismissed!"

He laughed—then as suddenly frowned.

"I swear as I stand here," he said emphatically, "that the press is not serving the people well! Do you know—no, of course you don't!—but I can tell you for a fact that a short time ago an offer was made from America through certain financial powers in the city, to buy up several of the London dailies, and run them on American lines! Germany had a finger in the pie, too, through her German Jews!"

Helmsley looked at his indignant face with a slight imperceptible smile.

"Well!" he said, with a purposely miscomprehending air.

"Well! You say 'Well,' David, as if such a proposition contained nothing remarkable. That's because you don't understand! Imagine for a moment the British Press being run by America!"

Helmsley stroked his beard thoughtfully.

"I *can't* imagine it,"—he said.

"No—of course you can't! But a few rascally city financiers *could* imagine it, and more than that, were prepared to carry the thing through. Then, the British people would have been led, guided, advised, and controlled by a Yankee syndicate! And the worst of it is that this same British people would have been kept in ignorance of the 'deal.' They would actually have been paying their pennies to keep up the shares of a gang of unscrupulous rascals whose sole end and object was to get the British press into their power! Think of it!"

"But did they succeed?" asked Helmsley.

"No, they didn't. Somebody somewhere had a conscience. Somebody somewhere refused to 'swop' the nation's much boasted 'liberty of the press' for so much cash down. I believe the 'Times' is backed by the Rothschilds, and managed by American advertisers—I don't know whether it is so or not—but I *do* know that the public ought to be put on their guard. If I were a powerful man and a powerful speaker I would call mass meetings everywhere, and urge the people not to purchase a single newspaper till each one published in its columns a full and honest list of the shareholders concerned in it. Then the public would have a chance of seeing where they are. At present they *don't* know where they are."

"Well, you know very well where *you* are!" said Mary, interrupting him at this juncture—"You are in my house,—it's Christmas Day, and dinner's ready!"

He laughed, and they all three sat down to table. It had been arranged for fully a week before that Angus should share his Christmas dinner with Mary and "old David"—and a very pleasant and merry meal they made of it. And in the afternoon and evening some of the villagers came in to gossip—and there was singing of songs, and one or two bashful attempts on the part of certain gawky lads to kiss equally gawky girls under the mistletoe. And Mary, as hostess of the haphazard little party, did her best to promote kindly feeling among them all, effacing herself so utterly, and playing the "old maid" with such sweet and placid loveliness that Angus became restless, and was moved by a feverish desire to possess himself of one of the little green twigs with white berries, which, looking so innocent, were apparently so provocative, and to try its effect by holding it suddenly above the glorious masses of her brown hair, which shone with the soft and shimmering hue of evening sunlight. But he dared not. Kissing under the mistletoe was all very well for boys and girls—but for a mature bachelor of thirty-nine and an "old maid" of thirty-five, these uncouth and calf-like gambollings lacked dignity. Moreover, when he looked at Mary's pure profile—the beautifully shaped eyes, classic mouth, and exquisite line of neck and shoulder, the very idea of touching those lips with a kiss given in mere lightness, seemed fraught with impertinence and irreverence. If ever he kissed Mary, he thought,—and then all the powers of his mind galloped off like wild horses let loose on a sun-baked ranch—if ever he kissed Mary! What a dream!—what a boldness unprecedented! But again—if ever he kissed her, it must be with the kiss of a lover, for whom such a token of endearment was the sign of a sacred betrothal. And he became so lost and abstracted in his musings that he almost forgot the simple village merriment around him, and only came back to himself a little when the party broke up altogether, and he himself had to say "good-night," and go with the rest. Mary, while giving him her hand in farewell, looked at him with a sisterly solicitude.

"You're tired, Mr. Reay,"—she said—"I'm afraid we've been too noisy for you, haven't we? But one can't keep boys and girls quiet!"

"I don't want them kept quiet,"—said Reay, holding her hand very hard—"And I'm not tired. I've only been thinking."

"Ah! Of your book?"

"Yes. Of my book."

He went then, and came no more to the cottage till a week later when it was New Year's Eve. This they celebrated very quietly—just they three alone. Mary thought it somewhat imprudent for "old David" to sit up till midnight in order to hear the bells "ring out the Old, ring in the New"—but he showed a sudden vigorous resolution about it which was not to be gainsaid.

"Let me have my way, my dear,"—he implored her—"I may never see another New Year!"

"Nonsense, David!" she said cheerily—"You will see many and many a one, please God!"

"Please God, I shall!" he answered, quietly—"But if it should not please God—then—"

"There!—you want to stay up, and you shall stay up!" she declared, smiling—"After all, as Mr. Reay is with us, the time won't perhaps seem so long for you."

"But for you,"—put in Angus—"it will seem very long won't it!"

"Oh, I always sit up for the coming-in of the New Year,"—she replied—"Father used to do it, and I like to keep up all father's ways. Only I thought David might feel too tired. You must sing to us, Mr. Reay, to pass the hours away."

"And so must you!" he replied.

And she did sing that night as she had never sung to them before, with a fuller voice and more passion than she had hitherto shown,—one little wild ballad in particular taking Reay's fancy so much that he asked her to sing it more than once. The song contained just three six-line stanzas, having little merit save in their suggestiveness.

> *Oh love, my love! I have giv'n you my heart*
> *Like a rose full-blown,*

With crimson petals trembling apart—
It is all your own—
What will you do with it. Dearest,—say?
Keep it for ever or throw it away?

Oh love, my love! I have giv'n you my life,
Like a ring of gold;
Symbol of peace in a world of strife,
To have and to hold.
What will you do with it, Dearest,—say?
Treasure it always, or throw it away?

Oh love, my love! Have all your will—
I am yours to the end;
Be false or faithful—comfort or kill,
Be lover or friend,—
Where gifts are given they must remain,
I never shall ask for them back again!

"Do you know that you have a very beautiful voice, Miss Mary?" said Angus, after hearing this for the second time.

"Oh, I don't think so at all,"—she answered, quickly; "Father used to like to hear me sing—but I can only just give ballads their meaning, and pronounce the words carefully so the people may know what I am trying to sing about. I've no real voice."

"You have!" And Angus turned to Helmsley for his opinion—"Hasn't she, David?"

"Her voice is the sweetest *I* ever heard,"—replied Helmsley—"But then I'm not much of a judge."

And his thoughts went roving back to certain entertainments in London which he had given for the benefit of his wealthy friends, when he had paid as much as five or six hundred guineas in fees to famous opera singers, that they might shriek or warble, as their respective talents dictated, to crowds of indifferent loungers in his rooms, who cared no more for music than they did for religion. He almost smiled as he recalled those nights, and contrasted them with this New Year's evening, when seated in an humble cottage, he had for his companions only a lowly-born poor woman, and an equally lowly-born poor man, both of whom evinced finer education, better manners, greater pride of spirit, and more resolute independence than nine-tenths of the "society" people who had fawned upon him and flattered him, simply because they knew he was a millionaire. And the charm of his present position was that these two, poor, lowly-born people were under the impression that even in their poverty and humility they were better off than he was, and that because fortune had been, as they considered, kind to them, they were bound to treat him in a way that should not remind him of his dependent and defenceless condition. It was impossible to imagine greater satisfaction than that which he enjoyed in the contemplation of his own actual situation as compared with that which he had impressed upon the minds of these two friends of his who had given him their friendship trustingly and frankly for himself alone. And he listened placidly, with folded hands and half shut eyes, while Angus, at Mary's request, trolled forth "The Standard on the Braes o' Mar" and "Sound the pibroch,"—varying those warlike ditties with "Jock o' Hazledean," and "Will ye no come back again,"—till all suddenly Mary rose from her chair, and with her finger to her lips said "Hark!" The church-bells were ringing out the Old Year, and glancing at the clock, they saw it wanted but ten minutes to midnight. Softly Mary stepped to the cottage door and opened it. The chime swung melodiously in, and Angus Reay went to the threshold, and stood beside Mary, listening. Had they glanced back that instant they would have seen Helmsley looking at them both, with an intensity of yearning in his pale face and sad old eyes that was pitiful and earnest beyond all expression—they would have seen his lips move, as he murmured—"God grant that I may make their lives beautiful! God give me this peace of mind before I die! God bless them!" But they were absorbed in listening—and presently with a deep clang the bells ceased. Mary turned her head.

"The Old Year's out, David!"

Then she went to him and knelt down beside him.

"It's been a kind old year!"—she said—"It brought you to me to take care of, and *me* to you to take care of you—didn't it?"

He laid one hand on hers, tremblingly, but was silent. She turned up her kind, sweet face to his.

"You're not tired, are you?"

He shook his head.

"No, my dear, no!"

A rush and a clang of melody swept suddenly through the open door—the bells had begun again.

MARIE CORELLI

"A Happy New Year, Miss Mary!" said Angus, looking towards her from where he stood on the threshold—"And to you, David!"

With an irrepressible movement of tenderness Helmsley raised his trembling hands and laid them gently on Mary's head.

"Take an old man's blessing, my dear!" he said, softly, "And from a most grateful heart!"

She caught his hands as he lifted them again from her brow, and kissed them. There were tears in her eyes, but she brushed them quickly away.

"You talk just like father!" she said, smiling—"He was always grateful for nothing!"

And rising from her kneeling attitude by Helmsley's chair, she went again towards the open cottage door, holding out her two hands to Reay. Looking at her as she approached he seemed to see in her some gracious angel, advancing with all the best possibilities of life for him in her sole power and gift.

"A Happy New Year, Mr. Reay! And success to the book!"

He clasped the hands she extended.

"If you wish success for it, success is bound to come!" he answered in a low voice—"I believe in your good influence!"

She looked at him, and whatever answer rose to her lips was suddenly silenced by the eloquence of his eyes. She coloured hotly, and then grew very pale. They both stood on the threshold of the open door, silent and strangely embarrassed, while the bells swung and clanged musically through the frosty air, and the long low swish of the sea swept up like a harmonious bass set to the silvery voice of the chimes. They little guessed with what passionate hope, yearning, and affection, Helmsley watched them standing there!—they little knew that on them the last ambition of his life was set!—and that any discovery of sham or falsehood in their natures would make cruel havoc of his dearest dreams! They waited, looking out on the dark quiet space, and listening to the rush of the stream till the clamour of the bells ceased again, and sounded no more. In the deep stillness that followed Angus said softly—

"There's not a leaf left on the old sweetbriar bush now!"

"No,"—answered Mary, in the same soft tone—"But it will be the first thing to bud with the spring."

"I've kept the little sprig you gave me,"—he added, apparently by way of a casual after-thought.

"Have you?"

Silence fell again—and not another word passed between them save a gentle "Good-night" when, the New Year having fully come in, they parted.

XVII

The dreariest season of the year had now set in, but frost and cold were very seldom felt severely in Weircombe. The little village lay in a deep warm hollow, and was thoroughly protected at the back by the hills, while in the front its shores were washed by the sea, which had a warming as well as bracing effect on the atmosphere. To invalids requiring an equable temperature, it would have been a far more ideal winter resort than any corner of the much-vaunted Riviera, except indeed for the fact that feeding and gambling dens were not among its attractions. To "society" people it would have proved insufferably dull, because society people, lacking intelligence to do anything themselves, always want everything done for them. Weircombe folk would not have understood that method of living. To them it seemed proper and reasonable that men, and women too, should work for what they ate. The theory that only a few chosen persons, not by any means estimable either as to their characters or their abilities, should eat what others were starved for, would not have appealed to them. They were a small and unimportant community, but their ideas of justice and principles of conduct were very firmly established. They lived on the lines laid down by their forefathers, and held that a simple faith in God, coupled with honest hard labour, was sufficient to make life well worth living. And, on the whole they were made of that robust human material of which in the days gone by there was enough to compose and consolidate the greatness of Britain. They were kindly of heart, but plain in speech,— and their remarks on current events, persons and things, would have astonished and perhaps edified many a press man had he been among them, when on Saturday nights they "dropped in" at the one little public-house of the village, and argued politics and religion till closing-time. Angus Reay soon became a favourite with them all, though at first they had looked upon him with a little distrust as a "gentleman *tow-rist*"; but when he had mixed with them freely and familiarly, making no secret of the fact that he was poor, and that he was endeavouring to earn a livelihood like all the rest of them, only in a different way, they abandoned all reserve, and treated him as one of themselves. Moreover, when it was understood that "Mis' Deane," whose reputation stood very high in the village, considered him not unworthy of her friendship, he rose up several degrees in the popular estimation, and many a time those who were the self-elected wits and wise-acres of the place, would "look in" as they termed it, at Mary's cottage, and pass the evening talking with him and with "old David," who, if he did not say much, listened the more. Mr. Bunce, the doctor, and Mr. Twitt, the stonemason, were in particular profoundly impressed when they knew that Reay had worked for two years on a London newspaper.

"Ye must 'ave a ter'uble knowledge of the world, Mister!" said Twitt, thoughtfully—"Just ter'uble!"

"Yes, I should assume it must be so,"—murmured Bunce—"I should think it could hardly fail to be so?"

Reay gave a short laugh.

"Well, I don't know!" he said—"You may call it a knowledge of the world if you like—I call it an unpleasant glimpse into the shady side of life. I'd rather walk in the sunshine."

"And what would you call the sunshine, sir?" asked Bunce, with his head very much on one side like a meditative bird.

Honesty, truth, belief in God, belief in good!"—answered Angus, with some passion—"Not perpetual scheming, suspicion of motives, personal slander, and pettiness—O Lord!—such pettiness as can hardly be believed! Journalism is the most educational force in the world, but its power is being put to wrong uses."

"Well,—said Twitt, slowly—"I aint so blind but I can see through a wall when there's a chink in it. An' when I gets my 'Daily' down from Lunnun, an' sees harf a page given up to a kind o' poster about Pills, an' another harf a page praisin' up somethin' about Tonics, I often sez to myself: 'Look 'ere, Twitt! What are ye payin' yer pennies out for? For a Patent Pill or for News? For a Nervy Tonic or for the latest pol'tics?' An' myself—me—Twitt—answers an' sez—'Why ye're payin' for news an' pol'tics, of course!' Well then, I sez, 'Twitt, ye aint gettin' nothin' o' the sort!' An' t' other day, blow'd if I didn't see in my paper a long piece about ''Ow to be Beautiful'—an' that 'adn't nothin' to do wi' me nor no man, but was just mere gabble for fool women. ''Ow to be Beautiful,' aint news o' the world!"

"No,"—said Reay—"You're not intended to know the news of the world. News, real news, is the property of the Stock Exchange. It's chiefly intended for company gambling purposes. The People are not expected to know much about it. Modern Journalism seeks to play Pope and assert the doctrine of infallibility. What It does not authorise, isn't supposed to exist."

"Is that truly so?" asked Bunce, solemnly.

"Most assuredly!"

"You mean to say,"—said Helmsley, breaking in upon the conversation, and speaking in quiet unconcerned tones—"that the actual national affairs of the world are not told to the people as they should be, but are jealously guarded by a few whose private interests are at stake?"

"Yes. I certainly do mean that."

"I thought you did. You see," went on Helmsley—"when I was in regular office work in London, I used to hear a good deal concerning the business schemes of this, that and the other great house in the city,—and I often wondered what the people would say if they ever came to know!"

"Came to know what?" said Mr. Bunce, anxiously.

"Why, the names of the principal shareholders in the newspapers,"— said Reay, placidly—"*That* might possibly open their eyes to the way their opinions are manufactured for them! There's very little 'liberty of the press' in Great Britain nowadays. The press is the property of a few rich men."

Mary, who was working very intently on a broad length of old lace she was mending, looked up at him—her eyes were brilliant and her cheeks softly flushed.

"I hope you will be brave enough to say that some day right out to the people as you say it to us,"—she observed.

"I will! Never fear about that! If I *am* ever anything—if I ever *can* be anything—I will do my level best to save my nation from being swallowed up by a horde of German-American Jews!" said Reay, hotly—"I would rather suffer anything myself than see the dear old country brought to shame."

"Right, very right!" said Mr. Bunce, approvingly—"And many—yes, I think we may certainly say many,—are of your spirit,—what do you think, David?"

Helmsley had raised himself in his chair, and was looking wonderfully alert. The conversation interested him.

"I quite agree,"—he said—"But Mr. Reay must remember that if he should ever want to make a clean sweep of German-American Jews and speculators as he says, and expose the way they tamper with British interests, he would require a great deal of money. A *very* great deal of money!" he repeated, slowly,—"Now I wonder, Mr. Reay, what you would do with a million?—two millions?—three millions?—four millions?"—

"Stop, stop, old David!"—interrupted Twitt, suddenly holding up his hand—"Ye takes my breath away!"

They all laughed, Reay's hearty tones ringing above the rest.

"Oh, I should know what to do with them!"—he said; "but I wouldn't spend them on my own selfish pleasures—that I swear! For one thing, I'd run a daily newspaper on *honest* lines—"

"It wouldn't sell!" observed Helmsley, drily.

"It would—it *should*!" declared Reay—"And I'd tell the people the truth of things,—I'd expose every financial fraud I could find—"

"And you'd live in the law-courts, I fear!" said Mr. Bunce, gravely shaking his head—"We may be perfectly certain, I think—may we not, David?—that the law-courts would be Mr. Reay's permanent address?"

They laughed again, and the conversation turned to other topics, though its tenor was not forgotten by anyone, least of all by Helmsley, who sat very silent for a long time afterwards, thinking deeply, and seeing in his thoughts various channels of usefulness to the world and the world's progress, which he had missed, but which others after him would find.

Meanwhile Weircombe suffered a kind of moral convulsion in the advent of the Reverend Mr. Arbroath, who arrived to "take duty" in the absence of its legitimate pastor. He descended upon the tiny place like an embodied black whirlwind, bringing his wife with him, a lady whose facial lineaments bore the strangest and most remarkable resemblance to those of a china cat; not a natural cat, because there is something soft and appealing about a real "pussy,"—whereas Mrs. Arbroath's countenance was cold and hard and shiny, like porcelain, and her smile was precisely that of the immovable and ruthless-looking animal designed long ago by old-time potters and named "Cheshire." Her eyes were similar to the eyes of that malevolent china creature— and when she spoke, her voice had the shrill tone which was but a few notes off the actual "*me-iau*" of an angry "Tom." Within a few days after their arrival, every cottage in the "coombe" had been "visited," and both Mr. and Mrs. Arbroath had made up their minds as to the neglected, wholly unspiritual and unregenerate nature of the little flock whom they had offered, for sake of their own health and advantage, to tend. The villagers had received them civilly, but without enthusiasm. When tackled on the subject of their religious opinions, most of them declined to answer, except Mr. Twitt, who, fixing a filmy eye sternly on the plain and gloomy face of Mr. Arbroath, said emphatically:

"We aint no 'Igh Jinks!"

"What do you mean, my man?" demanded Arbroath, with a dark smile.

"I mean what I sez"—rejoined Twitt—"I've been stonemason 'ere goin' on now for thirty odd years an' it's allus been the same 'ere—no 'Igh Jinks. Purcessin an' vestiments"—here Twitt spread out a broad dirty thumb and dumped it down with each word into the palm of his other hand—"candles, crosses, bobbins an' bowins—them's what we calls 'Igh Jinks, an' I make so bold as to say that if ye gets 'em up 'ere, Mr. Arbroath, ye'll be mighty sorry for yourself!"

"I shall conduct the services as I please!" said Arbroath. "You take too much upon yourself to speak to me in such a fashion! You should mind your own business!"

"So should you, Mister, so should you!" And Twitt chuckled contentedly—"An' if ye *don't* mind it, there's those 'ere as'll *make* ye!"

Arbroath departed in a huff, and the very next Sunday announced that "Matins" would be held at seven o'clock daily in the Church, and "Evensong" at six in the afternoon. Needless to say, the announcement was made in vain. Day after day passed, and no one attended. Smarting with rage, Arbroath sought to "work up" the village to a proper "'Igh Jink" pitch—but his efforts were wasted. And a visit to Mary Deane's cottage did not sweeten his temper, for the moment he caught sight of Helmsley sitting in his usual corner by the fire, he recognised him as the "old tramp" he had interviewed in the common room of the "Trusty Man."

"How did *you* come here?" he demanded, abruptly.

Helmsley, who happened to be at work basket-making, looked up, but made no reply. Whereupon Arbroath turned upon Mary—

"Is this man a relative of yours?" he asked.

Mary had risen from her chair out of ordinary civility as the clergyman entered, and now replied quietly.

"No, sir."

"Oh! Then what is he doing here?"

"You can see what he is doing,"—she answered, with a slight smile— "He is making baskets."

"He is a tramp!" said Arbroath, pointing an inflexible finger at him—"I saw him last summer smoking and drinking with a gang of low ruffians at a roadside inn called 'The Trusty Man'!" And he advanced a step towards Helmsley—"Didn't I see you there?"

Helmsley looked straight at him.

"You did."

"You told me you were tramping to Cornwall."

"So I was."

"Then what are you doing here?"

"Earning a living."

Arbroath turned sharply on Mary.

"Is that true?"

"Of course it is true,"—she replied—"Why should he tell you a lie?"

"Does he lodge with you?"

"Yes."

Arbroath paused a moment, his little brown eyes sparkling vindictively.

"Well, you had better be careful he does not rob you!" he said. "For I can prove that he seemed to be very good friends with that notorious rascal Tom o' the Gleam who murdered a nobleman at Blue Anchor last summer, and who would have hung for his crime if he had not fortunately saved the expense of a rope by dying."

Helmsley, bending over his basket-weaving, suddenly straightened himself and looked the clergyman full in the face.

"I never knew Tom o' the Gleam till that night on which you saw me at 'The Trusty Man,'" he said—"But I know he had terrible provocation for the murder he committed. I saw that murder done!"

"You saw it done!" exclaimed Arbroath—"And you are here?"

"Why should I not be here?" demanded Helmsley—"Would you have expected me to stay *there*? I was only one of many witnesses to that terrible deed of vengeance—but, as God lives, it was a just vengeance!"

"Just? You call murder just!" and Arbroath gave a gesture of scorn and horror—"And you,"—he continued, turning to Mary indignantly—"can allow a ruffian like this to live in your house?"

"He is no ruffian,"—said Mary steadily,—"Nor was Tom o' the Gleam a ruffian either. He was well-known in these parts for many and many a deed of kindness. The real ruffian was the man who killed his little child. Indeed I think he was the chief murderer."

"Oh, you do, do you?" and Mr. Arbroath frowned heavily—"And you call yourself a respectable woman?"

Mary smiled, and resuming her seat, bent her head intently over her lace work.

Arbroath stood irresolute, gazing at her. He was a sensual man, and her physical beauty annoyed him. He would have liked to sit down alone with her and take her hand in his own and talk to her about her "soul" while gloating over her body. But in the "old tramp's" presence there was nothing to be done. So he assumed a high moral tone.

"Accidents will happen,"—he said, sententiously—"If a child gets into the way of a motor going at full speed, it is bound to be unfortunate— for the child. But Lord Wrotham was a rich man—and no doubt he would have paid a handsome sum down in compensation—"

"Compensation!" And Helmsley suddenly stood up, drawing his frail thin figure erect—"Compensation! Money! Money for a child's life— money for a child's love! Are you a minister of Christ, that you can talk of such a thing as possible? What is all the wealth of the world compared to the life of one beloved human creature! Reverend sir, I am an old poor man,—a tramp as you say, consorting with rogues and ruffians— but were I as rich as the richest millionaire that ever 'sweated' honest labour, I would rather shoot myself than offer money compensation to a father for the loss of a child whom my selfish pleasure had slain!"

He trembled from head to foot with the force of his own eloquence, and Arbroath stared at him dumb-foundered.

"You are a preacher,"—went on Helmsley—"You are a teacher of the Gospel. Do you find anything in the New Testament that gives men licence to ride rough-shod over the hearts and emotions of their fellow-men? Do you find there that selfishness is praised or callousness condoned? In those sacred pages are we told that a sparrow's life is valueless, or a child's prayer despised? Sir, if you are a Christian, teach Christianity as Christ taught it—*honestly!*"

Arbroath turned livid.

"How dare you—!" he began—when Mary quietly rose.

"I would advise you to be going, sir,"—she said, quite courteously— "The old man is not very strong, and he has a trouble of the heart. It is little use for persons to argue who feel so differently. We poor folk do not understand the ways of the gentry."

And she held open the door of her cottage for him to pass out. He pressed his slouch-hat more heavily over his eyes, and glared at her from under the shadow of its brim.

"You are harbouring a dangerous customer in your house!" he said— "A dangerous customer! It will be my duty to warn the parish against him!"

She smiled.

"You are very welcome to do so, sir! Good-morning!"

And as he tramped away through her tiny garden, she quickly shut and barred the door after him, and hurried to Helmsley in some anxiety, for he looked very pale, and his breath came and went somewhat rapidly.

"David dear, why did you excite yourself so much over that man!" she said, kneeling beside him as he sank back exhausted in his chair—"Was it worth while?"

He patted her head with a tremulous hand.

"Perhaps not!" And he smiled—"Perhaps not, Mary! But the cold-blooded way in which he said that a money compensation might have been offered to poor Tom o' the Gleam for his little child's life—my God! As if any sort of money could compare with love!"

He stroked her hair gently, and went on murmuring to himself—

"As if all the gold in the world could make up for the loss of one loving heart!"

Mary was silent. She saw that he was greatly agitated, and thought it better to let him speak out his whole mind rather than suppress his feelings.

"What can a man do with wealth!" he went on, speaking more to himself than to her—"He can buy everything that is to be bought, certainly—but if he has no one to share his goods with him, what then? Eh, Mary? What then?"

"Why then he'd be a very miserable man, David!" she answered, smiling—"He'd wish he were poor, with some one to love him!"

He looked at her, and his sunken eyes flashed with quite an eager light.

"That's true!" he said—"He'd wish he were poor with some one to love him! Mary, you've been so kind to me—promise me one thing!"

"What's that?" and she patted his hand soothingly.

"Just this—if I die on your hands don't let that man Arbroath bury me! I think my very bones would split at the sound of his rasping voice!"

Mary laughed.

"Don't you worry about that!" she said—"Mr. Arbroath won't have the chance to bury you, David! Besides, he never takes the burials of the very poor folk even in his own parishes. He wrote a letter in one of the countryside papers not very long ago, to complain of the smallness of the burial fees, and said it wasn't worth his while to bury paupers!"

And she laughed again. "Poor, bitter-hearted man! He must be very wretched in himself to be so cantankerous to others."

"Well, don't let him bury *me*!" said Helmsley—"That's all I ask. I'd much rather Twitt dug a hole in the seashore and put my body into it himself, without any prayers at all, than have a prayer croaked over me by that clerical raven! Remember that!"

"I'll remember!" And Mary's face beamed with kindly tolerance and good-humour—"But you're really quite an angry old boy to-day, David! I never saw you in such a temper!"

Her playful tone brought a smile to his face at last.

"It was that horrible suggestion of money compensation for a child's life that angered me,"—he said, half apologetically—"The notion that pounds, shillings and pence could pay for the loss of love, got on my nerves. Why, love is the only good thing in the world!"

She had been half kneeling by his chair—but she now rose slowly, and stretched her arms out with a little gesture of sudden weariness.

"Do you think so, David?" and she sighed, almost unconsciously to herself—"I'm not so sure!"

He glanced at her in sudden uneasiness. Was she too going to say, like Lucy Sorrel, that she did not believe in love? He thought of Angus Reay, and wondered. She caught his look and smiled.

"I'm not so sure!" she repeated—"There's a great deal talked about love,—but it often seems as if there was more talk than deed. At least there is in what is generally called 'love.' I know there's a very real and beautiful love, like that which I had for my father, and which he had for me,—that was as near being perfect as anything could be in this world. But the love I had for the young man to whom I was once engaged was quite a different thing altogether."

"Of course it was!" said Helmsley—"And quite naturally, too. You loved your father as a daughter loves—and I suppose you loved the young man as a sweetheart loves—eh?"

"Sweetheart is a very pretty word,"—she answered, the smile still lingering about her lips—"It's quite old-fashioned too, and I love old-fashioned things. But I don't think I loved the young man exactly as a 'sweetheart.' It all came about in a very haphazard way. He took a fancy to me, and we used to go long walks together. He hadn't very much to say for himself—he smoked most of the time. But he was honest and respectable—and I got rather fond of him—so that when he asked me to marry him, I thought it would perhaps please father to see me provided for—and I said yes, without thinking very much about it. Then, when father failed in business and my man threw me over, I fretted a bit just for a day or two—mostly I think because we couldn't go any more Sunday walks together. I was in the early twenties, but now I'm getting on in the thirties. I know I didn't understand a bit about real love then. It was just fancy and the habit of seeing the one young man oftener than others. And, of course, that isn't love."

Helmsley listened to her every word, keenly interested. Surely, if he guided the conversation skilfully enough, he might now gain some useful hints which would speed the cause of Angus Reay?

"No—of course that isn't love,"—he echoed—"But what do you take to *be* love?—Can you tell me?"

Her eyes filled with a dreamy light, and her lips quivered a little.

"Can I tell you? Not very well, perhaps—but I'll try. Of course it's all over for me now—and I can only just picture what I think it ought to be. I never had it. I mean I never had that kind of love I have dreamed about, and it seems silly for an old maid to even talk of such a thing. But love to my mind ought to be the everything of life! If I loved a man—" Here she suddenly paused, and a wave of colour flushed her cheeks. Helmsley never took his eyes off her face.

"Yes?" he said, tentatively—"Well!—go on—if you loved a man?—"

"If I loved a man, David,"—she continued, slowly, clasping her hands meditatively behind her back, and looking thoughtfully into the glowing centre of the fire—"I should love him so completely that I should never think of anything in which he had not the first and greatest share. I should see his kind looks in every ray of sunshine—I should hear his loving voice in every note of music,—if I were to read a book alone, I should wonder which sentence in it would please *him* the most—if I plucked a flower, I should ask myself if he would like me to wear it,—I should live *through* him and *for* him—he would be my very eyes and heart and soul! The hours would seem empty without him—"

She broke off with a little sob, and her eyes brimmed over with tears.

"Why Mary! Mary, my dear!" murmured Helmsley, stretching out his hand to touch her—"Don't cry!"

"I'm not crying, David!" and a rainbow smile lighted her face—"I'm only just—*feeling*! It's like when I read a little verse of poetry that is very sad and sweet, I get tears into my eyes—and when I talk about love—especially now that I shall never know what it is, something rises in my throat and chokes me—"

"But you do know what it is,"—said Helmsley, powerfully moved by the touching simplicity of her confession of loneliness—"There isn't a more loving heart than yours in the world, I'm sure!"

She came and knelt down again beside him.

"Oh yes, I've a loving heart!" she said—"But that's just the worst of it! I can love, but no one loves or ever will love me—now. I'm past the age for it. No woman over thirty can expect to be loved by a lover, you know! Romance is all over—and one 'settles down,' as they say. I've never quite 'settled'—there's always something restless in me. You're such a dear old man, David, and so kind!—I can speak to you just as if you were my father—and I daresay you will not think it very wrong or selfish of me if I say I have longed to be loved sometimes! More than that, I've wished it had pleased God to send me a husband and children—I should have dearly liked to hold a baby in my arms, and soothe its little cries, and make it grow up to be happy and good, and a blessing to every one. Some women don't care for children—but I should have loved mine!"

She paused a moment, and Helmsley took her hand, and silently pressed it in his own.

"However,"—she went on, more lightly—"it's no good grieving over what cannot be helped. No man has ever really loved me—because, of course, the one I was engaged to wouldn't have thrown me over just because I was poor if he had cared very much about me. And I shall be thirty-five this year—so I must—I really *must*"—and she gave herself an admonitory little shake—"settle down! After all there are worse things in life than being an old maid. I don't mind it—it's only sometimes when I feel inclined to grizzle, that I think to myself what a lot of love I've got in my heart—all wasted!"

"Wasted?" echoed Helmsley, gently—"Do you think love is ever wasted?"

Her eyes grew serious and dreamy.

"Sometimes I do, and sometimes I don't"—she answered—"When I begin to like a person very much I often pull myself back and say 'Take care! Perhaps he doesn't like *you!*'"

"Oh! The person must be a 'he' then!" said Helmsley, smiling a little.

She coloured.

"Oh no—not exactly!—but I mean,—now, for instance,"—and she spoke rapidly as though to cover some deeper feeling—"I like *you* very much—indeed I'm fond of you, David!—I've got to know you so well, and to understand all your ways—but I can't be sure that you like *me* as much as I like *you*, can I?"

He looked at her kind and noble face with eyes full of tenderness and gratitude.

"If you can be sure of anything, you can be sure of that!"—he said—"To say I 'like' you would be a poor way of expressing myself. I owe my very life to you—and though I am only an old poor man, I would say I loved you if I dared!"

She smiled—and her whole face shone with the reflected sunshine of her soul.

"Say it, David dear! Do say it! I should like to hear it!"

He drew the hand he held to his lips, and gently kissed it.

"I love you, Mary!" he said—"As a father loves a daughter I love you, and bless you! You have been a good angel to me—and I only wish I were not so old and weak and dependent on your care. I can do nothing to show my affection for you—I'm only a burden upon your hands—"

She laid her fingers lightly across his lips.

"Sh-sh!" she said—"That's foolish talk, and I won't listen to it! I'm glad you're fond of me—it makes life so much pleasanter. Do you know, I sometimes think God must have sent you to me?"

"Do you? Why?"

"Well, I used to fret a little at being so much alone,—the days seemed so long, and it was hard to have to work only for one's wretched self, and see nothing in the future but just the same old round—and I missed my father always. I never could get accustomed to his empty chair. Then when I found you on the hills, lost and solitary, and ill, and brought you home to nurse and take care of, all the vacancy seemed filled—and I was quite glad to have some one to work for. I've been ever so much happier since you've been with me. We'll be like father and daughter to the end, won't we?"

She put one arm about him coaxingly. He did not answer.

"You won't go away from me now,—will you, David?" she urged—"Even when you've paid me back all you owe me as you wish by your own earnings, you won't go away?"

He lifted his head and looked at her as she bent over him.

"You mustn't ask me to promise anything,"—he said, "I will stay with you—as long as I can!"

She withdrew her arm from about him, and stood for a moment irresolute.

"Well—I shall be very miserable if you do go,"—she said—"And I'm sure no one will take more care of you than I will!"

"I'm sure of that, too, Mary!" and a smile that was almost youthful in its tenderness brightened his worn features—"I've never been so well taken care of in all my life before! Mr. Reay thinks I am a very lucky old fellow."

"Mr. Reay!" She echoed the name—and then, stooping abruptly towards the fire, began to make it up afresh. Helmsley watched her intently.

"Don't you like Mr. Reay?" he asked.

She turned a smiling face round upon him.

"Why, of course I like him!" she answered—"I think everyone in Weircombe likes him."

"I wonder if he'll ever marry?" pursued Helmsley, with a meditative air.

"Ah, I wonder! I hope if he does, he'll find some dear sweet little girl who will really love him and be proud of him! For he's going to be a great man, David!—a great and famous man some day!"

"You think so?"

"I'm sure of it!"

And she lifted her head proudly, while her blue eyes shone with enthusiastic fervour. Helmsley made a mental note of her expression, and wondered how he could proceed.

"And you'd like him to marry some 'dear sweet little girl'"—he went on, reflectively—"I'll tell him that you said so!"

She was silent, carefully piling one or two small logs on the fire.

"Dear sweet little girls are generally uncommonly vain of themselves," resumed Helmsley—"And in the strength of their dearness and sweetness they sometimes fail to appreciate love when they get it. Now Mr. Reay would love very deeply, I should imagine—and I don't think he could bear to be played with or slighted."

"But who would play with or slight such love as his?" asked Mary, with a warm flush on her face—"No woman that knew anything of his heart would wilfully throw it away!"

Helmsley stroked his beard thoughtfully.

"That story of his about a girl named Lucy Sorrel,"—he began.

"Oh, she was wicked—downright wicked!" declared Mary, with some passion—"Any girl who would plan and scheme to marry an old man for his money must be a worthless creature. I wish I had been in that Lucy Sorrel's place!"

"Ah! And what would you have done?" enquired Helmsley.

"Well, if I had been a pretty girl, in my teens, and I had been fortunate enough to win the heart of a splendid fellow like Angus Reay,"—said Mary, "I would have thanked God, as Shakespeare tells us to do, for a good man's love! And I would have waited for him years, if he had wished me to! I would have helped him all I could, and cheered him and encouraged him in every way I could think of—and when he had won his fame, I should have been prouder than a queen! Yes, I should!—I think any girl would have been lucky indeed to get such a man to care for her as Angus Reay!"

Thus spake Mary, with sparkling eyes and heaving bosom—and Helmsley heard her, showing no sign of any especial interest, the while he went on meditatively stroking his beard.

"It is a pity,"—he said, after a discreet pause—"that you are not a few years younger, Mary! You might have loved him yourself."

Her face grew suddenly scarlet, and she seemed about to utter an exclamation, but she repressed it. The colour faded from her cheeks as rapidly as it had flushed them, leaving her very pale.

"So I might!" she answered quietly,—and she smiled; "Indeed I think it would have been very likely! But that sort of thing is all over for me."

She turned away, and began busying herself with some of her household duties. Helmsley judged that he had said enough—and quietly exulted in his own mind at the discovery which he was confident he had made. All seemed clear and open sailing for Angus Reay—if—if she could be persuaded that it was for herself and herself alone that he loved her.

"Now if she were a rich woman, she would never believe in his love!" he thought—"There again comes in the curse of money! Suppose she were wealthy as women in her rank of life would consider it—suppose that she had a prosperous farm, and a reliable income of so much per annum, she would never flatter herself that a man loved her for her own good and beautiful self—especially a man in the situation of Reay, with only twenty pounds in the world to last him a year, and nothing beyond it save the dream of fame! She would think—and naturally too—that he sought to strengthen and improve his prospects by marrying a woman of some 'substance' as they call it. And even as it is the whole business requires careful handling. I myself must be on my guard. But I think I may give hope to Reay!—indeed I shall try and urge him to speak to her as soon as possible—before fortune comes to either of them! Love in its purest and most unselfish form, is such a rare blessing—such a glorious Angel of the kingdom of Heaven, that we should not hesitate to give it welcome, or delay in offering it reverence! It is all that makes life worth living—God knows how fully I have proved it!"

And that night in the quiet darkness of his own little room, he folded his worn hands and prayed—

"Oh God, before whom I appear as a wasted life, spent with toil in getting what is not worth the gaining, and that only seems as dross in Thy sight!—Give me sufficient time and strength to show my gratefulness to Thee for Thy mercy in permitting me to know the sweetness of Love at last, and in teaching me to understand, through Thy guidance, that those who may seem to us the unconsidered and lowly in this world, are often to be counted among Thy dearest creatures! Grant me but this, O God, and death when it comes, shall find me ready and resigned to Thy Will!"

Thus he murmured half aloud,—and in the wonderful restfulness which he obtained by the mere utterance of his thoughts to the Divine Source of all good, closed his eyes with a sense of abiding joy, and slept peacefully.

XVIII

A nd now by slow and beautiful degrees the cold and naked young
year grew warm, and expanded from weeping, shivering infancy
into the delighted consciousness of happy childhood. The first
snowdrops, the earliest aconites, perked up their pretty heads in Mary's
cottage garden, and throughout all nature there came that inexplicable,
indefinite, soft pulsation of new life and new love which we call the
spring. Tiny buds, rosy and shining with sap, began to gleam like rough
jewels on every twig and tree—a colony of rooks which had abode in
the elms surrounding Weircombe Church, started to make great ado
about their housekeeping, and kept up as much jabber as though they
were inaugurating an Irish night in the House of Commons,—and,
over a more or less tranquil sea, the gulls poised lightly on the heaving
waters in restful attitudes, as though conscious that the stress of winter
was past. To look at Weircombe village as it lay peacefully aslant down
the rocky "coombe," no one would have thought it likely to be a scene
of silent, but none the less violent, internal feud; yet such nevertheless
was the case, and all the trouble had arisen since the first Sunday of the
first month of the Reverend Mr. Arbroath's "taking duty" in the parish.
On that day six small choirboys had appeared in the Church, together
with a tall lanky youth in a black gown and white surplice—and to the
stupefied amazement of the congregation, the lanky youth had carried
a gilt cross round the Church, followed by Arbroath himself and the
six little boys, all chanting in a manner such as the Weircombe folk
had never heard before. It was a deeply resented innovation, especially
as the six little boys and the lanky cross-bearer, as well as the cross
itself, had been mysteriously "hired" from somewhere by Mr. Arbroath,
and were altogether strange to the village. Common civility, as well as
deeply rooted notions of "decency and order," kept the parishioners
in their seats during what they termed the "play-acting" which took
place on this occasion, but when they left the Church and went their
several ways, they all resolved on the course they meant to adopt with
the undesired introduction of "'Igh Jinks" for the future. And from
that date henceforward not one of the community attended Church.
Sunday after Sunday, the bells rang in vain. Mr. Arbroath conducted
the service solely for Mrs. Arbroath and for one ancient villager who
acted the double part of sexton and verger, and whose duties therefore

compelled him to remain attached to the sacred edifice. And the people read their morning prayers in their own houses every Sunday, and never stirred out on that day till after their dinners. In vain did both Mr. and Mrs. Arbroath run up and down the little village street, calling at every house, coaxing, cajoling, and promising,—they spoke to deaf ears. Nothing they could say or do made amends for the "insult" to which the parishioners considered they had been subjected, by the sudden appearance of six strange choirboys and the lanky youth in a black gown, who had carried a gilt cross round and round the tiny precincts of their simple little Church, which,—until the occurrence of this remarkable "mountebank" performance as they called it,— had been everything to them that was sacred in its devout simplicity. Finally, in despair, Mr. Arbroath wrote a long letter of complaint to the Bishop of the diocese, and after a considerable time of waiting, was informed by the secretary of that gentleman that the matter would be enquired into, but that in the meantime he had better conduct the Sunday services in the manner to which the parishioners had been accustomed. This order Arbroath flatly refused to obey, and there ensued a fierce polemical correspondence, during which the Church remained, as has been stated, empty of worshippers altogether. Casting about for reasons which should prove some contumacious spirit to be the leader of this rebellion, Arbroath attacked Mary Deane among others, and asked her if she was "a regular Communicant." To which she calmly replied—

"No, sir."

"And why are you not?" demanded the clergyman imperiously.

"Because I do not feel like it," she said; "I do not believe in going to Communion unless one really feels the spiritual wish and desire."

"Oh! Then that is to say that you are very seldom conscious of any spiritual wish or desire?"

She was silent.

"I am sorry for you!" And Arbroath shook his bullet head dismally. "You are one of the unregenerate, and if you do not amend your ways will be among the lost—"

"'I tell thee, churlish priest, A ministering angel shall my sister be, when thou liest howling!'" said Helmsley suddenly.

Arbroath turned upon him sharply.

"What's that?" he snarled.

"Shakespeare!" and Helmsley smiled.

"Shakespeare! Much you know about Shakespeare!" snapped out the irritated clergyman. "But atheists and ruffians always quote Shakespeare as glibly as they quote the New Testament!"

"It's lucky that atheists and ruffians have got such good authorities to quote from," said Helmsley placidly.

Arbroath gave an impatient exclamation, and again addressed Mary. "Why don't you come to Church?" he asked.

She raised her calm blue eyes and regarded him steadfastly.

"I don't like the way you conduct the service, sir, and I don't take you altogether for a Christian."

"What!" And he stared at her so furiously that his little pig eyes grew almost large for the moment—"You don't take me—*me*—for a Christian?"

"No, sir,—not altogether. You are too hard and too proud. You are not careful of us poor folk, and you don't seem to mind whether you hurt our feelings or not. We're only very humble simple people here in Weircombe, but we're not accustomed to being ordered about as if we were children, or as if our parson was a Romish priest wanting to get us all under his thumb. We believe in God with all our hearts and souls, and we love the dear gentle Saviour who came to show us how to live and how to die,— but we like to pray as we've always been accustomed to pray, just without any show, as our Lord taught us to do, not using any 'vain repetitions.'"

Helmsley, who was bending some stiff osiers in his hands, paused to listen. Arbroath stared gloomily at the noble, thoughtful face on which there was just now an inspired expression of honesty and truth which almost shamed him.

"I think," went on Mary, speaking very gently and modestly—"that if we read the New Testament, we shall find that our Lord expressly forbade all shows and ceremonies,—and that He very much disliked them. Indeed, if we strictly obeyed all His orders, we should never be seen praying in public at all! Of course it is pleasant and human for people to meet together in some place and worship God—but I think such a meeting should be quite without any ostentation—and that all our prayers should be as simple as possible. Pray excuse me if I speak too boldly—but that is the spirit and feeling of most of the Weircombe folk, and they are really very good, honest people."

The Reverend Mr. Arbroath stood inert and silent for about two minutes, his eyes still fixed upon her,—then, without a word, he turned on his heel and left the cottage. And from that day he did his best to sow small seeds of scandal against her,—scattering half-implied innuendoes,—faint breathings of disparagement, coarse jests as to her "old maid" condition, and other mean and petty calumnies, which, however, were all so much wasted breath on his part, as the Weircombe villagers were as indifferent to his attempted mischief as Mary herself. Even with the feline assistance of Mrs. Arbroath, who came readily to her husband's aid in his capacity of "downing" a woman, especially as that woman was so much better-looking than herself, nothing of any importance was accomplished in the way of either shaking Mary's established position in the estimation of Weircombe, or of persuading the parishioners to a "'Igh Jink" view of religious matters. Indeed, on this point they were inflexible, and as Mrs. Twitt remarked on one occasion, with a pious rolling-up of the whites of her eyes—

"To see that little black man with the 'igh stomach a-walkin' about this village is enough to turn a baby's bottle sour! It don't seem nat'ral like—he's as different from our good old parson as a rat is from a bird, an' you'll own, Mis' Deane, as there's a mighty difference between they two sorts of insecks. An' that minds me, on the Saturday night afore they got the play-actin' on up in the Church, the wick o' my candle guttered down in a windin' sheet as long as long, an' I sez to Twitt—'There you are! Our own parson's gone an' died over in Madery, an' we'll never 'ave the likes of 'im no more! There's trouble comin' for the Church, you mark my words.' An' Twitt, 'e says, 'G'arn, old 'ooman, it's the draught blowin' in at the door as makes the candle gutter,'—but all the same my words 'as come true!"

"Why no, surely not!" said Mary, "Our parson isn't dead in Madeira at all! The Sunday-school mistress had a letter from him only yesterday saying how much better he felt, and that he hoped to be home again with us very soon."

Mrs. Twitt pursed her lips and shook her head.

"That may be!" she observed—"I aint a-sayin' nuthin' again it. I sez to Twitt, there's trouble comin' for the Church, an' so there is. An' the windin' sheet in the candle means a death for somebody somewhere!"

Mary laughed, though her eyes were a little sad and wistful.

"Well, of course, there's always somebody dying somewhere, they say!" And she sighed. "There's a good deal of grief in the world that nobody ever sees or hears of."

"True enough, Mis' Deane!—true enough!" And Mrs. Twitt shook her head again—"But ye're spared a deal o' worrit, seein' ye 'aven't a husband nor childer to drive ye silly. When I 'ad my three boys at 'ome I never know'd whether I was on my 'ed or my 'eels, they kept up such a racket an' torment, but the Lord be thanked they're all out an' doin' for theirselves in the world now—forbye the eldest is thinkin' o' marryin' a girl I've never seen, down in Cornwall, which is where 'e be a-workin' in tin mines, an' when I 'eerd as 'ow 'e was p'raps a-goin' to tie hisself up in the bonds o' matterimony, I stepped out in the garden just casual like, an' if you'll believe me, I sees a magpie! Now, Mis' Deane, magpies is total strangers on these coasts—no one as I've ever 'eard tell on 'as ever seen one—an' they's the unlikeliest and unluckiest birds to come across as ever the good God created. An' of course I knows if my boy marries that gel in Cornwall, it'll be the worst chance and change for 'im that 'e's 'ad ever since 'e was born! That magpie comed 'ere to warn me of it!"

Mary tried to look serious, but Helmsley was listening to the conversation, and she caught the mirthful glance of his eyes. So she laughed, and taking Mrs. Twitt by the shoulders, kissed her heartily on both cheeks.

"You're a dear!" she said—"And I'll believe in the magpie if you want me to! But all the same, I don't think any mischief is coming for your son or for you. I like to hope that everything happening in this world is for the best, and that the good God means kindly to all of us. Don't you think that's the right way to live?"

"It may be the right way to live," replied Mrs. Twitt with a doubtful air—"But there's ter'uble things allus 'appenin', an' I sez if warnings is sent to us even out o' the mouths o' babes and sucklings, let's accept 'em in good part. An' if so be a magpie is chose by the Lord as a messenger we'se fools if we despises the magpie. But that little paunchy Arbroath's worse than a whole flock o' magpies comin' together, an' 'e's actin' like a pestilence in keepin' decent folk away from their own Church. 'Owsomever, Twitt reads prayers every Sunday mornin', an' t'other day Mr. Reay came in an' 'eerd 'im. An' Mr. Reay sez—'Twitt, ye're better than any parson I ever 'eerd!' An' I believe 'e is—'e's got real 'art an' feelin' for Scripter texes, an' sez 'em just as solemn as though 'e was carvin' 'em on tombstones. It's powerful movin'!"

Mary kept a grave face, but said nothing.

"An' last Sunday," went on Mrs. Twitt, encouraged, "Mr. Reay hisself read us a chapter o' the New Tesymen, an' 'twas fine! Twitt an' me, we felt as if we could 'a served the Lord faithful to the end of the world! An' we 'ardly ever feels like that in Church. In Church they reads the words so sing-songy like, that, bein' tired, we goes to sleep wi' the soothin' drawl. But Mr. Reay, he kep' us wide awake an' starin'! An' there's one tex which sticks in my 'ed an' comforts me for myself an' for everybody in trouble as I ever 'eerd on—"

"And what's that, Mrs. Twitt?" asked Helmsley, turning round in his chair, that he might see her better.

"It's this, Mister David," and Mrs. Twitt drew a long breath in preparation before beginning the quotation,—"an' it's beautiful! 'If the world hate you, ye know that it hated Me before it hated you.' Now if that aint enuff to send us on our way rejoicin', I don't know what is! For Lord knows if the dear Christ was hated, we can put up wi' a bit o' the hate for ourselves!"

There was a pause.

"So Mr. Reay reads very well, does he?" asked Mary.

"Fine!" said Mrs. Twitt,—"'E's a lovely man with a lovely voice! If 'e'd bin a parson 'e'd 'a drawed thousands to 'ear 'im! 'E wouldn't 'a wanted crosses nor candles to show us as 'e was speakin' true. Twitt sez to 'im t'other day—'Why aint you a parson, Mr. Reay?' an' 'e sez, 'Cos I'm goin' to be a preacher!' An' we couldn't make this out nohow, till 'e showed us as 'ow 'e was a-goin' to tell people things as they ought to know in the book 'e's writin'. An' 'e sez it's the only way, cos the parsons is gettin' so uppish, an' the Pope 'as got 'old o' some o' the newspapers, so that there aint no truth told nowheres, unless a few writers o' books will take 'art o' grace an' speak out. An' 'e sez there's a many as 'll do it, an' he tells Twitt—'Twitt,' sez he, 'Pin your faith on brave books! Beware o' newspapers, an' fight off the priest! Read brave books—books that were written centuries ago to teach people courage—an' read brave books that are written now to keep courage goin'!' An' we sez, so we will—for books is cheap enuff, God knows!—an' only t'other day Twitt went over to Minehead an' bought a new book by Sir Walter Scott called *Guy Mannering* for ninepence. It's a grand story! an' keeps us alive every evenin'! I'm just mad on that old woman in it—Meg Merrilies—she knew a good deal as goes on in the world, I'll warrant! All about signs an' omens too. It's just fine! I'd like to see Sir Walter Scott!"

"He's dead," said Mary, "dead long ago. But he was a good as well as a great man."

"'E must 'a bin," agreed Mrs. Twitt; "I'm right sorry 'e's dead. Some folks die as is bound to be missed, an' some folks lives on as one 'ud be glad to see in their long 'ome peaceful at rest, forbye their bein' born so grumblesome like. Twitt 'ud be at 'is best composin' a hepitaph for Mr. Arbroath now!"

As she said this the corners of her mouth, which usually drooped in somewhat lachrymose lines, went up in a whimsical smile. And feeling that she had launched a shaft of witticism which could not fail to reach its mark, she trotted off on further gossiping errands bent.

The tenor of her conversation was repeated to Angus Reay that afternoon when he arrived, as was often his custom, for what was ostensibly "a chat with old David," but what was really a silent, watchful worship of Mary.

"She is a dear old soul!" he said, "and Twitt is a rough diamond of British honesty. Such men as he keep the old country together and help to establish its reputation for integrity. But that man Arbroath ought to be kicked out of the Church! In fact, I as good as told him so!"

"You did!" And Helmsley's sunken eyes began to sparkle with sudden animation. "Upon my word, sir, you are very bold!"

"Bold? Why, what can he do to me?" demanded Angus. "I told him I had been for some years on the press, and that I knew the ins and outs of the Jesuit propaganda there. I told him he was false to the principles under which he had been ordained. I told him that he was assisting to introduce the Romish 'secret service' system into Great Britain, and that he was, with a shameless disregard of true patriotism, using such limited influence as he had to put our beloved free country under the tyranny of the Vatican. I said, that if ever I got a hearing with the British public, I meant to expose him, and all such similar wolves in sheep's clothing as himself."

"But—what did he say?" asked Mary eagerly.

"Oh, he turned livid, and then told me I was an atheist, adding that nearly all writers of books were of the same evil persuasion as myself. I said that if I believed that the Maker of Heaven and Earth took any pleasure in seeing him perambulate a church with a cross and six wretched little boys who didn't understand a bit what they were doing, I should be an atheist indeed. I furthermore told him I believed in God, who upheld this glorious Universe by the mere expressed power of His thought, and I said I believed in Christ, the Teacher who showed to men that the only way to obtain immortal life and happiness was by the conquest of Self. 'You may call that atheistical if you like,' I said,—'It's a firm faith that will help to keep *me* straight, and that will hold me to the paths of right and truth without any crosses or candles.' Then I told him that this little village of Weircombe, in its desire for simplicity in forms of devotion, was nearer heaven than he was. And—and I think," concluded Angus, ruffling up his hair with one hand, "that's about all I told him!"

Helmsley gave a low laugh of intense enjoyment.

"All!" he echoed, "I should say it was enough!"

"I hope it was," said Angus seriously, "I meant it to be." And moving to Mary's side, he took up the end of a lace flounce on which she was at work. "What a creation in cobwebs!" he exclaimed—"Who does it belong to, Miss Mary?"

"To a very great lady," she replied, working busily with her needle and avoiding the glance of his eyes; "her name is often in the papers." And she gave it. "No doubt you know her?"

"Know her? Not I!" And he shrugged his shoulders disdainfully. "But she is very generally known—as a thoroughly bad woman! I *hate* to see you working on anything for her!"

She looked up surprised, and the colour came and went in a delicate flush on her face.

"False to her husband, false to her children, and false to herself!" went on Angus hotly—"And disloyal to her king! And having turned on her own family and her own class, she seeks to truckle to the People under pretence of serving *them*, while all the time her sole object is to secure notoriety for herself! She is a shame to England!"

"You speak very hotly, sir!" said Helmsley, slowly. "Are you sure of your facts?"

"The facts are not concealed," returned Reay—"They are public property. That no one has the courage to denounce such women—women who openly flaunt their immoralities in our midst—is a bad sign of the times. Women are doing a great deal of mischief just now. Look at them fussing about Female Suffrage! Female Suffrage, quotha! Let them govern their homes properly, wisely, reasonably, and faithfully, and they will govern the nation!"

"That's true!" And Helmsley nodded gravely. "That's very true!"

"A woman who really loves a man," went on Angus, mechanically fingering the skeins of lace thread which lay on the table at Mary's side, ready for use—"governs him, unconsciously to herself, by the twin powers of sex and instinct. She was intended for his help-mate, to guide him in the right way by her finer forces. If she neglects to cultivate these finer forces—if she tramples on her own natural heritage, and seeks to 'best' him with his own weapons—she fails—she must fail—she deserves to fail! But as true wife and true mother, she is supreme!"

"But the ladies are not content with such a limited sphere," began Helmsley, with a little smile.

"Limited? Good God!—where does the limit come in?" demanded Reay. "It is because they are not sufficiently educated to understand their own privileges that women complain of limitations. An unthinking, unreasoning, unintelligent wife and mother is of course no higher than any other female of the animal species—but I do not uphold this class. I claim that the woman who *thinks*, and gives her intelligence full play—the woman who is physically sound and morally pure—the woman who devoutly studies the noblest side of life, and tries to bring herself into unison with the Divine intention of human progress towards the utmost good—she, as wife and mother, is the angel of the world. She *is* the world!—she makes it, she rejuvenates it, she gives it strength! Why should she condescend to mix with the passing political squabbles of her slaves and children?—for men are no more than her slaves and children. Love is her weapon—one true touch of that, and the wildest heart that ever beat in a man's breast is tamed."

There was a silence. Suddenly Mary pushed aside her work, and going to the door opened it.

"It's so warm to-day, don't you think?" she asked, passing her hand a little wearily across her forehead. "One would think it was almost June."

"You are tired, Miss Mary!" said Reay, somewhat anxiously.

"No—I'm not tired—but"—here all at once her eyes filled with tears. "I've got a bit of a headache," she murmured, forcing a smile—"I think I'll go to my room and rest for half an hour. Good-bye, Mr. Reay!"

"Good-bye—for the moment!" he answered—and taking her hand he pressed it gently. "I hope the headache will soon pass."

She withdrew her hand from his quickly and left the kitchen. Angus watched her go, and when she had disappeared heaved an involuntary but most lover-like sigh. Helmsley looked at him with a certain whimsical amusement.

"Well!" he said.

Reay gave himself a kind of impatient shake.

"Well, old David!" he rejoined.

"Why don't you speak to her?"

"I dare not! I'm too poor!"

"Is she so rich?"

"She's richer than I am."

"It is quite possible," said Helmsley slowly, "that she will always be richer than you. Literary men must never expect to be millionaires."

"Don't tell me that—I know it!" and Angus laughed. "Besides, I don't want to be a millionaire—wouldn't be one for the world! By the way, you remember that man I told you about—the old chap my first love was going to marry—David Helmsley?"

Helmsley did not move a muscle.

"Yes—I remember!" he answered quietly.

"Well, the papers say he's dead."

"Oh! the papers say he's dead, do they?"

"Yes. It appeared that he went abroad last summer,—it is thought that he went to the States on some matters of business—and has not since been heard of."

Helmsley kept an immovable face.

"He may possibly have got murdered for his money," went on Angus reflectively—"though I don't see how such an act could benefit the murderer. Because his death wouldn't stop the accumulation of his millions, which would eventually go to his heir."

"Has he an heir?" enquired Helmsley placidly.

"Oh, he's sure to have left his vast fortune to somebody," replied Reay. "He had two sons, so I was told—but they're dead. It's possible he may have left everything to Lucy Sorrel."

"Ah yes! Quite possible!"

"Of course," went on Reay, "it's only the newspapers that say he's dead—and there never was a newspaper yet that could give an absolutely veracious account of anything. His lawyers—a famous firm, Vesey and Symonds,—have written a sort of circular letter to the press stating that the report of his death is erroneous—that he is travelling for health's sake, and on account of a desire for rest and privacy, does not wish his whereabouts to be made publicly known."

Helmsley smiled.

"I knew I might trust Vesey!" he thought. Aloud he said—

"Well, I should believe the gentleman's lawyers more than the newspaper reporters. Wouldn't you?"

"Of course. I shouldn't have taken the least interest in the rumour, if I hadn't been once upon a time in love with Lucy Sorrel. Because if the old man is really dead and has done nothing in the way of providing for her, I wonder what she will do?"

"Go out charing!" said Helmsley drily. "Many a better woman than you have described her to be, has had to come to that."

There was a silence. Presently Helmsley spoke again in a quiet voice—

"I think, Mr. Reay, you should tell all your mind to Miss Mary."

Angus started nervously.

"Do you, David? Why?"

"Why?—well—because—" Here Helmsley spoke very gently—"because I believe she loves you!"

The colour kindled in Reay's face.

"Ah, don't fool me, David!" he said—"you don't know what it would mean to me—"

"Fool you!" Helmsley sat upright in his chair and looked at him with an earnestness which left no room for doubt. "Do you think I would 'fool' you, or any man, on such a matter? Old as I am, and lonely and friendless as I *was*, before I met this dear woman, I know that love is the most sacred of all things—the most valuable of all things—better than gold—greater than power—the only treasure we can lay up in heaven 'where neither moth nor rust do corrupt, and where thieves do not break through nor steal!' Do not"—and here his strong emotion threatened to get the better of him—"do not, sir, think that because I was tramping the road in search of a friend to help me, before Miss Mary found me and brought me home here and saved my life, God bless her!—do not think, I say, that I have no feeling! I feel very much—very strongly—" He broke off breathing quickly, and his hands trembled. Reay hastened to his side in some alarm, remembering what Mary had told him about the old man's heart.

"Dear old David, I know!" he said. "Don't worry! I know you feel it all—I'm sure you do! Now, for goodness' sake, don't excite yourself like this—she—she'll never forgive me!" and he shook up the cushion at the back of Helmsley's chair and made him lean upon it. "Only it would be such a joy to me—such a wonder—such a help—to know that she really loved me!—*loved* me, David!—you understand—why, I think I could conquer the world!"

Helmsley smiled faintly. He was suffering physical anguish at the moment—the old sharp pain at his heart to which he had become more or less wearily accustomed, had dizzied his senses for a space, but as the spasm passed he took Reay's hand and pressed it gently.

"What does the Great Book tell us?" he muttered. "'If a man would give all the substance of his house for love, it would utterly be contemned!' That's true! And I would never 'fool' or mislead you on a matter of such life and death to you, Mr. Reay. That's why I tell you to speak to Miss Mary as soon as you can find a good opportunity—for I am sure she loves you!"

"Sure, David?"

"Sure!"

Reay stood silent,—his eyes shining, and "the light that never was on sea or land" transfigured his features.

At that moment a tap came at the door. A hand, evidently accustomed to the outside management of the latch, lifted it, and Mr. Twitt entered, his rubicund face one broad smile.

"'Afternoon, David!' Afternoon, Mister! Wheer's Mis' Deane?"

"She's resting a bit in her room," replied Helmsley.

"Ah, well! You can tell 'er the news when she comes in. Mr. Arbroath's away for 'is life wi' old Nick in full chase arter 'im! It don't do t'ave a fav'rite gel!"

Helmsley and Reay stared at him, and then at one another.

"Why, what's up?" demanded Reay.

"Oh, nuthin' much!" and Twitt's broad shoulders shook with internal laughter. "It's wot 'appens often in the fam'lies o' the haris-to-crazy, an' aint taken no notice of, forbye 'tis not so common among poor folk. Ye see Mr. Arbroath he—he—he—he—he—he—" and here the pronoun "he" developed into a long chuckle. "He's got a sweet'art on the sly, an'—an'—an'—*'is wife's found it out*! Ha-ha-ha-he-he-he! 'Is wife's found it out! That's the trouble! An' she's gone an' writ to the Bishop 'erself! Oh lor'! Never trust a woman wi' cat's eyes! She's writ to the Bishop, an' gone 'ome in a tearin' fit o' the rantin' 'igh-strikes,— an' Mister Arbroath 'e's follerd 'er, an' left us wi' a curate—a 'armless little chap wi' a bad cold in 'is 'ed, an' a powerful red nose—but 'onest an' 'omely like 'is own face. An' 'e'll take the services till our own vicar comes 'ome, which'll be, please God, this day fort*night*. But oh lor'!— to think o' that grey-'aired rascal Arbroath with a fav'rite gel on the sly! Ha-ha-ha-he-he-he! We'se be all mortal!" and Twitt shook his head with profound solemnity. "Ef I was a-goin' to carve a tombstone for that 'oly 'igh Churchman, I'd write on it the old 'ackneyed sayin', 'Man wants but little 'ere below, Nor wants that little long!' Ha-ha-ha-he-he-he!"

His round jolly face beamed with merriment, and Angus Reay caught infection from his mirth and laughed heartily.

"Twitt, you're an old rascal!" he exclaimed. "I really believe you enjoy showing up Mr. Arbroath's little weaknesses!"

"Not I—not I, Mister!" protested Twitt, his eyes twinkling. "I sez, be fair to all men! I sez, if a parson wants to chuck a gel under the chin, let 'im do so by all means, God willin'! But don't let 'im purtend as 'e *couldn't* chuck 'er under the chin for the hull world! Don't let 'im go round lookin' as if 'e was vinegar gone bad, an' preach at the parish as if we was all mis'able sinners while 'e's the mis'ablest one hisself. But old Arbroath—damme!" and he gave a sounding slap to his leg in sheer ecstacy. "Caught in the act by 'is wife! Oh lor', oh lor'! 'Is wife! An' *aint* she a tartar!"

"But how did all this happen?" asked Helmsley, amused.

"Why, this way, David—quite 'appy an' innocent like, Missis Arbroath, she opens a letter from 'ome, which 'avin' glanced at the envelope casual-like she thinks was beggin' or mothers' meetin', an' there she finds it all out. Vicar's fav'rite gel writin' for money or clothes or summat, an' endin' up 'Yer own darlin'!' Ha-ha-ha-he-he-he! Oh Lord! There was an earthquake up at the rect'ry this marnin'—the cook there sez she never 'eerd sich a row in all 'er life—an' Missis Arbroath she was a-shriekin' for a divorce at the top of 'er voice! It's a small place, Weircombe Rect'ry, an' a woman can't shriek an' 'owl in it without bein' 'eerd. So both the cook an' 'ousemaid worn't by no manner o' means surprised when Mister Arbroath packed 'is bag an' went off in a trap to Minehead—an' we'll be left with a cheap curate in charge of our pore souls! Ha-ha-ha! But 'e's a decent little chap,—an' there'll be no 'igh falutin' services with '*im*, so we can all go to Church next Sunday comfortable. An' as for old Arbroath, we'll be seein' big 'edlines in the papers by and by about 'Scandalous Conduck of a Clergyman with 'is Fav'rite Gel!'" Here he made an effort to pull a grave face, but it was no use,—his broad smile beamed out once more despite himself. "Arter all," he said, chuckling, "the two things does fit in nicely together an' nat'ral like—'Igh Jinks an' a fav'rite gel!"

It was impossible not to derive a sense of fun from his shining eyes and beaming countenance, and Angus Reay gave himself up to the enjoyment of the moment, and laughed again and again.

"So you think he's gone altogether, eh?" he said, when he could speak.

"Oh, 'e's gone all right!" rejoined Twitt placidly. "A man may do lots o' queer things in this world, an' so long as 'is old 'ooman don't find 'im out, it's pretty fair sailin'; but once a parson's wife gets 'er nose on to the parson's fav'rite, then all the fat's bound to be in the fire! An' quite right as it should be! I wouldn't bet on the fav'rite when it come to a neck-an'-neck race atween the two!"

He laughed again, and they all talked awhile longer on this unexpected event, which, to such a village as Weircombe, was one of startling importance and excitement, and then, as the afternoon was drawing in and Mary did not reappear, Angus Reay took his departure with Twitt, leaving Helmsley sitting alone in his chair by the fire. But he did not go without a parting word—a word which was only a whisper.

"You think you are *sure*, David!" he said—"Sure that she loves me! I wish you would make doubly, trebly sure!—for it seems much too good to be true!"

Helmsley smiled, but made no answer.

When he was left alone in the little kitchen to which he was now so accustomed, he sat for a space gazing into the red embers of the fire, and thinking deeply. He had attained what he never thought it would be possible to attain—a love which had been bestowed upon him for himself alone. He had found what he had judged would be impossible to find—two hearts which, so far as he personally was concerned, were utterly uninfluenced by considerations of self-interest. Both Mary Deane and Angus Reay looked upon him as a poor, frail old man, entirely defenceless and dependent on the kindness and care of such strangers as sympathised with his condition. Could they now be suddenly told that he was the millionaire, David Helmsley, they would certainly never believe it. And even if they were with difficulty brought to believe it, they would possibly resent the deception he had practised on them. Sometimes he asked himself whether it was quite fair or right to so deceive them? But then,—reviewing his whole life, and seeing how at every step of his career men, and women too, had flattered him and fawned upon him as well as fooled him for mere money's sake,—he decided that surely he had the right at the approaching end of that career to make a fair and free trial of the world as to whether any thing or any one purely honest could be found in it.

"For it makes me feel more at peace with God," he said—"to know and to realise that there *are* unselfish loving hearts to be found, if only in the very lowliest walks of life! I,—who have seen Society,—the modern Juggernaut,—rolling its great wheels recklessly over the hopes and joys and confidences of thousands of human beings—I, who know that even kings, who should be above dishonesty, are tainted by their secret speculations in the money-markets of the world,—surely I may be permitted to rejoice for my few remaining days in the finding of two truthful and simple souls, who have no motive for their kindness to me,—who see nothing in me but age, feebleness and poverty,—and whom I have perhaps been the means, through God's guidance, of bringing together. For it was to me that Reay first spoke that day on the seashore—and it was at my request that he first entered Mary's home. Can this be the way in which Divine Wisdom has chosen to redeem me? I,—who have never been loved as I would have desired to be loved,—am I now instructed how,—leaving myself altogether out of the question,—I may prosper the love of others and make two noble lives happy? It may be so,—and that in the foundation of their joy, I shall win my own soul's peace! So—leaving my treasures on earth,—I shall find my treasure in heaven, 'where neither moth nor rust doth corrupt, and where thieves do not break through nor steal!'"

Still looking at the fire he watched the glowing embers, now reddening, now darkening—or leaping up into sparks of evanescent flame,—and presently stooping, picked up the little dog Charlie from his warm corner on the hearth and fondled him.

"You were the first to love me in my loneliness!" he said, stroking the tiny animal's soft ears—"And,—to be quite exact,—I owe my life and all my present surroundings to you, Charlie! What shall I leave you in my will, eh?"

Charlie yawned capaciously, showing very white teeth and a very red tongue, and winked one bright eye.

"You're only a dog, Charlie! You've no use for money! You rely entirely upon your own attractiveness and the kindness of human nature! And so far your confidence has not been misplaced. But your fidelity and affection are only additional proofs of the powerlessness of money. Money bought you, Charlie, no doubt, in the first place—but money failed to keep you! And now, though by your means Mary found me where I lay helpless and unconscious on the hills in the storm, I can neither make you richer nor happier, Charlie! You're only a dog!—and a millionaire is no more to you than any other man!"

Charlie yawned comfortably again. He seemed to be perfectly aware that his master was talking to him, but what it was about he evidently did not know, and still more evidently did not care. He liked to be petted and made much of—and presently curled himself up in a soft silken ball on Helmsley's knee, with his little black nose pointed towards the fire, and his eyes blinking lazily at the sparkle of the flames. And so Mary found them, when at last she came down from her room to prepare supper.

"Is the headache better, my dear?" asked Helmsley, as she entered.

"It's quite gone, David!" she answered cheerily—"Mending the lace often tries one's eyes—it was nothing but that."

He looked at her intently.

"But you've been crying!" he said, with real concern.

"Oh, David! Women always cry when they feel like it!"

"But did *you* feel like it?"

"Yes. I often do."

"Why?"

She gave a playful gesture with her hands.

"Who can tell! I remember when I was quite a child, I cried when I saw the first primrose of the spring after a long winter. I knelt down and kissed it, too! That's me all over. I'm stupid, David! My heart's too big for me—and there's too much in it that never comes out!"

He took her hand gently.

"All shut up like a volcano, Mary! But the fire is there!"

She laughed, with a touch of embarrassment.

"Oh yes! The fire is there! It will take years to cool down!"

"May it never cool down!" said Helmsley—"I hope it will always burn, and make life warm for you! For without the fire that is in *your* heart, my dear, Heaven itself would be cold!"

XIX

The scandal affecting the Reverend Mr. Arbroath's reputation which had been so graphically related by Twitt, turned out to be true in every respect, and though considerable efforts were made to hush it up, the outraged feelings of the reverend gentleman's wife were not to be silenced. Proceedings for divorce were commenced, and it was understood that there would be no defence. In due course the "big 'edlines" which announced to the world in general that one of the most imperious "High" Anglicans of the Church had not only slipped from moral rectitude, but had intensified that sin by his publicly aggressive assumption of hypocritical virtue, appeared in the newspapers, and the village of Weircombe for about a week was brought into a certain notoriety which was distinctly displeasing to itself. The arrival of the "dailies" became a terror to it, and a general feeling of devout thankfulness was experienced by the whole community, when the rightful spiritual shepherd of the little flock returned from his sojourn abroad to take up the reigns of government, and restore law and order to his tiny distracted commonwealth. Fortunately for the peace of Weircombe, the frantic rush of social events, and incidents in which actual "news" of interest has no part, is too persistent and overwhelming for any one occurrence out of the million to occupy more than a brief passing notice, which is in its turn soon forgotten, and the "Scandalous Conduck of a Clergyman," as Mr. Twitt had put it, was soon swept aside in other examples of "Scandalous Conduck" among all sorts and conditions of men and women, which, caught up by flying Rumour with her thousand false and blatant tongues, is the sort of useless and pernicious stuff which chiefly keeps the modern press alive. Even the fact that the Reverend Mr. Arbroath was summarily deprived of his living and informed by the Bishop in the usual way, that his services would no longer be required, created very little interest. Some months later a small journalistic flourish was heard on behalf of the discarded gentleman, upon the occasion of his being "received" into the Church of Rome, with all his sins forgiven,—but so far as Weircombe was concerned, the story of himself and his "fav'rite" was soon forgotten, and his very name ceased to be uttered. The little community resumed its normal habit of cheerful attendance at Church every Sunday, satisfied to have shown to the ecclesiastical powers that be, the fact that "'Igh

Jinks" in religion would never be tolerated amongst them; and the life of Weircombe went on in the usual placid way, divided between work and prayer, and governed by the twin forces of peace and contentment.

Meantime, the secret spells of Mother Nature were silently at work in the development and manifestation of the Spring. The advent of April came like a revelation of divine beauty to the little village nestled in the "coombe," and garlanded it from summit to base with tangles of festal flowers. The little cottage gardens and higher orchards were smothered in the snow of plum and cherry-blossom,—primroses carpeted the woods which crowned the heights of the hills, and the long dark spikes of bluebells, ready to bud and blossom, thrust themselves through the masses of last year's dead leaves, side by side with the uncurling fronds of the bracken and fern. Thrushes and blackbirds piped with cheerful persistence among the greening boughs of the old chestnut which shaded Mary Deane's cottage, and children roaming over the grassy downs above the sea, brought news of the skylark's song and the cuckoo's call. Many a time in these lovely, fresh and sunny April days Angus Reay would persuade Mary away from her lace-mending to take long walks with him across the downs, or through the woods—and on each occasion when they started on these rambles together, David Helmsley would sit and watch for their return in a curious sort of timorous suspense— wondering, hoping, and fearing,—eager for the moment when Angus should speak his mind to the woman he loved, and yet always afraid lest that woman should, out of some super-sensitive feeling, put aside and reject that love, even though she might long to accept it. However, day after day passed and nothing happened. Either Angus hesitated, or else Mary was unapproachable—and Helmsley worried himself in vain. They, who did not know his secret, could not of course imagine the strained condition of mind in which their undeclared feelings kept him,—and and he found himself more perplexed and anxious over their apparent uncertainty than he had ever been over some of his greatest financial schemes. Facts and figures can to a certain extent be relied upon, but the fluctuating humours and vagaries of a man and woman in love with each other are beyond the most precise calculations of the skilled mathematician. For it often happens that when they seem to be coldest they are warmest—and cases have been known where they have taken the greatest pains to avoid each other at a time when they have most deeply longed to be always together. It was during this uncomfortable period of uneasiness and hesitation for Helmsley, that Angus and Mary were perhaps most supremely happy. Dimly, sweetly conscious that the gate of Heaven was open for them and that it was Love, the greatest angel of all God's mighty host, that waited for them there, they hovered round and round upon the threshold of the glory, eager, yet afraid to enter. Up in the primrose-carpeted woods together they talked, like good friends, of a thousand things,—of the weather, of the promise of fruit in the orchards, of the possibilities of a good fishing year, and of the general beauty of the scenery around Weircombe. Then, of course, there was the book which Angus was writing—a book now nearing completion. It was a very useful book, because it gave them a constant and safe topic of conversation. Many chapters were read and re-read—many passages written and re-written for Mary's hearing and criticism,—and it may at once be said that what had at first been merely clever, brilliant, and intellectual writing, was now becoming not so much a book as an artistic creation, through which the blood and colour of human life pulsed and flowed, giving it force and vitality. Sometimes they persuaded Helmsley to accompany them on some of their shorter rambles,—but he was not strong enough to walk far, and he often left them half-way up the "coombe," returning to the cottage alone. Mary had frequently expressed a great wish to take him to a favourite haunt of hers, which she called the "Giant's Castle"—but he was unable to make the steep ascent—so on one fine afternoon she took Angus there instead. "The Giant's Castle" had no recognised name among the Weircombe villagers save this one which Mary had bestowed upon it, and which the children repeated after her so often that it seemed highly probable that the title would stick to it for ever. "Up Giant's Castle way" was quite a familiar direction to any one ascending the "coombe," or following the precipitous and narrow path which wound along the edge of the cliffs to certain pastures where shepherds as well as sheep were in daily danger of landslips, and which to the ordinary pedestrian were signalled by a warning board as "Dangerous." But "Giant's Castle" itself was merely the larger and loftier of the two towering rocks which guarded the sea-front of Weircombe village. A tortuous grassy path led up to its very pinnacle, and from here, there was an unbroken descent as straight and smooth as a well-built wall, of several hundred feet sheer down into the sea, which at this point swirled round the rocky base in dark, deep, blackish-green eddies, sprinkled with trailing sprays of brown and crimson weed. It was a wonderful sight to look down upon this heaving mass of water, if it could be done without the head swimming and the eyes growing blind with the light of the sky striking sharp against the restless heaving of the waves, and Mary was one of the few who could stand fearlessly on almost the very brink of the parapet of the "Giant's Castle," and watch the sweep of the gulls as they flew under and above her, uttering their brief plaintive cries of gladness or anger as the wild wind bore them to and fro. When Reay first saw her run eagerly to the very edge, and stand there, a light, bold, beautiful figure, with the wind fluttering her garments and blowing loose a long rippling tress of her amber-brown hair, he could not refrain from an involuntary cry of terror, and an equally involuntary rush to her side with his arms outstretched. But as she turned her sweet face and grave blue eyes upon him there was something in the gentle dignity and purity of her look that held him back, abashed, and curiously afraid. She made him feel the power of her sex,—a power invincible when strengthened by modesty and reserve,— and the easy licence which modern women, particularly those of a degraded aristocracy, permit to men in both conversation and behaviour nowadays, would have found no opportunity of being exercised in her presence. So, though his impulse moved him to catch her round the waist and draw her with forcible tenderness away from the dizzy eminence on which she stood, he dared not presume so far, and merely contented himself with a bounding stride which brought him to the same point of danger as herself, and the breathless exclamation—

"Miss Mary! Take care!"

She smiled.

"Oh, there is nothing to be frightened of!" she said. "Often and often I have come here quite alone and looked down upon the sea in all weathers. Just after my father's death, this used to be the place I loved best, where I could feel that I was all by myself with God, who alone understood my sadness. At night, when the moon is at the full, it is very beautiful here. One looks down into the water and sees a world of waving light, and then, looking up to the sky, there is a heaven of stars!—and all the weary ways of life are forgotten! The angels seem so near!"

A silent agreement with this latter statement shone in Reay's eyes as he looked at her.

"It's good sometimes to find a woman who still believes in angels," he said.

"Don't *you* believe in them?"

"Implicitly,—with all my heart and soul!" And again his eyes were eloquent.

A wave of rosy colour flitted over her face, and shading her eyes from the strong glare of the sun, she gazed across the sea.

"I wish dear old David could see this glorious sight!" she said. "But he's not strong—and I'm afraid—I hardly like to think it—that he's weaker than he knows."

"Poor old chap!" said Angus, gently. "Any way, you've done all you can for him, and he's very grateful. I hope he'll last a few years longer."

"I hope so too," she answered quickly. "For I should miss him very much. I've grown quite to love him."

"I think he feels that," and Angus seated himself on a jutting crag of the "Giant's Castle" and prepared for the utterance of something desperate. "Any one would, you know!"

She made no reply. Her gaze was fixed on the furthest silver gleaming line of the ocean horizon.

"Any one would be bound to feel it, if you loved—if you were fond of him," he went on in rather a rambling way. "It would make all the difference in the world—"

She turned towards him quickly with a smile. Her breathing was a little hurried.

"Shall we go back now?" she said.

"Certainly!—if—if you wish—but isn't it rather nice up here?" he pleaded.

"We'll come another day," and she ran lightly down the first half of the grassy path which had led them to the summit. "But I mustn't waste any more time this afternoon."

"Why? Any pressing demands for mended lace?" asked Angus, as he followed her.

"Oh no! Not particularly so. Only when the firm that employs me, sends any very specially valuable stuff worth five or six hundred pounds or so, I never like to keep it longer that I can help. And the piece I'm at work on is valued at a thousand guineas."

"Wouldn't you like to wear it yourself?" he asked suddenly, with a laugh.

"I? I wouldn't wear it for the world! Do you know, Mr. Reay, that I almost hate beautiful lace! I admire the work and design, of course—no one could help that—but every little flower and leaf in the fabric speaks to me of so many tired eyes growing blind over the intricate stitches—

so many weary fingers, and so many aching hearts—all toiling for the merest pittance! For it is not the real makers of the lace who get good profit by their work, it is the merchants who sell it that have all the advantage. If I were a great lady and a rich one, I would refuse to buy any lace from the middleman,—I would seek out the actual poor workers, and give them my orders, and see that they were comfortably fed and housed as long as they worked for me."

"And it's just ten chances to one whether they would be grateful to you—" Angus began. She silenced him by a slight gesture.

"But I shouldn't care whether they were grateful or not," she said. "I should be content to know that I had done what was right and just to my fellow-creatures."

They had no more talk that day, and Helmsley, eagerly expectant, and watching them perhaps more intently than a criminal watches the face of a judge, was as usual disappointed. His inward excitement, always suppressed, made him somewhat feverish and irritable, and Mary, all unconscious of the cause, stayed in to "take care of him" as she said, and gave up her afternoon walks with Angus for a time altogether, which made the situation still more perplexing, and to Helmsley almost unbearable. Yet there was nothing to be done. He felt it would be unwise to speak of the matter in any way to her—she was a woman who would certainly find it difficult to believe that she had won, or could possibly win the love of a lover at her age;—she might even resent it,— no one could tell. And so the days of April paced softly on, in bloom and sunlight, till May came in with a blaze of colour and radiance, and the last whiff of cold wind blew itself away across the sea. The "biting nor'easter," concerning which the comic press gives itself up to senseless parrot-talk with each recurrence of the May month, no matter how warm and beautiful that month may be, was a "thing foregone and clean forgotten,"—and under the mild and beneficial influences of the mingled sea and moorland air, Helmsley gained a temporary rush of strength, and felt so much better, that he was able to walk down to the shore and back again once or twice a a day, without any assistance, scarcely needing even the aid of his stick to lean upon. The shore remained his favourite haunt; he was never tired of watching the long waves roll in, edged with gleaming ribbons of foam, and roll out again, with the musical clatter of drawn pebbles and shells following the wake of the backward sweeping ripple,—and he made friends with many of the Weircombe fisherfolk, who were always ready to chat with him concerning themselves and the difficulties and dangers of their trade. The children, too, were all eager to run after "old David," as they called him,—and many an afternoon he would sit in the sun, with a group of these hardy little creatures gathered about him, listening entranced, while he told them strange stories of foreign lands and far travels,— travels which men took "in search of gold"—as he would say, with a sad little smile—"gold, which is not nearly so much use as it seems to be."

"But can't us buy everything with plenty of money?" asked a seven-year-old urchin, on one of these occasions, looking solemnly up into his face with a pair of very round, big brown eyes.

"Not everything, my little man," he answered, smoothing the rough locks of the small inquirer with a very tender hand. "I could not buy *you*, for instance! Your mother wouldn't sell you!"

The child laughed.

"Oh, no! But I didn't mean me!"

"I know you didn't mean me!" and Helmsley smiled. "But suppose some one put a thousand golden sovereigns in a bag on one side, and you in your rough little torn clothes on the other, and asked your mother which she would like best to have—what do you think she would say?"

"She'd 'ave *me*!" and a smile of confident satisfaction beamed on the grinning little face like a ray of sunshine.

"Of course she would! The bag of sovereigns would be no use at all compared to you. So you see we cannot buy everything with money."

"But—most things?" queried the boy—"Eh?"

"Most things—perhaps," Helmsley answered, with a slight sigh. "But those 'most things' are not things of much value even when you get them. You can never buy love,—and that is the only real treasure,—the treasure of Heaven!"

The child looked at him, vaguely impressed by his sudden earnestness, but scarcely understanding his words.

"Wouldn't *you* like a little money?" And the inquisitive young eyes fixed themselves on his face with an expression of tenderest pity. "You'se a very poor old man!"

Helmsley laughed, and again patted the little curly head.

"Yes—yes—a very poor old man!" he repeated. "But I don't want any more than I've got!"

One afternoon towards mid-May, a strong yet soft sou'wester gale blew across Weircombe, bringing with it light showers of rain, which, as they fell upon the flowering plants and trees, brought out all the perfume of the spring in such rich waves of sweetness, that, though as yet there were no roses, and the lilac was only just budding out, the whole countryside seemed full of the promised fragrance of the blossoms that were yet to be. The wind made scenery in the sky, heaping up snowy masses of cloud against the blue in picturesque groups resembling Alpine heights, and fantastic palaces of fairyland, and when,—after a glorious day of fresh and invigorating air which swept both sea and hillside, a sudden calm came with the approach of sunset, the lovely colours of earth and heaven, melting into one another, where so pure and brilliant, that Mary, always a lover of Nature, could not resist Angus Reay's earnest entreaty that she would accompany him to see the splendid departure of the orb of day, in all its imperial panoply of royal gold and purple.

"It will be a beautiful sunset," he said—"And from the 'Giant's Castle' rock, a sight worth seeing."

Helmsley looked at him as he spoke, and looking, smiled.

"Do go, my dear," he urged—"And come back and tell me all about it."

"I really think you want me out of your way, David!" she said laughingly. "You seem quite happy when I leave you!"

"You don't get enough fresh air," he answered evasively. "And this is just the season of the year when you most need it."

She made no more demur, and putting on the simple straw hat, which, plainly trimmed with a soft knot of navy-blue ribbon, was all her summer head-gear, she left the house with Reay. After a while, Helmsley also went out for his usual lonely ramble on the shore, from whence he could see the frowning rampart of the "Giant's Castle" above him, though it was impossible to discern any person who might be standing at its summit, on account of the perpendicular crags that intervened. From both shore and rocky height the scene was magnificent. The sun, dipping slowly down towards the sea, shot rays of glory around itself in an aureole of gold, which, darting far upwards, and spreading from north to south, pierced the drifting masses of floating fleecy cloud like arrows, and transfigured their whiteness to splendid hues of fiery rose and glowing amethyst, while just between the falling Star of Day and the ocean, a rift appeared of smooth and delicate watery green, touched here and there with flecks of palest pink and ardent violet. Up on the parapet of the "Giant's Castle," all this loyal panoply of festal colour was seen at its best, sweeping in widening waves across the whole surface of the Heavens; and there was a curious stillness everywhere, as though earth itself were conscious of a sudden and intense awe. Standing on the dizzy edge of her favourite point of vantage, Mary Deane gazed upon the sublime spectacle with eyes so passionately tender in their far-away expression, that, to Angus Reay, who watched those eyes with much more rapt admiration than he bestowed upon the splendour of the sunset, they looked like the eyes of some angel, who, seeing heaven all at once revealed, recognised her native home, and with the recognition, was prepared for immediate flight And on the impulse which gave him this fantastic thought, he said softly—

"Don't go away, Miss Mary! Stay with us—with me—as long as you can!"

She turned her head and looked at him, smiling.

"Why, what do you mean? I'm not going away anywhere—who told you that I was?"

"No one,"—and Angus drew a little nearer to her—"But just now you seemed so much a part of the sea and the sky, leaning forward and giving yourself entirely over to the glory of the moment, that I felt as if you might float away from me altogether." Here he paused—then added in a lower tone—"And I could not bear to lose you!"

She was silent. But her face grew pale, and her lips quivered. He saw the tremor pass over her, and inwardly rejoiced,—his own nerves thrilling as he realised that, after all, *if*—if she loved him, he was the master of her fate.

"We've been such good friends," he went on, dallying with his own desire to know the best or worst—"Haven't we?"

"Indeed, yes!" she answered, somewhat faintly. "And I hope we always will be."

"I hope so, too!" he answered in quite a matter-of-fact way. "You see I'm rather a clumsy chap with women—"

She smiled a little.

"Are you?"

"Yes,—I mean I never get on with them quite as well as other fellows do somehow—and—er—and—what I want to say, Miss Mary, is that I've never got on with any woman so well as I have with you—and—"

He paused. At no time in his life had he been at such a loss for language. His heart was thumping in the most extraordinary fashion, and he prodded the end of his walking-stick into the ground with quite a ferocious earnestness. She was still looking at him and still smiling.

MARIE CORELLI

"And," he went on ramblingly, "that's why I hope we shall always be good friends."

As he uttered this perfectly commonplace remark, he cursed himself for a fool. "What's the matter with me?" he inwardly demanded. "My tongue seems to be tied up!—or I'm going to have lockjaw! It's awful! Something better than this has got to come out of me somehow!" And acting on a brilliant flash of inspiration which suddenly seemed to have illumined his brain, he said—

"The fact is, I want to get married. I'm thinking about it."

How quiet she was! She seemed scarcely to breathe.

"Yes?" and the word, accentuated without surprise and merely as a question, was spoken very gently. "I do hope you have found some one who loves you with all her heart!"

She turned her head away, and Angus saw, or thought he saw, the bright tears brim up from under her lashes and slowly fall. Without another instant's pause he rushed upon his destiny, and in that rush grew strong.

"Yes, Mary!" he said, and moving to her side he caught her hand in his own—"I dare to think I have found that some one! I believe I have! I believe that a woman whom I love with all my heart, loves me in return! If I am mistaken, then I've lost the whole world! Tell me, Mary! Am I wrong?"

She could not speak,—the tears were thick in her eyes.

"Mary—dear, dearest Mary!" and he pressed the hand he held— "You know I love you!—you know—"

She turned her face towards him—a pale, wondering face,—and tried to smile.

"How do I know?" she murmured tremulously—"How can I believe? I'm past the time for love!"

For all answer he drew her into his arms.

"Ask Love itself about that, Mary!" he said. "Ask my heart, which beats for you,—ask my soul, which longs for you!—ask me, who worship you, you, best and dearest of women, about the time for love! That time for us is now, Mary!—now and always!"

Then came a silence—that eloquent silence which surpasses all speech. Love has no written or spoken language—it is incommunicable as God. And Mary, whose nature was open and pure as the daylight, would not have been the woman she was if she could have expressed in words the deep tenderness and passion which at that supreme moment silently responded to her lover's touch, her lover's embrace. And when,—lifting her face between his two hands, he gazed at it long and earnestly, a smile, shining between tears, brightened her sweet eyes.

"You are looking at me as if you never saw me before, Angus!" she said, her voice sinking softly, as she pronounced his name.

"Positively, I don't think I ever have!" he answered "Not as you are now, Mary! I have never seen you look so beautiful! I have never seen you before as my love! my wife!"

She drew herself a little away from him.

"But, are you sure you are doing right for yourself?" she asked—"You know you could marry anybody—"

He laughed, and threw one arm round her waist.

"Thanks!—I don't want to marry 'anybody'—I want to marry *you*! The question is, will you have me?"

She smiled.

"If I thought it would be for your good—"

Stooping quickly he kissed her.

"*That's* very much for my good!" he declared. "And now that I've told you my mind, you must tell me yours. Do you love me, Mary?"

"I'm afraid you know that already too well!" she said, with a wistful radiance in her eyes.

"I don't!" he declared—"I'm not at all sure of you—"

She interrupted him.

"Are you sure of yourself?"

"Mary!"

"Ah, don't look so reproachful! It's only for you I'm thinking! You see I'm nothing but a poor working woman of what is called the lower classes—I'm not young, and I'm not clever. Now you've got genius; you'll be a great man some day, quite soon perhaps—you may even become rich as well as famous, and then perhaps you'll be sorry you ever met me—"

"In that case I'll call upon the public hangman and ask him to give me a quick despatch," he said promptly; "Though I shouldn't be worth the expense of a rope!"

"Angus, you won't be serious!"

"Serious? I never was more serious in my life! And I want my question answered."

"What question?"

"Do you love me? Yes or no!"

He held her close and looked her full in the face as he made this peremptory demand. Her cheeks grew crimson, but she met his searching gaze frankly.

"Ah, though you are a man, you are a spoilt child!" she said. "You know I love you more than I can say!—and yet you want me to tell you what can never be told!"

He caught her to his heart, and kissed her passionately.

"That's enough!" he said—"For if you love me, Mary, your love is love indeed!—it's no sham; and like all true and heavenly things, it will never change. I believe, if I turned out to be an utter wastrel, you'd love me still!"

"Of course I should!" she answered.

"Of course you would!" and he kissed her again. "Mary, *my* Mary, if there were more women like you, there would be more men!—men in the real sense of the word—manly men, whose love and reverence for women would make them better and braver in the battle of life. Do you know, I can do anything now, with you to love me! I don't suppose,"—and here he unconsciously squared his shoulders—"I really don't suppose there is a single difficulty in my way that I won't conquer!"

She smiled, leaning against him.

"If you feel like that, I am very happy!" she said.

As she spoke, she raised her eyes to the sky, and uttered an involuntary exclamation.

"Look, look!" she cried—"How glorious!"

The heavens above them were glowing red,—forming a dome of burning rose, deepening in hue towards the sea, where the outer rim of the nearly vanished sun was slowly disappearing below the horizon— and in the centre of this ardent glory, a white cloud, shaped like a dove with outspread wings, hung almost motionless. The effect was marvellously beautiful, and Angus, full of his own joy, was more than ever conscious of the deep content of a spirit attuned to the infinite joy of nature.

"It is like the Holy Grail," he said, and, with one arm round the woman he loved, he softly quoted the lines:—

> *"And down the long beam stole the Holy Grail,*
> *Rose-red, with beatings in it as if alive!"*

"That is Tennyson," she said.

"Yes—that is Tennyson—the last great poet England can boast," he answered. "The poet who hated hate and loved love."

"All poets are like that," she murmured.

"Not all, Mary! Some of the modern ones hate love and love hate!"

"Then they are not poets," she said. "They would not see any beauty in that lovely sky—and they would not understand—"

"Us!" finished Angus. "And I assure you, Mary at the present moment, we are worth understanding!"

She laughed softly.

"Do we understand ourselves?" she asked.

"Of course we don't! If we did, we should probably be miserable. It's just because we are mysterious one to another, that we are so happy. No human being should ever try to analyse the fact of existence. It's enough that we exist—and that we love each other. Isn't it, Mary?"

"Enough? It is too much,—too much happiness altogether for *me*, at any rate," she said. "I can't believe in it yet! I can't really, Angus! Why should you love me?"

"Why, indeed!" And his eyes grew dark and warm with tenderness— "Why should you love *me*?"

"Ah, there's so much to love in you!" and she made her heart's confession with a perfectly naïve candour. "I daresay you don't see it yourself, but I do!"

"And I assure you, Mary," he declared, with a whimsical solemnity, "that there's ever so much more to love in you! I know you don't see it for yourself, but I do!"

Then they laughed together like two children, and all constraint was at an end between them. Hand in hand they descended the grassy steep of the "Giant's Castle"—charmed with one another, and at every step of the way seeing some new delight which they seemed to have missed before. The crimson sunset burned about them like the widening petals of a rose in fullest bloom,—earth caught the fervent glory and reflected it back again in many varying tints of brilliant colour, shading from green to gold, from pink to amethyst—and as they walked through the splendid vaporous light, it was as though they were a living part of the glory of the hour.

"We must tell David," said Mary, as they reached the bottom of the hill. "Poor old dear! I think he will be glad."

"I know he will!" and Angus smiled confidently. "He's been waiting for this ever since Christmas Day!"

Mary's eyes opened in wonderment.

"Ever since Christmas Day?"

"Yes. I told him then that I loved you, Mary,—that I wanted to ask you to marry me,—but that I felt I was too poor—"

Her hand stole through his arm.

"Too poor, Angus! Am I not poor also?"

"Not as poor as I am," he answered, promptly possessing himself of the caressing hand. "In fact, you're quite rich compared to me. You've got a house, and you've got work, which brings you in enough to live upon,—now I haven't a roof to call my own, and my stock of money is rapidly coming to an end. I've nothing to depend upon but my book,—and if I can't sell that when it's finished, where am I? I'm nothing but a beggar—less well off than I was as a wee boy when I herded cattle. And I'm not going to marry you—"

She stopped in her walk and looked at him with a smile.

"Oh Angus! I thought you were!"

He kissed the hand he held.

"Don't make fun of me, Mary! I won't allow it! I *am* going to marry you!—but I'm *not* going to marry you till I've sold my book. I don't suppose I'll get more than a hundred pounds for it, but that will do to start housekeeping together on. Won't it?"

"I should think it would indeed!" and she lifted her head with quite a proud gesture—"It will be a fortune!"

"Of course," he went on, "the cottage is yours, and all that is in it. I can't add much to that, because to my mind, it's just perfect. I never want any sweeter, prettier little home. But I want to work *for* you, Mary, so that you'll not have to work for yourself, you understand?"

She nodded her head gravely.

"I understand! You want me to sit with my hands folded in my lap, doing nothing at all, and getting lazy and bad-tempered."

"Now you know I don't!" he expostulated.

"Yes, you do, Angus! If you don't want me to work, you want me to be a perfectly useless and tiresome woman! Why, my dearest, now that you love me, I should like to work all the harder! If you think the cottage pretty, I shall try to make it even prettier. And I don't want to give up all my lace-mending. It's just as pleasant and interesting as the fancy-work which the rich ladies play with You must really let me go on working, Angus! I shall be a perfectly unbearable person if you don't!"

She looked so sweetly at him, that as they were at the moment passing under the convenient shadow of a tree he took her in his arms and kissed her.

"When *you* become a perfectly unbearable person," he said, "then it will be time for another deluge, and a general renovation of human kind. You shall work if you like, my Mary, but you shall not work for *me*. See?"

A tender smile lingered in her eyes.

"I see!" and linking her arm through his again, she moved on with him over the thyme-scented grass, her dress gently sweeping across the stray clusters of golden cowslips that nodded here and there. "*I* will work for myself, *you* will work for *me*, and old David will work for both of us!"

They laughed joyously.

"Poor old David!" said Angus. "He's been wondering why I have not spoken to you before,—he declared he couldn't understand it. But then I wasn't quite sure whether you liked me at all—"

"Weren't you?" and her glance was eloquent.

"No—and I asked him to find out!"

She looked at him in a whimsical wonderment.

"You asked him to find out? And did he?"

"He seems to think so. At any rate, he gave me courage to speak."

Mary grew suddenly meditative.

"Do you know, Angus," she said, "I think old David was sent to me for a special purpose. Some great and good influence guided him to me—I am sure of it. You don't know all his history. Shall I tell it to you?"

"Yes—do tell me—but I think I know it. Was he not a former old friend of your father's?"

"No—that's a story I had to invent to satisfy the curiosity of the villagers. It would never have done to let them know that he was only an old tramp whom I found ill and nearly dying out on the hills during a great storm we had last summer. There had been heavy thunder and lightning all the afternoon, and when the storm ceased I went to my door to watch the clearing off of the clouds, and I heard a dog yelping pitifully on the hill just above the coombe. I went out to see what was the matter, and there I found an old man lying quite unconscious on the wet grass, looking as if he were dead, and a little dog—you know Charlie?—guarding him and barking as loudly as it could. Well, I brought him back to life, and took him home and nursed him—and—

that's all. He told me his name was David—and that he had been 'on the tramp' to Cornwall to find a friend. You know the rest."

"Then he is really quite a stranger to you, Mary?" said Angus wonderingly.

"Quite. He never knew my father. But I am sure if Dad had been alive, he would have rescued him just as I did, and then he *would* have been his 'friend,'—he could not have helped himself. That's the way I argued it out to my own heart and conscience."

Angus looked at her.

"You darling!" he said suddenly.

She laughed.

"That doesn't come in!" she said.

"It does come in! It comes in everywhere!" he declared. "There's no other woman in the world that would have done so much for a poor forlorn old tramp like that, adrift on the country roads. And you exposed yourself to some risk, too, Mary! He might have been a dangerous character!"

"Poor dear, he didn't look it," she said gently—"and he hasn't proved it. Everything has gone well for me since I did my best for him. It was even through him that you came to know me, Angus!—think of that! Blessings on the dear old man!—I'm sure he must be an angel in disguise!"

He smiled.

"Well, we never know!" he said. "Angels certainly don't come to us with all the celestial splendour which is supposed to belong to them— they may perhaps choose the most unlikely way in which to make their errands known. I have often—especially lately—thought that I have seen an angel looking at me out of the eyes of a woman!"

"You *will* talk poetry!" protested Mary.

"I'm not talking it—I'm living it!" he answered.

There was nothing to be said to this. He was an incorrigible lover, and remonstrances were in vain.

"You must not tell David's real history to any of the villagers," said Mary presently, as they came in sight of her cottage—"I wouldn't like them to know it."

"They shall never know it so far as I am concerned," he answered. "He's been a good friend to me—and I wouldn't cause him a moment's trouble. I'd like to make him happier if I could!"

"I don't think that's possible,"—and her eyes were clouded for a moment with a shadow of melancholy—"You see he has no money, except the little he earns by basket-making, and he's very far from strong. We must be kind to him, Angus, as long as he needs kindness."

Angus agreed, with sundry ways of emphasis that need not here be narrated, as they composed a formula which could not be rendered into set language. Arriving at the cottage they found the door open, and no one in the kitchen,—but on the table lay two sprigs of sweetbriar. Angus caught sight of them at once.

"Mary! See! Don't you think he knows?"

She stood hesitating, with a lovely wavering colour in her cheeks.

"Don't you remember," he went on, "you gave me a bit of sweetbriar on the evening of the first day we ever met?"

"I remember!" and her voice was very soft and tremulous.

"I have that piece of sweetbriar still," he said; "I shall never part with it. And old David must have known all about it!"

He took up the little sprays set ready for them, and putting one in his own buttonhole, fastened the other in her bodice with a loving, lingering touch.

"It's a good emblem," he said, kissing her—"Sweet Briar—sweet Love!—not without thorns, which are the safety of the rose!"

A slow step sounded on the garden path, and they saw Helmsley approaching, with the tiny "Charlie" running at his heels. Pausing on the threshold of the open door, he looked at them with a questioning smile.

"Well, did you see the sunset?" he asked, "Or only each other?"

Mary ran to him, and impulsively threw her arms about his neck.

"Oh David!" she said. "Dear old David! I am so happy!"

He was silent,—her gentle embrace almost unmanned him. He stretched out a hand to Angus, who grasped it warmly.

"So it's all right!" he said, in a low voice that trembled a little. "You've settled it together?"

"Yes—we've settled it, David!" Angus answered cheerily. "Give us your blessing!"

"You have that—God knows you have that!"—and as Mary, in her usual kindly way, took his hat and stick from him, keeping her arm through his as he went to his accustomed chair by the fireside, he glanced at her tenderly. "You have it with all my heart and soul, Mr. Reay!—and as for this dear lady who is to be your wife, all I can say is that you have won a treasure—yes, a treasure of goodness and sweetness and patience, and most heavenly kindness—"

His voice failed him, and the quick tears sprang to Mary's eyes.

"Now, David, please stop!" she said, with a look between affection and remonstrance. "You are a terrible flatterer! You mustn't spoil me."

"Nothing will spoil you!" he answered, quietly. "Nothing could spoil you! All the joy in the world, all the prosperity in the world, could not change your nature, my dear! Mr. Reay knows that as well as I do,— and I'm sure he thanks God for it! You are all love and gentleness, as a woman should be,—as all women would be if they were wise!"

He paused a moment, and then, raising himself a little more uprightly in his chair, looked at them both earnestly.

"And now that you have made up your minds to share your lives together," he went on, "you must not think that I will be so selfish as to stay on here and be a burden to you both. I should like to see you married, but after that I will go away—"

"You will do nothing of the sort!" said Mary, dropping on her knees beside him and lifting her serene eyes to his face. "You don't want to make us unhappy, do you? This is your home, as long as it is ours, remember! We would not have you leave us on any account, would we, Angus?"

"Indeed no!" answered Reay, heartily. "David, what are you talking about? Aren't *you* the cause of my knowing Mary? Didn't *you* bring me to this dear little cottage first of all? Don't I owe all my happiness to *you*? And you talk about going away! It's pretty evident you don't know what's good for you! Look here! If I'm good for anything at all, I'm good for hard work—and for that matter I may as well go in for the basket-making trade as well as the book-making profession. We've got Mary to work for, David!—and we'll both work for her—together!"

Helmsley turned upon him a face in which the expression was difficult to define.

"You really mean that?" he said.

"Really mean it! Of course I do! Why shouldn't I mean it?"

There was a moment's silence, and Helmsley, looking down on Mary as she knelt beside him, laid his hand caressingly on her hair.

"I think," he said gently, "that you are both too kind-hearted and impulsive, and that you are undertaking a task which should not be imposed upon you. You offer me a continued home with you after your marriage—but who am I that I should accept such generosity from you? I am not getting younger. Every day robs me of some strength—and my work—such work as I can do—will be of very little use to you. I may suffer from illness, which will cause you trouble and expense,—death is closer to me than life—and why should I die on your hands? It can only mean trouble for you if I stay on,—and though I am grateful to you with all my heart—more grateful than I can say"—and his voice trembled—"I know I ought to be unselfish,—and that the truest and best way to thank you for all you have done for me is to go away and leave you in peace and happiness—"

"We should not be happy without you, David!" declared Mary. "Can't you, won't you understand that we are both fond of you?"

"Fond of me!" And he smiled. "Fond of a useless old wreck who can scarcely earn a day's wage!"

"That's rather wide of the mark, David!" said Reay. "Mary's not the woman—and I'm sure I'm not the man—to care for any one on account of the money he can make. We like you for yourself,—so don't spoil this happiest day of our lives by suggesting any separation between us. Do you hear?"

"I hear!"—and a sudden brightness flashed up in Helmsley's sunken eyes, making them look almost young—"And I understand! I understand that though I am poor and old, and a stranger to you,—you are giving me friendship such as rich men often seek for and never find!—and I will try,—yes, I will try, God helping me,—to be worthy of your trust! If I stay with you—"

"There must be no 'if' in the case, David!" said Mary, smiling up at him.

He stroked her bright hair caressingly.

"Well, then, I will put it not 'if,' but as long as I stay with you," he answered—"as long as I stay with you, I will do all I can to show you how grateful I am to you,—and—and—I will never give you cause"—here he spoke more slowly, and with deliberate emphasis—"I will never give you cause to regret your confidence in me! I want you both to be glad—not sorry—that you spared a lonely old man a little of your affection!"

"We *are* glad, David!"—and Mary, as he lifted his hand from her head, caught it and kissed it lightly. "And we shall never be sorry! And here is Charlie"—and she picked up the little dog as she spoke and fondled it playfully,—"wondering why he is not included in the family party! For, after all, it is quite your affair, isn't it, Charlie? *You* were the cause of my finding David out on the hills!—and David was the cause of my knowing Angus—so if it hadn't been for *you*, nothing would have happened at all, Charlie!—and I should have been a lonely old maid all the days of my life! And I can't do anything to show my gratitude to you, you quaint wee soul, but give you a saucer of cream!"

She laughed, and springing up, began to prepare the tea. While she was moving quickly to and fro on this household business, Helmsley beckoned Reay to come closer to him.

"Speak frankly, Mr. Reay!" he said. "As the master of her heart, you are the master of her home. I can easily slip away—and tramping is not such hard work in summer time. Shall I go?"

"If you go, I shall start out and bring you back again," replied Reay, shaking his head at him determinedly. "You won't get so far but that I shall be able to catch you up in an hour! Please consider that you belong to us,—and that we have no intention of parting with you!"

Tears rose in Helmsley's eyes, and for a moment he covered them with his hand. Angus saw that he was deeply moved, and to avoid noticing him, especially as he was somewhat affected himself by the touching gratefulness of this apparently poor and lonely old man, went after Mary with all the pleasant ease and familiarity of an accepted lover, to help her bring in the tea. The tiny "Charlie," meanwhile, sitting on the hearth in a vigilantly erect attitude, with quivering nose pointed in a creamward direction, waited for the approach of the expected afternoon refreshment, trembling from head to tail with nervous excitement. And Helmsley, left alone for those few moments, presently mastered the strong emotion which made him long to tell his true history to the two sincere souls who, out of his whole life's experience, had alone proved themselves faithful to the spirit of a friendship wherein the claims of cash had no part. Regaining full command of himself, and determining to act out the part he had elected to play to whatever end should most fittingly arrive,—an end he could not as yet foresee,—he sat quietly in his chair as usual, gazing into the fire with the meditative patience and calm of old age, and silently building up in a waking dream the last story of his House of Love,—which now promised to be like that house spoken of in the Divine Parable—"And the rain descended, and the floods came, and the winds blew and beat upon that house, and it fell not, for it was founded upon a rock." For as he knew,—and as we all must surely know,—the greatest rains and floods and winds of a world of sorrow, are powerless to destroy love, if love be true.

XX

Three days later, when the dawn was scarcely declared and the earliest notes of the waking birds trembled on the soft air with the faint sweetness of a far-off fluty piping, the door of Mary Deane's cottage opened stealthily, and David Helmsley, dressed ready for a journey, stepped noiselessly out into the little garden. He wore the same ordinary workman's outfit in which he had originally started on his intended "tramp," including the vest which he had lined with banknotes, and which he had not used once since his stay with Mary Deane. For she had insisted on his wearing the warmer and softer garments which had once belonged to her own father,—and all these he had now taken off and left behind him, carefully folded up on the bed in his room. He had examined his money and had found it just as he had placed it,—even the little "surprise packet" which poor Tom o' the Gleam had collected for his benefit in the "Trusty Man's" common room, was still in the side-pocket where he had himself put it. Unripping a corner of the vest lining, he took out two five-pound notes, and with these in a rough leather purse for immediate use, and his stout ash stick grasped firmly in his hand, he started out to walk to the top of the coombe where he knew the path brought him to the verge of the highroad leading to Minehead. As he moved almost on tip-toe through Mary's garden, now all fragrant with golden wall-flowers, lilac, and mayblossom, he paused a moment,—looking up at the picturesque gabled eaves and latticed windows. A sudden sense of loneliness affected him almost to tears. For now he had not even the little dog Charlie with him to console him— that canine friend slept in a cushioned basket in Mary's room, and was therefore all unaware that his master was leaving him.

"But, please God, I shall come back in a day or two!" he murmured. "Please God, I shall see this dear shrine of peace and love again before I die! Meanwhile—good-bye, Mary! Good-bye, dearest and kindest of women! God bless you!"

He turned away with an effort—and, lifting the latch of the garden gate, opened it and closed it softly behind him. Then he began the ascent of the coombe. Not a soul was in sight,—the actual day had not yet begun. The hill torrent flowed along with a subdued purling sound over the rough stones and pebbles,—there had been little rain of late and the water was shallow, though clear and bright enough to gleam like a wavering silver ribbon in the dimness of the early morning,—and as he followed it upward and finally reached a point from whence the open sea was visible he rested a moment, leaning on his stick and looking backward on the way he had come. Strangely beautiful and mystical was the scene his eyes dwelt upon,—or rather perhaps it should be said that he saw it in a somewhat strange and mystical fashion of his own. There, out beyond the furthest edge of land, lay the ocean, shadowed just now by a delicate dark grey mist, which, like a veil, covered its placid bosom,—a mist which presently the rising sun would scatter with its glorious rays of gold;—here at his feet nestled Weircombe,—a cluster of simple cottages, sweetly adorned by nature with her fairest garlanding of springtime flowers,—and behind him, just across a length of barren moor, was the common highroad leading to the wider, busier towns. And he thought as he stood alone,—a frail and solitary figure, gazing dreamily out of himself, as it were, to things altogether beyond himself,—that the dim and shadowy ocean was like the vast Unknown which we call Death,—which we look upon tremblingly,—afraid of its darkness, and unable to realise that the sun of Life will ever rise again to pierce its gloom with glory. And the little world—the only world that can be called a world,—namely, that special corner of the planet which holds the hearts that love us—a world which for him, the multi-millionaire, was just a tiny village with one sweet woman living in it—resembled a garland of flowers flung down from the rocks as though to soften their ruggedness,—a garland broken asunder at the shoreline, even as all earthly garlands must break and fade at the touch of the first cold wave of the Infinite. As for the further road in which he was about to turn and go, that, to his fancy, was a nearer similitude of an approach to hell than any scene ever portrayed in Dante's *Divine Comedy*. For it led to the crowded haunts of men—the hives of greedy business,—the smoky, suffocating centres where each human unit seeks to over-reach and outrival the other—where there is no time to be kind—no room to be courteous; where the passion for gain and the worship of self are so furious and inexhaustible, that all the old fair virtues which make nations great and lasting, are trampled down in the dust, and jeered at as things contemptible and of no value,—where, if a man is honourable, he is asked "What do you get by it?"—and where, if a woman would remain simple and chaste, she is told she is giving herself "no chance." In this whirl of avarice, egotism, and pushfulness, Helmsley had lived nearly all his life, always conscious of, and longing for, something better—something truer and more productive of peace and lasting good. Almost everything he had touched had turned to money,—while nothing he had ever gained had turned to love. Except now—now when the end was drawing nigh—when he must soon say farewell to the little earth, so replete with natural beauty—farewell to the lovely sky, which whether in storm or calm, ever shows itself as a visible reflex of divine majesty and power—farewell to the sweet birds, which for no thanks at all, charm the ear by their tender songs and graceful wingëd ways—farewell to the flowers, which, flourishing in the woods and fields without care, lift their cups to the sun, and fill the air with fragrance,—and above all, farewell to the affection which he had found so late!—to the heart whose truth he had tested—to the woman for whose sake, could he in some way have compassed her surer and greater happiness, he would gladly have lived half his life over again, working with every moment of it to add to her joy. But an instinctive premonition warned him that the sands in Time's hour-glass were for him running to an end,—there was no leisure left to him now for any new scheme or plan by which he could improve or strengthen that which he had already accomplished. He realised this fully, with a passing pang of regret which soon tempered itself into patient resignation,—and as the first arrowy beam of the rising sun shot upwards from the east, he slowly turned his back on the quiet hamlet where in a few months he had found what he had vainly sought for in many long and weary years, and plodded steadily across the moor to the highroad. Here he sat down on the bank to wait till some conveyance going to Minehead should pass by—for he knew he had not sufficient strength to walk far. "Tramping it" now was for him impossible,—moreover, his former thirst for adventure was satisfied; he had succeeded in his search for "a friend" without going so far as Cornwall. There was no longer any cause for him to endure unnecessary fatigue—so he waited patiently, listening to the first wild morning carol of a skylark, which, bounding up from its nest hard by, darted into the air with quivering wings beating against the dispersing vapours of the dawn, and sang aloud in the full rapture of a joy made perfect by innocence. And he thought of the lovely lines of George Herbert:—

> *"How fresh, O Lord, how sweet and clean*
> *Are Thy returns! Ev'n as the flowers in Spring,*
> *To which, besides their own demean,*

The late-past frosts tributes of pleasure bring;
Grief melts away
Like snow in May,
As if there were no such cold thing.

"Who would have thought my shrivell'd heart
Could have recover'd greenness? It was gone
Quite under ground; as flowers depart
To see their mother-root, when they have blown,
Where they together
All the hard weather,
Dead to the world, keep house unknown.

"These are Thy wonders, Lord of power,
Killing and quick'ning, bringing down to Hell
And up to Heaven in an hour;
Making a chiming of a passing bell.
We say amiss
This or that is;
Thy Word is all, if we could spell!"

"If we could spell!" he murmured, half aloud. "Ay, if we could learn even a quarter of the alphabet which would help us to understand the meaning of that 'Word!'—the Word which 'was in the beginning, and the word was with God, and the word *was* God!' Then we should be wise indeed with a wisdom that would profit us,—we should have no fears and no forebodings,—we should know that all is, all *must* be for the best!" And he raised his eyes to the slowly brightening sky. "Yet, after all, the attitude of simple faith is the right one for us, if we would call ourselves children of God—the faith which affirms—'Though He slay me, yet will I trust in Him!'"

As he thus mused, a golden light began to spread around him,— the sun had risen above the horizon, and its cheerful radiance sparkled on every leaf and every blade of grass that bore a drop of dew. The morning mists rose hoveringly, paused awhile, and then lightly rolled away, disclosing one picture after another of exquisite sylvan beauty,— every living thing took up anew its burden of work and pleasure for the day, and "Now" was again declared the acceptable time. To enjoy the moment, and to make much of the moment while it lasts, is the very keynote of Nature's happiness, and David Helmsley found himself on this particular morning more or less in tune with the general sentiment. Certain sad thoughts oppressed him from time to time, but they were tempered and well-nigh overcome by the secret pleasure he felt within himself at having been given the means wherewith to ensure happiness for those whom he considered were more deserving of it than himself. And he sat patiently watching the landscape grow in glory as the sun rose higher and higher, till presently, struck by a sudden fear lest Mary Deane should get up earlier than usual, and missing him, should come out to seek for him, he left the bank by the roadside, and began to trudge slowly along in the direction of Minehead. He had not walked for a much longer time than about ten minutes, when he heard the crunching sound of heavy wheels behind him, and, looking back, saw a large mill waggon piled with sacks of flour and drawn by two sturdy horses, coming leisurely along. He waited till it drew near, and then called to the waggoner—

"Will you give me a lift to Minehead for half a crown?"

The waggoner, stout, red-faced, and jolly-looking, nodded an emphatic assent.

"I'd do it for 'arf the money!" he said. "Gi' us yer 'and, old gaffer!"

The "old gaffer" obeyed, and was soon comfortably seated between the projecting corners of two flour sacks, which in their way were as comfortable as cushions.

"'Old on there," said the waggoner, "an' ye'll be as safe as though ye was in Abram's bosom. Not that I knows much about Abram anyway. Wheer abouts d'ye want in Minehead?"

"The railway station."

"Right y' are! That's my ticket too. Tired o' trampin' it, I s'pose, aint ye?"

"A bit tired—yes. I've walked since daybreak."

The waggoner cracked his whip, and the horses plodded on. Their heavy hoofs on the dusty road, and the noise made by the grind of the cart wheels, checked any attempt at prolonged conversation, for which Helmsley was thankful. He considered himself lucky in having met with a total stranger, for the name of the owner of the waggon, which was duly displayed both on the vehicle itself and the sacks of flour it contained, was unknown to him, and the place from which it had come was an inland village several miles away from Weircombe. He was therefore safe—so far—from any chance of recognition. To be driven along in a heavy mill cart was a rumblesome, drowsy way of travelling, but it was restful, and when Minehead was at last reached, he did not feel himself at all tired. The waggoner had to get his cargo of flour off by rail, so there was no lingering in the town itself, which was as yet scarcely astir. They were in time for the first train going to Exeter, and Helmsley, changing one of his five-pound notes at the railway station, took a third-class ticket to that place. Then he paid the promised half-crown to his friendly driver, with an extra threepence for a morning "dram," whereat the waggoner chuckled.

"Thankee! I zee ye be no temp'rance man!"

Helmsley smiled.

"No. I'm a sober man, not a temperance man!"

"Ay! We'd a parzon in these 'ere parts as was temp'rance, but 'e took 'is zpirits different like! 'E zkorned 'is glass, but 'e loved 'is gel! Har—ar—ar! Ivir 'eerd o' Parzon Arbroath as woz put out o' the Church for 'avin' a fav'rite?"

"I saw something about it in the papers," said Helmsley.

"Ay, 'twoz in the papers. Har—ar—ar! 'E woz a temp'rance man. But wot I sez is, we'se all a bit o' devil in us, an' we can't be temp'rance ivry which way. An' zo, if not the glass, then the gel! Har—ar—ar! Good-day t' ye, an' thank ye kindly!"

He went off then, and a few minutes later the train came gliding in. The whirr and noise of the panting engine confused Helmsley's ears and dazed his brain, after his months of seclusion in such a quiet little spot as Weircombe,—and he was seized with quite a nervous terror and doubt as to whether he would be able, after all, to undertake the journey he had decided upon, alone. But an energetic porter put an end to his indecision by opening all the doors of the various compartments in the train and banging them to again, whereupon he made up his mind quickly, and managed, with some little difficulty, to clamber up the high step of a third-class carriage and get in before the aforesaid porter had the chance to push him in head foremost. In another few minutes the engine whistle set up a deafening scream, and the train ran swiftly out of the station. He was off;—the hills, the sea, were left behind—and Weircombe—restful, simple little Weircombe, seemed not only miles of distance, but ages of time away! Had he ever lived there, he hazily wondered? Would he ever go back? Was he "old David the basket-maker," or David Helmsley the millionaire? He hardly knew. It did not seem worth while to consider the problem of his own identity. One figure alone was real,—one face alone smiled out of the cloudy vista of thoughts and memories, with the true glory of an ineffable tenderness— the sweet, pure face of Mary, with her clear and candid eyes lighting every expression to new loveliness. On Angus Reay his mind did not dwell so much—Angus was a man—and as a man he regarded him with warm liking and sympathy—but it was as the future husband and protector of Mary that he thought of him most—as the one out of all the world who would care for her, when he, David Helmsley, was no more. Mary was the centre of his dreams—the pivot round which all his last ambitions in this world were gathered together in one focus,— without her there was, there could be nothing for him—nothing to give peace or comfort to his last days—nothing to satisfy him as to the future of all that his life had been spent to gain.

Meantime,—while the train bearing him to Exeter was rushing along through wide and ever-varying stretches of fair landscape,— there was amazement and consternation in the little cottage he had left behind him. Mary, rising from a sound night's sleep, and coming down to the kitchen as usual to light the fire and prepare breakfast, saw a letter on the table addressed to her, and opening, it read as follows:—

My Dear Mary,

Do not be anxious this morning when you find that I am gone. I shall not be long away. I have an idea of getting some work to do, which may be more useful to you and Angus than my poor attempts at basket-making. At any rate I feel it would be wrong if I did not try to obtain some better paying employment, of a kind which I can do at home, so that I may be of greater assistance to you both when you marry and begin your double housekeeping. Old though I am and ailing, I want to feel less of a burden and more of a help. You will not think any the worse of me for wishing this. You have been so good and charitable to me in my need, that I should not die happy if I, in my turn, did not make an effort to give you some substantial proof of gratitude. This is Tuesday morning, and I shall hope to be home again with you before Sunday. In the meanwhile, do not worry at all about me, for I feel quite strong enough to do what I have in my mind. I leave Charlie with you. He is safest and happiest in your

care. Good-bye for a little while, dear, kind friend, and God
bless you!

DAVID

She read this with amazement and distress, the tears welling up in
her eyes.

"Oh, David!" she exclaimed. "Poor, poor old man! What will he
do all by himself, wandering about the country with no money! It's
dreadful! How could he think of such a thing! He is so weak, too!—he
can't possibly get very far!"

Here a sudden thought struck her, and picking up Charlie, who had
followed her downstairs from her bedroom and was now trotting to and
fro, sniffing the air in a somewhat disconsolate and dubious manner,
she ran out of the house bareheaded, and hurried up to the top of the
"coombe." There she paused, shading her eyes from the sun and looking
all about her. It was a lovely morning, and the sea, calm and sparkling
with sunbeams, shone like a blue glass flecked with gold. The sky was
clear, and the landscape fresh and radiant with the tender green of the
springtime verdure. But everything was quite solitary. Vainly her glance
swept from left to right and from right to left again,—there was no
figure in sight such as the one she sought and half-expected to discover.
Putting Charlie down to follow at her heels, she walked quickly across
the intervening breadth of moor to the highroad, and there paused,
looking up and down its dusty length, hoping against hope that she
might see David somewhere trudging slowly along on his lonely way,
but there was not a human creature visible. Charlie, assuming a highly
vigilant attitude, cocked his tiny ears and sniffed the air suspiciously,
as though he scented the trail of his lost master, but no clue presented
itself as likely to serve the purpose of tracking the way in which he had
gone. Moved by a sudden loneliness and despondency, Mary slowly
returned to the cottage, carrying the little dog in her arms, and was
affected to tears again when she entered the kitchen, because it looked
so empty. The bent figure, the patient aged face, on which for her there
was ever a smile of grateful tenderness—these had composed a picture
by her fireside to which she had grown affectionately accustomed,—
and to see it no longer there made her feel almost desolate. She lit the
fire listlessly and prepared her own breakfast without interest—it was
a solitary meal and lacked flavour. She was glad when, after breakfast,
Angus Reay came in, as was now his custom, to say good-morning, and

to "gain inspiration,"—so he told her,—for his day's work. He was no less astonished than herself at David's sudden departure.

"Poor old chap! I believe he thinks he is in our way, Mary!" he said, as he read the letter of explanation which their missing friend had left behind him. "And yet he says quite plainly here that he will be back before Sunday. Perhaps he will. But where can he have gone to?"

"Not far, surely!" and Mary looked, as she felt, perplexed. "He has no money!"

"Not a penny?"

"Not a penny! He makes me take everything he earns to help pay for his keep and as something towards the cost of his illness last year. I don't want it—but it pleases him that I should have it—"

"Of course—I understand that,"—and Angus slipped an arm round her waist, while he read the letter through again. "But if he hasn't a penny, how can he get along?"

"He must be on the tramp again," said Mary. "But he isn't strong enough to tramp. I went up the coombe this morning and right out to the highroad, for I thought I might see him and catch up with him—because I know it would take him ever so long to walk a mile. But he had gone altogether."

Reay stood thinking.

"I tell you what, Mary," he said at last, "I'll take a brisk walk down the road towards Minehead. I should think that's the only place where he'd try for work. I daresay I shall overtake him."

Her eyes brightened.

"Yes, that's quite possible,"—and she was evidently pleased at the suggestion. "He's so old and feeble, and you're so strong and quick on your feet—"

"Quick with my lips, too," said Angus, promptly kissing her. "But I shall have to be on my best behaviour now you're all alone in the cottage, Mary! David has left you defenceless!"

He laughed, but as she raised her eyes questioningly to his face, grew serious.

"Yes, my Mary! You'll have to stay by your own sweet lonesome! Otherwise all the dear, kind, meddlesome old women in the village will talk! Mrs. Twitt will lead the chorus, with the best intentions, unless—and this is a dreadful alternative!—you can persuade her to come up and play propriety!"

The puzzled look left her face, and she smiled though a wave of colour flushed her cheeks.

"Oh! I see what you mean, Angus! But I'm too old to want looking after—I can look after myself."

"Can you?" And he took her into his arms and held her fast. "And how will you do it?"

She was silent a moment, looking into his eyes with a grave and musing tenderness. Then she said quietly—

"By trusting you, my love, now and always!"

Very gently he released her from his embrace—very reverently he kissed her.

"And you shall never regret your trust, you dear, sweet angel of a woman! Be sure of that! Now I'm off to look for David—I'll try and bring him back with me. By the way, Mary, I've told Mr. and Mrs. Twitt and good old Bunce that we are engaged—so the news is now the public property of the whole village. In fact, we might just as well have put up the banns and secured the parson!"

He laughed his bright, jovial laugh, and throwing on his cap went out, striding up the coombe with swift, easy steps, whistling joyously "My Nannie O" as he made the ascent. Twice he turned to wave his hand to Mary who stood watching him from her garden gate, and then he disappeared. She waited a moment among all the sweetly perfumed flowers in her little garden, looking at the bright glitter of the hill stream as it flowed equably by.

"How wonderful it is," she thought, "that God should have been so good to me! I have done nothing to deserve any love at all, and yet Angus loves me! It seems too beautiful to be real! I am not worthy of such happiness! Sometimes I dare not think too much of it lest it should all prove to be only a dream! For surely no one in the world could wish for a better life than we shall live—Angus and I—in this dear little cottage together,—he with his writing, which I know will some day move the world,—and I with my usual work, helping as much as I can to make his life sweet to him. For we have the great secret of all joy—we love each other!"

With her eyes full of the dreamy light of inward heart's content, she turned and went into the house. The sight of David's empty chair by the fire troubled her,—but she tried to believe that Angus would succeed in finding him on the highroad, and in persuading him to return at once. Towards noon Mrs. Twitt came in, somewhat out of breath, on account of having climbed the village street more rapidly than was her custom on such a warm day as it had turned out to be, and straightway began conversation.

"Wonders 'ull never cease, Mis' Deane, an' that's a fact!" she said, wiping her hot face with the corner of her apron—"An' while there's life there's 'ope! I'd as soon 'a thought o' Weircombe Church walkin' down to the shore an' turnin' itself into a fishin' smack, as that you'd a' got engaged to be married! I would, an' that's a Gospel truth! Ye seemed so steady like an' settled—lor' a mussy me!" And here, despite her effort to look serious, a broad smile got the better of her. "An' a fine man too you've got,—none o' your scallywag weaklings as one sees too much of nowadays, but a real upright sort o' chap wi' no nonsense about 'im. An' I wishes ye well, Mary, my dear,"—and the worthy soul took Mary's hand in hers and gave her a hearty kiss. "For it's never too late to mend, as the Scripter tells us, an' forbye ye're not in yer green gooseberry days there's those as thinks ripe fruit better than sour-growin' young codlings. An' ye may take 'art o' grace for one thing—them as marries young settles quickly old—an' to look at the skin an' the 'air an' the eyes of ye, you beat ivery gel I've ivir seen in the twenties, so there's good preservin' stuff in ye wot'll last. An' I bet you're more fond o' the man ye've got late than if ye'd caught 'im early!"

Mary laughed, but her eyes were full of wistful tenderness.

"I love him very dearly," she said simply—"And I know he's a great deal too good for me."

Mrs. Twitt sniffed meaningly.

"Well, I'm not in any way sure o' that," she observed. "When a man's too good for a woman it's what we may call a Testymen' miracle. For the worst wife as ivir lived is never so bad as a bad 'usband. There's a suthin' in a man wot's real devil-like when it gits the uppermost of 'im—an' 'e's that crafty born that I've known 'im to be singin' hymns one hour an' drinkin' 'isself silly the next. 'Owsomever, Mister Reay seems a decent chap, forbye 'e do give 'is time to writin' which don't appear to make 'is pot boil—"

"Ah, but he will be famous!" interrupted Mary exultantly. "I know he will!"

"An' what's the good o' that?" enquired Mrs. Twitt. "If bein' famous is bein' printed about in the noospapers, I'd rather do without it if I wos 'im. Parzon Arbroath got famous that way!" And she chuckled. "But the great pint is that you an' 'e is a-goin' to be man an' wife, an' I'm right glad to 'ear it, for it's a lonely life ye've been leadin' since yer father's death, forbye ye've got a bit o' company in old David. An' wot'll ye do with David when you're married?"

"He'll stay on with us, I hope," said Mary. "But this morning he has gone away—and we don't know where he can have gone to."

Mrs. Twitt raised her eyes and hands in astonishment.

"Gone away?"

"Yes." And Mary showed her the letter Helmsley had written, and explained how Angus Reay had started off to walk towards Minehead, in the hope of overtaking the wanderer.

"Well, I never!" And Mrs. Twitt gave a short gasp of wonder. "Wants to find employment, do 'e? The poor old innercent! Why, Twitt would 'a given 'im a job in the stoneyard if 'e'd 'a known. He'll never find a thing to do anywheres on the road at 'is age!"

And the news of David's sudden and lonely departure affected her more powerfully than the prospect of Mary's marriage, which had, in the first place, occupied all her mental faculties.

"An' that reminds me," she went on, "of 'ow the warnin' came to me yesterday when I was a-goin' out to my wash-tub an' I slipt on a bit o' potato peelin'. That's allus a sign of a partin' 'twixt friends. Put that together with the lump o' clinkers as flew out o' the fire last week and split in two in the middle of the kitchen, an' there ye 'ave it all writ plain. I sez to Twitt—'Suthin's goin' to 'appen'—an' 'e sez in 'is fool way—'G'arn, old woman, suthin's allus a-'appenin' somewheres'— then when Mister Reay looked in all smiles an' sez 'Good-mornin', Twitt! I'm goin' to marry Miss Mary Deane! Wish us joy!' Twitt, 'e up an' sez, 'There's your suthin', old gel! A marriage!' an' I sez, 'Not at all, Twitt—not at all, Mister Reay, if I may make so bold, but slippin' on peel don't mean marriage, nor yet clinkers, though two spoons in a saucer does convey 'ints o' the same, an' two spoons was in Twitt's saucer only this very mornin'. Which I wishes both man an' woman as runs the risk everlastin' joy!' An' Twitt, as is allus puttin' in 'is word where 'taint wanted, sez, 'Don't talk about everlastin' joy, mother, 'tis like a hepitaph'—which I answers quick an' sez, 'Your mind may run on hepitaphs, Twitt, seein' 'tis your livin', but mine don't do no such thing, an' when I sez everlastin' joy for man an' wife, I means it.' An' then Mister Reay comes an' pats me on the shoulder cosy like an' sez, 'Right you are, Mrs. Twitt!' an' 'e walks off laughin', an' Twitt 'e laughs too an' sez, 'Good luck to the bridegroom an' the bride,' which I aint denyin', but there was still the thought o' the potato peel an' the clinker, an' it's come clear to-day now I've 'eerd as 'ow poor old David's gone!" She paused to take breath, and shook her head solemnly. "It's my opinion 'e'll never come back no more!"

"Oh, don't say that!" exclaimed Mary, distressed. "Don't even think it!"

But Mrs. Twitt was not to be shaken in her pronouncement.

"'E'll never come back no more!" she said. "An' the children on the shore 'ull miss 'im badly, for 'e was a reg'lar Father Christmas to 'em, not givin' presents by any manner o' means, 'avin' none to give, but tellin' 'em stories as kep' 'em quiet an' out of 'arms way for 'ours,—an' mendin' their toys an' throwin' their balls an' spinnin' their tops like the 'armless old soul 'e was! I'm right sorry 'e's gone! Weircombe 'll miss 'im for sartin sure!"

And this was the general feeling of the whole village when the unexpected departure of "old David" became known. Angus Reay, returning in the afternoon, reported that he had walked half the way, and had driven the other half with a man who had given him a lift in his trap, right into Minehead, but had seen and heard nothing of the missing waif and stray. Coming back to Weircombe with the carrier's cart, he had questioned the carrier as to whether he had seen the old man anywhere along the road, but this inquiry likewise met with failure.

"So the only thing to do, Mary," said Angus, finally, "is to believe his own written word,—that he will be back with us before Sunday. I don't think he means to leave you altogether in such an abrupt way,—that would be churlish and ungrateful—and I'm sure he is neither."

"Oh, he's anything but churlish!" she answered quickly. "He has always been most thoughtful and kind to me; and as for gratitude!— why, the poor old dear makes too much of it altogether—one would think I had given him a fortune instead of just taking common human care of him. I expect he must have worked in some very superior house of business, for though he's so poor, he has all the ways of a gentleman."

"What are the ways of a gentleman, my Mary?" demanded Angus, gaily. "Do you know? I mean, do you know what they are nowadays? To stick a cigar in one's mouth and smoke it all the time a woman is present—to keep one's hat on before her, and to talk to her in such a loose, free and easy fashion as might bring one's grandmother out of her grave and make her venerable hair curl! Those are the 'ways' of certain present-time 'gentlemen' who keep all the restaurants and music-halls of London going—and I don't rank good old David with these. I know what *you* mean—you mean that he has all the fine feeling, delicacy and courtesy of a gentleman, as 'gentlemen' used to be before our press was degraded to its present level by certain clowns and jesters who make it their business to jeer at every "gentlemanly" feeling that ever inspired humanity—yes, I understand! He is a gentleman of the old school,—well,—I think he is—and I think he would always be that, if he tramped the road till he died. He must have seen better days."

"Oh yes, I'm sure of that!" said Mary. "So many really capable men get turned out of work because they are old—"

"Well, there's one advantage about my profession," interrupted Angus. "No one can turn *me* out of literature either for young or old age, if I choose to make a name in it! Think of that, my Mary! The glorious independence of it! An author is a law unto himself, and if he succeeds, he is the master of his own fate. Publishers are his humble servants—waiting eagerly to snatch up his work that they may get all they can for themselves out of it,—and the public—the great public which, apart from all 'interested' critical bias, delivers its own verdict, is always ready to hearken and to applaud the writer of its choice. There is no more splendid and enviable life!—if I could only make a hundred pounds a year by it, I would rather be an author than a king! For if one has something in one's soul to say—something that is vital, true, and human as well as divine, the whole world will pause to listen. Yes, Mary! In all its toil and stress, its scheming for self-advantage, its political changes, its little temporary passing shows of empires and monarchies, the world will stop to hear what the Thinker and the Writer tells it! The words of old Socrates still ring down the ages—the thoughts of Shakespeare are still the basis of English literature!—what a grand life it is to be among the least of one of the writing band! I tell you, Mary, that even if I fail, I shall be proud to have at any rate *tried* to succeed!"

"You will not fail!" she said, her eyes glowing with enthusiasm. "I shall see you win your triumph!"

"Well, if I cannot conquer everything with you by my side, I shall be but a poor and worthless devil!" he answered. "And now I must be off and endeavour to make up for my lost time this morning, running after David! Poor old chap! Don't worry about him, Mary. I think you may take his word for it that he means to be back before Sunday."

He left her then, and all the day and all the evening too she spent the time alone. It would have been impossible to her to express in words how greatly she missed the companionship of the gentle old man who had so long been the object of her care. There was a sense of desolate emptiness in the little cottage such as had not so deeply affected her for years—not indeed since the first months following immediately on her own father's death. That Angus Reay kept away was, she knew, care for her on his part. Solitary woman as she was, the villagers, like all people who live in very small, mentally restricted country places, would have idly gossiped away her reputation had she received her lover into her house alone. So she passed a very dismal time all by herself; and closing up the house early, took little Charlie in her arms and went to bed, where, much to her own abashment, she cried herself to sleep.

Meanwhile, David himself, for whom she fretted, had arrived in Exeter. The journey had fatigued him considerably, though he had been able to get fairly good food and a glass of wine at one of the junctions where he had changed *en route*. On leaving the Exeter railway station, he made his way towards the Cathedral, and happening to chance on a very small and unpretending "Temperance Hotel" in a side street, where a placard intimating that "Good Accommodation for Travellers" might be had within, he entered and asked for a bedroom. He obtained it at once, for his appearance was by no means against him, being that of a respectable old working man who was prepared to pay his way in a humble, but perfectly honest fashion. As soon as he had secured his room, which was a curious little three-cornered apartment, partially obscured by the shadows of the many buttresses of the Cathedral, his next care was to go out into the High Street and provide himself with a good stock of writing materials. These obtained, he returned to his temporary lodging, where, after supper, he went to bed early in order to rise early. With the morning light he was up and dressed, eager to be at work,—an inrush of his old business energy came back on him,— his brain was clear, his mental force keen and active. There happened to be an old-fashioned oak table in his room, and drawing this to the window, he sat down to write the document which his solicitor and friend, Sir Francis Vesey, had so often urged him to prepare—his Will. He knew what a number of legal technicalities might, or could be involved in this business, and was therefore careful to make it as short, clear, and concise as possible, leaving no chance anywhere open of doubt or discussion. And with a firm, unwavering pen, in his own particularly distinct and characteristic caligraphy, he disposed of everything of which he died possessed "absolutely and without any conditions whatsoever" to Mary Deane, spinster, at present residing in Weircombe, Somerset, adding the hope that she would, if she saw fit to do so, carry out certain requests of his, the testator's, as conveyed privately to her in a letter accompanying the Will. All the morning long he sat thoughtfully considering and weighing each word he used—till at last, when the document was finished to his satisfaction, he folded it up, and putting it in his pocket, started out to get his midday meal and find a lawyer's office. He was somewhat surprised at his own alertness and vigour as he walked through the streets of Exeter on this quest;—excitement buoyed him up to such a degree that be was not conscious of the slightest fatigue or lassitude—he felt almost young. He took his lunch at a small restaurant where he saw city clerks and others of that type going in, and afterwards, strolling up a dull little street which ended in a *cul de sac*, he spied a dingy archway, offering itself as an approach to a flight of equally dingy stairs. Here a brass plate, winking at the passer-by, stated that "Rowden and Owlett, Solicitors," would be found on the first floor. Helmsley paused, considering a moment—then, making up his mind that "Rowden and Owlett" would suit his purpose as well as any other equally unknown firm, he slowly climbed the steep and unwashed stair. Opening the first door at the top of the flight, he saw a small boy leaning both arms across a large desk, and watching the gyrations of two white mice in a revolving cage.

"Hullo!" said the boy sharply, "what d' ye want?"

"I want to see Mr. Rowden or Mr. Owlett," he replied.

"Right y' are!" and the boy promptly seized the cage containing the white mice and hid it in a cupboard. "You're our first caller to-day. Mr. Rowden's gone to Dawlish,—but Mr. Owlett's in. Wait a minute."

Helmsley obeyed, sitting down in a chair near the door, and smiling to himself at the evidences of slack business which the offices of Messrs. Rowden and Owlett presented. In about five minutes the boy returned, and gave him a confidential nod.

"You can go in now," he said; "Mr. Owlett was taking his after-dinner snooze, but he's jumped up at once, and he's washed his hands and face, so he's quite ready for business. This way, please!"

He beckoned with a rather dirty finger, and Helmsley followed him into a small apartment where Mr. Owlett, a comfortably stout, middle-aged gentleman, sat at a large bureau covered with papers, pretending to read. He looked up as his hoped-for client entered, and flushed redly in the face with suppressed vexation as he saw that it was only a working man after all—"Some fellow wanting a debt collected," he decided, pushing away his papers with a rather irritated movement. However, in times when legal work was so scarce, it did not serve any good purpose to show anger, so, smoothing his ruffled brow, he forced a reluctantly condescending smile, as his office-boy, having ushered in the visitor, left the room.

"Good afternoon, my man!" he said, with a patronising air. "What can I do for you?"

"Well, not so very much, sir," and Helmsley took off his hat deferentially, standing in an attitude of humility. "It's only a matter of making my Will,—I've written it out myself, and if you would be so good as to see whether it is all in order, I'm prepared to pay you for your trouble."

"Oh, certainly, certainly!" Here Mr. Owlett took off his spectacles and polished them. "I suppose you know it's not always a wise thing to draw up your own Will yourself? You should always let a lawyer draw it up for you."

"Yes, sir, I've heard that," answered Helmsley, with an air of respectful attention—"And that's why I've brought the paper to you, for if there's anything wrong with it, you can put it right, or draw it up again if you think proper. Only I'd rather not be put to more expense than I can help."

"Just so!" And the worthy solicitor sighed, as he realised that there were no "pickings" to be made out of his present visitor—"Have you brought the document with you?"

"Yes, sir!" Helmsley fumbled in his pocket, and drew out the paper with a well-assumed air of hesitation; "I'm leaving everything I've got to a woman who has been like a daughter to me in my old age—my wife and children are dead—and I've no one that has any blood claim on me—so I think the best thing I can do is to give everything I've got to the one that's been kind to me in my need."

"Very right—very proper!" murmured Mr. Owlett, as he took the offered document from Helmsley's hand and opened it—"Um—um!—let me see!—" Here he read aloud—"I, David Helmsley,—um—um!—Helmsley—Helmsley!—that's a name that I seem to have heard somewhere!—David Helmsley!—yes!—why that's the name of a multi-millionaire!—ha-ha-ha! A multi-millionaire! That's curious! Do you know, my man, that your name is the same as that of one of the richest men in the world?"

Helmsley permitted himself to smile.

"Really, sir? You don't say so!"

"Yes, yes!" And Mr. Owlett fixed his spectacles on his nose and beamed at his humble client through them condescendingly—"One of the richest men in the world!" And he smacked his lips as though he had just swallowed a savoury morsel—"Amazing! Now if you were he, your Will would be a world's affair—a positively world's affair!"

"Would it indeed?" And again Helmsley smiled.

"Everybody would talk of it," proceeded Owlett, lost in rapturous musing—"The disposal of a rich man's millions is always a most interesting subject of conversation! And you actually didn't know you had such a rich namesake?"

"No, sir, I did not."

"Ah well! I suppose you live in the country, and people in the country seldom hear of the names that are famous in towns. Now let me consider this Will again—'I, David Helmsley, being in sound health of mind and body, thanks be to God, do make this to be my Last Will and Testament, revoking all former Wills, Codicils and Testamentary Dispositions. First I commend my soul into the hands of God my Creator, hoping and believing, through the merits of Jesus Christ my Saviour, to be made partaker of life everlasting'—Dear me, dear me!" and Mr. Owlett took off his spectacles. "You must be a very old-fashioned man! This sort of thing is not at all necessary nowadays!"

"Not necessary, perhaps," said Helmsley gently—"But there is no harm in putting it in, sir, I hope?"

"Oh, there's no harm! It doesn't affect the Will itself, of course,—but—but—it's odd—it's unusual! You see nobody minds what becomes of your Soul, or your Body either—the only question of importance to any one is what is to be done with your Money!"

"I see!" And Helmsley nodded his head and spoke with perfect mildness—"But I'm an old man, and I've lived long enough to be fonder of old-fashioned ways than new, and I should like, if you please, to let it be known that I died a Christian, which is, to me, not a member of any particular church or chapel, but just a Christian—a man who faithfully believes in the teaching of our Lord Jesus Christ."

The attorney stared at him astonished, and moved by a curious sense of shame. There was something both pathetic and dignified in the aspect of this frail old "working man," who stood before him so respectfully with his venerable white hair uncovered, and his eyes full of an earnest resolution which was not to be gainsaid. Coughing a cough of nervous embarrassment, he again glanced at the document before him.

"Of course," he said—"if you wish it, there is not the slightest objection to your making this—this public statement as to your religious convictions. It does not affect the disposal of your worldly goods in any way. It used—yes, it used to be quite the ordinary way of beginning a Last Will and Testament—but we have got beyond any special commendation of our souls to God, you know—"

"Oh yes, I quite understand that," rejoined Helmsley. "Present-day people like to think that God takes no interest whatever in His own creation. It's a more comfortable doctrine to believe that He is indifferent rather than observant. But, so far as I'm concerned, I don't go with the time."

"No, I see you don't," and Mr. Owlett bent his attention anew on the Will—"And the religious preliminary being quite unimportant, you shall have it your own way. Apart from that, you've drawn it up quite correctly, and in very good form. I suppose you understand that you have in this Will left 'everything' to the named legatee, Mary Deane, spinster, that is to say, excluding no item whatsoever? That she becomes the possessor, in fact, of your whole estate?"

Helmsley bent his head in assent.

"That is what I wish, sir, and I hope I have made it clear."

"Yes, you have made it quite clear. There is no room for discussion on any point. You wish us to witness your signature?"

"If you please, sir."

And he advanced to the bureau ready to sign. Mr. Owlett rang a bell sharply twice. An angular man with a youngish face and a very elderly manner answered the summons.

"My confidential clerk," said Owlett, briefly introducing him. "Here, Prindle! I want you to be witness with me to this gentleman's Will."

Prindle bowed, and passed his hand across his mouth to hide a smile. Prindle was secretly amused to think that a working man had anything to leave worth the trouble of making a Will at all. Mr. Owlett dipped a pen in ink, and handed it to his client. Whereat, Helmsley wrote his signature in a clear, bold, unfaltering hand. Mr. Owlett appended his own name, and then Prindle stepped up to sign. As he saw the signature "David Helmsley," he paused and seemed astonished. Mr. Owlett gave a short laugh.

"We know that name, don't we, Prindle?"

"Well, sir, I should say all the world knew it!" replied Prindle.

"All the world—yes!—all except our friend here," said Owlett, nodding towards Helmsley. "You didn't know, my man, did you, that there was a multi-millionaire existing of the same name as yourself?"

"No, sir, I did not!" answered Helmsley. "I hope he's made his Will!"

"I hope he has!" laughed the attorney. "There'll be a big haul for the Crown if he hasn't!"

Prindle, meanwhile, was slowly writing "James George Prindle, Clerk to the aforesaid Robert Owlett" underneath his legal employer's signature.

"I should suggest," said Mr. Owlett, addressing David, jocosely, "that you go and make yourself known to the rich Mr. Helmsley as a namesake of his!"

"Would you, sir? And why?"

"Well, he might be interested. Men as rich as he is always want a new 'sensation' to amuse them. And he might, for all you know, make you a handsome present, or leave you a little legacy!"

Helmsley smiled—he very nearly laughed. But he carefully guarded his equanimity.

"Thank you for the hint, sir! I'll try and see him some day!"

"I hear he's dead," said Prindle, finishing the signing of his name and laying down his pen. "It was in the papers some time back."

"But it was contradicted," said Owlett quickly.

"Ah, but I think it was true all the same," and Prindle shook his head obstinately. "The papers ought to know."

"Oh yes, they ought to know, but in nine cases out of ten they *don't* know," declared Owlett. "And if you contradict their lies, they're so savage at being put in the wrong that they'll blazon the lies all the more rather than confess them. That will do, Prindle! You can go."

Prindle, aware that his employer was not a man to be argued with, at once retired, and Owlett, folding up the Will, handed it to Helmsley.

"That's all right," he said, "I suppose you want to take it with you? You can leave it with us if you like."

"Thank you, but I'd rather have it about me," Helmsley answered. "You see I'm old and not very strong, and I might die at any time. I'd like to keep my Will on my own person."

"Well, take care of it, that's all," said the solicitor, smiling at what he thought his client's rustic *naïveté*. "No matter how little you've got to leave, it's just as well it should go where you want it to go without trouble or difficulty. And there's generally a quarrel over every Will."

"I hope there's no chance of any quarrel over mine," said Helmsley, with a touch of anxiety.

"Oh no! Not the least in the world! Even if you were as great a millionaire as the man who happens to bear the same name as yourself, the Will would hold good."

"Thank you!" And Helmsley placed on the lawyer's desk more than his rightful fee, which that respectable personage accepted without any hesitation. "I'm very much obliged to you. Good afternoon!"

"Good afternoon!" And Mr. Owlett leaned back in his chair, blandly surveying his visitor. "I suppose you quite understand that, having made your legatee, Mary Deane, your sole executrix likewise, you give her absolute control?"

"Oh yes, I quite understand that!" answered Helmsley. "That is what I wish her to have—the free and absolute control of all I die possessed of."

"Then you may be quite easy in your mind," said the lawyer. "You have made that perfectly clear."

Whereat Helmsley again said "Good afternoon," and again Mr. Owlett briefly responded, sweeping the money his client had paid him off his desk, and pocketing the same with that resigned air of injured virtue which was his natural expression whenever he thought of how little good hard cash a country solicitor could make in the space of twenty-four hours. Helmsley, on leaving the office, returned at once to his lodging under the shadow of the Cathedral and resumed his own work, which was that of writing several letters to various persons connected with his financial affairs, showing to each and all what a grip he held, even in absence, on the various turns of the wheel of fortune, and dating all his communications from Exeter, "at which interesting old town I am making a brief stay," he wrote, for the satisfaction of such curiosity as his correspondents might evince, as well as for the silencing of all rumours respecting his supposed death. Last of all he wrote to Sir Francis Vesey, as follows:—

My Dear Vesey,

On this day, in the good old city of Exeter, I have done what you so often have asked me to do. I have made my

Will. It is drawn up entirely in my own handwriting, and has been duly declared correct and valid by a legal firm here, Messrs. Rowden and Owlett. Mr. Owlett and Mr. Owlett's clerk were good enough to witness my signature. I wish you to consider this communication made to you in the most absolute confidence, and as I carry the said document, namely my 'Last Will and Testament,' upon my person, it will not reach your hands till I am no more. Then I trust you will see the business through without unnecessary trouble or worry to the person who, by my desire, will inherit all I have to leave.

"I have spent nearly a year of almost perfect happiness away from London and all the haunts of London men, and I have found what I sought, but what you probably doubted I could ever find—Love! The treasures of earth I possess and have seldom enjoyed—but the treasure of Heaven,—that pure, disinterested, tender affection, which bears the stress of poverty, sickness, and all other kindred ills,—I never had till now. And now the restless craving of my soul is pacified. I am happy,—moreover, I am perfectly at ease as regards the disposal of my wealth when I am gone. I know you will be glad to hear this, and that you will see that my last wishes and instructions are faithfully carried out in every respect—that is, if I should die before I see you again, which I hope may not be the case.

"It is my present intention to return to London shortly, and tell you personally the story of such adventures as have chanced to me since I left Carlton House Terrace last July, but 'man proposes, and God disposes,' and one can be certain of nothing. I need not ask you to keep all my affairs going as if I myself were on the scene of action, and also to inform the servants of my household to prepare for my return, as I may be back in town any day. I must thank you for your prompt and businesslike denial of the report of my death, which I understand has been circulated by the press. I am well—as well as a man of my age can expect to be, save for a troublesome heart-weakness, which threatens a brief and easy ending to my career. But for this, I should esteem myself stronger than some men who are still young. And one of the strongest feelings in me at the present moment (apart altogether from the deep affection and devout gratitude I have towards the one who under my Will is to inherit all I have spent my life to gain) is my friendship for you, my dear Vesey,—a friendship cemented by the experience of years, and which I trust may always be unbroken, even remaining in your mind as an unspoilt memory after I am gone where all who are weary, long, yet fear to go! Nevertheless, my faith is firm that the seeming darkness of death will prove but the veil which hides the light of a more perfect life, and I have learned, through the purity of a great and unselfish human love, to believe in the truth of the Love Divine.

Your friend always,
DAVID HELMSLEY

This letter finished, he went out and posted it with all the others he had written, and then passed the evening in listening to the organist practising grave anthems and voluntaries in the Cathedral. Every little item he could think of in his business affairs was carefully gone over during the three days he spent in Exeter,—nothing was left undone that could be so arranged as to leave his worldly concerns in perfect and unquestionable order—and when, as "Mr. David," he paid his last daily score at the little Temperance hotel where he had stayed since the Tuesday night, and started by the early train of Saturday morning on his return to Minehead, he was at peace with himself and all men. True it was that the making of his will had brought home to him the fact that it was not the same thing as when, being in the prime of life, he had made it in favour of his two sons, who were now dead,—it was really and truly a final winding-up of his temporal interests, and an admitted approach to the verge of the Eternal,—but he was not depressed by this consciousness. On the contrary, a happy sense of perfect calm pervaded his whole being, and as the train bore him swiftly through the quiet, lovely land back to Minehead, that sea-washed portal to the little village paradise which held the good angel of his life, he silently thanked God that he had done the work which he had started out to do, and that he had been spared to return and look again into the beloved face of the one woman in all the world who had given him a true affection without any "motive," or hope of reward. And he murmured again his favourite lines:—

"Let the sweet heavens endure,
Not close nor darken above me,
Before I am quite, quite sure
That there is one to love me!
Then let come what come may,
To a life that has been so sad,
I shall have had my day!"

"That is true!" he said—"And being 'quite, quite sure' beyond all doubt, that I have found 'one to love me' whose love is of the truest, holiest and purest, what more can I ask of Divine goodness!"

And his face was full of the light of a heart's content and peace, as the dimpled hill coast of Somerset came into view, and the warm spring sunshine danced upon the sea.

XXI

Arriving at Minehead, Helmsley passed out of the station unnoticed by any one, and made his way easily through the sunny little town. He was soon able to secure a "lift" towards Weircombe in a baker's cart going half the way; the rest of the distance he judged he could very well manage to walk, albeit slowly. A fluttering sense of happiness, like the scarcely suppressed excitement of a boy going home from school for the holidays, made him feel almost agile on his feet,—if he had only had a trifle more strength he thought he could have run the length of every mile stretching between him and the dear cottage in the coombe, which had now become the central interest of his life. The air was so pure, the sun so bright—the spring foliage was so fresh and green, the birds sang so joyously—all nature seemed to be in such perfect tune with the deep ease and satisfaction of his own soul, that every breath he took was more or less of a thanksgiving to God for having been spared to enjoy the beauty of such halcyon hours. By the willing away of all his millions to one whom he knew to be of a pure, noble, and incorruptible nature, a great load had been lifted from his mind,—he had done with world's work for ever; and by some inexplicable yet divine compensation it seemed as though the true meaning of the life to come had been suddenly disclosed to him, and that he was allowed to realise for the first time not only the possibility, but the certainty, that Death is not an End, but a new Beginning. And he felt himself to be a free man,—free of all earthly confusion and worry—free to recommence another cycle of nobler work in a higher and wider sphere of action, And he argued with himself thus:—

"A man is born into this world without his own knowledge or consent. Yet he finds himself—also without his own knowledge or consent—surrounded by natural beauty and perfect order—he finds nothing in the planet which can be accounted valueless—he learns that even a grain of dust has its appointed use, and that not a sparrow shall fall to the ground without 'Our Father.' Everything is ready to his hand to minister to his reasonable wants—and it is only when he misinterprets the mystic meaning of life, and puts God aside as an 'unknown quantity,' that things go wrong. His mission is that of progress and advancement—but not progress and advancement in base material needs and pleasures,—the progress and advancement required of him is primarily spiritual. For the spiritual, or Mind, is the only Real. Matter is merely the husk in which the seed of Spirit is enclosed—and Man's mistake is always that he attaches himself to the perishable husk instead of the ever germinating seed. He advances, but advances wrongly, and therefore has to go back upon his steps. He progresses in what he calls civilisation, which so long as it is purely self-aggrandisement, is but a common circle, bringing him back in due course to primitive savagery. Now I, for example, started in life to make money—I made it, and it brought me power, which I thought progress; but now, at the end of my tether, I see plainly that I have done no good in my career save such good as will come from my having placed all my foolish gainings under the control of a nature simpler and therefore stronger than my own. And I, leaving my dross behind me, must go forward and begin again—spiritually the wiser for my experience of this world, which may help me better to understand the next."

Thus he mused, as he slowly trudged along under the bright and burning sun—happy enough in his thoughts except that now and then a curious touch of foreboding fear came over him as to whether anything ill had happened to Mary in his absence.

"For one never knows!"—and a faint shudder came over him as he remembered Tom o' the Gleam, and the cruel, uncalled-for death of his child, the only human creature left to him in the world to care for. "One can never tell, whether in the scheme of creation there is such a being as a devil, who takes joy in running counter to the beneficent intentions of the Creator! Light exists—and Darkness. Good seems co-equal with Evil. It is all mystery! Now, suppose Mary were to die? Suppose she were, at this very moment, dead?"

Such a horror came over him as this idea presented itself to his mind that he trembled from head to foot, and his brain grew dizzy. He had walked for a longer time than he knew since the cart in which he had ridden part of the way had left him at about four miles away from Weircombe, and he felt that he must sit down on the roadside and rest for a bit before going further. How cruel, how fiendish it would be, he continued to imagine, if Mary were dead! It would be devil's work!—and he would have no more faith in God! He would have lost his last hope,—and he would fall into the grave a despairing atheist and blasphemer! Why, if Mary were dead, then the world was a snare, and heaven a delusion!—truth a trick, and goodness a lie! Then—was all the past, the present, and future hanging for him like a jewel on the finger of one woman? He was bound to admit that it was so. He was also bound to admit that all the past, present, and future had, for poor Tom o' the Gleam, been centred in one little child. And—God?—no, not God—but a devil, using as his tools devilish men,—had killed that child! Then, might not that devil kill Mary? His head swam, and a sickening sense of bafflement and incompetency came over him. He had made his will,—that was true!—but who could guarantee that she whom he had chosen as his heiress would live to inherit his wealth?

"I wish I did not think of such horrible things!" he said wearily—"Or I wish I could walk faster, and get home—home to the little cottage quickly, and see for myself that she is safe and well!"

Sitting among the long grass and field flowers by the roadside, he grasped his stick in one hand and leaned his head upon that support, closing his eyes in sheer fatigue and despondency. Suddenly a sound startled him, and he struggled to his feet, his eyes shining with an intent and eager look. That clear, tender voice!—that quick, sweet cry!

"David!"

He listened with a vague and dreamy sense of pleasure. The soft patter of feet across the grass—the swish of a dress against the leaves, and then—then—why, here was Mary herself, one tress of her lovely hair tumbling loose in the sun, her eyes bright and her cheeks crimson with running.

"Oh, David, dear old David! Here you are at last! Why *did* you go away! We have missed you dreadfully! David, you look *so* tired!—where have you been? Angus and I have been waiting for you ever so long,— you said in your letter you would be back by Sunday, and we thought you would likely choose to-day to come—oh, David?—you are quite worn out! Don't—don't give way!"

For with the longed-for sight of her, the world's multi-millionaire had become only a weak, over-wrought old man, and his tired heart had leaped in his breast with quite a poor and common human joy which brought the tears falling from his eyes despite himself. She was beside him in a moment, her arm thrown affectionately about his shoulders, and her sweet face turned up close to his, all aglow with sympathy and tenderness.

"Why did you leave us?" she went on with a gentle playfulness, though the tears were in her own eyes. "Whatever made you think of getting work out of Weircombe? Oh, you dissatisfied old boy! I thought you were quite happy with me!"

He took her hand and held it a moment, then pressed it to his lips.

"Happy!" he murmured. "My dear, I was *too* happy!—and I felt that I owed you too much! I went away for a bit just to see if I could do something for you more profitable than basket-making—"

Mary nodded her head at him in wise-like fashion, just as if he were a spoilt child.

"I daresay you did!" she said, smiling. "And what's the end of it all, eh?"

He looked at her, and in the brightness of her smile, smiled also.

"Well, the end of it all is that I've come back to you in exactly the same condition in which I went away," he said. "No richer,—no poorer! I've got nothing to do. Nobody wants old people on their hands nowadays. It's a rough time of the world!"

"You'll always find the world rough on you if you turn your back on those that love you!" she said.

He lifted his head and gazed at her with such a pained and piteous appeal, that her heart smote her. He looked so very ill, and his worn face with the snow-white hair ruffled about it, was so pallid and thin.

"God forbid that I should do that!" he murmured tremulously. "God forbid! Mary, you don't think I would ever do that?"

"No—of course not!" she answered soothingly. "Because you see, you've come back again. But if you had gone away altogether—"

"You'd have thought me an ungrateful, worthless old rascal, wouldn't you?" And the smile again sparkled in his dim eyes. "And you and Angus Reay would have said—'Well, never mind him! He served one useful purpose at any rate—he brought us together!'"

"Now, David!" said Mary, holding up a warning finger, "You know we shouldn't have talked in such a way of you at all! Even if you had never come back, we should always have thought of you kindly—and I should have always loved you and prayed for you!"

He was silent, mentally pulling himself together. Then he put his arm gently through hers.

"Let us go home," he said. "I can walk now. Are we far from the coombe?"

"Not ten minutes off," she answered, glad to see him more cheerful and alert. "By the short cut it's just over the brow of the hill. Will you come that way?"

"Any way you like to take me," and leaning on her arm he walked bravely on. "Where is Angus?"

"I left him sitting under a tree at the top of the coombe near the Church," she replied. "He was busy with his writing, and I told him I would just run across the hill and see if you were coming. I had a sort of fancy you would be tramping home this morning! And where have you been all these days?"

"A good way," he answered evasively. "I'm rather a slow walker."

"I should think you were!" and she laughed good-humouredly. "You must have been pretty near us all the while!"

He made no answer, and together they paced slowly across the grass, sweet with the mixed perfume of thousands of tiny close-growing herbs and flowers which clung in unseen clumps to the soil. All at once the quaint little tower of Weircombe Church thrust its ivy-covered summit above the edge of the green slope which they were ascending, and another few steps showed the glittering reaches of the sunlit sea. Helmsley paused, and drew a deep breath.

"I am thankful to see it all again!" he said.

She waited, while leaning heavily on her arm he scanned the whole fair landscape with a look of eager love and longing. She saw that he was very tired and exhausted, and wondered what he had been doing with himself in his days of absence from her care, but she had too much delicacy and feeling for him to ask him any questions. And she was glad when a cheery "Hillo!" echoed over the hill and Angus appeared, striding across the grass and waving his cap in quite a jubilant fashion. As soon as he saw them plainly he exchanged his stride for a run and came up to them in a couple of minutes.

"Why, David!" he exclaimed. "How are you, old boy? Welcome back! So Mary is right as usual! She said she was sure you would be home to-day!"

Helmsley could not speak. He merely returned the pressure of Reay's warm, strong hand with all the friendly fervour of which he was capable. A glance from Mary's eyes warned Angus that the old man was sorely tired—and he at once offered him his arm.

"Lean on me, David," he said. "Strong as bonnie Mary is, I'm just a bit stronger. We'll be across the brae in no time! Charlie's at home keeping house!"

He laughed, and Helmsley smiled.

"Poor wee Charlie!" he said. "Did he miss me?"

"That he did!" answered Mary. "He's been quite lonesome, and not contented at all with only me. Every morning and every night he went into your room looking for you, and whined so pitifully at not finding you that I had quite a trouble to comfort him."

"More tender-hearted than many a human so-called 'friend'!" murmured Helmsley.

"Why yes, of course!" said Reay. "There's nothing more faithful on earth than a faithful dog—except"—and he smiled—"a faithful husband!"

Mary laughed.

"Or a faithful wife—which?" she playfully demanded. "How does the old rhyme go—

> *'A wife, a dog, and a walnut tree,*
> *The more you beat 'em, the better they be!'*

Are you going to try that system when we are married, Angus?"

She laughed again, and without waiting for an answer, ran on a little in front, in order to be first across the natural bridge which separated them from the opposite side of the "coombe," and from the spot where the big chestnut-tree waved its fan-like green leaves and plumes of pinky white blossom over her garden gate. Another few steps made easily with the support of Reay's strong arm, and Helmsley found himself again in the simple little raftered cottage kitchen, with Charlie tearing madly round and round him in ecstasy, uttering short yelps of joy. Something struggled in his throat for utterance,—it seemed ages since he had last seen this little abode of peace and sweet content, and a curious impression was in his mind of having left one identity here to take up another less pleasing one elsewhere. A deep, unspeakable gratitude overwhelmed him,—he felt to the full the sympathetic environment of love,—that indescribable sense of security which satisfies the heart when it knows it is "dear to some one else."

> *"If I be dear to some one else,*
> *Then I should be to myself more dear."*

For there is nothing in the whole strange symphony of human life, with its concordances and dissonances, that strikes out such a chord of perfect music as the consciousness of love. To feel that there is one at least in the world to whom you are more dear than to any other living being, is the very centralisation of life and the mainspring of action. For that one you will work and plan,—for that one you will seek to be noble and above the average in your motives and character—for that one you will, despite a multitude of drawbacks, agree to live. But without this melodious note in the chorus all the singing is in vain.

Led to his accustomed chair by the hearth, Helmsley sank into it restfully, and closed his eyes. He was so thoroughly tired out mentally and physically with the strain he had put upon himself in undertaking his journey, as well as in getting through the business he had set out to do, that he was only conscious of a great desire to sleep. So that when he shut his eyes for a moment, as he thought, he was quite unaware that he fell into a dead faint and so remained for nearly half an hour. When he came to himself again, Mary was kneeling beside him with a very pale face, and Angus was standing quite close to him, while no less a personage than Mr. Bunce was holding his hand and feeling his pulse.

"Better now?" said Mr. Bunce, in a voice of encouraging mildness. "We have done too much. We have walked too far. We must rest."

Helmsley smiled—the little group of three around him looked so troubled, while he himself felt nothing unusual.

"What's the matter?" he asked. "I'm all right—quite all right. Only just a little tired!"

"Exactly!" And Mr. Bunce nodded profoundly. "Just a little tired! We have taken a very unnecessary journey away from our friends, and we are suffering for it! We must now be very good; we must stay at home and keep quiet!"

Helmsley looked from one to the other questioningly.

"Do you think I'm ill?" he asked. "I'm not, really! I feel very well."

"That's all right, David, dear!" said Mary, patting his hand. "But you *are* tired—you know you are!"

His eyes rested on her fondly.

"Yes, I'm tired," he confessed. "But that's nothing." He waited a minute, looking at them all. "That's nothing! Is it, Mr. Bunce?"

"When we are young it is nothing," replied Mr. Bunce cautiously. "But when we are old, we must be careful!"

Helmsley smiled.

"Shake hands, Bunce!" he said, suiting the action to the word. "I'll obey your orders, never fear! I'll sit quiet!"

And he showed so much cheerfulness, and chatted with them all so brightly, that, for the time, anxiety was dispelled. Mr. Bunce took his departure promptly, only pausing at the garden gate to give a hint to Angus Reay.

"He will require the greatest care. Don't alarm Miss Deane—but his heart was always weak, and it has grown perceptibly weaker. He needs complete repose."

Angus returned to the cottage somewhat depressed after this, and from that moment Helmsley found himself surrounded with evidences of tender forethought for his comfort such as no rich man could ever obtain for mere cash payment. The finest medical skill and the best trained nursing are, we know, to be had for money,—but the soothing touch of love,—the wordless sympathy which manifests itself in all the looks and movements of those by whom a life is really and truly held precious—these are neither to be bought nor sold. And David Helmsley in his assumed character of a man too old and too poor to have any so-called "useful" friends—a mere wayfarer on the road apparently without a home, or any prospect of obtaining one,—had, by the simplest, yet strangest chance in the world, found an affection such as he had never in his most successful and most brilliant days been able to win. He upon whom the society women of London and Paris had looked with greedy and speculative eyes, wondering how much they could manage to get out of him, was now being cared for by one simple-hearted sincere woman, who had no other motive for her affectionate solicitude save gentlest compassion and kindness;—he whom crafty kings had invited to dine with them because of his enormous wealth, and because is was possible that, for the "honour" of sitting at the same table with them he might tide them over a financial difficulty, was now tended with more than the duty and watchfulness of a son in the person of a poor journalist, kicked out of employment for telling the public certain important facts concerning financial "deals" on the part of persons of influence—a journalist, who for this very cause was likely never more to be a journalist, but rather a fighter against bitter storm and stress, for the fair wind of popular favour,—that being generally the true position of any independent author who has something new and out of the common to say to the world. Angus Reay, working steadily and hopefully on his gradually diminishing little stock of money, with all his energies bent on cutting a diamond of success out of the savagely hard rock of human circumstance, was more filial in his respect and thought for Helmsley than either of Helmsley's own sons had been; while his character was as far above the characters of those two ne'er-do-weel sprouts of their mother's treachery as light is above darkness. And the multi-millionaire was well content to rest in the little cottage where he had found a real home, watching the quiet course of events,—and waiting—waiting for something which he found himself disposed to expect—a something to which he could not give a name.

There was quite a little rejoicing in the village of Weircombe when it was known he had returned from his brief wanderings, and there was also a good deal of commiseration expressed for him when it was known that he was somewhat weakened in physical health by his efforts to find more paying work. Many of the children with whom he was a favourite came up to see him, bringing little knots of flowers, or curious trophies of weed and shells from the seashore—and now that the weather was settled fine and warm, he became accustomed to sit in his chair outside the cottage door in the garden, with the old sweetbriar bush shedding perfume around him, and a clambering rose breaking into voluptuous creamy pink blossom above his head. Here he would pursue his occupation of basket-making, and most of the villagers made it their habit to pass up and down at least once or twice a day in their turns, to see how he fared, or, as they themselves expressed it, "to keep old David going." His frail bent figure, his thin, intellectual face, with its composed expression of peace and resignation, his soft white hair, and his slow yet ever patiently working hands, made up a picture which, set in the delicate framework of leaf and blossom, was one to impress the imagination and haunt the memory. Mr. and Mrs. Twitt were constant visitors, and many were the would-be jocose remarks of the old stonemason on David's temporary truancy.

"Wanted more work, did ye?" And thrusting his hands deep in the pockets of his corduroys, Twitt looked at him with a whimsical complacency. "Well, why didn't ye come down to the stoneyard an' learn 'ow to cut a hepitaph? Nice chippy, easy work in its way, an' no 'arm in yer sittin' down to it. Why didn't ye, eh?"

"I've never had enough education for such work as that, Mr. Twitt," answered David mildly, with something of a humorous sparkle in his eyes. "I'm afraid I should spoil more than I could pay for. You want an artist—not an untrained clumsy old fellow like me."

"Oh, blow artists!" said Mr. Twitt irreverently. "They talks a lot—they talks yer 'ed off—but they doos onny 'arf the labour as they spends in waggin' their tongues. An' for a hepitaph, they none of 'em aint got an idee. It's allus Scripter texes with 'em,—they aint got no 'riginality. Now I'm a reg'lar Scripter reader, an' nowheres do I find it writ as we're to use the words o' God Himself to carve on tombstones for our speshul convenience, cos we aint no notions o' feelin' an' respect of our own. But artists can't think o' nothin', an' I never cares to employ 'em. Yet for all that there's not a sweeter, pruttier place than our little cemetery nowheres in all the world. There aint no tyranny in it, an' no pettifoggin' interference. Why, there's places in England where ye can't put what ye likes over the grave o' yer dead friends!—ye've got to 'submit' yer idee to the parzon, or wot's worse, the Corporation, if ser be yer last go-to-bed place is near a town. There's a town I know of," and here Mr. Twitt began to laugh,—"wheer ye can't 'ave a moniment put up to your dead folk without 'subjectin'' the design to the Town Council—an' we all knows the fine taste o' Town Councils! They'se 'artists,' an' no mistake! I've got the rules of the cemetery of that town for my own eddification. They runs like this—" And drawing a paper from his pocket, he read as follows:—

"'All gravestones, monuments, tombs, tablets, memorials, palisades, curbs, and inscriptions shall be subject to the approval of the Town Council; and a drawing, showing the form, materials, and dimensions of every gravestone, monument, tomb, tablet, memorial, palisades, or curb proposed to be erected or fixed, together with a copy of the inscription intended to be cut thereon (if any), on the form provided by the Town Council, must be left at the office of the Clerk at least ten days before the first Tuesday in any month. The Town Council reserve to themselves the right to remove or prevent the erection of any monument, tomb, tablet, memorial, etc., which shall not have previously received their sanction.' There! What d' ye think of that?"

Helmsley had listened in astonishment.

"Think? I think it is monstrous!" he said, with some indignation. "Such a Town Council as that is a sort of many-headed tyrant, resolved to persecute the unhappy townspeople into their very graves!"

"Right y' are!" said Twitt. "But there's a many on 'em! An' ye may thank yer stars ye're not anywheres under 'em. Now when *you* goes the way o' all flesh—"

He paused, suddenly embarrassed, and conscious that he had perhaps touched on a sore subject. But Helmsley reassured him.

"Yes, Twitt? Don't stop!—what then?"

"Why, then," said Twitt, almost tenderly, "ye'll 'ave our good old parzon to see ye properly tucked under a daisy quilt, an' wotever ye wants put on yer tomb, or wotever's writ on it, can be yer own desire, if ye'll think about it afore ye goes. An' there'll be no expense at all—for

I tell ye just the truth—I've grown to like ye that well that I'll carve ye the pruttiest little tombstone ye ever seed for nothin'!"

Helmsley smiled.

"Well, I shan't be able to thank you then, Mr. Twitt, so I thank you now," he said. "You know a good deed is always rewarded, if not in this world, then in the next."

"I b'leeve that," rejoined Twitt; "I b'leeve it true. And though I know Mis' Deane is that straight an' 'onest, she'd see ye properly mementoed an' paid for, I wouldn't take a penny from 'er—not on account of a kindly old gaffer like yerself. I'd do it all friendly."

"Of course you would!" and Helmsley shook his hand heartily; "And of course you *will*!"

This, and many other conversations he had with Twitt and a certain few of the villagers, showed him that the little community of Weircombe evidently thought of him as being not long for this world. He accepted the position quietly, and passed day after day peacefully enough, without feeling any particular illness, save a great weakness in his limbs. He was in himself particularly happy, for Mary was always with him, and Angus passed every evening with them both. Another great pleasure, too, he found in the occasional and entirely unobtrusive visits of the parson of the little parish—a weak and ailing man physically, but in soul and intellect exceptionally strong. As different from the Reverend Mr. Arbroath as an old-time Crusader would be from a modern jockey, he recognised the sacred character of his mission as an ordained minister of Christ, and performed that mission simply and faithfully. He would sit by Helmsley's chair of a summer afternoon and talk with him as friend to friend—it made no difference to him that to all appearances the old man was poor and dependent on Mary Deane's bounty, and that his former life was, to him, the clergyman, a sealed book; he was there to cheer and to comfort, not to inquire, reproach, or condemn. He was the cheeriest of companions, and the most hopeful of believers.

"If all clergymen were like you, sir," said Helmsley to him one day, "there would be no atheists!"

The good man reddened at the compliment, as though he had been accused of a crime.

"You think too kindly of my efforts," he said gently. "I only speak to you as I would wish others to speak to me."

"'For this is the Law and the Prophets!'" murmured Helmsley. "Sir, will you tell me one thing—are there many poor people in Weircombe?"

The clergyman looked a trifle surprised.

"Why, yes, to tell the exact truth, they are all poor people in Weircombe," he answered. "You see, it is really only a little fishing village. The rich people's places are situated all about it, here and there at various miles of distance, but no one with money lives in Weircombe itself."

"Yet every one seems happy," said Helmsley thoughtfully.

"Oh, yes, every one not only seems, but *is* happy!" and the clergyman smiled. "They have the ordinary troubles that fall to the common lot, of course—but they are none of them discontented. There's very little drunkenness, and as a consequence, very little quarrelling. They are a good set of people—typically English of England!"

"If some millionaire were to leave every man, woman, and child a thousand or more pounds apiece, I wonder what would happen?" suggested Helmsley.

"Their joy would be turned to misery!" said the clergyman—"and their little heaven would become a hell! Fortunately for them, such a disaster is not likely to happen!"

Helmsley was silent; and after his kindly visitor had left him that day sat for a long time absorbed in thought, his hands resting idly on the osiers which he was gradually becoming too weak to bend.

It was now wearing on towards the middle of June, and on one fine morning when Mary was carefully spreading out on a mending-frame a wonderful old flounce of priceless *point d'Alençon* lace, preparatory to examining the numerous repairs it needed, Helmsley turned towards her abruptly with the question—

"When are you and Angus going to be married, my dear?"

Mary smiled, and the soft colour flew over her face at the suggestion.

"Oh, not for a long time yet, David!" she replied. "Angus has not yet finished his book,—and even when it is all done, he has to get it published. He won't have the banns put up till the book is accepted."

"Won't he?" And Helmsley's eyes grew very wistful. "Why not?"

"Well, it's for quite a good reason, after all," she said. "He wants to feel perfectly independent. You see, if he could get even a hundred pounds down for his book he would be richer than I am, and it would be all right. He'd never marry me with nothing at all of his own."

"Yet *you* would marry him?"

"I'm not sure that I would," and she lifted her hand with a prettily proud gesture. "You see, David, I really love him! And my love is too strong and deep for me to be so selfish as to wish to drag him down. I wouldn't have him lower his own self-respect for the world!"

"Love is greater than self-respect!" said Helmsley.

"Oh, David! You know better than that! There's no love *without* self-respect—no real love, I mean. There are certain kinds of stupid fancies called love—but they've no 'wear' in them!" and she laughed. "They wouldn't last a month, let alone a lifetime!"

He sighed a little, and his lips trembled nervously.

"I'm afraid, my dear,—I'm afraid I shall not live to see you married!" he said.

She left her lace frame and came to his side.

"Don't say that, David! You mustn't think it for a moment. You're much better than you were—even Mr. Bunce says so!"

"Even Mr. Bunce!" And he took her hand in his own and studied its smooth whiteness and beautiful shape attentively—anon he patted it tenderly. "You have a pretty hand, Mary! It's a rare beauty!"

"Is it?" And she looked at her rosy palm meditatively. "I've never thought much about it—but I've noticed that Angus and you both have nice hands."

"Especially Angus!" said Helmsley, with a smile.

Her face reflected the smile.

"Yes. Especially Angus!"

After this little conversation Helmsley was very quiet and thoughtful. Often indeed he sat with eyes closed, pretending to sleep, in order inwardly to meditate on the plans he had most at heart. He saw no reason to alter them,—though the idea presented itself once or twice as to whether he should not reveal his actual identity to the clergyman who visited him so often, and who was, apart from his sacred calling, not only a thinking, feeling, humane creature, but a very perfect gentleman. But on due reflection he saw that this might possibly lead to awkward complications, so he still resolved to pursue the safer policy of silence.

One evening, when Angus Reay had come in as usual to sit awhile and chat with him before he went to bed, he could hardly control a slight nervous start when Reay observed casually—

"By the way, David, that old millionaire I told you about, Helmsley, isn't dead after all!"

"Oh—isn't he?" And Helmsley feigned to be affected with a troublesome cough which necessitated his looking away for a minute. "Has he turned up?"

"Yes—he's turned up. That is to say, that he's expected back in town for the 'season,' as the Cooing Column of the paper says."

"Why, what's the Cooing Column?" asked Mary, laughing.

"The fashionable intelligence corner," answered Angus, joining in her laughter. "I call it the Cooing Column, because it's the place where all the doves of society, soiled and clean, get their little grain of personal advertisement. They pay for it, of course. There it is that the disreputable Mrs. Mushroom Ketchup gets it announced that she wore a collar of diamonds at the Opera, and there the battered, dissipated Lord 'Jimmy' Jenkins has it proudly stated that his yacht is undergoing 'extensive alterations.' Who in the real work-a-day, sane world cares a button whether his lordship Jenkins sails in his yacht or sinks in it! And Mrs. Mushroom Ketchup's diamonds are only so much fresh fuel piled on the burning anguish of starving and suffering men,—anguish which results in anarchy. Any number of anarchists are bred from the Cooing Column!"

"What would you have rich men do?" asked Helmsley suddenly. "If all their business turns out much more successfully than they have ever expected, and they make millions almost despite their own desire, what would you have them do with their wealth?"

Angus thought a moment.

"It would be difficult to advise," he said at last. "For one thing I would not have them pauperise two of the finest things in this world and the best worth fighting for—Education and Literature. The man who has no struggle at all to get himself educated is only half a man. And literature which is handed to the people free of cost is shamed by being put at a lower level than beer and potatoes, for which every man has to *pay*. Andrew Carnegie I look upon as one of the world's big meddlers. A 'cute' meddler too, for he takes care to do nothing that hasn't got his name tacked on to it. However, I'm in great hopes that his pauperising of Scottish University education may in time wear itself out, and that Scotsmen will be sufficiently true to the spirit of Robert Burns to stick to the business of working and paying for what they get. I hate all things that are given *gratis*. There's always a smack of the advertising agent about them. God Himself gives nothing 'free'—you've got to pay with your very life for each gulp of air you breathe,—and rightly too! And if you try to get something out of His creation *without* paying for it, the bill is presented in due course with compound interest!"

"I agree with you," said Helmsley. "But what, then, of the poor rich men? You don't approve of Carnegie's methods of disbursing wealth. What would you suggest?"

"The doing of private good," replied Angus promptly. "Good that is never heard of, never talked of, never mentioned in the Cooing Column. A rich man could perform acts of the most heavenly and helpful kindness if he would only go about personally and privately among the very poor, make friends with them, and himself assist them. But he will hardly ever do this. Now the millionaire who is going to marry my first love, Lucy Sorrel—"

"Oh, *is* he going to marry her?" And Helmsley looked up with sudden interest.

"Well, I suppose he is!" And Angus threw back his head and laughed. "He's to be back in town for the 'season'—and you know what the London 'season' is!"

"I'm sure we don't!" said Mary, with an amused glance. "Tell us!"

"An endless round of lunches, dinners, balls, operas, theatres, card-parties, and inane jabber," he answered. "A mixture of various kinds of food which people eat recklessly with the natural results,—dyspepsia, inertia, mental vacuity, and general uselessness. A few Court 'functions,' some picture shows, and two or three great races—and—that's all. Some unfortunate marriages are usually the result of each year's motley."

"And you think the millionaire you speak of will be one of the unfortunate ones?" said Helmsley.

"Yes, David, I do! If he's going back to London for the season, Lucy Sorrel will never let him out of her sight again! She's made up her mind to be a Mrs. Millionaire, and she's not troubled by any over-sensitiveness or delicacy of sentiment."

"That I quite believe—from what you have told me,"—and Helmsley smiled. "But what do the papers—what does the Cooing Column say?"

"The Cooing Column says that one of the world's greatest millionaires, Mr. David Helmsley, who has been abroad for nearly a year for the benefit of his health, will return to his mansion in Carlton House Terrace this month for the 'season.'"

"Is that all?"

"That's all. Mary, my bonnie Mary,"—and Angus put an arm tenderly round the waist of his promised wife—"Your husband may, perhaps—only perhaps!—become famous—but you'll never, never be a Mrs. Millionaire!"

She laughed and blushed as he kissed her.

"I don't want ever to be rich," she said. "I'd rather be poor!"

They went out into the little garden then, with their arms entwined,—and Helmsley, seated in his chair under the rose-covered porch, watched them half in gladness, half in trouble. Was he doing well for them, he wondered? Or ill? Would the possession of wealth disturb the idyll of their contented lives, their perfect love? Almost he wished that he really were in very truth the forlorn and homeless wayfarer he had assumed to be,—wholly and irrevocably poor!

That night in his little room, when everything was quiet, and Mary was soundly sleeping in the attic above him, he rose quietly from his bed, and lighting a candle, took pen and ink and made a few additions to the letter of instructions which accompanied his will. Some evenings previously, when Mary and Angus had gone out for a walk together, he had taken the opportunity to disburden his "workman's coat" of all the banknotes contained in the lining, and, folding them up in one parcel, had put them in a sealed envelope, which envelope he marked in a certain fashion, enclosing it in the larger envelope which contained his will. In the same way he made a small, neatly sealed packet of the "collection" made for him at the "Trusty Man" by poor Tom o' the Gleam, marking that also. Now, on this particular night, feeling that he had done all he could think of to make business matters fairly easy to deal with, he packed up everything in one parcel, which he tied with a string and sealed securely, addressing it to Sir Francis Vesey. This parcel he again enclosed in another, equally tied up and sealed, the outer wrapper of which he addressed to one John Bulteel at certain offices in London, which were in truth the offices of Vesey and Symonds, Bulteel being their confidential clerk. The fact that Angus Reay knew the name of the firm which had been mentioned in the papers as connected with the famous millionaire, David Helmsley, caused him to avoid inscribing it on the packet which would have to be taken to its destination immediately after his death. As he had now arranged things, it would be conveyed to the office unsuspectingly, and Bulteel, opening the first wrapper, would see that the contents were for Sir Francis, and would take them to him at once. Locking the packet in the little cupboard in the wall which Mary had given him, as she playfully said, "to keep his treasures in"—he threw himself again on his bed, and, thoroughly exhausted, tried to sleep.

"It will be all right, I think!" he murmured to himself, as he closed his eyes wearily—"At any rate, so far as I am concerned, I have done with the world! God grant some good may come of my millions after I am dead! After I am dead! How strange it sounds! What will it seem like, I wonder,—to be dead?"

And he suddenly thought of a poem he had read some years back,— one of the finest and most daring thoughts ever expressed in verse, from the pen of a fine and much neglected poet, Robert Buchanan:—

> *"Master, if there be Doom,*
> *All men are bereaven!*
> *If in the Universe*
> *One Spirit receive the curse,*
> *Alas for Heaven!*
> *If there be Doom for one,*
> *Thou, Master, art undone!*
> *"Were I a Soul in Heaven,*
> *Afar from pain;—*
> *Yea, on thy breast of snow,*
> *At the scream of one below,*
> *I should scream again—*
> *Art Thou less piteous than*
> *The conception of a Man?"*

"No, no, not less piteous!" he murmured—"But surely infinitely more pitiful!"

XXII

A nd now there came a wondrous week of perfect weather. All the lovely Somersetshire coast lay under the warmth and brilliance of a dazzling sun,—the sea was smooth,—and small sailing skiffs danced merrily up and down from Minehead to Weircombe and back again with the ease and security of seabirds, whose happiest resting-place is on the waves. A lovely calm environed the little village,—it was not a haunt of cheap "trippers,"—and summer-time was not only a working-time, but a playing time too with all the inhabitants, both young and old. The shore, with its fine golden sand, warm with the warmth of the cloudless sky, was a popular resort, and Helmsley, though his physical weakness perceptibly increased, was often able to go down there, assisted by Mary and Angus, one on each side supporting him and guarding his movements. It pleased him to sit under the shelter of the rocks and watch the long shining ripples of ocean roll forwards and backwards on the shore in silvery lines, edged with delicate, lace-like fringes of foam,—and the slow, monotonous murmur of the gathering and dispersing water soothed his nerves and hushed a certain inward fretfulness of spirit which teased him now and then, but to which he bravely strove not to give way. Sometimes—but only sometimes—he felt that it was hard to die. Hard to be old just as he was beginning to learn how to live,—hard to pass out of the beauty and wonder of this present life with all its best joys scarcely experienced, and exchange the consciousness of what little he knew for something concerning which no one could honestly give him any authentic information.

"Yet I might have said the same, had I been conscious, before I was born!" he thought. "In a former state of existence I might have said, 'Why send me from this that I know and enjoy, to something which I have not seen and therefore cannot believe in?' Perhaps, for all I can tell, I did say it. And yet God had His way with me and placed me here— for what? Only to learn a lesson! That is truly all I have done. For the making of money is as nothing in the sight of Eternal Law,—it is merely man's accumulation of perishable matter, which, like all perishable things, is swept away in due course, while he who accumulated it is of no more account as a mere corpse than his poverty-stricken brother. What a foolish striving it all is! What envyings, spites, meannesses and miserable pettinesses arise from this greed of money! Yes, I have learned my lesson! I wonder whether I shall now be permitted to pass into a higher standard, and begin again!"

These inner musings sometimes comforted and sometimes perplexed him, and often he was made suddenly aware of a strange and exhilarating impression of returning youthfulness—a buoyancy of feeling and a delightful ease, such as a man in full vigour experiences when, after ascending some glorious mountain summit, he sees the panorama of a world below him. His brain was very clear and active— and whenever he chose to talk, there were plenty of his humble friends ready to listen. One day the morning papers were full of great headlines announcing the assassination of one of the world's throned rulers, and the Weircombe fishermen, discussing the news, sought the opinion of "old David" concerning the matter. "Old David" was, however, somewhat slow to be drawn on so questionable a subject, but Angus Reay was not so reticent.

"Why should kings spend money recklessly on their often filthy vices and pleasures," he demanded, "while thousands, ay, millions of their subjects starve? As long as such a wretched state of things exists, so long will there be Anarchy. But I know the head and front of the offending! I know the Chief of all the Anarchists!"

"Lord bless us!" exclaimed Mrs. Twitt, who happened to be standing by. "Ye don't say so! Wot's' 'ee like?"

"He's all shapes and sizes—all colours too!" laughed Angus. "He's simply the Irresponsible Journalist!"

"As you were once!" suggested Helmsley, with a smile.

"No, I was never 'irresponsible,'" declared Reay, emphatically. "I may have been faulty in the following of my profession, but I never wrote a line that I thought might cause uneasiness in the minds of the million. What I mean is, that the Irresponsible Journalist who gives more prominence to the doings of kings and queens and stupid 'society' folk, than to the actual work, thought, and progress of the nation at large, is making a forcing-bed for the growth of Anarchy. Consider the feelings of a starving man who reads in a newspaper that certain people in London give dinners to their friends at a cost of Two Guineas a head! Consider the frenzied passion of a father who sees his children dying of want, when he reads that the mistress of a king wears diamonds worth forty thousand pounds round her throat! If the balance of material things is for the present thus set awry, and such vile and criminal anachronisms exist, the proprietors of newspapers should have better sense than to flaunt them before the public eye as though they deserved admiration. The Anarchist at any rate has an ideal. It may be a mistaken ideal, but whatever it is, it is a desperate effort to break down a system which anarchists imagine is at the root of all the bribery, corruption, flunkeyism and money-grubbing of the world. Moreover, the Anarchist carries his own life in his hand, and the risk he runs can scarcely be for his pleasure. Yet he braves everything for the 'ideal,' which he fancies, if realised, will release others from the yoke of injustice and tyranny. Few people have any 'ideals' at all nowadays;—what they want to do is to spend as much as they like, and eat as much as they can. And the newspapers that persist in chronicling the amount of their expenditure and the extent of their appetites, are the real breeders and encouragers of every form of anarchy under the sun!"

"You may be right," said Helmsley, slowly. "Indeed I fear you are! If one is to judge by old-time records, it was a kinder, simpler world when there was no daily press."

"Man is an imitative animal," continued Reay. "The deeds he hears of, whether good or bad, he seeks to emulate. In bygone ages crime existed, of course, but it was not blazoned in headlines to the public. Good and brave deeds were praised and recorded, and as a consequence—perhaps as a result of imitation—there were many heroes. In our times a good or brave deed is squeezed into an obscure paragraph,—while intellect and brilliant talent receive scarcely any acknowledgment—the silly doings of 'society' and the Court are the chief matter,—hence, possibly, the preponderance of dunces and flunkeys, again produced by sheer 'imitativeness.' Is it pleasant for a man with starvation at his door, to read that a king pays two thousand a year to his cook? That same two thousand comes out of the pockets of the nation—and the starving man thinks some of it ought to fall in *his* way instead of providing for a cooker of royal victuals! There is no end to the mischief generated by the publication of such snobbish statements, whether true or false. This was the kind of irresponsible talk that set Jean-Jacques Rousseau thinking and writing, and kindling the first spark of the fire of the French Revolution. 'Royal-Flunkey' methods of journalism provoke deep resentment in the public mind,—for a king after all is only the paid servant of the people—he is not an idol or a deity to which an independent nation should for ever crook the knee. And from the smouldering anger of the million at what they conceive to be injustice and hypocrisy, springs Anarchy."

"All very well said,—but now suppose you were a wealthy man, what would you do with your money?" asked Helmsley.

Angus smiled.

"I don't know, David!—I've never realised the position yet. But I should try to serve others more than to serve myself."

The conversation ceased then, for Helmsley looked pale and exhausted. He had been on the seashore for the greater part of the afternoon, and it was now sunset. Yet he was very unwilling to return home, and it was only by gentle and oft-repeated persuasion that he at last agreed to leave his well-loved haunt, leaning as usual on Mary's arm, with Angus walking on the other side. Once or twice as he slowly ascended the village street he paused, and looked back at the tranquil loveliness of ocean, glimmering as with millions of rubies in the red glow of the sinking sun.

"'And there shall be no more sea!'" he quoted, dreamily—"I should be sorry if that were true! One would miss the beautiful sea!—even in heaven!"

He walked very feebly, and Mary exchanged one or two anxious glances with Angus. But on reaching the cottage again, his spirits revived. Seated in his accustomed chair, he smiled as the little dog, Charlie, jumped on his knee, and peered with a comically affectionate gravity into his face.

"Asking me how I am, aren't you, Charlie!" he said, cheerfully—"I'm all right, wee man!—all right!"

Apparently Charlie was not quite sure about it, for he declined to be removed from the position he had chosen, and snuggling close down on his master's lap, curled himself up in a silky ball and went to sleep, now and then opening a soft dark eye to show that his slumbers were not so profound as they seemed.

That evening when Angus had gone, after saying a prolonged good-night to Mary in the little scented garden under the lovely radiance of an almost full moon, Helmsley called her to his side.

"Mary!"

She came at once, and put her arm around him. He looked up at her, smiling.

"You think I'm very tired, I know," he said—"But I'm not. I—I want to say a word to you."

Still keeping her arm round him, she patted his shoulder gently.

"Yes, David! What is it?"

"It is just this. You know I told you I had some papers that I valued, locked away in the little cupboard in my room?"

"Yes. I know."

"Well now,—when—when I die—will you promise me to take these papers yourself to the address that is written on them? That's all I ask of you! Will you?"

"Of course I will!" she said, readily—"You know you've kept the key yourself since you got well from your bad fever last year—"

"There is the key," he said, drawing it from his pocket, and holding it up to her—"Take it now!"

"But why now—?" she began.

"Because I wish it!" he answered, with a slight touch of obstinacy—then, smiling rather wistfully, he added, "It will comfort me to know you have it in your own possession. And Mary—promise me that you will let no one—not even Angus—see or touch these papers!—that you will take the parcel just as you find it, straight to the person to whom it is addressed, and deliver it yourself to him! I don't want you to *swear*, but I want you to put your dear kind hand in mine, and say 'On my word of honour I will not open the packet old David has entrusted to me. When he dies I will take it my own self to the person to whom it is addressed, and wait till I am told that everything in it has been received and understood.' Will you, for my comfort, say these words after me, Mary?"

"Of course I will!"

And placing her hand in his, she repeated it slowly word for word. He watched her closely as she spoke, her eyes gazing candidly into his own. Then he heaved a deep sigh.

"Thank you, my dear! That will do. God bless you! And now to bed!"

He rose somewhat unsteadily, and she saw he was very weak.

"Don't you feel so well, David?" she asked, anxiously. "Would you like me to sit up with you?"

"No, no, my dear, no! All I want is a good sleep—a good long sleep. I'm only tired."

She saw him into his room, and, according to her usual custom, put a handbell on the small table which was at the side of his bed. Charlie, trotting at her heels, suddenly began to whimper. She stooped and picked the little creature up in her arms.

"Mind you ring if you want me," she said to Helmsley then,—"I'm just above you, and I can hear the least sound."

He looked at her earnestly. His eyes were almost young in their brightness.

"God bless you, Mary!" he said—"You've been a good angel to me! I never quite believed in Heaven, but looking at you I know there is such a place—the place where you were born!"

She smiled—but her eyes were soft with unshed tears.

"You think too well of me, David," she said. "I'm not an angel—I wish I were! I'm only a very poor, ordinary sort of woman."

"Are you?" he said, and smiled—"Well, think so, if it pleases you. Good-night—and again God bless you!"

He patted the tiny head of the small Charlie, whom she held nestling against her breast.

"Good-night, Charlie!"

The little dog licked his hand and looked at him wistfully.

"Don't part with him, Mary!" he said, suddenly—"Let him always have a home with you!"

"Now, David! You really are tired out and over-melancholy! As if I should ever part with him!" And she kissed Charlie's silky head— "We'll all keep together! Good-night, David!"

"Good-night!" he answered. He watched her as she went through the doorway, holding the dog in her arms and turning back to smile at him over her shoulder—anon he listened to her footfall ascending the stairway to her own room—then, to her gentle movements to and fro above his bed—till presently all was silent. Silence—except for the measured plash of the sea, which he heard distinctly echoing up through the coombe from the shore. A great loneliness environed him—touched by a great awe. He felt himself to be a solitary soul in the midst of some vast desert, yet not without the consciousness that a mystic joy, an undreamed-of glory, was drawing near that should make that desert "blossom like the rose." He moved slowly and feebly to the window—against one-half of the latticed pane leaned a bunch of white roses, shining with a soft pearl hue in the light of a lovely moon.

"It is a beautiful world!" he said, half aloud—"No one in his right mind could leave it without some regret!"

Then an inward voice seemed to whisper to him—

"You knew nothing of this world you call so beautiful before you entered it; may there not be another world still more beautiful of which you equally know nothing, but of which you are about to make an experience, all life being a process of continuous higher progress?"

And this idea now not only seemed to him possible but almost a certainty. For as our last Laureate expresses it:—

> *"Whatever crazy sorrow saith,*
> *No life that breathes with human breath*
> *Has ever truly longed for death.*
> *'Tis life whereof our nerves are scant,*
> *Oh life, not death, for which we pant—*
> *More life, and fuller, that I want!"*

His brain was so active and his memory so clear that he was somewhat surprised to feel his body so feeble and aching, when at last he undressed, and lay down to sleep. He thought of many things—of his boyhood's home out in Virginia—of the stress and excitement of his business career—of his extraordinary successes, piled one on the top of the other—and then of the emptiness of it all!

"I should have been happier and wiser," he said, "if I had lived the life of a student in some quiet home among the hills—where I should have seen less of men and learned more of God. But it is too late now—too late!"

And a curious sorrow and pity moved him for certain men he knew who were eating up the best time of their lives in a mad struggle for money, losing everything of real value in their scramble for what was, after all, so valueless,—sacrificing peace, honour, love, and a quiet mind, for what in the eternal countings is of no more consideration than the dust of the highroad. Not what a man *has*, but what he *is*,—this is the sole concern of Divine Equity. Earthly ideas of justice are in direct opposition to this law, but the finite can never overbalance the infinite. We may, if we so please, honour a king as king,—but with God there are no kings. There are only Souls, "made in His image." And whosoever defaces that Divine Image, whether he be base-born churl or crowned potentate, must answer for the wicked deed. How many of us view our social acquaintances from any higher standard than the extent of their cash accounts, or the "usefulness" of their influence? Yet the inexorable Law works silently on,—and day after day, century after century, shows us the vanity of riches, the fall of pride and power, the triumph of genius, the immutability of love! And we are still turning over the well-worn pages of the same old school-book which was set before Tyre and Sidon, Carthage and Babylon—the same, the very same, with one saving exception—that a Divine Teacher came to show us how to spell it and read it aright—and He was crucified! Doubtless were He to come again and once more try to help us, we should re-enact that old-time Jewish murder!

Lying quietly in his bed, Helmsley conversed with his inner self, as it were, reasoning with his own human perplexities and gradually unravelling them. After all, if his life had been, as he considered, only a lesson, was it not good for him that he had learned that lesson? A passing memory of Lucy Sorrel flitted across his brain—and he thought how singular it was that chance should have brought him into touch with the very man who would have given her that "rose of love" he desired she should wear, had she realised the value and beauty of that immortal flower. He, David Helmsley, had been apparently led by devious ways, not only to find an unselfish love for himself, but also to be the instrument of atoning to Angus Reay for his first love-disappointment, and uniting him to a woman whose exquisitely tender and faithful nature was bound to make the joy and sanctity of his life. In this, had not all things been ordered well? Did it not seem that, notwithstanding his, Helmsley's, self-admitted worthlessness, the Divine Power had used him for the happiness of others, to serve as a link of love between two deserving souls? He began to think that it was not by chance that he had been led to wander away from the centre of his business interests, and lose himself on the hills above Weircombe. Not accident, but a high design had been hidden in this incident—a design in which Self had been transformed to Selflessness, and loneliness to love. "I should like to believe in God—if I could!" This he had said to his friend Vesey, on the last night he had seen him. And now—did he believe? Yes!—for he had benefited by his first experience of what a truly God-like love may be—the love of a perfectly unselfish, tender, devout woman who, for no motive at all, but simply out of pure goodness and compassion for sorrow and suffering, had rescued one whom she judged to be in need of help. If therefore God could make one poor woman so divinely forbearing and gentle, it was certain that He, from whom all Love must emanate, was yet more merciful than the most merciful woman, as well as stronger than the strongest man. And he believed—believed implicitly;—lifted to the height of a perfect faith by the help of a perfect love. In the mirror of one sweet and simple human character he had seen the face of God—and he was of the same mind as the mighty musician who, when he was dying, cried out in rapture—"I believe I am only at the Beginning!" He was conscious of a strange dual personality,—some spirit within him urgently expressed itself as being young, clamorous, inquisitive, eager, and impatient of restraint, while his natural bodily self was so weary and feeble that he felt as if he could scarcely move a hand. He listened for a little while to the ticking of the clock in the kitchen which was next to his room,—and by and by, being thoroughly drowsy, he sank into a heavy slumber. He did not know that Mary, anxious about him, had not gone to bed at all, but had resolved to sit up all night in case he should call her or want for anything. But the hours wore on peacefully for him till the moon began her downward course towards the west, and the tide having rolled in to its highest mark, began to ebb and flow out again. Then—all at once— he awoke—smitten by a shock of pain that seemed to crash through his heart and send his brain swirling into a blind chaos. Struggling for breath, he sprang up in his bed, and instinctively snatched the handbell at his side. He was hardly aware of ringing it, so great was his agony— but presently, regaining a glimmering sense of consciousness, he found Mary's arms round him, and saw Mary's eyes looking tenderly into his own.

"David, dear David!" And the sweet voice was shaken by tears. "David!—Oh, my poor dear, don't you know me?"

Know her? In the Valley of the Shadow what other Angel could there be so faithful or so tender! He sighed, leaning heavily against her bosom.

"Yes, dear—I know you!" he gasped, faintly. "But—I am very ill— dying, I think! Open the window—give me air!"

She laid his head gently back on the pillow, and ran quickly to throw open the lattice. In that same moment, the dog Charlie, who had followed her downstairs from her room, jumped on the bed, and finding his master's hand lying limp and pallid outside the coverlet, fawned upon it with a plaintive cry. The cool sea-air rushed in, and Helmsley's sinking strength revived. He turned his eyes gratefully towards the stream of silvery moonlight that poured through the open casement.

"'Angels ever bright and fair!'" he murmured—then as Mary came back to his side, he smiled vaguely; "I thought I heard my little sister singing!"

Slipping her arm again under his head, she carefully administered a dose of the cordial which had been made up for him as a calmative against his sudden heart attacks.

He swallowed it slowly and with difficulty.

"I'm—I'm all right," he said, feebly. "The pain has gone. I'm sorry to have wakened you up, Mary!—but you're always kind and patient—"

His voice broke—and a grey pallor began to steal almost imperceptibly upwards over his wasted features. She watched him, her heart beating fast with grief and terror,—the tears rushing to her eyes in spite of her efforts to restrain them. For she saw that he was dying. The solemnly musical plash of the sea sounded rhythmically upon the quiet air like the soothing murmur of a loving mother's lullaby, and the radiance of the moonlight flooded the little room with mystical glory. In her womanly tenderness she drew him more protectingly into the embrace of her kind arm, as though seeking to hold him back from the abyss of the Unknown, and held his head close against her breast. He opened his eyes and saw her thus bending over him. A smile brightened his face—a smile of youth, and hope, and confidence.

"The end is near, Mary!" he said in a clear, calm voice; "but—it's not difficult! There is no pain. And you are with me. That is enough!—that is more than I ever hoped for!—more than I deserve! God bless you always!"

He shut his eyes again—but opened them quickly in a sudden struggle for breath.

"The papers!" he gasped. "Mary—Mary—you won't forget—your promise!"

"No, David!—dear David!" she sobbed. "I won't forget!"

The paroxysm passed, and his hand wandered over the coverlet, where it encountered the soft, crouching head of the little dog who was lying close to him, shivering in every limb.

"Why, here's Charlie!" he whispered, weakly. "Poor wee Charlie! 'Take care of me' is written on his collar. Mary will take care of you, Charlie!—good-bye, little man!"

He lay quiet then, but his eyes were wide open, gazing not upward, but straight ahead, as though they saw some wondrous vision in the little room.

"Strange!—strange that I did not know all this before!" he murmured—and then was silent, still gazing straight before him. All at once a great shudder shook his body—and his thin features grew suddenly pinched and wan.

"It is almost morning!" he said, and his voice was like an echo of itself from very far away. "The sun will rise—but I shall not be here to see the sun or you, Mary!" and rallying his fast ebbing strength he turned towards her. "Keep your arms about me!—pray for me!—God will hear you—God must hear His own! Don't cry, dear! Kiss me!"

She kissed him, clasping his poor frail form to her heart as though he were a child, and tenderly smoothing back his venerable snow-white hair. A slumbrous look of perfect peace softened the piteousness of his dying eyes.

"The only treasure!" he murmured, faintly. "The treasure of Heaven—Love! God bless you for giving it to me, Mary!—good-bye, my dear!"

"Not good-bye, David!" she cried. "No—not good-bye!"

"Yes—good-bye!" he said,—and then, as another strong shudder convulsed him, he made a last feeble effort to lay his head against her bosom. "Don't let me go, Mary! Hold me!—closer!—closer! Your heart is warm, ah, so warm, Mary!—and death is cold—cold—!"

Another moment—and the moonlight, streaming through the open window, fell on the quiet face of a dead man. Then came silence—broken only by the gentle murmur of the sea, and the sound of a woman's weeping.

XXIII

N ot often is the death of a man, who to all appearances was nothing more than a "tramp," attended by any demonstrations of sorrow. There are so many "poor" men! The roads are infested with them. It would seem, in fact, that they have no business to live at all, especially when they are old, and can do little or nothing to earn their bread. Such, generally and roughly speaking, is the opinion of the matter-of-fact world. Nevertheless, the death of "old David" created quite an atmosphere of mourning in Weircombe, though, had it been known that he was one of the world's famous millionaires, such kindly regret and compassion might have been lacking. As things were, he carried his triumph of love to the grave with him. Mary's grief for the loss of the gentle old man was deep and genuine, and Angus Reay shared it with her to the full.

"I shall miss him so much!" she sobbed, looking at the empty chair, which had been that of her own father. "He was always so kind and thoughtful for me—never wishing to give trouble!—poor dear old David!—and he did so hope to see us married, Angus!—you know it was through him that we knew each other!"

"I know!"—and Angus, profoundly moved, was not ashamed of the tears in his own eyes—"God bless him! He was a dear, good old fellow! But, Mary, you must not fret; he would not like to see your pretty eyes all red with weeping. This life was getting very difficult for him, remember,—he endured a good deal of pain. Bunce says he must have suffered acutely often without saying a word about it, lest you should be anxious. He is at rest now."

"Yes, he is at rest!"—and Mary struggled to repress her tears—"Come and see!"

Hand in hand they entered the little room where the dead man lay, covered with a snowy sheet, his waxen hands crossed peacefully outside it, and delicate clusters of white roses and myrtle laid here and there around him. His face was like a fine piece of sculptured marble in its still repose—the gravity and grandeur of death had hallowed the worn features of old age, and given them a great sweetness and majesty. The two lovers stood gazing at the corpse for a moment in silent awe—then Mary whispered softly—

"He seems only asleep! And he looks happy."

"He *is* happy, dear!—he must be happy!"—and Angus drew her gently away. "Poor and helpless as he was, still he found a friend in you at the last, and now all his troubles are over. He has gone to Heaven with the help and blessing of your kind and tender heart, my Mary! I am sure of that!"

She sighed, and her eyes were clouded with sadness.

"Heaven seems very far away sometimes!" she said. "And—often I wonder—what *is* Heaven?"

"Love!" he answered—"Love made perfect—Love that knows no change and no end! 'Nothing is sweeter than love; nothing stronger, nothing higher, nothing broader, nothing more pleasant, nothing fuller or better in heaven and in earth, for love is born of God, and can rest only in God above all things created.'"

He quoted the beautiful words from the *Imitation of Christ* reverently and tenderly.

"Is that not true, my Mary?" he said, kissing her.

"Yes, Angus! For *us* I know it is true!—I wish it were true for all the world!"

And then there came a lovely day, perfectly brilliant and intensely calm, on which "old David," was quietly buried in the picturesque little churchyard of Weircombe. Mary and Angus together had chosen his resting-place, a grassy knoll swept by the delicate shadows of a noble beech-tree, and facing the blue expanse of the ocean. Every man who had known and talked with him in the village offered to contribute to the expenses of his funeral, which, however, were very slight. The good Vicar would accept no burial fee, and all who knew the story of the old "tramp's" rescue from the storm by Mary Deane, and her gentle care of him afterwards, were anxious to prove that they too were not destitute of that pure and true charity which "suffereth long and is kind." Had David Helmsley been buried as David Helmsley the millionaire, it is more than likely that he might not have had one sincere mourner at his grave, with the exception of his friend, Sir Francis Vesey, and his valet Benson. There would have been a few "business" men,—and some empty carriages belonging to fashionable folk sent out of so-called "respect"; but of the many he had entertained, assisted and benefited, not one probably would have taken the trouble to pay him, so much as a last honour. As the poor tramping old basket-maker, whose failing strength would not allow him to earn much of a living, his simple funeral was attended by nearly a whole village,—honest men who stood respectfully bareheaded as the coffin was lowered into the grave—kind-hearted women who wept for "poor lonely soul"—as they expressed it,—and little children who threw knots of flowers into that mysterious dark hole in the ground "where people went to sleep for a little, and then came out again as angels"—as their parents told them. It was a simple ceremony, performed in a spirit of perfect piety, and without any hypocrisy or formality. And when it was all over, and the villagers had dispersed to their homes, Mr. Twitt on his way "down street," as he termed it, from the churchyard, paused at Mary Deane's cottage to unburden his mind of a weighty resolution.

"Ye see, Mis' Deane, it's like this," he said—"I as good as promised the poor old gaffer as I'd do 'im a tombstone for nuthin', an' I'm 'ere to say as I aint a-goin' back on that. But I must take my time on it. I'd like to think out a speshul hepitaph—an' doin' portry takes a bit of 'ard brain work. So when the earth's set down on 'is grave a bit, an' the daisies is a-growin' on the grass, I'll mebbe 'ave got an idea wot'll please ye. 'E aint left any mossel o' paper writ out like, with wot 'e'd like put on 'im, I s'pose?"

Mary felt the colour rush to her face.

"N—no! Not that I know of, Mr. Twitt," she said. "He has left a few papers which I promised him I would take to a friend of his, but I haven't even looked at them yet, and don't know to whom they are addressed. If I find anything I'll let you know."

"Ay, do so!" and Twitt rubbed his chin meditatively. "I wouldn't run agin' 'is wishes for anything if ser be I can carry 'em out. I considers as 'e wor a very fine sort—gentle as a lamb, an' grateful for all wot was done for 'im, an' I wants to be as friendly to 'im in 'is death as I wos in 'is life—ye understand?"

"Yes—I know—I quite understand," said Mary. "But there's plenty of time—"

"Yes, there's plenty of time!" agreed Twitt. "But, lor,' if you could only know what a pain it gives me in the 'ed to work the portry out of it, ye wouldn't wonder at my preparin' ye, as 'twere. Onny I wishes ye just to understand that it'll all be done for love—an' no charge."

Mary thanked him smiling, yet with tears in her eyes, and he strolled away down the street in his usual slow and somewhat casual manner.

That evening,—the evening of the day on which all that was mortal of "old David" had been committed to the gentle ground, Mary unlocked the cupboard of which he had given her the key on the last night of his life, and took out the bulky packet it contained. She read the superscription with some surprise and uneasiness. It was addressed to a Mr. Bulteel, in a certain street near Chancery Lane, London. Now Mary had never been to London in her life. The very idea of going to that vast unknown metropolis half scared her, and she sat for some minutes, with the sealed packet in her lap, quite confused and troubled.

"Yet I made the promise!" she said to herself—"And I dare not break it! I must go. And I must not tell Angus anything about it—that's the worst part of all!"

She gazed wistfully at the packet,—anon she turned it over and over. It was sealed in several places—but the seal had no graven impress, the wax having merely been pressed with the finger.

"I must go!" she repeated. "I'm bound to deliver it myself to the man for whom it is intended. But what a journey it will be! To London!"

Absorbed in thought, she started as a tap came at the cottage door,—and rising, she hurriedly put the package out of sight, just as Angus entered.

"Mary," he said, as he came towards her—"Do you know, I've been thinking we had better get quietly married as soon as possible?"

She smiled.

"Why? Is the book finished?" she asked.

"No, it isn't. I wish it was! But it will be finished in another month—"

"Then let us wait that other month," she said. "You will be happier, I know, if the work is off your mind."

"Yes—I shall be happier—but Mary, I can't bear to think of you all alone in this little cottage—"

She gently interrupted him.

"I was all alone for five years after my father died," she said. "And though I was sometimes a little sad, I was not dull, because I always had work to do. Dear old David was a good companion, and it was pleasant to take care of him—indeed, this last year has been quite a happy one for me, and I shan't find it hard to live alone in the cottage for just a month now. Don't worry about me, Angus!"

He stooped and picked up Charlie, who, since his master's death, had been very dispirited.

"You see, Mary," he said, as he fondled the little dog and stroked its silky hair—"nothing will alter the fact that you are richer than I am. You do regular work for which you get regular pay—now I have no settled work at all, and not much chance of pay, even for the book on which

I've been spending nearly a year of my time. You've got a house which you can keep going—and very soon I shall not be able to afford so much as a room!—think of that! And yet—I have the impertinence to ask you to marry me! Forgive me, dear! It is, as you say, better to wait."

She came and entwined her arms about him.

"I'll wait a month," she said—"No longer, Angus! By that time, if you don't marry me, I shall summons you for breach of promise!"

She smiled—but he still remained thoughtful.

"Angus!" she said suddenly—"I want to tell you—I shall have to go away from Weircombe for a day—perhaps two days."

He looked surprised.

"Go away!" he echoed. "What for? Where to?"

She told him then of "old David's" last request to her, and of the duty she had undertaken to perform.

He listened gravely.

"You must do it, of course," he said. "But will you have to travel far?"

"Some distance from Weircombe," she answered, evasively.

"May I not go with you?" he asked.

She hesitated.

"I promised—" she began.

"And you shall not break your word," he said, kissing her. "You are so true, my Mary, that I wouldn't tempt you to change one word or even half a word of what you have said to any one, living or dead. When do you want to take this journey?"

"To-morrow, or the next day," she said. "I'll ask Mrs. Twitt to see to the house and look after Charlie, and I'll be back again as quickly as I can. Because, when I've given the papers over to David's friend, whoever he is, I shall have nothing more to do but just come home."

This being settled, it was afterwards determined that the next day but one would be the most convenient for her to go, as she could then avail herself of the carrier's cart to take her as far as Minehead. But she was not allowed to start on her unexpected travels without a burst of prophecy from Mrs. Twitt.

"As I've said an' allus thought," said that estimable lady—"Old David 'ad suthin' 'idden in 'is 'art wot 'e never giv' away to nobody. Mark my words, Mis' Deane!—'e 'ad a sin or a sorrer at the back of 'im, an' whichever it do turn out to be I'm not a-goin' to blame 'im either way, for bein' dead 'e's dead, an' them as sez unkind o' the dead is apt to be picked morsels for the devil's gridiron. But now that you've got a packet to take to old David's friends somewheres, you may take my word for 't, Mis' Deane, you'll find out as 'e was wot ye didn't expect. Onny last night, as I was a-sittin' afore the kitchen fire, for though bein' summer I'm that chilly that I feels the least change in the temper o' the sea,—as I was a-sittin', I say, out jumps a cinder as long as a pine cone, red an' glowin' like a candle at the end. An' I stares at the thing, an' I sez: 'That's either a purse o' money, or a journey with a coffin at the end'—an' the thing burns an' shines like a reg'lar spark of old Nick's cookin' stove, an' though I pokes an' pokes it, it won't go out, but lies on the 'erth, frizzlin' all the time. An' I do 'ope, Mis' Deane, as now yer goin' off to 'and over old David's effecks to the party interested, ye'll come back safe, for the poor old dear 'adn't a penny to bless 'isself with, so the cinder must mean the journey, an' bein' warned, ye'll guard agin the coffin at the end."

Mary smiled rather sadly.

"I'll take care!" she said. "But I don't think anything very serious is likely to happen. Poor old David had no friends,—and probably the few papers he has left are only for some relative who would not do anything for him while he was alive, but who, all the same, has to be told that he is dead."

"Maybe so!" and Mrs. Twitt nodded her head profoundly—"But that cinder worn't made in the fire for nowt! Such a shape as 'twas don't grow out of the flames twice in twenty year!"

And, with the conviction of the village prophetess she assumed to be, she was not to be shaken from the idea that strange discoveries were pending respecting "old David." Mary herself could not quite get rid of a vague misgiving and anxiety, which culminated at last in her determination to show Angus Reay the packet left in her charge, in order that he might see to whom it was addressed.

"For that can do no harm," she thought—"I feel that he really ought to know that I have to go all the way to London."

Angus, however, on reading the superscription, was fully as perplexed as she was. He was familiar with the street near Chancery Lane where the mysterious "Mr. Bulteel" lived, but the name of Bulteel as a resident in that street was altogether unknown to him. Presently a bright idea struck him.

"I have it!" he said. "Look here, Mary, didn't David say he used to be employed in office-work?"

"Yes," she answered,—"He had to give up his situation, so I understand, on account of old age."

"Then that makes it clear," Angus declared. "This Mr. Bulteel is probably a man who worked with him in the same office—perhaps the only link he had with his past life. I think you'll find that's the way it will turn out. But I hate to think of your travelling to London all alone!—for the first time in your life, too!"

"Oh well, that doesn't matter much!" she said, cheerfully,—"Now that you know where I am going, it's all right. You forget, Angus!—I'm quite old enough to take care of myself. How many times must I remind you that you are engaged to be married to an old maid of thirty-five? You treat me as if I were quite a young girl!"

"So I do—and so I will!" and his eyes rested upon her with a proud look of admiration. "For you *are* young, Mary—young in your heart and soul and nature—younger than any so-called young girl I ever met, and twenty times more beautiful. So there!"

She smiled gravely.

"You are easily satisfied, Angus," she said—"But the world will not agree with you in your ideas of me. And when you become a famous man—"

"If I become a famous man—" he interrupted.

"No—not 'if'—I say 'when,'" she repeated. "When you become a famous man, people will say, 'what a pity he did not marry some one younger and more suited to his position—"

She could speak no more, for Angus silenced her with a kiss.

"Yes, what a pity it will be!" he echoed. "What a pity! When other men, less fortunate, see that I have won a beautiful and loving wife, whose heart is all my own,—who is pure and true as the sun in heaven,—'what a pity,' they will say, 'that we are not so lucky!' That's what the talk will be, Mary! For there's no man on earth who does not crave to be loved for himself alone—a selfish wish, perhaps—but it's implanted in every son of Adam. And a man's life is always more or less spoilt by lack of the love he needs."

She put her arms round his neck, and her true eyes looked straightly into his own.

"Your life will not be spoilt that way, dear!" she said. "Trust me for that!"

"Do I not know it!" he answered, passionately. "And would I not lose the whole world, with all its chances of fame and fortune, rather than lose *you*!"

And in their mutual exchange of tenderness and confidence they forgot all save

MARIE CORELLI

"The time and place
And the loved one all together!"

It was a perfect summer's morning when Mary, for the first time in many years, left her little home in Weircombe and started upon a journey she had never taken and never had thought of taking—a journey which, to her unsophisticated mind, seemed fraught with strange possibilities of difficulty, even of peril. London had loomed upon her horizon through the medium of the daily newspaper, as a vast over-populated city where (if she might believe the press) humanity is more selfish than generous, more cruel than kind,—where bitter poverty and starvation are seen side by side with criminal extravagance and luxury,—and where, according to her simple notions, the people were forgetting or had forgotten God. It was with a certain lingering and wistful backward look that she left her little cottage embowered among roses, and waved farewell to Mrs. Twitt, who, standing at the garden gate with Charlie in her arms, waved hearty response, cheerfully calling out "Good Luck!" after her, and adding the further assurance—"Ye'll find everything as well an' straight as ye left it when ye comes 'ome, please God!"

Angus Reay accompanied her in the carrier's cart to Minehead, and there she caught the express to London. On enquiry, she found there was a midnight train which would bring her back from the metropolis at about nine o'clock the next morning, and she resolved to travel home by it.

"You will be so tired!" said Angus, regretfully. "And yet I would rather you did not stay away a moment longer than you can help!"

"Don't fear!" and she smiled. "You cannot be a bit more anxious for me to come back than I am to come back myself! Good-bye! It's only for a day!"

She waved her hand as the train steamed out of the station, and he watched her sweet face smiling at him to the very last, when the express, gathering speed, rushed away with her and whirled her into the far distance. A great depression fell upon his soul,—all the light seemed gone out of the landscape—all the joy out of his life—and he realised, as it were suddenly, what her love meant to him.

"It is everything!" he said. "I don't believe I could write a line without her!—in fact I know I wouldn't have the heart for it! She is so different to every woman I have ever known,—she seems to make the world all warm and kind by just smiling her own bonnie smile!"

And starting off to walk part of the way back to Weircombe, he sang softly under his breath as he went a verse of "Annie Laurie"—

> *"Like dew on the gowan lyin'*
> *Is the fa' o' her fairy feet;*
> *And like winds in simmer sighin'*
> *Her voice is low an' sweet*
> *Her voice is low an' sweet;*
> *An' she's a' the world to me;*
> *An' for bonnie Annie Laurie*
> *I'd lay me doun and dee!"*

And all the beautiful influences of nature,—the bright sunshine, the wealth of June blossom, the clear skies and the singing of birds, seemed part of that enchanting old song, expressing the happiness which alone is made perfect by love.

Meanwhile, no adventures of a startling or remarkable kind occurred to Mary during her rather long and tedious journey. Various passengers got into her third-class compartment and got out again, but they were somewhat dull and commonplace folk, many of them being of that curiously unsociable type of human creature which apparently mistrusts its fellows. Contrary to her ingenuous expectation, no one seemed to think a journey to London was anything of a unique or thrilling experience. Once only, when she was nearing her destination, did she venture to ask a fellow-passenger, an elderly man with a kindly face, how she ought to go to Chancery Lane. He looked at her with a touch of curiosity.

"That's among the hornets' nests," he said.

She raised her pretty eyebrows with a little air of perplexity.

"Hornets' nests?"

"Yes. Where a good many lawyers live, or used to live."

"Oh, I see!" And she smiled responsively to what he evidently intended as a brilliant satirical joke. "But is it easy to get there?"

"Quite easy. Take a 'bus."

"From the station?"

"Of course!"

And he subsided into silence.

She asked no more questions, and on her arrival at Paddington confided her anxieties to a friendly porter, who, announcing that he was "from Somerset born himself and would see her through," gave her concise directions which she attentively followed; with the result that despite much bewilderment in getting in and getting out of omnibuses, and jostling against more people than she had ever seen in the course of her whole life, she found herself at last at the entrance of a rather obscure-looking smutty little passage, guarded by a couple of round columns, on which were painted in black letters a considerable number of names, among which were those of "Vesey and Symonds." The numeral inscribed above the entrance to this passage corresponded to the number on the address of the packet which she carried for "Mr. Bulteel"—but though she read all the names on the two columns, "Bulteel" was not among them. Nevertheless, she made her way perseveringly into what seemed nothing but a little blind alley leading nowhere, and as she did so, a small boy came running briskly down a flight of dark stairs, which were scarcely visible from the street, and nearly knocked her over.

"'Ullo! Beg pardon 'm! Which office d' ye want?"

"Is there," began Mary, in her gentle voice—"is there a Mr. Bulteel—?"

"Bulteel? Yes—straight up—second floor—third door—Vesey and Symonds!"

With these words jerked out of himself at lightning speed, the boy rushed past her and disappeared.

With a beating heart Mary cautiously climbed the dark staircase which he had just descended. When she reached the second floor, she paused. There were three doors all facing her,—on the first one was painted the name of "Sir Francis Vesey"—on the second "Mr. John Symonds"—and on the third "Mr. Bulteel." As soon as she saw this last, she heaved a little sigh of relief, and going straight up to it knocked timidly. It was opened at once by a young clerk who looked at her questioningly.

"Mr. Bulteel?" she asked, hesitatingly.

"Yes. Have you an appointment?"

"No. I am quite a stranger," she said. "I only wish to tell Mr. Bulteel of the death of some one he knows."

The clerk glanced at her and seemed dubious.

"Mr. Bulteel is very busy," he began—"and unless you have an appointment—"

"Oh, please let me see him!" And Mary's eyes almost filled with tears. "See!"—and she held up before him the packet she carried. "I've travelled all the way from Weircombe, in Somerset, to bring him this from his dead friend, and I promised to give it to him myself. Please, please do not turn me away!"

The clerk stared hard at the superscription on the packet, as he well might. For he had at once recognised the handwriting of David Helmsley. But he suppressed every outward sign of surprise, save such as might appear in a glance of unconcealed wonder at Mary herself. Then he said briefly—

"Come in!"

She obeyed, and was at once shut in a stuffy cupboard-like room which had no other furniture than an office desk and high stool.

"Name, please!" said the clerk.

She looked startled—then smiled.

"My name? Mary Deane."

"Miss or Mrs.?"

"'Miss,' if you please, sir," she answered, the colour flushing her cheeks with confusion at the sharpness of his manner.

The clerk gave her another up-and-down look, and opening a door behind his office desk vanished like a conjuror tricking himself through a hole.

She waited patiently for a couple of minutes—and then the clerk came back, with traces of excitement in his manner.

"Yes—Mr. Bulteel will see you. This way!"

She followed him with her usual quiet step and composed demeanour, and bent her head with a pretty air of respect as she found herself in the presence of an elderly man with iron-grey whiskers and a severely preoccupied air of business hardening his otherwise rather benevolent features. He adjusted his spectacles and looked keenly at her as she entered. She spoke at once.

"You are Mr. Bulteel?"

"Yes."

"Then this is for you," she said, approaching him, and handing him the packet she had brought. "They are some papers belonging to a poor old tramp named David, who lodged in my house for nearly a year—it will be a year come July. He was very weak and feeble and got lost in a storm on the hills above Weircombe—that's where I live—and I found him lying quite unconscious in the wet and cold, and took him home and nursed him. He got better and stayed on with me, making baskets for a living—he was too feeble to tramp any more—but he gave me no trouble, he was such a kind, good old man. I was very fond of him.

And—and—last week he died"—here her sweet voice trembled. "He suffered great pain—but at the end he passed away quite peacefully—in my arms. He was very anxious that I should bring his papers to you myself—and I promised I would so—"

She paused, a little troubled by his silence. Surely he looked very strangely at her.

"I am sorry," she faltered, nervously—"if I have brought you any bad news;—poor David seemed to have no friends, but perhaps you were a friend to him once and may have a kind recollection of him—"

He was still quite silent. Slowly he broke the seals of the packet, and drawing out a slip of paper which came first to his hand, read what was written upon it. Then he rose from his chair.

"Kindly wait one moment," he said. "These—these papers and letters are not for me, but—but for—for another gentleman."

He hurried out of the room, taking the packet with him, and Mary remained alone for nearly a quarter of an hour, vaguely perplexed, and wondering how any "other gentleman" could possibly be concerned in the matter. Presently Mr. Bulteel returned, in an evident state of suppressed agitation.

"Will you please follow me, Miss Deane?" he said, with a singular air of deference. "Sir Francis is quite alone and will see you at once."

Mary's blue eyes opened in amazement.

"Sir Francis—!" she stammered. "I don't quite understand—"

"This way," said Mr. Bulteel, escorting her out of his own room along the passage to the door which she had before seen labelled with the name of "Sir Francis Vesey"—then catching the startled and appealing glance of her eyes, he added kindly: "Don't be alarmed! It's all right!"

Thereupon he opened the door and announced—

"Miss Deane, Sir Francis."

Mary looked up, and then curtsied with quite an "out-of-date" air of exquisite grace, as she found herself in the presence of a dignified white-haired old gentleman, who, standing near a large office desk on which the papers she had brought lay open, was wiping his spectacles, and looking very much as if he had been guilty of the womanish weakness of tears. He advanced to meet her.

"How do you do!" he said, uttering this commonplace with remarkable earnestness, and taking her hand kindly in his own. "You bring me sad news—very sad news! I had not expected the death of my old friend so suddenly—I had hoped to see him again—yes, I had hoped very much to see him again quite soon! And so you were with him at the last?"

Mary looked, as she felt, utterly bewildered.

"I think," she murmured—"I think there must be some mistake,—the papers I brought here were for Mr. Bulteel—"

"Yes—yes!" said Sir Francis. "That's quite right! Mr. Bulteel is my confidential clerk—and the packet was addressed to him. But a note inside requested that Mr. Bulteel should bring all the documents at once to me, which he has done. Everything is quite correct—quite in order. But—I forgot! You do not know! Please sit down—and I will endeavour to explain."

He drew up a chair for her near his desk so that she might lean her arm upon it, for she looked frightened. As a matter of fact he was frightened himself. Such a task as he had now to perform had never before been allotted to him. A letter addressed to him, and enclosed in the packet containing Helmsley's Last Will and Testament, had explained the whole situation, and had fully described, with simple fidelity, the life his old friend had led at Weircombe, and the affectionate care with which Mary had tended him,—while the conclusion of the letter was worded in terms of touching farewell.

For," wrote Helmsley, "when you read this, I shall be dead and in my quiet grave at Weircombe. Let me rest there in peace,—for though my eyes will no more see the sun,—or the kindness in the eyes of the woman whose unselfish goodness has been more than the sunshine to me, I shall—or so I think and hope—be spiritually conscious that my mortal remains are buried where humble and simple folk think well of me. This last letter from my hand to you is one not of business so much as friendship—for I have learned that what we call 'business' counts for very little, while the ties of sympathy, confidence, and love between human beings are the only forces that assist in the betterment of the world. And so farewell! Let the beloved angel who brings you these last messages from me have all honour from you for my sake.

Yours,
David Helmsley

And now, to Sir Francis Vesey's deep concern, the "beloved angel" thus spoken of sat opposite to him, moved by evident alarm,—her blue eyes full of tears, and her face pale and scared. How was he to begin telling her what she was bound to know?

"Yes—I will—I must endeavour to explain," he repeated, bending his brows upon her and regaining something of his self-control. "You, of course, were not aware—I mean my old friend never told you who he really was?"

Her anxious look grew more wistful.

"No, and indeed I never asked," she said. "He was so feeble when I took him to my home out of the storm, and for weeks afterwards he was so dangerously ill, that I thought questions might worry him. Besides it was not my business to bother about where he came from. He was just old and poor and friendless—that was enough for me."

"I hope—I do very much hope," said Sir Francis gently, "that you will not allow yourself to be too much startled—or—or overcome by what I have to tell you. David—he said his name was David, did he not?"

She made a sign of assent. A strange terror was creeping upon her, and she could not speak.

"David—yes!—that was quite right—David was his name," proceeded Sir Francis cautiously. "But he had another name—a surname which perhaps you may, or may not have heard. That name was Helmsley—"

She sprang up with a cry, remembering Angus Reay's story about his first love, Lucy Sorrel, and her millionaire.

"Helmsley! Not David Helmsley!"

"Yes,—David Helmsley! The 'poor old tramp' you sheltered in your home,—the friendless and penniless stranger you cared for so unselfishly and tenderly, was one of the richest men in the world!"

She stood amazed,—stricken as by a lightning shock.

"One of the richest men in the world!" she faltered. "One of the richest—" and here, with a little stifled sob, she wrung her hands together. "Oh no—no! That can't be true! He would never have deceived me!"

Sir Francis felt an uncomfortable tightness in his throat. The situation was embarrassing. He saw at once that she was not so much affected by the announcement of the supposed "poor" man's riches, as by the overwhelming thought that he could have represented himself to her as any other than he truly was.

"Sit down again, and let me tell you all," he said gently—"You will, I am sure, forgive him for the part he played when you know his history.

David Helmsley—who was my friend as well as my client for more than twenty years—was a fortunate man in the way of material prosperity,—but he was very unfortunate in his experience of human nature. His vast wealth made it impossible for him to see much more of men and women than was just enough to show him their worst side. He was surrounded by people who sought to use him and his great influence for their own selfish ends,—and the emotions and sentiments of life, such as love, fidelity, kindness, and integrity, he seldom or never met with among either his so-called 'friends' or his acquaintances. His wife was false to him, and his two sons brought him nothing but shame and dishonour. They all three died—and then—then in his old age he found himself alone in the world without any one who loved him, or whom he loved—without any one to whom he could confidently leave his enormous fortune, knowing it would be wisely and nobly used. When I last saw him I urged upon him the necessity of making his Will. He said he could not make it, as there was no one living whom he cared to name as his heir. Then he left London,—ostensibly on a journey for his health." Here Sir Francis paused, looking anxiously at his listener. She was deadly pale, and every now and then her eyes brimmed over with tears. "You can guess the rest," he continued,—"He took no one into his confidence as to his intention,—not even me. I understood he had gone abroad—till the other day—a short time ago—when I had a letter from him telling me that he was passing through Exeter."

She clasped and unclasped her hands nervously.

"Ah! That was where he went when he told me he had gone in search of work!" she murmured—"Oh, David, David!"

"He informed me then," proceeded Sir Francis, "that he had made his Will. The Will is here,"—and he took up a document lying on his desk—"The manner of its execution coincides precisely with the letter of instructions received, as I say, from Exeter—of course it will have to be formally proved—"

She lifted her eyes wonderingly.

"What is it to me?" she said—"I have nothing to do with it. I have brought you the papers—but I am sorry—oh, so sorry to hear that he was not what he made himself out to be! I cannot think of him in the same way—"

Sir Francis drew his chair closer to hers.

"Is it possible," he said—"Is it possible, my dear Miss Deane, that you do not understand?"

She gazed at him candidly.

"Yes, of course I understand," she said—"I understand that he was a rich man who played the part of a poor one—to see if any one would care for him just for himself alone—and—I—I—did care—oh, I did care!—and now I feel as if I couldn't care any more—"

Her voice broke sobbingly, and Sir Francis Vesey grew desperate.

"Don't cry!" he said—"Please don't cry! I should not be able to bear it! You see I'm a business man"—here he took off his spectacles and rubbed them vigorously—"and my position is that of the late Mr. David Helmsley's solicitor. In that position I am bound to tell you the straight truth—because I'm afraid you don't grasp it at all. It is a very overwhelming thing for you,—but all the same, I am sure, quite sure, that my old friend had reason to rely confidently upon your strength of character—as well as upon your affection for him—"

She had checked her sobs and was looking at him steadily.

"And, therefore," he proceeded—"referring again to my own position—that of the late David Helmsley's solicitor, it is my duty to inform you that you, Mary Deane, are by his last Will and Testament, the late David Helmsley's sole heiress."

She started up in terror.

"Oh no, no!—not me!" she cried.

"Everything which the late David Helmsley died possessed of, is left to you absolutely and unconditionally," went on Sir Francis, speaking with slow and deliberate emphasis—"And—even as he was one of the richest men, so you are now one of the richest women in the world!"

She turned deathly white,—then suddenly, to his great alarm and confusion, dropped on her knees before him, clasping her hands in a passion of appeal.

"Oh, don't say that, sir!" she exclaimed—"Please, please don't say it! I cannot be rich—I would not! I should be miserable—I should indeed! Oh, David, dear old David! I'm sure he never wished to make me wretched—he was fond of me—he was, really! And we were so happy and peaceful in the cottage at home! There was so little money, but so much love! Don't say I'm rich, sir!—or, if I am, let me give it all away at once! Let me give it to the starving and sick people in this great city—or please give it to them for me,—but don't, don't say that I must keep it myself!—I could not bear it!—oh, I could not bear it! Help me, oh, do help me to give it all away and let me remain just as I am, quite, quite poor!"

XXIV

There was a moment's silence, broken only by the roar and din of the London city traffic outside, which sounded like the thunder of mighty wheels—the wheels of a rolling world. And then Sir Francis, gently taking Mary's hand in his own, raised her from the ground.

"My dear,"—he said, huskily—"You must not—you really must not give way! See,"—and he took up a sealed letter from among the documents on the desk, addressed "To Mary"—and handed it to her—"my late friend asks me in the last written words I have from him to give this to you. I will leave you alone to read it. You will be quite private in this room—and no one will enter till you ring. Here is the bell,"—and he indicated it—"I think—indeed I am sure, when you understand everything, you will accept the great responsibility which will now devolve upon you, in as noble a spirit as that in which you accepted the care of David Helmsley himself when you thought him no more than what in very truth he was—a lonely-hearted old man, searching for what few of us ever find—an unselfish love!"

He left her then—and like one in a dream, she opened and read the letter he had given her—a letter as beautiful and wise and tender as ever the fondest father could have written to the dearest of daughters. Everything was explained in it—everything made clear; and gradually she realised the natural, strong and pardonable craving of the rich, unloved man, to seek out for himself some means whereby he might leave all his world's gainings to one whose kindness to him had not been measured by any knowledge of his wealth, but which had been bestowed upon him solely for simple love's sake. Every line Helmsley had written to her in this last appeal to her tenderness, came from his very heart, and went to her own heart again, moving her to the utmost reverence, pity and affection. In his letter he enclosed a paper with a list of bequests which he left to her charge.

"I could not name them in my Will,"—he wrote—"as this would have disclosed my identity—but you, my dear, will be more exact than the law in the payment of what I have here set down as just. And, therefore, to you I leave this duty."

First among these legacies came one of Ten Thousand Pounds to "my old friend Sir Francis Vesey,"—and then followed a long list of legacies to servants, secretaries, and workpeople generally. The sum of Five Hundred Pounds was to be paid to Miss Tranter, hostess of "The Trusty Man,"—"for her kindness to me on the one night I passed under her hospitable roof,"—and sums of Two Hundred Pounds each were left to "Matthew Peke, Herb Gatherer," and Farmer Joltram, both these personages to be found through the aforesaid Miss Tranter. Likewise a sum of Two Hundred Pounds was to be paid to one "Meg Ross—believed to hold a farm near Watchett in Somerset." No one that had served the poor "tramp" was forgotten by the great millionaire;—a sum of Five Hundred Pounds was left to John Bunce, "with grateful and affectionate thanks for his constant care"—and a final charge to Mary was the placing of Fifty Thousand Pounds in trust for the benefit of Weircombe, its Church, and its aged poor. The money in bank notes, enclosed with the testator's last Will and Testament, was to be given to Mary for her own immediate use,—and then came the following earnest request;—"I desire that the sum of Half-a-crown, made up of coppers and one sixpence, which will be found with these effects, shall be enclosed in a casket of gold and inscribed with the words 'The "surprise gift" collected by "Tom o' the Gleam" for David Helmsley, when as a tramp on the road he seemed to be in need of the charity and sympathy of his fellow men and which to him was

MORE PRECIOUS THAN MANY MILLIONS.

And I request that the said casket containing these coins may be retained by Mary Deane as a valued possession in her family, to be handed down as a talisman and cornerstone of fortune for herself and her heirs in perpetuity."

Finally the list of bequests ended with one sufficiently unusual to be called eccentric. It ran thus:—"To Angus Reay I leave Mary Deane— and with Her, all that I value, and more than I have ever possessed!"

Gradually, very gradually, Mary, sitting alone in Sir Francis Vesey's office, realised the whole position,—gradually the trouble and excitation of her mind calmed down, and her naturally even temperament reasserted itself. She was rich,—but though she tried to realise the fact, she could not do so, till at last the thought of Angus and how she might be able now to help him on with his career, roused a sudden rush of energy within her—which, however, was not by any means actual happiness. A great weight seemed to have fallen on her life—and she was bowed down by its heaviness. Kissing David Helmsley's letter, she put it in her bosom,—he had asked that its contents might be held sacred, and that no eyes but her own should scan his last words, and to her that request of a dead man was more than the command of a living King. The list of bequests she held in her hand ready to show Sir Francis Vesey when he entered, which he did as soon as she touched the bell. He saw that, though very pale, she was now comparatively calm and collected, and as she raised her eyes and tried to smile at him, he realised what a beautiful woman she was.

"Please forgive me for troubling you so much,"—she said, gently—"I am very sorry! I understand it all now,—I have read David's letter,—I shall always call him David, I think!—and I quite see how it all happened. I can't help being sorry—very sorry, that he has left his money to me—because it will be so difficult to know how to dispose of it for the best. But surely a great deal of it will go in these legacies,"— and she handed him the paper she held—"You see he names you first."

Sir Francis stared at the document, fairly startled and overcome by his late friend's generosity, as well as by Mary's naïve candour.

"My dear Miss Deane,"—he began, with deep embarrassment.

"You will tell me how to do everything, will you not?" she interrupted him, with an air of pathetic entreaty—"I want to carry out all his wishes exactly as if he were beside me, watching me—I think—" and her voice sank a little—"he may be here—with us—even now!" She paused a moment. "And if he is, he knows that I do not want money for myself at all—but that if I can do good with it, for his sake and memory, I will. Is it a very great deal?"

"Is it great deal of money, you mean?" he queried.

She nodded.

"I should say that at the very least my late friend's personal estate must be between six and seven millions of pounds sterling."

She clasped her hands in dismay.

"Oh! It is terrible!" she said, in a low strained voice—"Surely God never meant one man to have so much money!"

"It was fairly earned,"—said Sir Francis, quietly—"David Helmsley, to my own knowledge, never wronged or oppressed a single human being on his way to his own success. His money is clean! There's no brother's blood on the gold—and no 'sweated' labour at the back of it. That I can vouch for—that I can swear! No curse will rest on the fortune you inherit, Miss Deane—for it was made honestly!"

Tears stood in her eyes, and she wiped them away furtively.

"Poor David!" she murmured—"Poor lonely old man! With all that wealth and no one to care for him! Oh yes, the more I think of it the more I understand it! But now there is only one thing for me to do—I must get home as quickly as possible and tell Angus"—here she pointed to the last paragraph in Helmsley's list of bequests—"You see,"—she went on—"he leaves Mary Deane—that's me—to Angus Reay, 'and with Her all that I value.' I am engaged to be married to Mr. Reay—David wished very much to live till our wedding-day—"

She broke off, passing her hand across her brow and looking puzzled.

"Mr. Reay is very much to be congratulated!"—said Sir Francis, gently.

She smiled rather sadly.

"Oh, I'm not sure of that," she said—"He is a very clever man—he writes books, and he will be famous very soon—while I—" She paused again, then went on, looking very earnestly at Sir Francis—"May I—would you—write out something for me that I might sign before I go away to-day, to make it sure that if I die, all that I have—including this terrible, terrible fortune—shall come to Angus Reay? You see anything might happen to me—quite suddenly,—the very train I am going back in to-night might meet with some accident, and I might be killed—and then poor David's money would be lost, and his legacies never paid. Don't you see that?"

Sir Francis certainly saw it, but was not disposed to admit its possibility.

"There is really no necessity to anticipate evil," he began.

"There is perhaps no necessity—but I should like to be sure, quite sure, that in case of such evil all was right,"—she said, with great feeling—"And I know you could do it for me—"

"Why, of course, if you insist upon it, I can draw you up a form of Will in ten minutes,"—he said, smiling benevolently—"Would that satisfy you? You have only to sign it, and the thing is done."

It was wonderful to see how she rejoiced at this proposition,—the eager delight with which she contemplated the immediate disposal of the wealth she had not as yet touched, to the man she loved best in the world—and the swift change in her manner from depression to joy, when Sir Francis, just to put her mind at ease, drafted a concise form of Will for her in his own handwriting, in which form she, with the same precision as that of David Helmsley, left "everything of which she died possessed, absolutely and unconditionally," to her promised husband.

With a smile on her face and sparkling eyes, she signed this document in the presence of two witnesses, clerks of the office called up for the purpose, who, if it had been their business to express astonishment, would undoubtedly have expressed it then.

"You will keep it here for me, won't you?" she said, when the clerks had retired and the business was concluded—"And I shall feel so much more at rest now! For when I have talked it over with Angus I shall realise everything more clearly—he will advise me what to do—he is so much wiser than I am! And you will write to me and tell me all that is needful for me to know—shall I leave this paper?"—and she held up the document in which the list of Helmsley's various legacies was written—"Surely you ought to keep it?"

Sir Francis smiled gravely.

"I think not!" he said—"I think I must urge you to retain that paper on which my name is so generously remembered, in your own possession, Miss Deane. You understand, I suppose, that you are not *by the law* compelled to pay any of these legacies. They are left entirely to your own discretion. They merely represent the last purely personal wishes of my late friend, David Helmsley, and you must yourself decide whether you consider it practical to carry them out."

She looked surprised.

"But the personal wishes of the dead are more than any law" she exclaimed—"They are sacred. How could I"—and moved by a sudden impulse she laid her hand appealingly on his arm—"How could I neglect or fail to fulfil any one of them? It would be impossible!

Responding to her earnest look and womanly gentleness, Sir Francis who had not forgotten the old courtesies once practised by gentlemen to women whom they honoured, raised the hand that rested so lightly on his arm, and kissed it.

"I know" he said—"that it would be impossible for you to do what is not right and true and just! And you will need no advice from me save such as is purely legal and technical. Let me be your friend in these matters—"

"And in others too,"—said Mary, sweetly—"I do hope you will not dislike me!"

Dislike her? Well, well! If any mortal man, old or young, could "dislike" a woman with a face like hers and eyes so tender, such an one would have to be a criminal or a madman! In a little while they fell into conversation as naturally as if they had known each other for years: Sir Francis listening with profound interest to the story of his old friend's last days. And presently, despatching a telegram to his wife to say that he was detained in the city by pressing business, he took Mary out with him to a quiet little restaurant where he dined with her, and finally saw her off from Paddington station by the midnight train for Minehead. Nothing would induce her to stay in London,—her one aim and object in life now was to return to Weircombe and explain everything to Angus as quickly as possible. And when the train had gone, Sir Francis left the platform in a state of profound abstraction, and was driven home in his brougham feeling more like a sentimentalist than a lawyer.

"Extraordinary!" he exclaimed—"The most extraordinary thing I ever heard of in my life? But I knew—I felt that Helmsley would dispose of his wealth in quite an unexpected way! Now I wonder how the man—Mary Deane's lover—will take it? I wonder! But what a woman she is!—how beautiful!—how simple and honest—above all how purely womanly!—with all the sweet grace and gentleness which alone commands, and ever will command man's adoration! Helmsley must have been very much at peace and happy in his last days! Yes!—the sorrowful 'king' of many millions must have at last found the treasure he sought and which he considered more precious than all his money! For Solomon was right: 'If a man would give all the substance of his house for love, it would be utterly contemned!'"

AT WEIRCOMBE NEXT DAY THERE was a stiff gale of wind blowing inland, and the village, with its garlands and pyramids of summer blossom, was swept from end to end by warm, swift, salty gusts, that bent the trees and shook the flowers in half savage, half tender sportiveness, while the sea, shaping itself by degrees into "wild horses" of blue water bridled with foam, raced into the shore with ever-increasing hurry and fury. But notwithstanding the strong wind, there was a bright sun, and a dazzling blue sky, scattered over with flying masses of cloud, like flocks of white birds soaring swiftly to some far-off region of rest. Everything in nature looked radiant and beautiful,—health and joy were exhaled from every breath of air—and yet in one place—one pretty rose-embowered cottage, where, until now, the spirit of content had held its happy habitation, a sudden gloom had fallen, and a dark cloud had blotted out all the sunshine. Mary's little "home sweet home" had been all at once deprived of sweetness,—and she sat within it like a mournful castaway, clinging to the wreck of that which had so long been her peace and safety. Tired out by her long night journey and lack of sleep, she looked very white and weary and ill—and Angus Reay, sitting opposite to her, looked scarcely less worn and weary than herself. He had met her on her return from London at the Minehead station, with all the ardour and eagerness of a lover and a boy,—and he had at once seen in her face that something unexpected had happened,—something that had deeply affected her—though she had told him nothing, till on their arrival home at the cottage, she was able to be quite alone with him. Then he learned all. Then he knew that "old David" had been no other than David Helmsley the millionaire,—the very man whom his first love, Lucy Sorrel, had schemed and hoped to marry. And he realised—and God alone knew with what a passion of despair he realised it!—that Mary—his bonnie Mary—his betrothed wife—had been chosen to inherit those very millions which had formerly stood between him and what he had then imagined to be his happiness. And listening to the strange story, he had sunk deeper and deeper into the Slough of Despond, and now sat rigidly silent, with all the light gone out of his features, and all the ardour quenched in his eyes. Mary looking at him, and reading every expression in that dark beloved face, felt the tears rising thickly in her throat, but bravely suppressed them, and tried to smile.

"I knew you would be sorry when you heard all about it, Angus,"—she said—"I felt sure you would! I wish it had happened differently—" Here she stopped, and taking up the little dog Charlie, settled him on her knee. He was whimpering to be caressed, and she bent over his small silky head to hide the burning drops that fell from her eyes despite herself. "If it could only be altered!—but it can't—and the only thing to do is to give the money away to those who need it as quickly as possible—"

"Give it away!" answered Angus, bitterly—"Good God! Why, to give away seven or eight millions of money in the right quarters would occupy one man's lifetime!"

His voice was harsh, and his hand clenched itself involuntarily as he spoke. She looked at him in a vague fear.

"No, Mary,"—he said—"You can't give it away—not as you imagine. Besides,—there is more than money—there is the millionaire's house—his priceless pictures, his books—his yacht—a thousand and one other things that he possessed, and which now belong to you. Oh Mary! I wish to God I had never seen him!"

She trembled.

"Then perhaps—you and I would never have met," she murmured.

"Better so!" and rising, he paced restlessly up and down the little kitchen—"Better that I should never have loved you, Mary, than be so parted from you! By money, too! The last thing that should ever have come between us! Money! Curse it! It has ruined my life!"

She lifted her tear-wet eyes to his.

"What do you mean, Angus?" she asked, gently—"Why do you talk of parting? The money makes no difference to our love!"

"No difference? No difference? Oh Mary, don't you see!" and he turned upon her a face white and drawn with his inward anguish—"Do you think—can you imagine that I would marry a woman with millions of money—I—a poor devil, with nothing in the world to call my own, and no means of livelihood save in my brain, which, after all, may turn out to be quite of a worthless quality! Do you think I would live on your bounty? Do you think I would accept money from you? Surely you know me better! Mary, I love you! I love you with my whole heart and soul!—but I love you as the poor working woman whose work I hoped to make easier, whose life it was my soul's purpose to make happy—but,—you have everything you want in the world now!—and I—I am no use to you! I can do nothing for you—nothing!—you are David Helmsley's heiress, and with such wealth as he has left you, you might marry a prince of the royal blood if you cared—for princes are to be bought,—like anything else in the world's market! But you are not of the world—you never were—and now—now—the world will take you! The world leaves nothing alone that has any gold upon it!"

She listened quietly to his passionate outburst. She was deadly pale, and she pressed Charlie close against her bosom,—the little dog, she thought half vaguely, would love her just as well whether she was rich or poor.

"How can the world take me, Angus?" she said—"Am I not yours?—all yours!—and what has the world to do with me? Do not speak in such a strange way—you hurt me—"

"I know I hurt you!" he said, stopping in his restless walk and facing her—"And I know I should always hurt you—now! If David Helmsley had never crossed our path, how happy we might have been—"

She raised her hand reproachfully.

"Do not blame the poor old man, even in a thought, Angus!" she said—"His dream—his last hope was that we two might be happy!

He brought us together,—and I am sure, quite sure, that he hoped we would do good in the world with the money he has left us—"

"Us!" interrupted Angus, meaningly.

"Yes,—surely us! For am I not to be one with you? Oh Angus, be patient, be gentle! Think kindly of him who meant so much kindness to those whom he loved in his last days!" She smothered a rising sob, and went on entreatingly—"He has forgotten no one who was friendly to him—and—and—Angus—remember!—remember in that paper I have shown to you—that list of bequests, which he has entrusted me to pay, he has left me to you, Angus!—me—with all I possess—"

She broke off, startled by the sorrow in his eyes.

"It is a legacy I cannot accept!" he said, hoarsely, his voice trembling with suppressed emotion—"I cannot take it—even though you, the most precious part of it, are the dearest thing to me in the world! I cannot! This horrible money has parted us, Mary! More than that, it has robbed me of my energy for work—I cannot work without you— and I must give you up! Even if I could curb my pride and sink my independence, and take money which I have not earned, I should never be great as a writer—never be famous. For the need of patience and grit would be gone—I should have nothing to work for—no object in view—no goal to attain. Don't you see how it is with me? And so—as things have turned out—I must leave Weircombe at once—I must fight this business through by myself—"

"Angus!" and putting Charlie gently down, she rose from her chair and came towards him, trembling—"Do you mean—do you really mean that all is over between us?—that you will not marry me?"

He looked at her straightly.

"I cannot!" he said—"Not if I am true to myself as a man!"

"You cannot be true to *me*, as a woman?"

He caught her in his arms and held her there.

"Yes—I can be so true to you, Mary, that as long as I live I shall love you! No other woman shall ever rest on my heart—here—thus— as you are resting now! I will never kiss another woman's lips as I kiss yours now!" And he kissed her again and again—"But, at the same time, I will never live upon your wealth like a beggar on the bounty of a queen! I will never accept a penny at your hands! I will go away and work—and if possible, will make the fame I have dreamed of—but I will never marry you, Mary—never! That can never be!" He clasped her more closely and tenderly in his arms—"Don't—don't cry, dear! You are tired with your long journey—and—and—with all the excitement and trouble. Lie down and rest awhile—and—don't—don't worry about me! You deserve your fortune—you will be happy with it by and by, when you find out how much it can do for you, and what pleasures you can have with it—and life will be very bright for you—I'm sure it will! Mary—don't cling to me, darling!—it—it unmans me!—and I must be strong—strong for your sake and my own"—here he gently detached her arms from about his neck—"Good-bye, dear!—you must—you must let me go!—God bless you!"

As in a dream she felt him put her away from his embrace—the cottage door opened and closed—he was gone.

Vaguely she looked about her. There was a great sickness at her heart—her eyes ached, and her brain was giddy. She was tired,—very tired—and hardly knowing what she did, she crept like a beaten and wounded animal into the room which had formerly been her own, but which she had so long cheerfully resigned for Helmsley's occupation and better comfort,—and there she threw herself upon the bed where he had died, and lay for a long time in a kind of waking stupor.

"Oh, dear God, help me!" she prayed—"Help me to bear it! It is so hard—so hard!—to have won the greatest joy that life can give—and then—to lose it all!"

She closed her eyes,—they were hot and burning, and now no tears relieved the pressure on her brain. By and by she fell into a heavy slumber. As the afternoon wore slowly away, Mrs. Twitt, on neighbourly thoughts intent, came up to the cottage, eager to hear all the news concerning "old David"—but she found the kitchen deserted; and peeping into the bedroom adjoining, saw Mary lying there fast asleep, with Charlie curled up beside her.

"She's just dead beat and tired out for sure!" and Mrs. Twitt stole softly away again on tip-toe. "'Twould be real cruel to wake her. I'll put a bit on the kitchen fire to keep it going, and take myself off. There's plenty of time to hear all the news to-morrow."

So, being left undisturbed, Mary slept on and on—and when she at last awoke it was quite dark. Dark save for the glimmer of the moon which shone with a white vividness through the lattice window—shedding on the room something of the same ghostly light as on the night when Helmsley died. She sat up, pressing her hands to her throbbing temples,—for a moment she hardly knew where she was. Then, with a sudden rush of recollection, she realised her surroundings—and smiled. She was one of the richest women in the world!—and—without Angus—one of the poorest!

"But he does not need me so much as I need him!" she said aloud— "A man has so many thing to live for; but a woman has only one—love!"

She rose from the bed, trembling a little. She thought she saw "old David" standing near the door,—how pale and cold he seemed!—what a sorrow there was in his eyes! She stretched out her arms to the fancied phantom.

"Don't,—don't be unhappy, David dear!" she said—"You meant all for the best—I know—I know! But even you, old as you were, tried to find some one to care for you—and you see—surely in Heaven you see how hard it is for me to have found that some one, and then to lose him! But you must not grieve!—it will be all right!"

Mechanically she smoothed her tumbled hair—and taking up Charlie from the bed where he was anxiously watching her, she went into the kitchen. A small fire was burning low—and she lit the lamp and set it on the table. A gust of wind rushed round the house, shaking the door and the window, then swept away again with a plaintive cry,— and pausing to listen, she heard the low, thunderous boom of the sea. Moving about almost automatically, she prepared Charlie's supper and gave it to him, and slipping a length of ribbon through his collar, tied him securely to a chair. The little animal was intelligent enough to consider this an unusual proceeding on her part—and as a consequence of the impression it made upon his canine mind, refused to take his food. She saw this—but made no attempt to coax or persuade him. Opening a drawer in her oaken press, she took out pen, ink, and paper, and sitting down at the table wrote a letter. It was not a long letter—for it was finished, put in an envelope and sealed in less than ten minutes. Addressing it "To Angus"—she left it close under the lamp where the light might fall upon it. Then she looked around her. Everything was very quiet. Charlie alone was restless—and sat on his tiny haunches, trembling nervously, refusing to eat, and watching her every movement. She stooped suddenly and kissed him—then without hat or cloak, went out, closing the cottage door behind her.

What a night it was! What a scene of wild sky splendour! Overhead the moon, now at the full, raced through clouds of pearl-grey, lightening to milky whiteness, and the wind played among the trees as though with giant hands, bending them to and fro like reeds, and rustling through the foliage with a swishing sound like that of falling water.

The ripple of the hill-torrent was almost inaudible, overwhelmed as it was by the roar of the gale and the low thunder of the sea—and Mary, going swiftly up the "coombe" to the churchyard, was caught by the blast like a leaf, and blown to and fro, till all her hair came tumbling about her face and almost blinded her eyes. But she scarcely heeded this. She was not conscious of the weather—she knew nothing of the hour. She saw the moon—the white, cold moon, staring at her now and then between pinnacles of cloud—and whenever it gleamed whitely upon her path, she thought of David Helmsley's dead face—its still smile—its peacefully closed eyelids. And with that face ever before her, she went to his grave. A humble grave—with the clods of earth still fresh and brown upon it—the chosen grave of "one of the richest men in the world!" She repeated this phrase over and over again to herself, not knowing why she did so. Then she knelt down and tried to pray, but could find no words—save "O God, bless my dear love, and make him happy!" It was foolish to say this so often,—God would be tired of it, she thought dreamily—but—after all—there was nothing else to pray for! She rose, and stood a moment—thinking—then she said aloud— "Good-night, David! Dear old David, you meant to make me so happy! Good-night! Sleep well!"

Something frightened her at this moment,—a sound—or a shadow on the grass—and she uttered a cry of terror. Then, turning, she rushed out of the churchyard, and away—away up the hills, towards the rocks that over-hung the sea.

Meanwhile, Angus Reay, feverish and miserable, had been shut up in his one humble little room for hours, wrestling with himself and trying to work out the way in which he could best master and overcome what he chose to consider the complete wreck of his life at what had promised to be its highest point of happiness. He could not shake himself free of the clinging touch of Mary's arms—her lovely, haunting blue eyes looked at him piteously out of the very air. Never had she been to him so dear—so unutterably beloved!—never had she seemed so beautiful as now when he felt that he must resign all claims of love upon her.

"For she will be sought after by many a better man than myself,"— he said—"Even rich men, who do not need her millions, are likely to admire her—and why should I stand in her way?—I, who haven't a penny to call my own! I should be a coward if I kept her to her promise. For she does not know yet—she does not see what the possession of Helmsley's millions will mean to her. And by and bye when she does know she will change—she will be grateful to me for setting her free—"

He paused, and the hot tears sprang to his eyes—"No—I am wrong! Nothing will change Mary! She will always be her sweet self—pure and faithful!—and she will do all the good with Helmsley's money that he believed and hoped she would. But I—I must leave her to it!"

Then the thought came to him that he had perhaps been rough in speech to her that day—abrupt in parting from her—even unkind in overwhelming her with the force of his abnegation, when she was so tired with her journey—so worn out—so weary looking. Acting on a sudden impulse, he threw on his cap.

"I will go and say good-night to her,"—he said—"For the last time!"

He strode swiftly up the village street and saw through the cottage window that the lamp was lighted on the table. He knocked at the door, but there was no answer save a tiny querulous bark from Charlie. He tried the latch; it was unfastened, and he entered. The first object he saw was Charlie, tied to a chair, with a small saucer of untasted food beside him. The little dog capered to the length of his ribbon, and mutely expressed the absence of his kind mistress, while Angus, bewildered, looked round the deserted dwelling in amazement. All at once his eyes caught sight of the letter addressed to him, and he tore it open. It was very brief, and ran thus—

My Dearest,

"When you read this, I shall be gone from you. I am sorry, oh, so sorry, about the money—but it is not my fault that I did not know who old David was. I hope now that everything will be right, when I am out of the way. I did not tell you—but before I left London I asked the kind gentleman, Sir Francis Vesey, to let me make a will in case any accident happened to me on my way home. He arranged it all for me very quickly—so that everything I possess, including all the dreadful fortune that has parted you from me,—now belongs to you. And you will be a great and famous man; and I am sure you will get on much better without me than with me—for I am not clever, and I should not understand how to live in the world as the world likes to live. God bless you, darling! Thank you for loving me, who am so unworthy of your love! Be happy! David and I will perhaps be able to watch you from 'the other side,' and we shall be proud of all you do. For you will spend those terrible millions in good deeds that must benefit all the world, I am sure. That is what I hoped we might perhaps have done together—but I see quite plainly now that it is best you should be without me. My love, whom I love so much more than I have ever dared to, say!—Good-bye!

MARY

With a cry like that of a man in physical torture or despair, Angus rushed out of the house.

"Mary! Mary!" he cried to the tumbling stream and the moonlit sky. "Mary!"

He paused. Just then the clock in the little church tower struck ten. The village was asleep—and there was no sound of human life anywhere. The faint, subtle scent of sweetbriar stole on the air as he stood in a trance of desperate uncertainty—and as the delicate odour floated by, a rush of tears came to his eyes.

"Mary!" he called again—"Mary!"

Then all at once a fearful idea entered his brain that filled him as it were with a mad panic. Rushing up the coombe, he sprang across the torrent, and raced over the adjoining hill, as though racing for life. Soon in front of him towered the "Giant's Castle" Rock, and he ran up its steep ascent with an almost crazy speed. At the summit he halted abruptly, looking keenly from side to side. Was there any one there? No. There seemed to be no one. Chilled with a nameless horror, he stood watching—watching and listening to the crashing noise of the great billows as they broke against the rocks below. He raised his eyes to the heavens, and saw—almost unseeingly—a white cloud break asunder and show a dark blue space between,—just an azure setting for one brilliant star that shone out with a sudden flash like a signal. And then—then he caught sight of a dark crouching figure in the corner of the rocky platform over-hanging the sea,—a dear, familiar figure that even while he looked, rose up and advanced to the extreme edge with outstretched arms,—its lovely hair loosely flowing and flecked with glints of gold by the light of the moon. Nearer, nearer to the very edge of the dizzy height it moved—and Angus, breathless with terror, and fearing to utter a sound lest out of sudden alarm it should leap from its footing and be lost for ever, crept closer and ever closer. Closer still,— and he heard Mary's sweet voice murmuring plaintively—

"I wish I did not love him so dearly! I wish the world were not so beautiful! I wish I could stay—but I must go—I must go!—"Here there was a little sobbing cry—"You are so deep and cruel, you sea!—you have drowned so many brave men! You will not be long in drowning poor me, will you?—I don't want to struggle with you! Cover me up quickly—and let me forget—oh, no, no! Dear God, don't let me forget Angus!—I want to remember him always—always!"

She swayed towards the brink—one second more—and then, with a swift strong clasp and passionate cry Angus had caught her in her arms.

"Mary! Mary, my love! My wife! Anything but that, Mary! Anything but that!"

Heart to heart they stood, their arms entwined, clasping each other in a wild passion of tenderness,—Angus trembling in all his strong frame with the excitement and horror of the past moment, and Mary sobbing out all her weakness, weariness and gladness on his breast. Above their heads the bright star shone, pendant between the snowy wings of the dividing cloud, and the sound of the sea was as a sacred psalm of jubilation in their ears.

"Thank God I came in time! Thank God I have you safe!" and Angus drew her closer and yet closer into his fervent embrace—"Oh Mary, my darling!—sweetest of women! How could you think of leaving me? What should I have done without you! Poverty or riches—either or neither—I care not which! But I cannot lose *you*, Mary! I cannot let my heavenly treasure go! Nothing else matters in all the world—I only want love—and you!"

THE END

A Note About the Author

Marie Corelli (1855–1924), born Mary Mackay, was a British writer from London, England. Educated at a Parisian convent, she later worked as a pianist before embarking on a literary career. Her first novel, *A Romance of Two Worlds* was published in 1886 and surpassed all expectations. Corelli quickly became one of the most popular fiction writers of her time. Her books featured contrasting themes rooted in religion, science and the supernatural. Some of Corelli's other notable works include *Barabbas: A Dream of the World's Tragedy* (1893) and *The Sorrows of Satan* (1895).

A Note from the Publisher

Spanning many genres, from non-fiction essays to literature classics to children's books and lyric poetry, Mint Edition books showcase the master works of our time in a modern new package. The text is freshly typeset, is clean and easy to read, and features a new note about the author in each volume. Many books also include exclusive new introductory material. Every book boasts a striking new cover, which makes it as appropriate for collecting as it is for gift giving. Mint Edition books are only printed when a reader orders them, so natural resources are not wasted. We're proud that our books are never manufactured in excess and exist only in the exact quantity they need to be read and enjoyed.

Discover more of your favorite classics with Bookfinity™.

- Track your reading with custom book lists.
- Get great book recommendations for your personalized Reader Type.
- Add reviews for your favorite books.
- AND MUCH MORE!

Visit **bookfinity.com** and take the fun Reader Type quiz to get started.

Enjoy our classic and modern companion pairings!